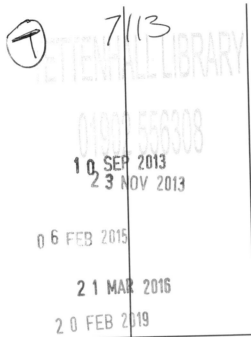

Lasting Damage

Also by Sophie Hannah

Little Face
Hurting Distance
The Point of Rescue
The Other Half Lives
A Room Swept White

SOPHIE HANNAH

Lasting Damage

First published in Great Britain in 2011 by Hodder & Stoughton
An Hachette UK company

1

A CIP catalogue record for this title is available from the British Library

Hardback ISBN 978 0 340 98065 1
Trade paperback ISBN 978 0 340 98066 8

Typeset in Sabon by Hewer Text UK Ltd, Edinburgh
Printed and bound by Clays Ltd, St Ives plc

Hodder & Stoughton policy is to use papers that are natural, renewable and recyclable products and made from wood grown in sustainable forests. The logging and manufacturing processes are expected to conform to the environmental regulations of the country of origin.

Hodder & Stoughton Ltd
338 Euston Road
London NW1 3BH

www.hodder.co.uk

For 7GR

11 Bentley Grove, Cambridge

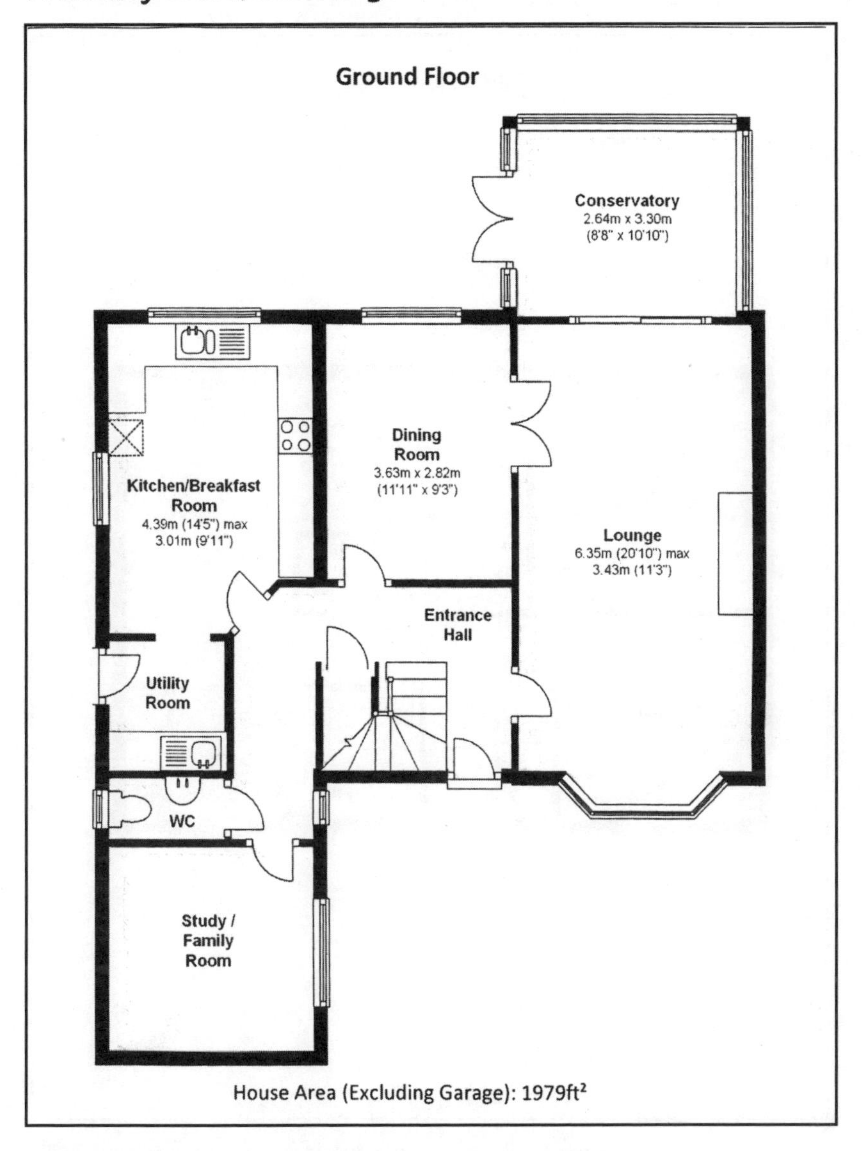

NOT TO SCALE: For guidance purposes only

Whilst every attempt has been made to ensure the accuracy of the floor plans contained here, measurements of doors, windows and rooms are approximate and no responsibility is taken for any error, omission or mis-statement. These plans are for representation purposes only as defined by RICS Code of Measuring Practice and should be used as such by any prospective purchaser. No services, systems or appliances have been tested, and no guarantee as to their operating ability or their efficiency can be given.

11 Bentley Grove, Cambridge

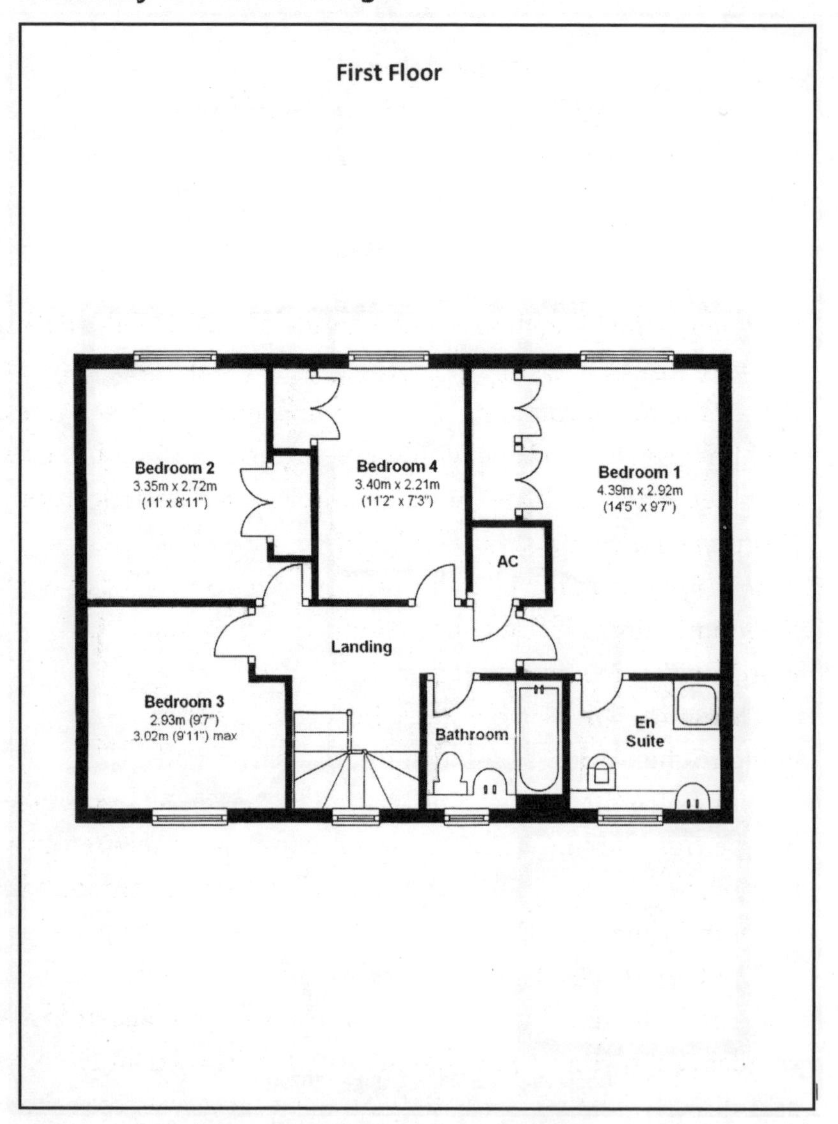

NOT TO SCALE: For guidance purposes only

Whilst every attempt has been made to ensure the accuracy of the floor plans contained here, measurements of doors, windows and rooms are approximate and no responsibility is taken for any error, omission or mis-statement. These plans are for representation purposes only as defined by RICS Code of Measuring Practice and should be used as such by any prospective purchaser. No services, systems or appliances have been tested, and no guarantee as to their operating ability or their efficiency can be given.

Saturday 24 July 2010

I'm going to be killed because of a family called the Gilpatricks.

There are four of them: mother, father, son and daughter. *Elise, Donal, Riordan and Tilly*. Kit tells me their first names, as if I'm keen to dispense with the formalities and get to know them better, when all I want is to run screaming from the room. *Riordan's seven*, he says. *Tilly's five*.

Shut up, I want to yell in his face, but I'm too scared to open my mouth. It's as if someone's clamped and locked it; no more words will come out, not ever.

This is it. This is where and how and when and why I'm going to die. At least I understand the why, finally.

Kit's as frightened as I am. More. That's why he keeps talking, because he knows, as all those who wait in terror know, that when silence and fear combine, they form a compound a thousand times more horrifying than the sum of its parts.

The Gilpatricks, he says, tears streaking his face.

I watch the door in the mirror above the fireplace. It looks smaller and further away than it would if I turned and looked at it directly. The mirror is shaped like a fat gravestone: three straight sides and an arch at the top.

I didn't believe in them. The name sounded made up. Kit laughs, chokes on a sob. All of him is shaking, even his voice. *Gilpatrick's the sort of name you'd make up if you were inventing a person. Mr Gilpatrick. If only I'd believed in him, none of this would have happened. We'd have been safe. If I'd only . . .*

He stops, backs away from the locked door. He hears the same footsteps I hear – rushing, a stampede. They're here.

One week earlier

I

Saturday 17 July 2010

I lie on my back with my eyes closed, waiting for Kit's breathing to change. I fake the deep, slow sleep-breaths I need to hear from him before I can get out of bed – *in and hold, out and hold* – and try to convince myself that it's a harmless deception. Am I the only woman who has ever done this, or does it happen all the time in houses all over the world? If it does, then it must be for different reasons, more common ones than mine: a cheating wife or girlfriend wanting to text a lover undetected, or sneak one last guilty glass of wine on top of the five she's had already. Normal things. Ordinary urgencies.

No woman on earth has ever been in the situation I'm in now.

You're being ridiculous. You're not 'in a situation', apart from the one you've brewed in your imagination. Ingredients: coincidence and paranoia.

Nothing I tell myself works. That's why I need to check, to put my mind at rest. Checking isn't crazy; missing the opportunity to check would be crazy. And once I've looked and found nothing, I'll be able to forget about it and accept that it's all in my head.

Will you?

It shouldn't be too long before I can move. Kit's usually dead to the world within seconds of the light going out. If I count to a hundred . . . but I can't. Can't make myself focus on something that doesn't interest me. If I could, I'd be able to do the reverse: banish 11 Bentley Grove from my mind. Will I ever be able to do that?

While I wait, I rehearse for the task ahead. What would this bedroom tell me about Kit and me, if I didn't know us? Huge bed, cast-iron fireplace, identical alcoves on either side of the chimney breast where our two identical wardrobes stand. Kit likes symmetry. One of his reservations, when I proposed buying the biggest bed we could find to replace our ordinary double, was that it might not leave room for our matching bedside cabinets. When I said I'd be happy to lose mine, Kit looked at me as if I was an anarchist agitator plotting to demolish his well-ordered world. 'You can't have a cabinet on one side and not the other,' he said. Both ended up going in the end; having first made me promise not to tell anyone, Kit admitted that, however inconvenient it was to have to lean down and put his book, watch, glasses and mobile phone under the bed, he would find it more irritating to have a bedroom that didn't 'look right'.

'Are you sure you're a genuine, bona fide heterosexual?' I teased him.

He grinned. 'Either I am, or else I'm pretending to be in order to get my Christmas cards written and posted for me every year. I guess you'll never know which is the truth.'

Floor-length cream silk curtains. Kit wanted a Roman blind, but I overruled him. Silk curtains are something I've wanted since childhood, one of those 'as soon as I have a home of my own' pledges I made to myself. And curtains in a bedroom have to pool on the floor – that's my look-right rule. I suppose everybody has at least one, and we all think our own are sensible and other people's completely ridiculous.

Above the fireplace, there's a framed tapestry of a red house with a green rectangle around it that's supposed to be the garden. Instead of flowers, the solid colour of the grass is broken up by stitched words: 'Melrose Cottage, Little Holling, Silsford' in orange, and then, in smaller yellow letters beneath, 'Connie and Kit, 13th July 2004'.

'But Melrose isn't red,' I used to protest, before I gave up. 'It's made of white clunch stone. Do you think Mum was picturing it drenched in blood?' Kit and I called our house 'Melrose' for short when we first bought it. Now that we've lived here for years and know it like we know our own faces, we call it 'Mellers'.

What would an impartial observer make of the tapestry? Would they think Kit and I were so stupid that we were in danger of forgetting our names and when we bought our house? That we'd decided to hang a reminder on the wall? Would they guess that it was a home-made house-warming present from Connie's mother, and that Connie thought it was twee and crass, and had fought hard to have it exiled to the loft?

Kit insisted we put it up, out of loyalty to our home and to Mum. He said our bedroom was the perfect place, so that then guests wouldn't see it. I don't think he notices it any more. I do – every night before I go to sleep and every morning when I wake up. It depresses me for a whole range of reasons.

Someone peering into our bedroom would see none of this – none of the wrangles, none of the compromises. They wouldn't see Kit's missing bedside table, the picture I'd have liked to put above the fireplace if only the hideous red house tapestry weren't there.

Which proves that looking at a room in someone else's house doesn't tell you anything, and there's no point in my doing what I'm about to do, now that I'm sure Kit's sound asleep. I ought to go to sleep too.

As quietly as I can, I fold back my side of the duvet, climb out of bed and tiptoe to the second bedroom, which we've turned into a home office. We run our business from here, which is a little absurd given that it's about eleven feet long by ten feet wide. Like Kit's and my bedroom, it has a cast-iron fireplace. We've managed to cram two desks in here, a chair for each of us, three filing cabinets. When our certificate of incorporation arrived from Companies House, Kit bought a frame for it and hung it on the wall opposite the door, so that it's the first thing that catches your eye when you walk into the room. 'It's a legal requirement,' he told me when I complained that it looked uninspiring and bureaucratic. 'Has to be displayed at company headquarters. Do you want Nulli to start life as an outlaw?'

Nulli Secundus Ltd. It means 'second to none', and was Kit's choice. 'Talk about tempting fate and dooming us to failure,' I said when we were discussing what to call ourselves, imagining how much worse liquidation would feel with such a conceited name. I suggested 'C & K Bowskill Ltd'. 'Those are *our* names,' Kit said scathingly, as if this fact might have passed me by. 'Have a bit of imagination, for God's sake. Confidence would help, too. Are we launching this company in order to go bankrupt? I don't know about you, but I'm planning to make a success of it.'

What else have you made a success of, Kit? What else that I don't know about?

You're being ridiculous, Connie. Your ridiculousness is second to none.

I tap my laptop's touchpad and it springs to life. The

Google screen appears. I type 'houses for sale' into the search box, press enter, and wait. The first result that comes up is Roundthehouses.co.uk, which declares itself the UK's leading property website. I click on it, thinking that obviously the Roundthehouses people subscribe to Kit's way of thinking rather than mine: they have no worries about bankruptcy-induced humiliation.

The home page loads: exterior shots of houses for sale beneath a dark red border filled in with lots of tiny pictures of magnifying glasses, each with a disembodied pair of eyes inside it. The eyes look eerie, alien, and make me think of people hiding in the darkness, spying on one another.

Isn't that exactly what you're doing?

I type 'Cambridge' into the location box, and click on the 'For Sale' button. Another screen comes up, offering me more choices. I work my way through them impatiently – search radius: this area only; property type: houses; number of bedrooms: any; price range: any; added to site . . . When would 11 Bentley Grove have been added? I click on 'last 7 days'. The 'For Sale' board I saw in the front garden today – or yesterday, since it's now quarter past one in the morning – wasn't there a week ago.

I click on 'Find properties', tapping my bare feet on the floor, and close my eyes for a second. When I open them, there are houses on the screen: one on Chaucer Road for 4 million pounds, one on Newton Road for 2.3 million. I know both streets – they're near Bentley Grove, off Trumpington Road. I've seen them, on my many trips to Cambridge that nobody knows about.

11 Bentley Grove is the third house on the list. It's on for 1.2 million pounds. I'm surprised it's so expensive. It's big

enough, but nothing spectacular. Obviously that part of Cambridge is regarded as a choice area, though it's always looked fairly ordinary to me, and the traffic on Trumpington Road is often waiting to move rather than moving. There's a Waitrose nearby, an Indian restaurant, a specialist wine shop, a couple of estate agents. *And lots of enormous expensive mansions*. If the asking prices for all the houses in this part of town are into the millions, that means there must be plenty of people who can afford to pay that much. Who are they? Sir Cliff Richard springs to mind; I've no idea why. Who else? People who own football clubs, or have oil wells in their back gardens? Certainly not me and Kit, and we're doing about as well, professionally, as we could ever hope to do . . .

I shake these thoughts from my mind. *You could be asleep now, you lunatic. Instead, you're sitting hunched over a computer in the dark, feeling inferior to Cliff Richard. Get a grip.*

To bring up the full details, I click on the picture of this house I know so well, and yet not at all. I don't believe anyone in the world has spent as much time staring at the outside of 11 Bentley Grove as I have; I know its façade brick by brick. It's strange, almost shocking, to see a photograph of it on my computer – in my house, where it doesn't belong.

Inviting the enemy into your home . . .

There is no enemy, I tell myself firmly. *Be practical, get it over with, and go back to bed.* Kit has started to snore. Good. I've no idea what I'd say if he caught me doing this, how I'd defend my sanity.

The page has loaded. I'm not interested in the big photograph on the left, the one taken from across the road. It's the inside of the house I need to see. One by one, I click on the little pictures on the right-hand side of the screen to enlarge them. First, a kitchen with wooden worktops, a double Belfast sink, blue-painted unit fronts, a blue-sided wooden-topped island . . .

Kit hates kitchen islands. He thinks they're ugly and pretentious – an affectation imported from America. The avocado bathroom suites of the future, he calls them. He'd got rid of the one in our kitchen within a fortnight of our moving in, and commissioned a local joiner to make us a big round oak table to take its place.

This kitchen I'm looking at can't be Kit's, not with that island in it.

Of course it's not Kit's. Kit's kitchen is downstairs – it also happens to be your kitchen.

I click on a picture of a lounge. I've seen 11 Bentley Grove's lounge before, though only briefly. On one of my visits, I was brave enough – or stupid enough, depending on your point of view – to open the gate, walk up the long path that's bordered by lavender bushes on both sides and divides the square front lawn into two triangles, and peer in through the front window. I was afraid I'd be caught trespassing and couldn't really concentrate. A few seconds later an elderly man with the thickest glasses I've ever seen emerged from the house next door and turned his excessively enlarged eyes in my direction. I hurried back to my car before he could ask me what I was doing, and, afterwards, remembered little about the room I'd seen apart from that it had white walls and a grey L-shaped sofa with some kind of intricate red embroidery on it.

I'm looking at that same sofa now, on my computer screen. It's not so much grey as a sort of cloudy silver. It looks expensive, unique. I can't imagine there's another sofa like it.

Kit loves unique. He avoids mass-produced as far as is

possible. All the mugs in our kitchen were made and painted individually by a potter in Spilling.

Every piece of furniture in the lounge at 11 Bentley Grove looks like a one-off: a chair with enormous curved wooden arms like the bottoms of rowing boats; an unusual coffee table with a glass surface, and, beneath the glass, a structure resembling a display cabinet with sixteen compartments, lying on its back. Each compartment contains a small flower with a red circle at its centre and blue petals pointing up towards the glass.

Kit would like all of these things. I swallow, tell myself this proves nothing.

There's a tiled fireplace with a large map above it in a frame, a chimney breast, matching alcoves on either side. A symmetrical room, a Kit sort of room. I feel a little nauseous.

Christ, this is insane. How many living rooms, up and down the country, follow this basic format: fireplace, a chimney breast, alcoves left and right? It's a classic design, replicated all over the world. It appeals to Kit, and to about a trillion other people.

It's not as if you've seen his jacket draped over the banister, his stripy scarf over the back of a chair . . .

Quickly, wanting to be finished with this task I've set myself – aware that it's making me feel worse, not better – I work my way through the other rooms, enlarging their pictures. Hall and stairs, carpeted in beige; chunky dark wood banister. A utility room with sky-blue unit fronts, similar to those in the kitchen. Honey-coloured marble for the house bathroom – clean and ostentatiously expensive.

I click on a picture of what must be the back garden. It's a lot bigger than I'd have imagined, having only seen the house from the front. I scroll down to the text beneath the photographs and see that the garden is described as being just over an acre. It's the sort of garden I'd love to have: decking for a table and chairs, two-seater swing with a canopy, vast lawn, trees at the bottom, lush yellow fields beyond. An idyllic countryside view, ten minutes' walk from the centre of Cambridge. Now I'm starting to understand the 1.2-million-pound price tag. I try not to compare what I'm looking at to Melrose Cottage's garden, which is roughly the size of half a single garage. It's big enough to accommodate a wrought-iron table, four chairs, a few plants in terracotta pots, and not a lot else.

That's it. I've looked at all the pictures, seen all there is to see.

And found nothing. Satisfied now?

I yawn and rub my eyes. I'm about to shut down the Roundthehouses website and go back to bed when I notice a row of buttons beneath the picture of the back garden: 'Street View', 'Floorplan', 'Virtual Tour'. I don't need a view of Bentley Grove – I've seen more than enough of it in the past six months – but I might as well have a look at number 11's floorplan, since I've got this far. I click on the button, then hit the 'x' to shut down the screen within seconds of it opening. It isn't going to help me to know which room is where; I'd be better off taking the virtual tour. Will it make me feel as if I'm walking around the house myself, looking into every room? That's what I'd like to do.

Then I'd be satisfied.

I hit the button and wait for the tour to load. Another button pops up: 'Play Tour'. I click on it. The kitchen appears first, and I see what I've already seen in the photograph, then a bit more as the camera does a 360-degree turn to reveal the rest of the room. Then another turn, then another. The spinning effect makes me feel dizzy, as if I'm on a roundabout that won't stop. I close my eyes, needing a break. I'm so tired. Travelling to Cambridge and back in a day nearly every Friday is doing me no good; it's not the physical effort that's draining, it's the secrecy. I have to move on, let it go.

I open my eyes and see a mass of red. At first I don't know what I'm looking at, and then ... *Oh, God. It can't be. Oh, fuck, oh, God.* Blood. A woman lying face down in the middle of the room, and blood, a lake of it, all over the beige carpet. For a second, in my panic, I mistake the blood for my own. I look down at myself. *No blood.* Of course not – it's not my carpet, not my house. It's 11 Bentley Grove. The lounge, spinning. The fireplace, the framed map above it, the door open to the hall ...

The dead woman, face down in a sea of red. As if all the blood inside her has been squeezed out, every drop of it ...

I make a noise that might be a scream. I try to call Kit's name, but it doesn't work. Where's the phone? Not on its base. Where's my BlackBerry? Should I ring 999? Panting, I reach out for something, I'm not sure what. I can't take my eyes off the screen. The blood is still turning, the dead woman slowly turning. *She must be dead; it must be her blood. Red around the outside, almost black in the middle. Black-red, thick as tar. Make it stop spinning.*

I stand up, knock my chair over. It falls to the floor with a thud. I back away from my desk, wanting only to escape. *Out, out!* a voice in my head screams. I'm stumbling in the wrong direction, nowhere near the door. *Don't look. Stop looking.* I can't help it. My back hits the wall; something hard presses into my skin. I hear a crash, step on something that crunches.

Pain pricks the soles of my feet. I look down and see broken glass. Blood. Mine, this time.

Somehow, I get myself out of the room and close the door. Better; now there's a barrier between it and me. *Kit.* I need Kit. I walk into our bedroom, switch on the light and burst into tears. How dare he be asleep? 'Kit!'

He groans. Blinks. 'Light off,' he mumbles, groggy with sleep. 'Fuck's going on? Time is it?'

I stand there crying, my feet bleeding onto the white rug.

'Con?' Kit hauls himself up into a sitting position and rubs his eyes. 'What's wrong? What's happened?'

'She's dead,' I tell him.

~

'Who's dead?' He's alert now. He reaches under the bed for his glasses, puts them on.

'I don't know! A woman,' I sob. 'On the computer.'

'What woman? What are you talking about?' He throws back the covers, gets out of bed. 'Your . . . what have you done to your feet? They're bleeding.'

'I don't know.' It's the best I can do. 'I did a virtual . . .' I'm having trouble breathing and speaking at the same time.

'Just tell me if everybody's okay. Your sister, Benji . . .'

'What?' My sister? 'It's nothing to do with them, it's a woman. I can't see her face.'

'You're white as a sheet, Con. Did you have a nightmare?'

'On my laptop. She's there now,' I sob. 'She's dead. She must be. We should call the police.'

'Sweetheart, there's no dead woman on your laptop,' Kit says. I hear the impatience beneath the reassurance. 'You had a bad dream.'

'Go and look!' I scream at him. 'It's not a dream. Go in there and see it for yourself!'

He looks down at my feet again, at the trail of blood on the rug and the floorboards – a dotted red line leading to the bedroom door. 'What happened to you?' he asks. I wonder how guilty I look. 'What's going on?' The concerned tone has gone; his voice is hard with suspicion. Without waiting to hear my answer, he heads for the spare room.

'No!' I blurt out.

He stops on the landing. Turns. 'No? I thought you wanted me to look at your computer.' I've made him angry. Anything that interrupts his sleep makes him angry.

I can't let him go in there until I've explained, or tried to. 'I did a virtual tour of 11 Bentley Grove,' I say.

'*What?* For fuck's sake, Connie.'

'Listen to me. Just listen, okay? It's for sale, 11 Bentley Grove is for sale.'

'How do you know that?'

'I . . . I just know, all right?' I wipe my face. If I'm under attack, I can't cry. I have to concentrate on defending myself.

'This is just . . . Connie, this is *so* fucked up, I don't know where to . . .' Kit pushes past me, tries to get back into bed.

I grab his arm to stop him. 'Be angry later, but first listen to me. Okay? That's all I'm asking.'

He shakes me off him. I hate the way he's staring at me.

What do you expect him to do?

'I'm listening,' he says quietly. 'I've been listening to you talk about 11 Bentley Grove for six months. When's it going to stop?'

'It's for sale,' I say, as calmly as I can. 'I looked it up on Roundthehouses, a property website.'

'When?'

'Now, just . . . before.'

'You waited until I was asleep?' Kit shakes his head in disgust.

'There was a virtual tour, and I . . . I thought I'd . . .' It's better if I don't tell him what I was thinking. Not that he couldn't guess. 'There was a woman, in the lounge, face down on the floor, blood all around her, a huge pool . . .' Describing it makes me feel as if I might throw up.

Kit takes a step back, looks at me as if he's never seen me before. 'Let's get this straight: you went onto Roundthehouses, took a virtual tour of 11 Bentley Grove, which you happen to know is for sale, and saw a dead woman in one of the rooms?'

'In the lounge.'

He laughs. 'This is inventive, even for you,' he says.

'It's still up on the screen,' I tell him. 'Go and look if you don't believe me.' I'm shaking, freezing cold suddenly.

He's going to refuse. He's going to ignore what I've told him and go back to sleep, to punish me, and because it can't possibly be true. There can't be a dead woman lying in a sea of blood on the Roundthehouses website.

Kit sighs. 'Okay,' he says. 'I'll go and look. Evidently I'm as big an idiot as you think I am.'

'I'm not making it up!' I shout after him. I want to go with him, but my body won't move. *Any second now he'll see what I saw*. I can't bear the waiting, knowing it's going to happen.

'Great,' I hear Kit say to himself. Or maybe he's talking to me. 'I've always wanted to look at a stranger's dishwasher in the middle of the night.'

Dishwasher. The tour must be on a loop. In my absence, it's started again at the beginning. 'The obligatory kitchen island,' Kit mutters. 'Why do people do it?'

'The lounge is after the kitchen,' I tell him. I force myself onto the landing; that's as close as I'm willing to go. I can't breathe. I hate the thought that Kit's about to see what I saw – no one should have to see it. It's too horrible. At the same time, I need him to . . .

To what? Confirm that it was real, that you didn't imagine it?

I don't imagine things that aren't there. *I don't.* I sometimes worry about things that maybe don't need to be worried about, but that's not the same thing. I know what's true and what isn't. My name is Catriona Louise Bowskill. *True.* I'm thirty-four years old. *True.* I live at Melrose Cottage in Little Holling, Silsford, with my husband Christian, but he's always been known as Kit, just as I've always been known as Connie. We have our own business – it's called Nulli Secundus. We're data management consultants, or rather, Kit is. My official title is Business and Financial Director. Kit works for Nulli full-time. I'm part-time: three days a week. On Tuesdays and Thursdays, I work for my mum and dad's business, Monk & Sons Fine Furnishings, where I have a more old-fashioned job title: book-keeper. My mum and dad are Val and Geoff Monk. They live down the road. I have a sister, Fran, who's thirty-two. She also works for Monk & Sons; she runs the curtain and blind department. She has a partner, Anton, and they have a five-year-old son, Benji. All these things are true, and it's also true – true in exactly the same way – that less than ten minutes ago I took a virtual tour of 11 Bentley Grove, Cambridge, and saw a dead woman lying on a blood-soaked carpet.

'Bingo: the lounge,' I hear Kit say. His tone sends a chill shooting up my spine. How can he sound so flippant, unless . . .

'Interesting choice of coffee table. Trying a bit too hard, I'd say. No dead woman, no blood.'

What? What's he talking about? He's wrong. I know what I saw.

I push open the door and make myself walk into the room. *No. It's not possible.* 11 Bentley Grove's lounge turns slowly on the screen, but there's no body in it – no woman lying face down, no pool of red. The carpet's beige. Moving closer, I see that there's a faint mark on it in one corner, but . . . 'It's not there,' I say.

Kit stands up. 'I'm going back to bed,' he says, his voice stiff with fury.

'But . . . how could it disappear?'

'Don't.' He raises his fist, smacks it against the wall. 'We're not going to talk about this now. I've got a good idea: let's never talk about it. Let's pretend it didn't happen.'

'Kit . . .'

'I can't go on like this, Con. *We* can't go on like this.'

He pushes past me. I hear our bedroom door slam. Too shocked to cry, I sit down in the chair that's still warm from Kit's body, and stare at the screen. When the lounge disappears, I wait for it to come back, in case the dead woman and the blood also come back. It seems unlikely, but then what's happened already is also unlikely, and yet it happened.

I sit through the tour of 11 Bentley Grove four times. Each time the kitchen fades, I hold my breath. Each time the lounge returns spotless, with no dead woman or blood in it. Eventually, because I don't know what else to do, I click on the 'x' in the top right-hand corner of the screen, shut the tour down.

Not possible.

One last time, starting from scratch. I click on the internet

Explorer icon, go back to Roundthehouses, retrace my steps: find 11 Bentley Grove again, click on the virtual tour button again, sit and watch. There's no woman. No blood. Kit is still right. I am still wrong.

I slam my laptop shut. I ought to clear up the broken glass, and the real bloodstains on my own carpet. I stare down at Nulli's certificate of incorporation, lying on the floor in its shattered frame. In my shock at seeing the dead woman, I must have knocked it off the wall. Kit will be upset about that. *As if he hasn't got enough to be upset about.*

Reframing a certificate is easy. Deciding what to do about a disappearing dead woman that you might have imagined in the first place – not so easy.

As far as I can see, I have two choices. I can either try to forget about it, talk myself into believing that the horrific scene I saw only ever existed in my mind. Or I can ring Simon Waterhouse.

POLICE EXHIBIT REF: CB13345/432/19IG

CAVENDISH LODGE PRIMARY SCHOOL
BULLETIN NO. 581
Date: Monday 19th October 2009

Autumn Thoughts from Mrs Kennedy's class

Conkers are . . .
Silky smooth,
Velvety and chocolate brown
And rusty red on the outside.
Their shiny shells are crusty
Creamy and cool to touch.
I love Autumn because
Conkers fall off the trees in Autumn.
I love conkers SO much!

by Riordan Gilpatrick

Conkers
They fall off trees
Hit you on the head.
You can tie them on strings
Have fights with them
You can collect them
And put them on your shelf.
Green-brown-orange-red, that's the colour of . . .
Conkers!

by Emily Sabine

Well done to both of you – you have really brought Autumn to life in all our minds!
Thank you!

2

17/07/10

Betting man that he was, DC Chris Gibbs would have put the odds against Olivia's persuading the concierge to serve them yet another drink, long after the hotel bar had officially closed, at several thousand to one. Happily, he'd have been wrong.

'Just one more *titchy* little nightcap,' she breathed, as if confiding a secret. Where did she get that voice? It couldn't be natural; nothing about her seemed natural.

'Well, perhaps not quite so titchy,' Olivia quickly amended, once she'd secured an agreement in principle. 'A double Laphroaig for Chrissy and a double Baileys for me, since we're celebrating.'

Gibbs tensed. No one had ever referred to him as 'Chrissy' before. He prayed it wouldn't happen again, but didn't want to make an issue of it. *Fuck*. Did the concierge think he called himself Chrissy? He hoped it was obvious from his appearance that he didn't and wouldn't.

Olivia draped herself across the bar while she waited, revealing even more of her world-class cleavage. Gibbs noticed the concierge looking while pretending not to. All men did it all the time, but none as skilfully as Gibbs, in his own not-so-humble opinion.

'No ice in either,' Olivia said. 'Oh, and whatever you're having, obviously – let's not forget you! A double of something yummy and *hugely* alcoholic for you!'

Gibbs was glad she was as drunk as she was. Sober, earlier, she'd been a bit much for him, but he knew how to deal with drunks; he'd arrested enough of them. Admittedly, most weren't wearing funny-shaped gold dresses that had cost two thousand pounds, as Olivia had told him hers had. He'd done a double-take, expressed disbelief, and she'd laughed at him.

'Kind of you, madam, but I'm fine, thank you,' said the concierge.

'Did I say no ice? I can't remember if I said it or only thought it. That's always happening to me. Neither of us likes ice, do we?' Olivia turned to Gibbs, then, before he had a chance to respond, back to the concierge. 'We didn't know we had anything in common – I mean, look at us! We're so different! – but then it turned out that we both hate ice.'

'A lot of people do,' said the concierge, smiling. Perhaps there was nothing he liked more than to stay up all night, dressed like a butler from the 1920s, serving drinks to a loud posh woman and an unfriendly copper who'd had way too many already. 'Then again, a lot of people don't.'

Give us the drinks and spare us the tedious observations. Gibbs had grabbed his Laphroaig and was on his way back to their table when he heard Olivia say, 'Aren't you going to ask what we're celebrating?' He didn't know whether it'd be rude to leave her to it, whether he ought to go back and join her; it took him less than a second to decide he didn't care. If she and the Jeeves lookalike wanted to bore each other to death, that was their lookout. Gibbs had his drink, the extra one that he hadn't thought he was going to get; that was all he wanted.

'We've been to a wedding today, and guess what?' Olivia's voice blared out behind him. 'There was no one else there!

Apart from the bride and groom, I mean. My sister Charlie was the bride. Chris and I were the two witnesses and the only guests.'

No more 'Chrissy', then. Thank God for that.

'They chose one each,' Olivia went on. 'Charlie chose me and Simon chose . . . Sorry, did I mention Simon? He's my sister's husband – as of today! Simon Waterhouse. The groom.' She said it as if the concierge ought to have heard of him.

Gibbs felt a bit irked, probably only because he was hammered, that she hadn't finished her sentence: *and Simon chose Chris*. It was clear enough, even though she hadn't spelled it out. If they'd chosen one witness each and Charlie had chosen Olivia, then Waterhouse must have chosen Gibbs. Not that the hotel concierge needed to know that. It was true whether he knew it or not.

Yesterday, before setting off to Torquay, Gibbs had asked his wife Debbie why she thought Waterhouse had picked him. 'Why not you?' she'd said without lifting her eyes from the shirt she was ironing, clearly not interested in discussing it. There was no room in her head for anything but her IVF at the moment. She'd gone in for the embryo transfer on Tuesday – two had been implanted, the two healthiest specimens. Gibbs hoped to God he didn't end up with twins. One would be . . .

Bad enough? No, not bad, exactly. Hard, though. And if the embryos didn't take, if Debbie still wasn't pregnant after all the hassle they'd had and all the cash they'd handed over, that would be even harder. The worst thing was having to talk about the lack of a baby endlessly, when it bored Gibbs so much and he wasn't allowed to say that it did. He didn't care any more. He'd agreed that a baby was a nice idea when he'd thought it would be straightforward, but if it wasn't straightforward, if it was a never-ending nightmare, as it was proving to be, then why bother? What was so special about his or Debbie's genes that they needed to be passed on?

Olivia plonked herself down next to him. 'He's left the bottles on the bar in case we want a top-up, said we can settle up in the morning. What a lovely man!'

Earlier, Gibbs had wished she would stop gushing and lower her voice. Now that they were the only people left, it didn't matter. The music had stopped more than an hour ago. The wall-candles had been put out at the same time, and the bright overhead lights switched on. There was a morning-after feel to the hotel bar, even though, as far as Gibbs was concerned, it was still the night before.

'So, are you going to tell me, then?' he asked.

'Tell you what?'

'Where they are. Waterhouse and Charlie.' If Olivia knew, Gibbs figured, then he had a right to know too. As the two witnesses, they ought to have equal access to all relevant information.

'If I wouldn't tell you at ten o'clock, or eleven, or midnight, or one, why would I tell you now?'

'You've had more to drink. Your defences are down.'

Olivia raised an eyebrow and laughed. 'My defences are never down. The downer they seem, the upper they are. If that makes sense.' She leaned forward. *Cleavage alert.* 'Why do you call him Waterhouse?'

'It's his name.'

'Why don't you call him Simon?'

'Dunno. We call each other by our surnames: Gibbs, Waterhouse. Sellers. We all do.'

'Sam Kombothekra doesn't,' said Olivia. 'He calls you Chris

– I've heard him. He calls Simon Simon. And Simon calls him Sam, but you don't – you still call him Stepford. That was your original nickname for him and you're sticking with it.' Her eyes narrowed. 'You fear change.'

Gibbs wondered what had happened to the inebriated airhead he'd been drinking with a few minutes ago. Obviously she wasn't as far gone as he'd thought. 'It's a good nickname,' he told her. 'He'll always be Stepford to me.' He'd go to bed after this drink, bottle on the bar or no bottle on the bar. A woman like Olivia Zailer couldn't possibly be interested in anything he had to say. Knowing that made it hard to talk to her.

'Aren't you surprised that I know who calls who what, and I don't even work with you?'

'Not really.'

'Hm.' She sounded dissatisfied. 'Why do you think Simon chose you and not Sam? To be a witness.'

Gibbs was careful not to give himself away by looking as if it mattered to him. 'Your guess is as good as mine,' he said.

'It's obvious why he didn't choose Colin Sellers, a dedicated adulterer,' said Olivia. 'Simon'd think it was a jinx on his and Charlie's marriage to have a lowly fornicator involved in the proceedings.'

'That's stupid,' said Gibbs. 'It's up to Sellers what he does.' The Fornicator, *starring DC Colin Sellers. DC Colin Sellers is back in* Fornicator II. Gibbs smiled. A whole new world of piss-taking possibilities had just opened up. He wished he'd thought of it himself.

'With Colin out of the picture, Simon's options were you or Sam,' said Olivia. 'At first I wondered whether he didn't want Sam because Sam's chatty. He knew he and Charlie would be jetting off mid-evening and leaving us alone together – me and the other witness. Simon would hate the thought of Sam and me gossiping about him.'

'Stepford doesn't gossip,' said Gibbs.

'Maybe not normally, but he would with me, especially after a few drinks. And he'd tell himself he wasn't gossiping, just *discussing*, you know how people do.'

'You reckon I was chosen because I don't gossip?'

'Gossip?' Olivia chuckled. 'You barely speak. You make a point of saying as little as possible. Anyway, no, that was only my first theory.' She sipped her drink. 'My second was that Simon ruled Sam out on the grounds of his superior rank – asking his skipper to be a witness at his wedding might have looked like sucking up, even though it wouldn't have been – Simon's the least suck-up-y person I've ever known, and he'd hate for anyone to think otherwise.'

So Sellers was a non-starter and Stepford was a non-starter. Which had left only Gibbs.

'Then I decided – my third theory – that Simon chose you because he has more respect for you than he has for Sam, even if he thinks Sam's *nicer*. He thinks you're more intelligent. Or more like him, maybe. You're a puzzle, whereas Sam's an open book.'

Gibbs couldn't understand why she cared. She seemed to have given it as much thought as he had, and made more progress: three answers to his none.

'I couldn't bear the suspense, so I made Charlie ask him,' she said.

Gibbs' hand tightened around his glass. 'And?'

'Simon told her he feels closer to you than to Colin or Sam.' Olivia laughed. 'Which I thought was *just* hilarious, given that I bet the two of you have never had a single conversation about anything other than work.'

'We haven't,' Gibbs confirmed. He downed the rest of his drink and went to pour himself another one, unwilling to notice or reflect on the sudden improvement in his mood. 'If you're so keen on talking, why don't you tell me where the happy couple are?' he said. 'I'm not going to give the game away to Waterhouse's mum.'

Gibbs had met Kathleen Waterhouse only once, at the engagement party. She'd seemed timid, unassuming – a fade-into-the-background sort of person. Gibbs couldn't understand why she hadn't been allowed to attend her son's wedding, why it was so crucial that she shouldn't find out where he was going on his honeymoon.

'I'll answer any question but that one.' Olivia sounded apologetic. 'Sorry, but Charlie made me swear.'

'I'm not asking any other questions. That's the question I'm asking, and I'm going to keep asking. Though I reckon I know where they are. It doesn't take a genius.'

'You can't possibly know, unless you're psychic.' Olivia looked worried.

'You mentioned them 'jetting off' before, to put me off the scent. They haven't jetted off anywhere, have they? They're still here.' Gibbs grinned, pleased with his theory.

'*Here?* In Torquay, you mean?'

'Here: the Blue Horizon Hotel – the last place I'd expect them to be, after they made a big show of leaving a few hours ago.'

Olivia rolled her eyes in mock exasperation. Or maybe it was the real thing. 'They're not here, and this isn't the Blue Horizon Hotel,' she said. 'It's Blue Horizon.'

Was she taking the piss? 'That's what I said.'

'No, you called it the Blue Horizon Hotel.'

'It's called Blue Horizon, it's a hotel,' said Gibbs impatiently. 'That makes it the Blue Horizon Hotel.'

'No, it doesn't.' Olivia was inspecting him as if he was from another planet. 'Blue Horizon is the name of a top-notch establishment, which is what this is. Call it the Blue Horizon Hotel and it morphs into a shabby seaside B&B.'

'Right. I guess I'm too shabby to know the difference.'

'No, I didn't mean . . . Oh, God, I'm such an idiot! Now I've offended you and you'll clam up again, just when I'd got you warmed up.'

'I'm going to have to go bed,' said Gibbs. 'I can't listen to you any more. You're like a Sunday colour supplement – full of all kinds of shit.'

Olivia's eyes widened. She stared at him in silence.

Fuck. Talk about ending the day on a high note.

'Look, I didn't mean . . .'

'It's okay. I probably deserved it,' said Olivia briskly. 'Typical – the man who doesn't speak manages to say *one* thing, and it turns out to be something horrible about me that I'm going to have to carry around with me and feel rubbish about for at least the next year.'

'I didn't mean it in a bad way,' said Gibbs. 'It was just an observation.'

'You want to know where Simon and Charlie are? Fine. I can do better than tell you – I can show you a picture of their villa.' Olivia pulled her mobile phone out of her handbag and started to press buttons. Was she expecting Gibbs to say, 'No, forget it, it doesn't matter'? If so, she'd be disappointed. If he'd wanted to know before, why should that have changed now, just because she was upset and angry with him?

After a few seconds of finger-jabbing, Olivia thrust her

phone in front of his face. 'There you go. Los Delfines – the honeymoon villa.'

Gibbs looked at a small photograph of a long, white two-storey building that might have been designed to accommodate twenty people. There were balconies at most of the windows. Landscaped gardens, an outdoor bar and barbecue area, a swimming pool that looked big enough for an Olympic contest, all glowing in bright sunlight.

'Spain?' Gibbs guessed.

'Puerto Banus. Near Marbella.'

'All that for just the two of them? Not bad.'

'Insurance against unhappiness,' said Olivia. She still sounded annoyed. 'Fifteen grand's worth. No one could possibly be unhappy in a place like that, right?'

'Why would they be unhappy? They're on their honeymoon.'

Gibbs didn't think she was going to answer. Then she said, 'For years, Charlie's mobilising grievance has been *not having* Simon, in any and every sense. Now that they're married, she's got him. Sometimes, when you get something, you stop wanting it.'

'Sometimes you stop wanting it before you get it,' said Gibbs.

'Do you? I don't.'

'My wife Debbie's – what did you call it? – mobilising grievance is not being able to have a baby. I've stopped wanting one.'

'Has she?' Olivia asked.

'No.' *If only.*

'There you go, then. And you probably didn't want one all that much in the first place.'

'Come upstairs with me,' Gibbs said.

'Upstairs?'

'To my room. Or yours.'

'Why?' Olivia asked.

'Why do you think?' *What are you playing at, dickhead? Don't you know a bad idea when you have one?*

'Why?' she asked again.

'I could say, "Because for once, just for a change, I'd like to have sex with someone who isn't obsessed with getting pregnant." Or I could say, "Because I'm drunk and horny", or "Today's a special occasion and tomorrow it'll be back to normal life for both of us." How about, "Because you're the most beautiful, sexy woman I've ever met"? Risky – you might not believe me.'

Olivia frowned. 'Ideally, you ought to be going through your answer options in silence, in the privacy of your own head. Not out loud to me.'

In the privacy of your own head. It was because of the things she said. Not that he'd ever tell her that.

He took her glass from her hand and put it down on the table. 'Say yes,' he said. 'It's easy.'

3

Saturday 17 July 2010

'Why did you want to speak to Simon Waterhouse?' the detective called Sam asks. His surname is something long and unusual beginning with a K – he spelled it for me when he introduced himself. I didn't take it in, and didn't feel I could ask again. He's tall, good-looking, with black hair and a dark complexion. He's wearing a black suit and a white shirt with thin lilac stitched stripes, like perforated lines. No tie. I can't stop looking at his Adam's apple. It looks sharp enough to break skin. I imagine it slicing through his neck, an arc of blood spurting out. I shake my head to banish the morbid fantasy.

Does he want me to tell him again? 'I saw a woman lying face down—'

'You misunderstand me,' he interrupts, smiling to show that he doesn't mean to be rude. 'I meant why Simon Waterhouse in particular?'

Kit is in the kitchen making tea for us all. I'm glad. I'd find it harder to answer the question with him listening. If I didn't feel so horrible, this might be funny, like a weird sort of pantomime: *The Policeman Who Came to Tea*. It's only half past eight; we ought to be offering him breakfast. It's good of him to come so early. Maybe Kit will bring some croissants in with the drinks. If he doesn't, I won't offer. I can't think about anything apart from the dead woman. Who is she?

Does anybody know or care that she's been murdered, apart from me?

'I've been seeing a homeopath for the past six months. I've got a couple of minor health problems, nothing serious.' Was there any need to tell him that? I stop short of adding that the problems relate to my emotional health, and that my homeopath is also a counsellor. My desire to evade the truth makes me angry – with myself, Kit, Sam K, everyone. There's nothing shameful about needing to talk to somebody.

Then why are you ashamed?

'Alice – that's my homeopath – she suggested I talk to Simon Waterhouse. She said . . .' *Don't say it. You'll prejudice him against you.*

'Go on.' Sam K is doing his very best to look kind and unthreatening.

I decide to reward his efforts with an honest answer. 'She said he was like no other policeman. She said he'd believe the unbelievable, if it was true. And it *is* true. I saw a dead woman in that room. I don't know why it . . . why she wasn't there any more by the time Kit went and looked. I can't explain it, but that doesn't mean there isn't an explanation. There must be one.'

Sam K nods. His face is unreadable. Maybe he makes a point of encouraging mad people. If he thinks I'm mad, I wish he'd say it straight out: *You're a nutter, Mrs Bowskill.* I told him to call me Connie, but I don't think he wants to. Since I said it, he hasn't called me anything.

'Where is Simon?' I ask. When I rang his mobile last night, his recorded voice told me that he was unavailable – not for how long, or why – and gave a number to ring in an emergency: Sam K's number, as it turned out.

'He's on his honeymoon.'

'Oh.' He didn't tell me he was getting married. No reason why he would, I suppose. 'When will he be back?'

'He's gone for a fortnight.'

'I'm sorry I rang you at 2 a.m.,' I say. 'I should have waited till the morning, but . . . Kit had gone back to sleep, and I couldn't just do nothing. I had to tell someone what I'd seen.'

A fortnight. Of course – that's how long honeymoons are. Mine and Kit's was even longer: three weeks in Sri Lanka. I remember Mum asking if the third week was 'strictly necessary'. Kit told her politely but firmly that it was. He'd made all the arrangements and didn't appreciate her picking holes in the plan. The hotels he chose were so beautiful, I could hardly believe they were real and not something out of a dream. We stayed a week in each. Kit dubbed the last one 'the Strictly Necessary Hotel'.

Simon Waterhouse is entitled to his honeymoon, just as Kit is entitled to his sleep. Just as Sam K is entitled to deal with my concerns quickly and early, so that he can enjoy the rest of his Saturday. It can't be the case that everyone I come into contact with lets me down; it must be something I'm doing wrong.

'He didn't mention your name in his voicemail message – only the phone number,' I say. 'I thought it might be some kind of out-of-hours service, like doctors have.'

'Don't worry about it. Really. It made a nice change to get an emergency call that wasn't from Simon's mother.'

'Is she all right?' I ask. I sense it's expected of me.

'That depends on your point of view.' Sam K smiles. 'She's phoned me twice since Simon set off yesterday, crying and saying she needs to speak to him. He warned her that he and Charlie weren't going to be taking their mobiles, but I don't think she believed him. And now she doesn't believe me when I say I don't know where he is, which I don't.'

I wonder if the Charlie sharing Simon Waterhouse's honeymoon is a man or a woman. Not that it makes any difference to anything.

Kit comes in with the tea things and a plate of chocolate biscuits on a wooden tray. 'Help yourself,' he says to Sam K. 'Where are we up to?' He wants progress, solutions. He wants to hear that this expert has cured his wife of her lunacy during the ten minutes that he was in the kitchen.

Sam K straightens up. 'I was waiting for you, and then I was going to explain . . .' He turns from Kit to me. 'I'm happy to help as much as I can, and I can put you in touch with the right person if you decide to take this further, but . . . it's not something I can deal with directly. Simon Waterhouse couldn't deal with it either, even if he wasn't on his honeymoon, and even if . . .' He runs out of words, bites his lip.

Even if it weren't the most far-fetched story I've ever heard, and bound to be a load of rubbish. That's what he stopped himself from saying.

'If there's a woman lying injured or dead in a house in Cambridge, then it's Cambridgeshire Police you need to speak to,' he says.

'She wasn't injured,' I tell him. 'She was dead. That amount of blood can't come out of a person and them not be dead. And I'm willing to speak to whoever I need to – tell me a name and where I can find them, and I will.'

Did Kit sigh, or did I imagine it?

'All right.' Having poured himself a cup of tea, Sam K gets out a notebook and a pen. 'Why don't we go over a few details? The house in question is 11 Bentley Grove, correct?'

'11 Bentley Grove, Cambridge. CB2 9AW.' *You see, Kit? I even know the postcode by heart.*

'Tell me exactly what happened, Connie. In your own words.'

Who else's am I likely to use? 'I was looking on a property website, Roundthehouses.'

'What time was this?'

'Late. Quarter past one.'

'Do you mind if I ask why so late?'

'Sometimes I have difficulty sleeping.'

A sneer contorts Kit's face for a second; only I notice its fleeting presence. He's thinking that, if it's true, it's my own fault for giving in to my paranoia: I've chosen to torment myself with imaginary problems. He is sane and normal, therefore he sleeps well.

How can I know him well enough to read his thoughts, and, at the same time, fear that I don't know him at all? If I looked at an X-ray of his personality, would I see only the bits I know are there – his conviction that tea tastes better from a teapot and if you put the milk into the cup first, his ambition and perfectionism, his surreal sense of humour – or would there be an unfamiliar black mass at the centre, malignant and terrifying?

'Why a property website, and why Cambridge?' Sam K asks me. 'Are you thinking of moving there?'

'Definitely not,' says Kit with feeling. 'We've only just put the finishing touches to this place, six years after buying it. I want to spend at least that long enjoying it. I've told Connie: if we have a baby in the next six years, it'll have to bed down in a filing cabinet drawer.' He grins and reaches for a biscuit. 'I didn't do all that work only to sell up and let someone else get the benefit. Plus we run a business that's based here, and Connie got a bit carried away with the headed stationery, so we can't move until we've written at least another four thousand letters.'

I know what's going to happen before it happens: Sam K is going to ask about Nulli. Kit will answer at length; it's impossible to explain our work quickly, and my husband is nothing if not a lover of detail. I will have to wait to talk about the dead woman.

Connie got a bit carried away.

Did he say that deliberately, to plant the idea in Sam K's mind that I'm an easily-carried-away sort of person? Someone who orders six times more headed notepaper than she needs might also hallucinate a dead body lying in a pool of blood.

I listen as Kit describes our work. For the past three years, Nulli's twenty-odd full-time staff have been working for the London Allied Capital banking group. The US government is in the process of prosecuting the group, which, like many UK banks, has a long history of breaking American rules about dealing with sponsors of terrorism, and unwittingly allowing blacklisted people and companies to carry out wire-transfer transactions in the US in dollars. London Allied Capital is currently bending over backwards to right the wrong, ingratiate itself with OFAC, the American office of foreign asset control, and minimise the eventual damage, which will almost certainly be a multi-million-dollar fine. Nulli was taken on to build data-filtering systems that will enable the bank to unearth all the questionable transactions that lie hidden in its history, so that it can come clean to the US Department of Justice.

Like everyone Kit tells, Sam K looks impressed and confused in equal parts. 'So do you have a base in London, then?' he asks. 'Or do you commute?'

'Connie's based here, I'm half and half,' says Kit. 'I rent a flat in Limehouse – a box with a bed in it, basically. As far as I'm concerned, I only have one home, and that's Melrose Cottage.' He glances at me as he says this. Does he expect a round of applause?

'I can see that a small flat in London would have a job competing with this place.' Sam K looks around our lounge. 'It's got bags of character.' He turns to study the framed print on the wall behind him – a photograph of King's College Chapel, with a laughing girl sitting on the steps. Does he know he's looking at a picture of Cambridge? If he does, he says nothing.

The print was a present from Kit and I've always hated it. On the mount, at the bottom, someone has written '4/100'. 'That's not a very good mark,' I said when Kit first gave it to me. 'Four per cent.'

He laughed. 'It's the fourth in a run of a hundred prints, you fool. There are only a hundred of these in the world. Isn't it beautiful?'

'I thought you didn't like mass-produced things,' I said, determinedly ungrateful.

He was hurt. 'The handwritten "4/100" makes it unique. That's why prints are numbered.' He sighed. 'You don't like it, do you?'

I realised how selfish I was being and pretended that I did.

'My wife calls houses like this "camera-ready",' Sam K says. 'The minute I stepped over your threshold, I felt inferior.'

'You should see the insides of our cars,' Kit tells him. 'Or rather, our two dustbin-spillover areas on wheels. I've thought about leaving them on the pavement next to the wheelie bin on collection day, doors open – maybe the council'd take pity on us.'

I stand up. Blood rushes to my head and the room tilts, blurs.

I feel as if the different parts of my body are detaching from one another, breaking off and floating away. My head fills with a woolly throbbing. This keeps happening. My GP has no idea what the cause might be. I've had blood tests, scans, everything. Alice, my homeopath, thinks it's a physical manifestation of emotional distress.

It takes a few seconds for the dizziness to pass. 'You might as well go,' I say to Sam K, as soon as I'm able to speak. 'You obviously don't believe me, so why should we both waste our time?'

He looks at me thoughtfully. 'What makes you think I don't believe you?'

'I might be delusional but I'm not stupid,' I snap at him. 'You're sitting there eating biscuits, chatting about wheelie bins and interior décor . . .'

'It helps me to find out a little about you and Kit.' He's unruffled by my outburst. 'I want to know who you are as well as what you saw.'

The holistic approach. Alice would be on his side.

'I saw nothing.' Kit shrugs.

'That's not true,' I tell him. 'You didn't see *nothing* – you saw a lounge with no woman's body in it. That's not nothing.'

'Why a property website, Connie?' Sam K asks again. 'Why Cambridge?'

'A few years ago we thought about moving there,' I say, unable to look him in the eye. 'We decided not to, but . . . sometimes I still think about it, and . . . I don't know, it was a spur of the moment thing – there was no particular reason behind it. I look up all sorts of strange things on the internet when I'm restless and can't sleep.'

'So, last night, you logged onto Roundthehouses and . . . what? Talk me through it, step by step.'

'I searched for properties for sale in Cambridge, saw 11 Bentley Grove, called up the details . . .'

'Did you look at any other houses?'

'No.'

'Why not? What made you pick 11 Bentley Grove?'

'I don't know. It was third on the list that came up. I liked the look of it, so I clicked on it.' I sit down again. 'First I looked at the photographs of the rooms, and then I saw there was a virtual tour, so I thought I might as well have a look at that too.'

Kit reaches over and squeezes my hand.

'How much was it on for?' Sam K asks.

Why does he want to know that? '1.2 million.'

'Would that be affordable for you?'

'No. Not even close,' I say.

'So you have no plans to move to Cambridge, and 11 Bentley Grove would be out of reach price-wise, but you were still interested enough to take the virtual tour, even after you'd looked at the photographs?'

'You must know what it's like.' I try not to sound defensive. 'You find yourself clicking on one thing after another. Not for any good reason, just . . .'

'She was wilfing,' Kit tells Sam K. 'Wilf as in "What was I Looking For?" – aimless web-surfing. I do it all the time, when I should be working.' He's covering for me. Does he expect me to be grateful for his support? It's his fault that I've had to make up a story. *I'm not the liar here.*

'All right,' says Sam K. 'So you took the virtual tour of 11 Bentley Grove.'

'The kitchen came up first. The picture kept turning – it made my eyes feel tired, so I closed them, and then when I opened them I saw all this . . . red. I realised I was looking at the lounge, and there was a woman's body—'

'How did you know it was the lounge?' Sam K cuts me off.

I don't mind the interruption. It calms me, pulls me out of the horror that's still so vivid in my mind, and back into the present. 'I'd seen it in one of the photographs – it was the same room.' Haven't I just told him I looked at the photographs first? Is he trying to catch me out?

'But there was no woman's body and no blood in the photograph, correct?'

I nod.

'Let's leave aside the blood and the body for a second. In every other respect, the virtual tour's lounge was the same as the lounge in the photograph, yes?'

'Yes. I'm almost sure. I mean, I'm as sure as I can be.'

'Describe it.'

'What's the point?' I ask, frustrated. 'You can log onto Roundthehouses and see it for yourself. Why don't you ask me to describe the woman?'

'I know this is hard for you, Connie, but you have to trust that anything I ask, it's for a good reason.'

'You want me to describe the lounge?' I feel as if I'm at a kids' party, playing a stupid game.

'Please.'

'White walls, beige carpet. A fireplace at the centre of one wall, tiles around it. I couldn't see the tiles in detail, but I think they had some kind of flower pattern on them. They were too old-fashioned for the room.' I realise this only as I hear myself say it, and feel relieved. Kit might choose tiles like that for our house, which was built in 1750, but never for a modern house like 11 Bentley Grove that can't be more than ten years old.

He believes new buildings should be wholeheartedly contemporary, inside and out.

Therefore 11 Bentley Grove is nothing to do with him.

'Go on,' says Sam K.

'Alcoves on either side of the chimney breast. A silver L-shaped sofa with red embroidery on it, a chair with funny wooden arms, a coffee table with a glass top and flowers in a sort of horizontal display case under the glass – blue and red flowers.' *To match the tiles*. There was something else, something I can't call to mind. What was it? What else did I see, while the room was slowly circling? 'Oh, and a map above the fireplace – a framed map.' That wasn't it, but I might as well mention it. *What else?* Should I tell Sam K there was something else but I don't know what? Is there any point?

'A map of?' he asks.

'I couldn't see – it was too small in the picture. In the top left-hand corner there were some shields – about ten maybe.'

'Shields?'

'Like upside-down gravestones.'

'You mean crests?' says Kit. 'Like when a family has a crest?'

'Yes.' That's it. I couldn't think of the word. 'Most of them were colourful and patterned, but one was empty – just an outline.'

Was the empty crest the missing detail? I could pretend it was, but I'd be kidding myself. My mind took something else from that room, something it won't put back.

'Anything else?'

'A dead woman in a pool of blood,' I say, hating the belligerence in my voice. Why am I so angry? *Because you're powerless*, Alice would say. *We manufacture anger to give ourselves the illusion of power when we feel weak and helpless.*

At last, I hear the words I've been waiting for. 'Describe the woman,' Sam K says.

~

Words begin to pour out of me, an uncontrollable flow. 'When I saw her, and all that blood, when I realised what I was looking at, I looked down at myself – that was the first thing I did. I panicked. For a second I thought I was looking at a picture of myself – I looked down to check I wasn't bleeding. I didn't understand it afterwards – why would I do that? She was lying on her front – I couldn't see her face. She was small, petite, my size and build. She had dark hair, same colour as mine, straight like mine. It was . . . messy, sort of fanned out, as if she'd fallen and . . .' I shudder, hoping I don't need to spell it out: dead women can't make adjustments to their hair.

'I couldn't see her face, and I imagined – just for a second, until I got my bearings – that she was me, that I was the one lying there. Stop writing,' I hear myself say. *Too loud.* 'Can't you just listen, and make notes afterwards?'

Sam K puts down his notebook and pen.

'I don't want to build it up into more than it was,' I say. 'I knew she wasn't me, of course I did, but . . . it was as if my perception played a trick on me. It must have been the shock. She was lying in the most blood I've ever seen. It was like a big red rug under her. At first I thought it couldn't be blood because there was so much of it, it covered about a third of the room, but then I thought . . . Well, you must know. You must have seen dead people lying in their own blood, people who've bled to death.'

'Jesus, Con,' Kit mutters.

I ignore him. 'How much blood is there, normally?'

Sam K clears his throat. 'What you're describing doesn't sound implausible, in a bleeding-to-death scenario, though I've never seen it first-hand. What size is the lounge?'

'Twenty foot ten by eleven foot three,' I tell him.

He looks surprised. 'That's very exact.'

'It's on the floorplan.'

'On the Roundthehouses website?'

'Yes.'

'Do you know the dimensions of all the rooms?'

'No. Only the lounge.'

'Tell him what you did last night, once I'd gone back to bed,' says Kit.

'First I rang Simon Waterhouse, then, when I couldn't get him, I rang you,' I tell Sam K. 'After talking to you, I went back to my laptop and . . . looked at 11 Bentley Grove again. I studied every photograph, I studied the floorplan. I watched the virtual tour over and over.' *Yes, that's right. I hereby declare myself obsessive and insane.*

'For six hours she did that, until I woke up and dragged her away from the computer,' says Kit quietly.

'I kept closing down the internet, then opening it up again. A few times I turned off the laptop, unplugged it, then plugged it in again and rebooted it. I . . . I was exhausted and not thinking straight, and . . . I kind of got the idea into my head that if I persisted, I'd see it again – the woman's body.' Am I being too honest? So my behaviour last night was out of control – so what? Does that make me an unreliable witness? Do the police only listen to people who take mugs of Ovaltine to bed at ten o'clock and spend the rest of the night sensibly asleep in their flannel pyjamas? 'I've never seen a dead body before. A *murdered* body, that then disappears. I was in shock. I probably still am.'

'Why do you say "murdered"?' Sam K asks.

'It's hard to imagine how she could end up like that by accident. I suppose she might have plunged a knife into her stomach, laid herself face down on the floor and waited to die, but it seems unlikely. It's not the most obvious way to commit suicide.'

'Did you see a stomach wound?'

'No, but the blood looked thickest around her middle. It was almost black. I suppose I just assumed . . .' *A deep tarry blackness, thinning to red. A small window, rectangles of light on the dark surface . . .*

'Connie?' Kit's face is swimming in front of mine. 'Are you okay?'

'No. No, not really. I saw the window . . .'

'Don't try to talk until the dizziness passes.'

'. . . in the blood.'

'What does she mean?' Sam K asks.

'No idea. Con, put your head between your knees and breathe.'

'I'm fine.' I push him away. 'I'm fine now. If nothing else I've said has convinced you both, this will,' I say. 'I saw the lounge window reflected on the surface of the blood. As the room turned, the blood turned, and so did the little window. That proves I didn't imagine it! No one would imagine such a stupid, pedantic detail. I *must* have seen it. It must have been real.'

'For Christ's sake.' Kit covers his face with his hands.

'And her dress – why would I have imagined a dress like that? It was pale green and lilac, and had a pattern that was like lots of hourglass shapes going down her body in vertical lines, curved lines going in and out, in and out.' I try to demonstrate with my hands.

Sam K nods. 'Was she wearing shoes, or tights? Any jewellery that you noticed?'

'No tights. Her legs were bare. I don't think she was wearing shoes either. She had a wedding ring on. Her arms were up, over her head. I remember looking at her fingers and . . . Yes. Definitely a wedding ring.'

And something else, something my mind's eye refuses to bring into focus. The more I try and fail to identify it, the more aware I am of its hidden presence, like a dark shape that's slipped off the edge and out of sight.

'What happened when you saw the body on your laptop?' Sam K asks. 'What did you do, after you'd examined yourself to check you weren't bleeding?'

'I woke Kit and made him go and look.'

'When I went in, there was a rotating kitchen on the screen,' Kit says. 'Then the lounge came on, and there was no woman's body in it, and no blood. I told Connie, and she came in to look.'

'The body had gone,' I say.

'I didn't reload the tour,' says Kit. 'It was still running when I walked into the room, the same one Connie had started, on a repeating loop. I'm not saying changes can't be made to a virtual tour of a house – of course they can – but they wouldn't affect a tour already playing. It's just not possible—'

'Of course it's possible,' I cut him off. 'You're telling me someone can't arrange a virtual tour so that once in every hundred or thousand times, a different picture of the lounge comes up?' *Come on, Kit. Aren't you proud of your pupil? It's thanks to you that I no longer underestimate what's technically possible. A computer, instructed by the right person, can do almost anything.*

'Well?' I demand. 'Isn't it possible?'

Grudgingly, Kit concedes that it is. 'Please tell me you're not going to spend the rest of the day sitting through the tour a thousand times,' he says. 'Please.'

'Can I have a look at the laptop?' Sam K asks.

While Kit takes him upstairs, I pace up and down, picturing 11 Bentley Grove's lounge, trying to uncover the missing detail. *The woman disappeared. The blood disappeared. And something else . . .*

I'm so wrapped up in my thoughts that I don't notice Kit has returned, and I jump when he says, 'I know everyone hates estate agents, but you've taken it to a whole new level. What you haven't done is considered the why. *Why* would some evil genius estate agent, sitting in his office in Cambridge, want to include an elusive dead woman complete with own pool of blood on the virtual tour of a house he's trying to sell? Is it, what, a daring new marketing technique? Maybe you should see which agent the house is on with, ring up and ask them.'

'No,' I say, feeling calmer as he loses his cool. 'It's the police who ought to do that.' I won't let him turn this into something to be laughed at.

'You say she was murdered. Most murderers want to cover up what they've done, not broadcast it via one of the country's most popular websites.'

'I'm aware of that, Kit. I also know what I saw.' I need to ask him something, but every question I ask is another opportunity for him to lie. 'Why didn't you tell him?'

'Tell him?'

'Sam. That I was obsessed with 11 Bentley Grove long before last night. The whole story.'

Kit looks caught out. 'Why didn't *you* tell him? I assumed

you didn't want him to know, because . . .' He stops himself, looks away.

'Because?'

'You know damn well why! If I'd told him what's been going on since January, he wouldn't have given your dead woman the time of day – he'd have assumed the vanishing body was a figment of your imagination, just like the rest of it's a figment of your imagination!'

'Would he? Mightn't he have assumed the opposite – that something must be going on, something involving 11 Bentley Grove and you?' I wasn't willing to take the risk; perhaps Kit wasn't either.

His eyes fill with tears. 'I can't take much more of this, Con. I keep telling you, and you don't listen.' He falls into a chair, rubs his temples with his fingers. He looks so much older than he did six months ago. His face has new lines; there's more grey in his hair; his eyes are duller. Have I done that to him? The alternatives are too horrible to contemplate: either he's the kind, funny, loyal, honourable man I fell in love with and I'm slowly but surely destroying him, or he's a stranger who has been wearing a disguise for months, maybe years – a stranger who will eventually destroy me.

'I love you, Con,' he says in a hollow voice. I start to cry. His love for me is his most effective weapon. 'I always will, even if you succeed in driving me out of this house and out of your life. That's why I didn't tell' – he gestures towards upstairs – 'the whole story. If you want the police to take you seriously, if you want them to go to 11 Bentley Grove and check there's no dead woman lying on the carpet, then, however crazy it is, that's what I want too. I want you to feel better.'

'I know,' I say, numb inside. I don't know what I know any more.

'Do you have any idea how hard it is, living under a cloud of suspicion when you've done nothing wrong? You think I don't know what you're thinking? "Kit's a computer geek. Maybe he can make a body appear and disappear in a matter of seconds. Maybe he killed the body himself." '

'I don't think that!' I sob. *Because I didn't let myself go that far*. 'I hate being suspicious of you, I *hate* it. If 11 Bentley Grove was anywhere but Cambridge . . .'

Sam K is back, standing in the doorway. How much has he overheard? 'I'll tell you what I'll do,' he says. 'I'm going to speak to Cambridge police myself. They're more likely to pay attention if I make the initial contact.'

My heart jolts. 'Did you . . . ?' I point upwards, towards our office.

'I didn't see a body, no. Or any blood.'

'But . . .'

'The strong likelihood is that you were tired and had some kind of . . . transitory hallucination. What did you call it before? A trick of perception. But, at the same time, I don't want to dismiss what you've told me, because . . .' He sighs. 'Because you rang Simon Waterhouse, not me. Simon's the one you wanted. I can't turn myself into him, but I can do the next best thing, do what I know he'd do: take you seriously.'

'Thank you,' I say.

'Don't thank me – I'm only the stand-in.' Sam K smiles. 'You can thank Simon, the next time you see him.'

It's only once he's gone that it occurs to me what those words must mean: he knows I've met Simon before.

POLICE EXHIBIT REF: CB13345/432/20IG

CAVENDISH LODGE PRIMARY SCHOOL
BULLETIN NO. 586
Date: Monday 30th November 2009

Kittens at Cavendish Lodge!

We had an assembly with a difference on Wednesday in Class 1! Marcus's cat Bess has had five kittens, and his mum and dad brought them all into school! We had a marvellous time playing with these cute furry visitors, and a very interesting talk afterwards about pets and how to care for them, so huge thanks to Marcus and his family for allowing us to have this super treat! Below are two lovely write-ups from Class 1 children . . .

yesterday afternoon Marcus kittens came into school. They looked so cute they were black with white patches. I got to hold one of them they were lovely and furry but they had very sarp pink claws. One of them runed of beind the piona. I herd one of them purring. They had little blue eyes. It was a lovely afternoon.

by Harry Bradshaw

yesterday Marcus and his mummy brought some kittens to our asembaly we were talking about how to look after pets they were so lovely some were black with wight patches. The mummy cat Bess was not there. I got to hold four of them they felt soft just like fethers.

by Tilly Gilpatrick

4

17/07/10

Charlie didn't know what to do about her surname. It hadn't occurred to her that it was an issue until Simon had brought it up at the airport. He'd nodded at her passport and said, 'I suppose you'll have to get a new one now.' She hadn't known what he'd meant, and must have done a dismal job of concealing her shock when he'd explained. Simon had laughed at her. 'Don't worry,' he said. 'I assumed you'd be changing your name to mine, but if you don't want to, I don't mind.'

'Really?' Charlie had asked, immediately anxious about his happiness, which she perceived as fragile and endangered at the best of times. She had assumed the opposite: that she would remain Charlie Zailer; frankly, she was amazed Simon hadn't also. Annoyed with herself for being unprepared for such an important discussion, she'd decided on the spot that she would do whatever he wanted. There were worse names than Waterhouse.

It seemed, though, that for once Simon's feelings were uncomplicated. 'Really,' he'd assured her. 'What does it matter what you're called? It's only a label, isn't it?'

'Exactly,' she'd replied, straight-faced. 'I mean, thinking about it, I could just be called Female Police Sergeant number 54,437, couldn't I?'

The matter of her surname had been preoccupying her ever

since. What did other married women do? Charlie's next-door neighbour Marion Gregory, Kate Kombothekra, Stacey Sellers, Debbie Gibbs – they had all changed their names. Olivia, Charlie's sister, who was getting married next year, was trying to persuade Dominic, her husband-to-be, that they should become the Zailer-Lunds. 'Or he can stay as he is, and I'll be Zailer-Lund on my own,' she'd told Charlie defiantly. 'If Dom wants to wrap himself in the mouldering fetters of outmoded tradition, that's up to him. He can't stop me from adopting a more progressive approach.' Knowing Olivia as she did, Charlie suspected her determination had less to do with principle and more to do with a desire to be double-barrelled.

Charlie Zailer-Waterhouse. No, it was out of the question. Unlike Liv, Charlie did not hanker after the trappings of aristocracy; a double-barrelled surname would be an embarrassment to her, as well as an opportunity for everyone at the nick to take the piss.

'Why don't we pick a new name?' she called out to Simon, who was in the pool – or, rather, on it, lying in an inflatable boat that they'd found bobbing on the surface when they arrived. His arms and legs trailed in the water as he drifted aimlessly. Sometimes he used his hands as oars to turn himself round or push himself along; once or twice he'd kicked back from the edge, to see if he could propel himself all the way to the other side. He couldn't; the pool was too big.

Charlie had been secretly watching him, pretending to read her book, for nearly an hour and a half. What was going on in his mind? 'Simon?'

'Hm?'

'You're miles away.'

'Did you say something?'

'Instead of me taking your name, why don't we choose a new one? For both of us.'

'Don't be daft. No one does that.'

'Charlie and Simon Herrera.'

'Isn't that Domingo's surname?'

'Exactly. We could start a new tradition: the first person you meet on your honeymoon, their surname becomes your married name.' Domingo was the villa's caretaker: a young muscly chain-smoker with a deep tan, who spoke little English and appeared to live in a small wooden chalet-style building at the far end of the garden. He had picked Simon and Charlie up at the airport and driven them to Los Delfines, then given them a tour of the house and grounds without asking – perhaps because he lacked the vocabulary – whether they would prefer to wait until morning. The tour had taken nearly an hour; Domingo had insisted on stopping in front of every appliance and pointing at it, before demonstrating, in total silence, how it ought to be used.

Charlie hadn't cared. She had walked through the wooden gate set into the high, pantile-topped white wall, smelled the warm, spicy air in the garden, seen the pool lit up like an enormous glowing aquamarine stone, and fallen in love with Los Delfines on the spot. If she had to watch Domingo mime the turning of keys in front of keyholes and the setting and unsetting of the burglar alarm in order to be allowed to stay here for a fortnight, it was a price she was more than happy to pay.

Everything about this place was perfect. So perfect that it made Charlie worry about herself and Simon in comparison. What if the only thing wrong was them? She knew it was stupid to compare oneself with other people – to compare herself and Simon with other married couples – but it was hard to avoid doing so. Charlie knew of no other newlyweds who had approached their honeymoon in the way ex-mobsters-turned-informers might approach entry into the witness protection programme. Kathleen, Simon's mother, was as terrified of flying as she was of most things in life, and wouldn't have been able to cope with the thought of her son getting on a plane, so Simon had told her he and Charlie were going to Torquay for their honeymoon – by train. Kathleen had asked where they were staying, in case she needed to contact him in an emergency. He could have named a hotel in Torquay, real or imaginary, but he knew Kathleen would try to reach him there within a couple of days and discover he'd lied, which had left him with no alternative but to refuse to tell her. 'There won't be an emergency,' he'd said firmly. 'And if there is, it'll have to wait.'

Kathleen had sulked, wept, begged. At one point, after one of her trademark soggy Sunday lunches, she had fallen to her knees and grabbed Simon's legs. He'd had to pull her off him. Charlie had been shocked, as much by Simon's apparent lack of surprise as by anything else. Michael, his dad, hadn't seemed surprised either. His only verbal contribution had been the occasional muttered, 'Please, son,' to Simon. *Please, son, give her a way of contacting you. Make my life easier.*

To Charlie's great relief, Simon had stood firm. To her utter bafflement, he had accepted an invitation to lunch at his parents' house the following Sunday. 'Are you mental?' Charlie had snapped at him. 'It'll happen again – exactly what happened last week.' Simon had shrugged and said, 'Then I'll walk out like I did last week.'

He liked to believe that his mother didn't control him, but

then he did things like insist they go all the way to Torquay to get married – 'to make the lie a bit more true,' he'd said, unwilling to acknowledge the irrationality. Charlie would have preferred to get married at Spilling Register Office; she hated the thought that anything about their wedding was dictated by her pathetic mother-in-law. Simon had shouted her down: 'I thought you loved Torquay. Isn't that why we're pretending to go there for our honeymoon?'

Oddly enough, Kathleen hadn't tried to impose a church wedding on them, as Charlie had feared she might. She'd voiced no objection when Simon had told her that the wedding would involve only himself, Charlie and two witnesses, neither of whom would be her. 'She's relieved,' he'd explained. 'Nothing's expected of her. Think about it: most weddings, the mother of the groom spends the best part of a day being friendly and welcoming to the guests. Mum'd never have managed it. There'd have been a sudden illness, and Dad would have had to stay at home and look after her.'

Charlie's parents had also been thankful to hear that their attendance wouldn't be required. Her father would rather play golf than do anything else. He'd have taken a day off, for Charlie's sake, and tried to enjoy her wedding, but he'd soon have found an excuse to sink into a foul mood. Any day that involved no golf was a disastrous day for Howard Zailer, and for all those unlucky enough to encounter him in his golfless state.

'What about Melville?' Simon shouted from the swimming pool.

'Hm?'

'Our new surname.'

'Why Melville?'

'As in Herman Melville.'

'What about Dick?'

Simon stuck two fingers up at her. *Moby Dick* was his favourite novel. He read it once a year. He'd brought it with him to Spain; it was supposed to be his honeymoon reading, so why wasn't he reading it? Why was he content to float aimlessly, as if there was nothing else he wanted to do? The leaves and petals on the pool's surface looked as if they were making more of an effort.

Why wasn't he having sex with his wife?

Weren't you supposed to spend most of your honeymoon in bed? Or was that only if you hadn't slept together before the wedding?

Charlie sighed. Was she expecting too much? After years of avoiding all physical contact with her, Simon had decided last year that it was time they consummated their relationship. Since then, everything had been fine. Well, fine-ish. Charlie still didn't dare make the first move; she sensed Simon wouldn't like it. It was equally clear that talking – during, immediately afterwards, or on the subject of – was forbidden. Or was Charlie imagining barriers that weren't there? Maybe Simon wanted nothing more than for her to say, 'Do you like having sex with me, or do you only do it because you feel you have to?' Physically it seemed to work for him, but he always seemed so removed – eyes closed, silent, almost robotic at times.

The mid-afternoon sun was scorching. Charlie considered telling Simon to go inside and put on more sun-cream. And then she could go in after him and . . . No. The rule of never initiating sex was a good one, and she was determined to stick to it. Once – years ago at a party, long before they were officially together – Simon had rejected her advances in a particularly brutal way. Charlie was determined never to allow it to happen again.

She heard a noise behind her – footsteps. Domingo. She tensed, then exhaled with relief when she saw that he was holding a rake and a hoe; he was here to work, that was all. The garden that surrounded Los Delfines on all sides was evidently somebody's pride and joy – perhaps Domingo's, perhaps the owners'. It was bursting with more colours than Charlie had ever seen together in one place before: flame red, burgundy, purple, lilac, royal blue, orange, yellow, every shade of green. It made most English gardens look anaemic. Charlie's favourite thing in it was what she thought of as 'the upside-down lily tree', from which white lilies hung like little lampshades.

She put down her book and headed for the pool. Not because she wanted to be closer to Simon, but because the heat was blistering and she needed to cool off. She walked down the marble Roman steps into the water. 'Exactly the right temperature,' she said. 'Not cold, but not warm. Like a hot bath someone ran two hours ago.'

Simon didn't reply.

'Simon?' What was he so focused on, that he couldn't hear her when she was right next to him?

'Hm? Sorry. What did you say?'

It was hardly worth repeating. It seemed a shame to waste this opportunity; she ought to say something more important while she had his attention. 'Every time I see Domingo heading in our direction, I panic.'

'Scared he's going to try and show us some more light switches?'

'No, it's not that, it's . . . His mobile number's on the website. That means we're contactable via him, doesn't it?'

Simon struggled to sit up in his boat. 'Are you worried about my mum? She doesn't know where we are. No one does.'

'Olivia does.' Would he be angry that she'd told her sister what was supposed to be their secret? Apparently not. Charlie battled against the urge to ask him if she had his full attention. 'When I told Liv how much this place cost, she insisted on seeing pictures. I had to show her the website.'

'She's not going to tell my mum, is she?'

'It's not Kathleen I'm worried about,' said Charlie. 'It's work.'

Simon made a dismissive noise. 'The Safer Communities Forum can manage without you for fourteen days.'

'I mean *your* work. No one cares if I'm not there.'

'What, the Snowman? After months of looking forward to his Waterhouse sabbatical, as he calls it? He's hardly going to seek me out. You know the last thing he said to me before I left? "Let's both make the most of our two weeks off, Waterhouse. I might not be going anywhere more exotic than my office and the canteen, but without your constant plaguing presence wherever I turn, I shall be on holiday in my heart." '

'Believe me, Proust can't *wait* for you to get back. He's counting the days.'

'Don't say that,' Simon warned her. He hated the idea that his DI might feel anything but loathing for him.

'We left Liv and Gibbs alone together,' said Charlie. 'What if Liv got even more pissed than she was already and told Gibbs, and what if . . . ?' She didn't want to put it into words, in case that would make it more likely to come true.

'Gibbs?' Simon laughed. 'Gibbs makes no effort to speak to me when I'm sitting next to him. He's not going to go to the trouble of tracking me down in Spain. Why would he?'

'All it would take would be for something a bit less mundane than usual to come up at work, and everyone would think, "If only Simon were here, if only we could ask him what he thinks . . ." '

'No, they wouldn't. They'd think, "Thank God Waterhouse isn't here to over-complicate things." '

'You know that's not true. Sam Kombothekra doesn't think like that. And if Gibbs—'

'For fuck's sake, Charlie! Olivia isn't going to tell Gibbs where we are, Gibbs isn't going to tell Sam, Sam isn't going to stumble over a problem in the next fortnight that he needs to talk to me about. Okay? Relax.'

He was right; it was unlikely they'd be disturbed by anyone from home. So why couldn't Charlie shift the anxiety that was taking up space in her lungs, space she needed for breathing?

'I'm all yours for a fortnight, so count yourself unlucky,' said Simon. 'What's that Mark Twain quote? "I've worried about thousands of things in my life, a few of which have actually happened." Or words to that effect. Look.' He pointed to the gap between two trees, to a large mountain in the distance.

'What am I supposed to be looking at?' Charlie asked.

'The mountain. See the face?'

'The mountain face?'

'No, an actual face. It looks like it's got a face.'

'I can't see anything. What, you mean like eyes, nose, mouth?'

'And eyebrows, and I can see an ear, I think. Can't you see it?'

'No.' Charlie tried not to sound cross. 'I can't see a face in the mountain. Is it attractive?'

'It's got to be a trick of the light, but . . . I wonder whether it'll change as the sun moves. It must be something to do with the shadows cast by the rocky ridges.'

Charlie stared for a long time, but no face made itself apparent to her. Stupidly, she felt left out. Simon and his boat had floated to the other side of the pool. Might as well do a few lengths, she decided, keep herself fit. She resolved not to panic from now on when she saw Domingo coming her way, even if she did have a startlingly clear image in her mind of him ambushing her and Simon with the words, 'Phone, England,' waving his mobile in the air.

'Charlie?'

'Mm?'

'What would you do if . . . ?' Simon shook his head. 'Nothing,' he said.

'What would I do if what?'

'Never mind. Forget it.'

'I can't forget it, and you know I can't,' she said. 'Tell me.'

'There's nothing to tell.'

'*Tell* me!'

What would you do if I asked you for a divorce? What would you do if I said I wanted us to sleep in separate rooms?

'I'm imagining bad things here. Do you want to put me out of my misery?'

'It's nothing bad,' he said. 'It's nothing to do with you and me.'

Meaning that if it was something relating to the two of them it would, by necessity, be bad?

Stop creating problems where none exist, Zailer.

Charlie swore under her breath. She knew she was about to spend at least the next two hours trying to make him tell her, and she knew she would fail.

~

'You've got to *go*,' Olivia told Gibbs, pressing her hands against his ribcage. For the past hour she'd been trying to push him out of her bed, but he was stronger than she was, and resisting.

'No, I haven't.' He was lying on his back, arms folded behind his head.

'Yes, you have! We've got to start pretending not to be wicked Godless degenerates. If we start now, it won't take too long for it to become convincing – we might believe it by this evening if we're lucky.' Gibbs almost smiled, but didn't move. It was two o'clock in the afternoon, according to Olivia's phone. Her hotel room was as dark as it had been when they'd stumbled in here twelve hours ago. The black-out blinds and thick curtains were more serious about the preservation of night than any window-dressings Olivia had ever previously encountered, and had joined forces against the daylight.

'Don't you have to get home at some point? Haven't you got a life, plans, a curfew? I've got all three.' She gave up pushing. It wasn't going to work, and it was hurting her hands.

Gibbs rolled onto his side so that he was facing her. It was funny: though she called him Chris, she could only think of him as Gibbs, which was what Simon called him. Would that change? Silently, she reprimanded herself for thinking about him in the future tense. She needed to pull herself together, but how could she, with him lying next to her, radiating heat?

'Trying to get rid of me?' he asked.

'Yes, but . . . not in a bad way.'

'Is there a good way?'

'Of course. There are loads. There's the self-sacrificing "cut me loose and save yourself while you still can" good way, and there's . . .' Olivia stopped, remembering that he'd compared her to a Sunday colour supplement, and his reason for doing so. 'We've got to be out by three o'clock,' she said briskly, to disguise her embarrassment. 'I can't ring and ask for another extension.'

'What are the other good ways?' Gibbs asked. Could he really be interested?

She couldn't tell him the truth. She'd just had sex with him, three times. If ever a situation called for the opposite of the truth, this was surely it.

'I'm going nowhere unless you tell me,' he threatened.

'For God's sake! All right, then, maybe this'll do the trick where trying to push you out of bed failed. Another good way is: I need you to go so that I can spend the rest of the day thinking obsessively about all aspects of you, and going over your every word and action in my mind, to the exclusion of all else, for the foreseeable future.'

Gibbs grinned. 'It'll be easier for you to think about me if I stay here.'

'Wrong. For as long as you're here, I'll be too busy wondering what you're thinking to do any thinking myself.'

'I'm not thinking anything, apart from I want to fuck you again, but I'm too knackered.'

'Not listening, not listening!' Olivia covered her ears with her hands. 'Stop adding more words to the ones I already have to think about. I need to deal with the backlog. Don't laugh – I'm being serious. Please just go. Don't say anything else.'

'So that you can think about me?'

'Yes.'

'And about nothing else?'

'Not until I've cleared the backlog, no.'

Gibbs nodded as if her request were entirely reasonable. He

sat up and started gathering his clothes together. Olivia looked at her phone again. Five past two. She felt excitement welling up inside her at the prospect of him leaving. There were things she needed to attend to, urgently. First on the agenda was the letting off of steam in an undignified manner: running in circles round the room screaming, 'Oh my God, oh my God, oh my God!' Second was standing in front of the full-length mirror by the door and studying her face and body as if she'd never seen them before and never would again; trying to see them as Gibbs saw them, through his eyes. Then she would ring Charlie. Or rather, she would ring the caretaker at Los Delfines, the one whose number was on the website, and ask him to pass on a message for Charlie to ring her. Any decent sister – and Charlie was, generally – would want to hear this sort of news straight away.

Guess who's been a complete and utter slapper? Me!

Some gossip was so momentous that it demolished all considerations of honeymoon privacy that stood in its path; by pure chance, this was exactly such an instance. Olivia knew she would enjoy gossiping about herself as much as she enjoyed gossiping about other people. More, even. She so rarely did anything that would shock anyone. How refreshing, to be a scandal-maker at her age – to do something indescribably stupid when, in forty-one years, no one had ever feared she might.

Could she ask Charlie not to tell Simon? Some people kept no secrets from their spouses. Would her sister become fanatical about sharing everything, now that she was married? Simon would disapprove, in the way that people who lacked life experience always disapproved of others having adventures they had so far missed out on. He would feel that in some obscure way, his and Charlie's wedding day had been ruined, degraded, by their two witnesses ending up in bed together.

Olivia sighed as she realised the implications. For Simon's sake, Charlie would have to be livid and wounded. She wouldn't see Olivia's one-night stand with Gibbs as something that had happened to Olivia, but as something bad that had happened to her all-important husband. Perhaps she would also object on her own account, and accuse Olivia of trespassing; Gibbs was police, and therefore belonged to Charlie and Simon, and not to Olivia, who'd had no right to barge in to a world that wasn't hers, into which she was only invited from time to time, at Charlie's discretion.

Had she hijacked the most important day of her sister's life? Was it unforgivable to cast oneself as a rival leading lady without consulting anybody, when one was supposed to be playing a supporting role? Olivia couldn't decide whether she'd done a terrible thing to Charlie, or nothing at all. She would never know, unless she told Charlie what had happened; she couldn't work it out on her own, not without knowing what the reaction would be.

I ought to be feeling guilty about Dom, she thought, and about Debbie Gibbs. They're the wronged parties here.

Gibbs was dressed. 'I'm off,' he said. 'You can start thinking.'

'So can you,' said Olivia, wanting a way of attaching him to her, now that he was going. 'Think about me, I mean.'

'To the exclusion of all else,' he said. 'For the foreseeable future.'

It sounded like a quote. Because it was, Olivia realised. He was quoting her.

~

Sam Kombothekra wasn't used to feeling guilty, but that was how he felt as he sat at a window table in Chompers café bar, waiting for Alice Bean. This was – or would be, assuming she turned up – an entirely unnecessary meeting, yet Sam had chosen it in preference to an afternoon at home with his family. He already knew the answers Alice would give to the questions he planned to ask her. He could have asked them over the phone, but he'd been keen to see her in the flesh, keener than he cared to admit even to himself. Few women were more legendary than Alice in the small world that was Spilling nick. Sam had heard from at least ten different sources that Simon Waterhouse had been romantically fixated on her several years ago. She'd been Alice Fancourt then.

Sam knew that her involvement with Simon (which, according to Colin Sellers, had been 'a shagless waste of time') had ended badly, that the two of them no longer spoke to one another. How much of the story would Alice tell him today? On the phone this morning, she had asked within seconds of Sam introducing himself if he worked with Simon. She'd suggested Chompers as the venue for this afternoon's meeting, saying, 'That's where Simon and I always met.' Sam felt guilty about that too: not only was he abandoning his family on one of his days off, he would also very probably be stirring up painful memories for a stranger, for no more noble reason than to satisfy his unwholesome curiosity.

He looked at his watch. She was ten minutes late. Should he ring her? No, he'd leave it until quarter past. Maybe he'd ask one of the waiters to turn down the music. Presumably it was intended to cover the noise from the corner of the room, where there was a fenced-off play area full of howling soggy-faced toddlers, a handful of mothers whose stiff smiles sizzled with repressed fury, tables and chairs in the shape of toadstools, and an assortment of unrecognisable plastic objects in primary colours. Sam didn't blame the children for wailing; he might soon be doing the same if he had to sit through many more Def Leppard hits from the 1980s.

He stared out of the window at the car park. Any second now, Alice would pull into one of the empty spaces. This might be her, slamming shut the boot of a red Renault Clio. Sunglasses, strappy sandals . . . No. Simon would never fall for a face like that. Sam wondered if Alice looked anything like Charlie. *So what if she does? And so what if she doesn't?* Why did he find everything to do with Simon so compelling? He wouldn't have put himself out to meet a woman Chris Gibbs used to be in love with, or Colin Sellers. Come to think of it, he would probably travel a reasonable distance to see the rare woman that *didn't* inspire longing in Colin, assuming such a person existed.

Ashamed of his own prurience, Sam tried to focus instead on Connie Bowskill. He soon found himself thinking about Simon Waterhouse again. Nothing wrong with that, he decided, not in this context. Simon was the best detective Sam knew; he was the best detective anyone knew, though most people were reluctant to admit it, and preferred to dismiss him as a rude, unpredictable troublemaker. On the first of January this year, at five past midnight, Sam had made a resolution: instead of constantly feeling inferior to Simon, and allowing more and more resentment to build, he would try to learn from him, to put aside his ego and see if he could acquire by imitation – by studying Simon's behaviour and attitudes as if he might one day be examined on both – a small fraction of that brilliance.

Simon would not have dismissed Connie Bowskill in a hurry, Sam was certain of that. Would he have believed her, though?

In Sam's position, having met Connie and heard what she had to say, would Simon be leaning more towards thinking she was suffering from stress and seeing things that weren't there, or would he be convinced she was lying? Maybe he'd think her story's implausibility made it likely to be true, because few people would have the confidence to tell so outrageous a lie.

You're not Simon – that's the whole problem. You've no idea what he'd think.

No, that wasn't true. You couldn't work closely with someone for years and not have an inkling as to how their mind worked. Simon would think there was at least a chance that a crime had been committed. If he'd gone with Sam to talk to the Bowskills this morning, he'd have come away certain that there was something badly wrong in that house – Melrose Cottage, not 11 Bentley Grove, Cambridge. Sam agreed, in so far as one can agree with one's imaginary projection of an absent person. Something was going on: Connie and Kit Bowskill hadn't told him everything, not by a long way. He'd overheard enough of the conversation he wasn't supposed to hear to be sure that they were conspiring to hide something from him.

The idea of somebody putting an image of a dead body on an estate agent's website was laughable. Beyond crazy. In his mind, Sam heard Simon say, 'Crazy doesn't have to mean made up. Insanity's as real as sanity. It doesn't need our understanding in order to fuck up and end lives – it only needs to understand itself. Sometimes it doesn't even need that.' Immediately, Sam wished he hadn't remembered the comment; with it came the memory of yet another instance of Simon being proved right and him wrong, despite his more sensible belief in what had seemed so much more likely.

He sighed. As Simon's temporary stand-in, he would do everything he could to find a dead woman that he didn't believe in – a woman in a green and lilac dress. He'd already put in a call to Cambridge police and made it clear to them that he expected them to take action, once they'd stopped laughing.

'Sam?'

He looked up and saw a woman with cropped peroxide blonde hair, maroon plastic-framed glasses and shiny London-bus-red lipstick. She was wearing a long pink sleeveless dress and flat gold sandals, carrying a bag with holes in it that looked as if it was made from lots of offcuts of rope knotted together; the holes were a design feature, not the result of wear and tear, and enabled Sam to see some of the bag's contents: a red wallet, an envelope, some keys.

'Alice Bean.' She smiled and held out her hand. 'You have no idea how weird this is for me. I haven't set foot in this place for nearly seven years. If I have a funny turn, you'll know why.'

'Can I get you a drink?' Sam asked, shaking her hand.

'Lime cordial and lemonade would be lovely. Lots of ice. I know it's a kid's drink, but in this heat, nothing else will do. I must have sweated at least a pint in the car on the way here.'

Sam watched her out of the corner of his eye as he queued at the bar. She was undeniably pretty, but the hair had surprised him – its shortness and its colour. And the maroon glasses, and the lipstick most of all. He wouldn't have thought Simon would . . . But that was assuming she'd looked the same seven years ago, and that Simon's taste in women would be easy to predict. Why should it be, when nothing else about him was? He'd proposed marriage to Charlie when she wasn't even his girlfriend.

'So Connie gave you my number?' Alice said as Sam put her drink down on the table in front of her.

'She didn't. I didn't ask her for it. I looked you up in the *Yellow Pages*, under "Alternative Health – Homeopaths". There were no Alice Fancourts, but I figured Alice Bean might work, and it did.'

'Bean's my maiden name. I haven't been Fancourt for years.'

'Do you normally work Saturdays?'

'No. I wasn't working today. I popped into the centre to pick up a remedy for my daughter, Florence, who's got a tummy bug. You were lucky to catch me. And I hope you don't catch the bug, but you might, so don't say I didn't warn you. I had it before Florence and everyone at work had it before me. It's a spreader, that's for sure. Passes out of your system quickly, though, on the plus side. Twenty-four hours of vomiting and diarrhoea and then it moves on to the next poor sucker.'

Great. Something to look forward to.

'I won't keep you long,' Sam told her. 'If your daughter's ill.'

'She'll be fine. She's with my friend Briony, who's like a second mum to her. Keep me as long as you like. I promise not to make it hard for you by asking awkward questions.'

Sam tried not to look surprised. Wasn't he supposed to be the one with the questions? 'Like what?' he said.

'About Simon. He wouldn't want you to talk about him to me – I know he wouldn't.' Alice reached into her bag, pulled out the envelope Sam had seen through the holes, and held it out for him to take. He saw Simon's name on the front in blue handwriting, underlined. 'Could you give him this?'

Sam was aware of not wanting to take it from her, but couldn't think why at first. Then his brain caught up with his gut. *No thanks.* Whatever the drama was, he didn't want even a minor role. His hands stayed where they were, wrapped round his coffee mug. Eventually Alice put the envelope back in her bag, and he felt petty and self-important, knowing that he'd turned the focus from her and Simon to himself and his scruples; he wished he'd taken the damn thing. Ought he to tell her Simon got married yesterday, that he was on his honeymoon? Did it make it worse that it had happened only yesterday? Sam didn't think it should make a difference, but felt that it did, somehow.

He opened his mouth to try and explain why he didn't think it was a good idea for him to act as go-between, but Alice talked over him, smiling to show she wasn't offended. 'What did you want to ask me about Connie? Is she okay?'

'When did you last speak to her?'

'I see her once a fortnight. The last time was . . . Hang on, I can tell you exactly.' She pulled a small pink diary out of her miniature fisherman's net. 'Last Monday, four o'clock.'

'As in the one just gone? Monday 12 July?'

Alice nodded.

'Since then, have you spoken to her on the phone? Emailed or texted her?'

'No. Nothing.'

'And she didn't ring you in the early hours of this morning?'

Alice looked worried. She leaned forward. 'No. Why? Has something happened?'

'She's fine, as far as I can tell,' said Sam. He wasn't prepared to say more than that.

'Why the early hours of this morning?' Alice persisted. 'Why did you ask that?'

Because that was when a dead woman appeared on her computer screen, and then disappeared. And she told me you'd recommended she contact Simon Waterhouse, who would believe the unbelievable, if it were true. Except that you couldn't have recommended him at two this morning, because Alice didn't ring you then. She hasn't spoken to you since seeing the woman's body. Unless she lied about when she saw it.

'Did you advise Connie to speak to Simon?' Sam asked.

'I can't really discuss what I say to my patients or what they say to me. Sorry.'

'I'm not asking you to tell me anything Connie hasn't told me herself. She said you recommended Simon as being unlike any other detective, willing to believe what most people would find implausible.'

Alice nodded. 'That's right. That's what I said, almost word for word.'

'Would I be right in thinking, then – and I'm not asking for details – that Connie was in some kind of . . . situation, or had a problem, and was worried that no one would believe her?'

'I really can't go into the specifics, but . . . Connie came to see me initially because she'd had a shock – she didn't want to believe that something was the case, and yet she feared it was.'

'When was this?' Sam asked.

'January, so . . . six months ago.'

'And you told her to go to Simon? Was there a criminal angle, then?'

Alice frowned as she considered it. 'There was no evidence of anything illegal, but . . . Connie thought there might have been a crime involved, yes. But at the same time, she feared she was mad for thinking it.'

'What did you think?'

'I honestly had no idea. All I knew was that being psychologically and emotionally split in two was doing her no good whatsoever. I thought that if she spoke to Simon, he could find out for her one way or the other.'

'Whether a crime had been committed?'

Alice smiled. 'I realise there's no great master list headed "All the crimes that have been committed ever", but this particular crime would have been documented. Simon could have tracked down the evidence of it in a way that Connie couldn't.'

'Do you remember when you first mentioned his name to her?' Sam asked.

'Oh, not straight away. About a month ago, six weeks maybe. I tried to help her myself first, obviously, as I do with all my patients, but nothing I said or did seemed to work with Connie. If anything, she started to feel worse as time went on. That was when I realised she might need more than Anacardium or Medorrhinum. Sorry, they're homeopathic remedies – I forget sometimes that not everyone's as familiar with them as I am.'

'Did Connie take your advice?' Sam asked. 'Did she share her problem with Simon?' *Was that why he took two days off a couple of weeks ago?* He'd mumbled something vague about 'wedding preparations', not making eye-contact. At the time, Sam had put it down to embarrassment; Simon was undoubtedly, if inexplicably, mortified to be in a relationship, and avoided referring to his attached status.

Alice looked apologetic. 'Ask Connie,' she said. 'I'm sure she'll tell you the whole story, if you're willing to listen sympathetically.'

'Did her unlikely-sounding and possibly criminal problem involve a virtual tour of a house on a property website?' Sam asked. Alice's facial expression was the only answer he needed: she didn't know what he was talking about.

So Connie Bowskill had two impossible-to-believe problems, one since January and one since thirteen hours ago. Interesting.

Impossible to believe.

'Did you advise Connie to talk to Simon because you genuinely believed she needed police help, or because you hoped he would contact you to ask about her?' As soon as the words were out of his mouth, Sam knew he'd overstepped the mark. 'I'm sorry,' he said, holding up his hands. 'That's a question I have no right to ask. Ignore it.'

'Why, when it's one I can answer freely?' said Alice. 'I genuinely believed Simon ought to hear about Connie's problem, because . . . well, because it was so odd, so unusual. It was either something truly horrible or nothing at all. I . . .' She stopped, stared down at the table. Sam was starting to wonder if he ought to prompt her when she said, 'I've only just this second realised it, but I told her to speak to Simon because that was what *I* wanted to do. I wanted to talk to him about it. He and I haven't spoken since 2003, and – this, Connie's . . . issue that she had, made me want to be in touch with him again more than anything else ever has. It made me *miss* him, though I never really knew him in the first place. Oh, it's crazy! The funny thing is, I've always known absolutely for sure that one day he'd reappear in my life. And when you rang this morning . . .' She shook her head, looking past Sam out of the window.

He could guess what was coming next. When he'd rung this morning and asked her to meet him, she'd given her sick daughter to a friend and devoted the next two hours to writing the letter she'd wanted to write for the last seven years, the one Sam had refused to deliver.

'Look, I'm sorry about—'

'Don't be,' said Alice. 'I shouldn't have tried to turn you into the very-likely-to-get-shot messenger. It was unethical. And unnecessary – I don't need you. I know where Simon works – I could post the letter to him. I won't, though.' She nodded, as if to formalise the decision. 'I'm a firm believer in fate, and today fate's made it clear to me that now's not the right time. I bet you're not used to thinking of yourself as an agent of fate, are you?' She grinned.

'I'm not.' Colin Sellers would have had a jokey response ready, but Sam couldn't think of one.

Alice closed her eyes and took a sip of her drink. 'The right time will come,' she said.

5

Saturday 17 July 2010

'1.2 *million* pounds? Oh . . . *Ow!* Ouch.' My mother has missed the five mugs lined up on the worktop and poured boiling water over her left hand instead. Deliberately, though I can't prove it. She has burned herself, and it's my fault for causing her more worry than she can cope with. *Again*. She wants everybody to notice and blame me. If they do, if Fran or Anton or Dad says, 'Look what you've done, Con,' Mum will stick up for me, but her defence will be a veiled attack: 'It wasn't Connie's fault – I should have known better than to look away, with a kettle full of boiling water in my hand, but I was so shocked, I couldn't help it.'

Is this what being close to someone means – knowing their limitations, their ego-boosting delusions and self-serving grottiness, as well as you know your own? Being able to predict their reactions, their facial expressions, down to the last word and grimace, so that disappointment and a sickening sense of predictability surge up and crush the breath out of you the moment you clap eyes on them, before anyone's uttered a word? Kit would say that was too pessimistic an analysis, but then he was never close to his parents, and now he has no relationship with them at all. He is for ever saying he envies me my membership of what he calls 'the Monk clan'. I don't dare tell him the truth; he would accuse me of being ungrateful. He'd probably be right.

The truth is that I would rather be less close to my family, so that they could surprise me from time to time. So that their disapproval, when it came, wouldn't have the capacity to burrow so deeply into me and plant seeds of self-doubt, pre-programmed to grow to the size of large oak trees. At least Kit is free.

'Come on, Benji,' Fran whispers. 'One more bit of broccoli and then you can have a chocolate finger. Just the curly bit at the top. *Please.*'

'Go on, Benji, mate – show Mummy and Daddy how brave you are. Like a superhero!' Anton doesn't bother to lower his voice. It hasn't occurred to him that there's anything more important going on in his parents-in-law's kitchen today than Benji's war on green vegetables; he feels no need to confine the broccoli negotiations to the background. Making a loud-speaker out of his hands, he puts on a booming voice and says, 'Can one little boy defeat the broccoli monster? Is Benji brave enough to eat . . . his . . . broccoli? If he proves that he's as brave as a superhero, his reward will be two . . . chocolate . . . fingers!'

Am I going mad? Didn't Anton hear any of what I said, about seeing a murdered woman lying in a pool of blood, and talking to a detective this morning? Why is no one telling him to shut up? Did nobody hear me? That none of them should have anything to say on the subject seems as impossible to me as what I saw on my laptop last night – impossible, yet real, unless I've lost my capacity to distinguish reality from its opposite.

Kit thinks I have. Maybe my family do also, and that's why they're ignoring me.

'Don't say two,' Fran admonishes Anton in a sing-song voice, wearing an exaggerated smile in order, presumably, to prevent their son from wondering if the emotional carnage of a broken home might be all he has to look forward to. 'One's enough, isn't it, Benji?'

'I want two chocolate fingers!' my five-year-old nephew wails, red in the face.

I open my mouth, then close it. Why waste my breath? I've done what I came here to do: told my family what they need to know. In order not to look as if I'm waiting to be asked questions, I glance out of the window at the swing, slide, climbing-frame, treehouse, free-standing sandpit and two trampolines in my parents' back garden: Benji's private playground. Kit calls it 'Neverland'.

'Ow,' Mum says again, making a big show of examining the red skin on her hand. She's wasting her time with Fran and Anton; she ought to know that the ordeal of Benji's supper has driven away all other thoughts, as well as their normal powers of observation.

'All right, two chocolate fingers,' says Fran wearily. 'Sorry about this, everybody. Come on, though, Benji – eat this first.' She takes the fork from his hand, impales the broccoli on it and holds it in front of his mouth, so that it's touching his lips.

He yanks his head away, spitting, and nearly falls off his chair. Together, like anxious cheerleaders, Fran and Anton yell, 'Don't fall off your chair!'

'I hate broccoli! It looks like a yucky lumpy snot tree!'

Privately, Kit and I refer to him as Benjamin Rigby. Kit started it, and, after a few cursory protests, I went along with it. His full name is Benji Duncan Geoffrey Rigby-Monk. 'You're joking,' Kit said, when I first told him. '*Benji*? Not even Benjamin?' Duncan and Geoffrey are his two grandads' names – both unglamorous and old-dufferish, in Kit's view, and not worth inflicting on a new generation – and Rigby-Monk is a fusion of Fran's surname and Anton's. 'As far as I'm concerned, he's Benjamin Rigby,' said Kit, after the first time we met him. 'He seems like a decent baby and he deserves a decent name. Not that his father's got one, so I suppose I shouldn't be surprised.' Kit thinks it's only acceptable to 'go around calling yourself Anton', as he puts it, if you're Spanish, Mexican or Colombian, or if you're a hairdresser or a professional ice-skater.

He tells me I ought to be grateful for my family, and pleased to live so near to them, and then he mocks them mercilessly in front of me, and avoids seeing them whenever he can, sending me round here on my own instead. I never complain; I feel guilty for entangling him. I would hate to marry someone with a family as overwhelming and ever-present as mine.

'Leave the poor child alone, Fran,' says my mum. 'It's not worth the effort, for one measly floret of broccoli. I'll make him ch—'

'Don't!' Fran cuts her off with a frantic wave of the arm, before the fatal words 'chicken nuggets and chips' are spoken aloud. 'We're fine, aren't we, Benj? You're going to eat your nice yummy healthy greens, aren't you, darling? You want to grow big and strong, don't you?'

'Like Daddy,' Anton adds, flexing his muscles. He used to be a personal trainer at Waterfront, but gave up his job when Benji was born. Now he lifts weights and hones his biceps, or sinews, or whatever fit people call the parts of their body that need honing, on various odd-looking machines in his and Fran's garage, which he's turned into a home gym. 'Daddy ate all his greens when he was little, and look at him now!'

At this point my father would normally pipe up with, 'The only way to turn children into good eaters is to present them with a simple choice: they eat what everyone else is eating, or nothing at all. That soon teaches them. It worked with you two. You'll eat anything, both of you. You'd eat your mother if she was on the plate!' He's said that, or a version of it, at least fifty times. Even when Fran hasn't been there, he still says 'you two' rather than 'you and Fran', because he's so used to all of us being together in this room, exactly as we are now: him sitting at the rickety pine trestle table that's been in Thorrold House's kitchen since before I was born, with the *Times* in front of him; Mum bustling around preparing food and drinks and waiting on everybody, refusing all offers of help so that she can sigh and rub the small of her back when she finally finishes loading the dishwasher; Anton leaning diagonally – in the manner of some-one too cool to stand upright – against the rail of the Aga, which was once red but is now cross-hatched with silver from years of scratches; Fran fussing over Benji, trying to force one Brussels sprout, one leaf of spinach, one pea into his mouth, offering him vats of chocolate mousse, mountains of crisps and endless sugary butter balls as an incentive.

And me sitting in the rocking-chair by the window, fantasis-ing about wrapping a thick blanket around my head and smothering myself, biting back the urge to say, 'Wouldn't it be better for him to have fish, potatoes and no courgette rather than fish, potatoes, a bit of courgette, twenty Benson and Hedges, a bottle of vodka and some crack cocaine? Just wondering.'

I'm at my most vicious when I'm with my family. *One good reason why I shouldn't live a hundred and fifty yards down the road from them.*

'Do you think I ought to run it under the cold tap,' Mum says to Dad, stroking her hand. 'Isn't that what they say you should do with burns? Or are you supposed to put butter on them? I haven't burned myself for years.' She's given up hope of attracting Fran's or Anton's attention, but she's a fool if she can't see that Dad's too angry with me to listen to anything she might say. The extent of his fury is clear from his posture: head bowed, forehead pulled into a tight frown, shoulders hard and hunched, hands balled into fists. He's wearing a blue and yellow striped shirt, but I'm sure if Alice were here she would agree with me that the energy radiating from him is a stony grey. He hasn't moved at all for nearly fifteen minutes; the grinning, back-slapping Dad who ushered me in here when I arrived has vanished and been replaced by a statue, or sculpture, which, if I were the artist, I would call 'Enraged Man'.

'Have you lost your marbles?' He spits the words at me. 'You can't afford a house for 1.2 million!'

'I know that,' I tell him. It isn't only the prospect of my financial recklessness that's bothering him. He resents the upheaval I've brought into his life without consulting him. We used to be a family that, between us, had never seen a murdered woman who then inexplicably disappeared. Now, thanks to me, that's no longer true.

'If you know you can't afford a 1.2-million-pound house, then why were you looking at one?' Mum says, as if she's caught me out with a particularly clever logical manoeuvre. She shakes her head from side to side slowly, rhythmically, as if she intends to carry on for ever, as if I've given her more than enough cause for eternal anguish. In her mind, I've already bankrupted myself and brought shame on the family. She has the capacity to enter a dimension that's inaccessible to most ordinary mortals: the ten-years-into-the-future worst-case scenario. It's as real to her as the present moment; so vivid is it, in fact, that most of the time the present doesn't stand a chance against it.

'Don't you ever look at things you can't afford?' I ask her.

'No, I certainly do not!' *Conversation over*. Like the metal clasp of an old-fashioned purse, clipping shut. I should have known. My mother never does anything apart from the most sensible thing. 'And nor should you, and nor *would* you, unless you were tempted, and considering mortgaging yourself up to the hilt for the—'

'Mum, there's no way they'd get a mortgage for that much,' Fran chips in. 'You're worrying about nothing, as usual. They won't buy that house because they can't. In the current climate, Melrose Cottage would sell for maximum three hundred thousand, most of which would go back to the Rawndesley and Silsford Building Society. Even if Con and Kit put in all their savings, no lender in their right mind would let them borrow over a million quid.'

It makes me want to scream that my sister knows as much about Kit's and my finances as we do. When she says 'savings', she has an exact figure in mind – the correct one. I know about her and Anton's money in the same way: their ISAs, their mortgage, their exact monthly income now that Anton has stopped working, how much they pay in school fees for Benji (hardly anything), how much Mum and Dad pay (almost all of it). 'I don't know why some families are so cagey about all things financial,' Mum has been saying for as long as I can remember. 'Why treat the people closest to you like strangers?'

When I was twelve and Fran ten, Mum showed us the blue pocket-book for her and Dad's Halifax savings account, so that we could see that they'd saved four hundred and seventy-three thousand pounds and fifty-two pence. I remember staring at the blue handwritten figure and being impressed and somewhat stunned by it, thinking my parents must be geniuses, that I could never hope to be as clever as them. 'We're always going to be okay, because we've got this money as a cushion,' Mum said. Both Fran and I fell for her propaganda, and spent our teenage years hoarding our pocket money in our savings accounts, while our friends were blowing every penny they had on lipstick and cider.

'If you think your mother and I are going to lend you money so that you can live beyond your means, you can forget it,' says Dad. In his and Mum's eyes, living beyond one's means is on a par, ethically, with tipping small babies out of windows.

'I don't think that,' I tell him. I wouldn't ask my parents to lend me a hundred pounds, let alone a million. 'I wouldn't want to buy 11 Bentley Grove even if I could afford it ten times over and there were no other houses in the world.' I stop short of explaining why. It ought to be obvious.

'Do you really think my hypothetical extravagance is what we ought to be talking about? What about the dead woman lying in her own blood? Why don't we talk about that instead? Why are you all avoiding it? I did tell you, didn't I? I could have sworn I told you what I saw on Roundthehouses, and about the detective who came round—'

'You didn't see a dead woman on Roundthehouses or anywhere else,' Dad cuts me off. 'I've never heard such a load of twaddle in my life. You said yourself: when Kit came to look, there was no body. Right?'

'That's what you said,' Mum adds nervously, as if she fears I'm a loose cannon, likely to change my story.

I nod.

'Then there was no body – you imagined it,' says Dad. 'You ought to ring that copper and apologise for wasting his time.'

'I'm sure if I stayed up until goodness knows what time of night, I'd start hallucinating too,' Mum contributes. 'I keep telling you, but you never listen: you need to look after yourself better. You and Kit both work too hard, you stay up too late, you don't always eat properly . . .'

'Give it a rest, Mum,' says Fran. 'You don't do yourself any favours. Come on, Benji, open your mouth, for Christ's sake. Big wide mouth!'

'Do you think I imagined it, Fran?'

'I don't know,' she says. 'Not necessarily. Maybe. *Three* chocolate fingers, Benji, if you open your mouth and eat this yummy . . . That's right! Bit wider . . .'

'What do you think, Anton?' I ask him.

'I don't think you'd have seen it if it wasn't there,' he says. I'm considering leaping out of my chair and throwing my arms around him when he ruins it by adding, 'Sounds like someone's idea of a practical joke to me. I wouldn't let it worry you.' As answers go, it's only a fraction less dismissive than, 'I can't be bothered with this – it's too much effort.'

'You shouldn't be looking at houses in Cambridge at any price,' says Mum. 'Millionaires' Row or . . . Paupers' Parade. Have you forgotten what happened last time you went down that route?'

'Mum, for God's sake!' says Fran.

'At least there was a reason last time – Kit being offered a promotion.'

Which he couldn't accept, because I ruined everything for him. Thanks for reminding me.

'Why now, all of a sudden?' Mum pleads, adopting what's

probably her favourite of her many voices: the frail, reedy warble of a broken woman. 'You and Kit have got a thriving business, a lovely home, you've got all of us right on your doorstep, your sister, lovely Benji – why would you want to move to Cambridge *now*? I mean, if it was London, I could understand it, with Kit working there as much as he does – though heaven knows why anyone would want to live in such a noisy, scruffy hell-hole – but Cambridge . . .'

'Because we should have moved in 2003, and we didn't, and I've regretted it ever since.' I'm on my feet, and I'm not sure why. Did I plan to storm out of the room? Out of the house? Mum and Dad stare at me as if they don't understand what I've just said. Dad turns away, makes a breathy, growling noise I haven't heard before. It frightens me.

Why do I always ruin things for everybody? What's wrong with me?

'Hooray! Benji ate his broccoli!' Anton cheers, again through a pretend loudspeaker, apparently oblivious to the invisible strings of tension stretched tautly from one end of the kitchen to the other. Maybe I am suffering from a disease that makes you hallucinate; I can see those strings as clearly as if they were real, with unspoken threats and glowing grudges hanging from them like Christmas decorations.

'Benji's the champion!' Anton bellows, as Fran waves the empty fork in the air in triumph.

'Benji's five, not two,' I snap. 'Why don't you try talking to him normally, instead of like a low-budget children's party entertainer?'

'Because' – Anton continues in his false booming voice – 'it's only when Daddy talks like this and makes him *laugh* . . . that he eats his *broccoli*!'

Benji isn't laughing. He's trying not to gag on the food he hates.

Anton's impermeable jollity makes me want to scream a torrent of insults at him. The only time I've ever seen the mildest of frowns pass across his face was when a Monk & Sons customer referred to him as a house-husband. Fran quickly corrected her in a way that sounded forced, learned by heart. I made the mistake of repeating the story to Kit, who instantly developed a Pavlovian response to hearing Anton's name: 'Anton – not a house-husband, but a personal trainer taking an open-ended career break.'

'Low-budget!' Mum pounces on the phrase. 'Of course, you're high-end now, aren't you, with your 1.2-million-pound house?'

'Completely unaffordable 1.2-million-pound house,' Fran is quick to say. It bothers her that Kit and I are better off than she and Anton are, though I'm not sure she would admit it to herself. It's been worse since Kit left Deloitte and we started our own business. If Nulli came a cropper, Fran would be sympathetic, upset on our behalf, but also relieved. I'm certain of this, but I can't prove it. I can't prove a lot of things at the moment.

Fran and Anton live in a cottage called Thatchers that's smaller than my house, and closer to my parents – almost directly opposite Thorrold House, across the green. Like Melrose Cottage, Thatchers is a two-up two-down, but the kitchen is no more than a tiny strip at one end of the lounge, and the bedrooms are in the thatched roof and therefore triangular, difficult to stand up in. As it happens, Anton and Fran suffer hardly at all from a lack of space – effectively, they have lived with Mum and Dad since Benji was born. Thatchers, which they persist in referring to as 'home', is empty almost all the time.

Why does nobody ever point out how crazy it is to have an empty house just standing there? *Crazier than looking at houses in Cambridge on the internet. Crazier than considering moving to one of England's most beautiful, vibrant cities instead of spending the rest of your life in Little Holling, Silsford, with its one pub and its population of fewer than a thousand people.*

'Ignore Connie, Anton,' Mum says. 'She's clearly taken leave of her senses.'

'She can make it up to me.' Anton winks at me. 'Extra babysitting, Con, yeah?'

I try to smile, though the prospect of any more babysitting makes me swell with resentment. I already babysit for Benji every Tuesday night. In my family, if something happens once and goes well, it's only a matter of time before someone suggests that it ought to become a tradition.

'One choccie finger, *two* choccie fingers, *three* choccie fingers!' Fran is hamming up her dealings with Benji now, to demonstrate her support for Anton and his silly voices. She's on his side, Dad and Mum are on each other's, and nobody's on mine. Suits me fine; anything that makes me feel less like one of the Little Holling Monks has to be a good thing.

'There's nothing wrong with my senses,' I tell Mum. 'I know what I saw. I saw a dead woman in that room, lying in a pool of her own blood. The detective I spoke to this morning is taking it seriously. If you don't want to, that's up to you.'

'Oh, Connie, listen to yourself!' Mum says sorrowfully.

'Don't waste your breath, Val,' Dad mutters. 'When does she ever pay attention to what we say?' He lifts his right arm and studies the table beneath as if he expects to find something there. 'What happened to that cuppa you were making?'

'I'm sorry, but it makes no sense, love,' Mum says to me in a hushed voice as she refills the kettle, shooting guilty glances in Dad's direction, hoping he won't notice her continued willingness to engage with the daughter he just dismissed as not worth bothering with. 'I mean, you only have to think about it for two seconds to realise it's a non-starter, don't you? Why would anyone put a murdered woman's body on a property website? A murderer wouldn't do it, would he, because he'd want to hide what he'd done. An estate agent wouldn't do it because he'd want to sell the house, and no one's going to buy a—'

'Except my eldest daughter,' Dad announces loudly. 'Not only my daughter – also my book-keeper, which is even more worrying. Oh, she's more than happy to mortgage herself into penury to buy the gruesome death house for 1.2 million pounds!' I don't know why he's glaring at Benji as he says this, as if it's his fault.

'Dad, I don't want to buy 11 Bentley Grove. I can't afford to buy it. You're not listening to me.' *As usual.* What did he mean by the book-keeper comment? That he's afraid I might steal from Monk & Sons? That my profligate tendencies are likely to bankrupt the family business? I've never done anything but a brilliant job for him, and it counts for nothing. I needn't have bothered.

And now I'm thinking like a martyr. Don't they say all women turn into their mothers?

Tell them all you're leaving Monk & Sons. Resigning. Work full-time for Nulli – that's what you want to do, isn't it? What is it about these people that makes it impossible to say what you mean and do what you want?

'You're contradicting yourself,' I say to Dad. 'If I imagined the body, then it's not a gruesome death house, is it?'

'So you *do* want to buy it. I knew it!' He thumps his fist down on the table, making it rock.

'The vendor wouldn't do it,' Mum burbles to herself, wrapping her burned hand in a piece of kitchen roll while she waits for the kettle to boil. 'Presumably he or she wants the house to sell as much as the estate agent does.'

'Please stop cataloguing everyone who wouldn't put a dead body up on a website, Mum,' Fran groans. 'You've made your point: no one would do it.'

'Well, if no one would do it, Connie can't have seen it, can she?' Mum nods triumphantly at me, as if that ought to be the end of the matter.

Why do my family always make me feel like this? Whenever I talk to them for any length of time, I end up wriggling in discomfort, desperately searching for a pocket of air as the oxygen is slowly squeezed from the conversation.

I can't bear to be around them any longer. Nor can I stand the thought of going home to Kit, who will ask me how it went, and laugh as though at a sitcom when I bring it to life for him, as he will expect me to, as if I am a comedian and my family entertaining and harmless, joke-fodder. There's only one person I want to talk to at the moment, and although it's a Saturday, it's also an emergency.

Is it? Are you sure?

When was I last sure of anything?

I pull my mobile phone out of my bag and leave the room. Mum shouts after me, 'You don't have to go into another room. We won't listen.'

~

'And the ridiculous thing was, I nearly didn't do it. I found myself thinking, "But it's not a real emergency – you're not bleeding to death, or hanging from a cliff by your fingernails. Save your permission to ring in an emergency for a life-or-death situation, don't squander it on this.' But why not? I mean, it *is* a life-and-death situation: the woman I saw had been murdered – she must have been. And why did I decide it was a once-only thing and that after I'd used up my ringing-in-an-emergency allowance, it would be gone for ever? Would you be angry if I rang you outside working hours in a few months, or even years, if I was unlucky enough to feel as bad as this again?'

'Are you noticing the words you're choosing?' Alice asks. ' "Saving", "squandering"?'

No, I didn't notice. Admitting as much would be too depressing, so I say nothing. When I first started to see Alice, the long silences unsettled me. Now I'm used to them. I've grown to like them. Sometimes I count how long they last: *one elephant, two elephants, three elephants*. Sometimes I go into a kind of trance, staring at the clear glass beads that run along the bottom of the cream silk blind, or at the pink butterflies chandelier.

'Why did you tell your family about seeing the woman and the blood?' Alice says eventually.

'Kit asked me the same thing. "Why tell them?" he said. "They'll give you a hard time and make you feel a hundred times worse." I knew he was right, but I still went round and put myself in the firing line.'

'You often describe your parents as suffocating.' Alice remembers every word I have uttered in her presence since we first met, without the help of notes. Maybe the pink butterflies are hiding some kind of recording device. 'Why did you go round to be suffocated, on no sleep and after the worst shock of your life?'

'I had to tell them. A detective came to interview me. It was . . . too big to keep from them, too important. I can't be involved with the police and hide it from my family.'

'Can't?'

No secrets between people who love each other. I've had it drummed into me all my life. I'm not sure it's possible to explain that sort of programming to someone who hasn't experienced it.

'Yet you've kept quiet about the other big, important thing in your life at the moment,' says Alice. 'The problem that's been preoccupying you since January.'

I laugh, though I feel like crying. 'It's not the same. That might be nothing. It probably is.'

'The dead woman you saw might be nothing, if you imagined her.'

'I didn't. I know I didn't.'

Alice takes off her glasses, drops them in her lap. 'You didn't imagine what happened in January, either,' she says. 'You don't know what it means, but you didn't imagine it.'

'I can't tell Mum and Dad that I'm afraid Kit might have a whole other life that I don't know about,' I say, loathing the sound of the words. 'It's just not an option. You don't understand. I might have changed my surname, but I'm still a Monk. Everything in the Monk family is nice and normal and happy. That's not a coincidence, it's a rule. There are no problems, ever, apart from Benji not eating his sodding broccoli – that's the worst thing that's allowed to happen. It's out of the question, absolutely forbidden, for there to be anything weird going on – really bad weird, I mean. Weird funny is okay, as long as it makes a good anecdote.'

I wipe my face, try to compose myself. 'The only thing worse than bad-weird is uncertain. My parents don't accept ambiguity of any kind – literally, as soon as it dares to make an appearance, they show it the door in no uncertain terms. And, yes, I said that deliberately. Everything Mum and Dad do, they do in no uncertain terms. Uncertainty is the enemy. One of the enemies,' I correct myself. 'Change is the other. And spontaneity, and risk; there's a whole gang of them.'

'No wonder your parents are scared,' says Alice. 'You said it yourself: they're being persecuted by a gang.'

Is she going to give me the same remedy she gave me last time? Kali Phos, it was called. For people who have an aversion to their own relatives. Kit threatened to steal the bottle for himself when I told him that.

'Kit's so unhappy,' I tell Alice. 'I've *made* him unhappy. He can't understand why I don't believe him. Neither can I. Why can't I accept that strange things happen sometimes, and put it behind me? I *know* Kit loves me, I know he's desperate for things to go back to normal. I'm all he's got, and . . . I love him. It'll sound crazy, but I love him more than ever – I feel outraged on his behalf.'

'Because he's probably innocent, and his own wife doesn't believe in him?' Alice guesses.

I nod. 'How can I tell Mum and Dad, and Fran, and make them suspect him too, when there's no way to end that suspicion, *ever*? Haven't I made him miserable enough already?'

'So it's for Kit's sake that you're keeping it from your family?'

'His and theirs. Mum and Dad couldn't live with it – I know they couldn't. They'd try not to allow me to live with it. They'd hire a private detective . . . No, that would mean admitting they were mixed up in something unsavoury, if they did that. I know what they'd do.' It feels like a revelation, though on one level I know I'm making it up. 'They'd put pressure on me to leave him and move back to Thorrold House. Just in case. They'd say, "If you're not a hundred per cent sure he's trustworthy, you can't stay with him." '

'Is that such a stupid thing to say?'

'Yes. I'd rather have the rest of my life ruined by suspicions that achieve nothing than leave a man I love who's very probably done nothing wrong.'

Alice puts her glasses back on and leans forward. Her leather swivel chair creaks. 'Explain something to me,' she says. 'You say there's no way for the suspicion to end, ever, but in the next breath you mention the possibility of hiring a private detective. You might not want to do that, and I'd understand if you didn't, but wouldn't that be one way to find out for sure if Kit's lying?'

'Are you saying you think I should hire a detective?' If she says yes, I'm never coming back here. 'Wouldn't it be dangerous for someone as paranoid as me to imagine that I can pay for certainty whenever I need it? Wouldn't I be better off trying to cultivate trust? What if the detective followed Kit for a month and found nothing? Would I finally accept that nothing's going on, or would I worry that the detective had been slapdash and missed something?'

Alice smiles. 'And yet only this morning, you told a detective all about seeing a dead woman on the internet. He might be slapdash – he might miss something.'

'Then I'll go to Cambridge and find a conscientious detective, and make him listen to me,' I say fiercely.

'Because you want to find out the truth.'

'It's not about me, it's about the woman I saw, whoever she is. Someone murdered her. I can't just—'

'You want to find out the truth,' Alice says again.

'All right, then, yes! I saw a dead woman on the floor in *that* house. Wouldn't you want the truth, in my position?'

'Connie, can I speak frankly? When it comes to the dead woman, your truth-seeking energy is really strong. I can feel it – it's tangible in this room. Normally, that would help to attract the truth to you. When we focus on something we want with all our energy, believe we're going to get it one day and pursue it with great determination, resolved that we will never give up, usually what we're seeking comes to us – it's just a matter of how long it takes to reach us. In your case, there's a complication: in another area of your life, you're terrified of finding out the truth, and you're transmitting an equally strong truth-*repelling* energy.' She folds her arms, waits for my reaction.

'Kit, you mean? That's not fair. You know how hard I've tried.'

'You haven't,' says Alice gently. 'You're lying to yourself if you think you have.'

I must be quite exceptionally convincing, in that case. 'What, so you're saying that the contradictory energies are getting mixed up and sending out a muddled signal? That my fear of finding out the truth about Kit is repelling *all* truth?'

Alice says nothing.

'So, whoever's in charge of all this energy and attraction stuff, up there in the cockpit of the universe – God, or Fate, or whatever you want to call him – he's short-sighted, is he?' I say irritably. 'He can't *quite* read the shopping list – item one: truth about dead woman; item two: no truth about possibly treacherous husband. They blur together, do they, so that he doesn't know what exactly he's supposed to deliver? Can't he focus really hard and attract a decent pair of reading glasses? As the all-powerful controller of the universe, that shouldn't be beyond him.'

'Nothing has blurred together,' says Alice. 'The two items were never separate. They're linked by an address: 11 Bentley Grove, Cambridge.'

I feel as if I'm going to throw up.

Kit didn't kill her. He can't have. He's not a killer. I wouldn't love a killer.

'Do you want only part of the truth, or do you want all of it?' Alice asks. 'What if it was all or nothing? Which would you choose?'

'All,' I whisper. My stomach twists.

'Good. Your phone's ringing.'

I didn't hear it.

'Nothing like an immediate result to convince a hardened sceptic,' Alice says.

'Do you mind if I . . .? Hello?'

'Is that Connie Bowskill?'

'Speaking.'

'Sam Kombothekra.'

'Oh.' My heart jolts. *Kombothekra, Kombothekra.* I try to remember the name.

'Can you get to Spilling police station by nine thirty, Monday morning?'

'I . . . Has something happened? Have you spoken to Cambridge police?'

'I'd like to speak to you face to face,' he says. 'Monday morning, nine thirty?'

'All right. Can't you even—?'

'I'll see you then.'

He's gone.

Alice raises her water glass in what looks like a toast. 'Well done,' she says, beaming at me. I have no idea what she's congratulating me for.

POLICE EXHIBIT REF: CB13345/432/21IG

D,

Don't forget to nip to supermarket and buy:

Pitta breads, passata, bag of salad, lamb mince, feta cheese, cinnamon, chargrilled artichokes (in oil in jar, from deli section – NOT a tin of artichokes from canned veg section) new pencil case for Riordan, something for Tilly so she doesn't feel left out – Barbie mag or something. Ta!

E xx

6

19/07/2010

'Okay. You've put your house up for sale . . .'

'No, I haven't,' said Gibbs.

'Suppose you have. You want to move, and you've put your house on the market,' said Sam. 'Why might you go and stay in a hotel?' For the past ten minutes, he'd been orbiting Gibbs' desk – glancing at him occasionally, then looking away, as if he had something on his mind but wasn't sure how to broach it.

Gibbs had been waiting for him to spit it out, whatever it was. 'If I fancied a holiday, and self-catering felt like too much effort . . .'

'No, not a holiday. You wouldn't choose a hotel within walking distance of your house, would you? Sorry, I'm not explaining myself very well.'

You're not explaining yourself at all.

'Why would you decide to go and stay in a hotel while you waited for your house to sell? However long that took.'

'I wouldn't,' said Gibbs, annoyed that Stepford was his skipper and therefore couldn't be told to piss off and stop wasting his time. 'I'd stay in my house until it sold, and then I'd move to my new house. Isn't that what most people do?'

'It is. Exactly.'

'Even if you were lucky and your house sold quickly, you'd

be looking at minimum six weeks, I reckon. Six weeks in a hotel'd be unaffordable for most people – it would for me, anyway.'

'Let's say you could afford it – you're a high earner, or you've got private wealth.'

'I still wouldn't do it. No one would. Why not just stay in your house?'

'What about if you couldn't stand the thought of prospective buyers and surveyors getting under your feet all the time, traipsing in and out while you were trying to entertain friends, ringing the doorbell at 9 a.m. on a Saturday when you were hoping for a lie-in? Mightn't it be more convenient to shift to a hotel?'

'No,' said Gibbs flatly. Entertain friends? Debbie's mates popped round for a cup of tea now and then – did that count as entertaining? Who did Stepford think Gibbs was, Nigella Lawson?

Colin Sellers slouched in looking worse than he'd looked last week, which Gibbs wouldn't have believed possible if the evidence hadn't been looming in front of him. 'Your hair looks like a furball a cat coughed up,' he called out. No reaction. He tried again. 'Some barbers'll slit your throat for the price of a haircut – solve all your problems in one go.'

Sellers grunted and headed for his desk. Suki, his girlfriend of many years, had dumped him a fortnight ago. Gibbs had tried to cheer him up at first, pointing out that he still had his wife, Stacey, and at least she'd never found out about the affair, but Sellers wasn't so easily consoled. 'I've got a gaping girlfriend gap,' he'd mumbled gloomily. 'If you want to help, find me a new woman. Can you think of anyone?' Gibbs couldn't. 'Anyone,' Sellers had repeated, dejectedly. 'Old, young, flabby, bony, a minger if that's all you can find – as long as she's new.' The idea that there were females in the world that he might never get to have sex with was Sellers' mobilising grievance.

Gibbs liked that phrase. It was a useful way of pinning people down in your mind. Stepford was tricky: he didn't have any grievances, as far as Gibbs knew. The Snowman had too many. Gibbs wondered if there needed to be one that stood out above the rest in order for it to count. Could you have a mobilising cluster of grievances?

'Poor old Colin,' Stepford muttered. 'He's taken it really badly, hasn't he?'

'How big's my house?'

'I don't know. I've never seen it.'

'The house I've put up for sale,' Gibbs clarified.

'Oh, sorry. For one person living alone, it's big. Four bedrooms, lounge, family room, conservatory, dining room, decent size kitchen. Massive garden.'

'Then I'm used to having the space, aren't I? I wouldn't be prepared to live in one room in a hotel for however long my gaff took to sell. I'd get cabin fever.'

'Imagine you're a woman . . .'

'Keep your voice down,' said Gibbs, nodding in Sellers' direction. 'I don't want to be mounted by the Fornicator.'

'You're sentimental. You're moving because you have to relocate to another part of the country for work, but you love your house. You can't stand to carry on living in it knowing you'll be leaving soon – you'd rather move out immediately and . . . No?'

Gibbs was shaking his head. 'I might do it if I *hated* my house and couldn't stand to live there any more,' he said. 'If I'd lived there for years with a bloke who beat the shit out of me, or if something fucked-up had happened there – my kids had died in a fire, or I'd been burgled and gang-raped . . .'

DI Giles Proust stomped past without looking up. When he reached his glass office-cubicle in the far corner of the room, he turned, raised his briefcase in the air and said, 'Don't mind me, Gibbs. Continue with your edifying and uplifting conversation, your inspirational Monday morning thought for the day.' He went in and slammed the door.

Go fuck yourself, Frosty.

Stepford was rubbing his forehead, looking worried. 'I can't believe I'm in this situation,' he said. 'In a minute, a woman called Connie Bowskill's going to walk in here and very probably tell me a pack of lies, or a mixture of lies and half-truths, and I won't know if she's lying or not because I can't get hold of Simon Waterhouse. I've no way of reaching him – can't be done, simple as that. Whereas if I could speak to him for two minutes – one minute, even – I'd be able to get my bearings.'

Gibbs knew where Waterhouse was. What he didn't have was permission to pass that knowledge on.

The Snowman's office door opened and he stuck out his bald head. He was still holding his briefcase. 'Are you expecting a visitor, Sergeant? There was a woman at reception asking for you. Youngish, dark, attractive. Connie Bowler, I think her name was. I avoided her.'

'Connie Bowskill,' said Stepford. Gibbs heard the reluctance in his voice; no doubt Proust did too.

'I'm good with names, and hers didn't ring a bell. Who is she?'

'Connie Bowskill?' Sellers looked up from the Mars bar he was unwrapping. 'Never heard of her.'

You're itching to shag her, though, aren't you? Sight unseen.

Stepford shifted from one foot to the other, avoiding Proust's eye.

'Who is she, Sergeant? A clairvoyant? Your flute teacher? I could stand here guessing all day, or you could make life easier for both of us by answering the question.'

'She's . . . someone I'm trying to help. It's a long story, sir, and about to get longer. It involves a possible murder.'

'So do the staff-training initiatives I devise in my mind every night before falling asleep. If it's a murder, why don't I know about it?'

'It's not our patch.'

'Then what's she doing here? Why isn't she in St Anne's-on-Sea? Why isn't she in Nether Stowey, Somerset?'

'I haven't got time to explain, if she's at reception,' said Stepford. 'Let me talk to her and then I'll put you in the picture.'

A possible murder. Did that mean Gibbs was duty-bound to tell Stepford where Waterhouse was? Possibly. Probably.

'I already don't like the sound of it,' Proust barked. 'You should try being less helpful, in future – to everyone but me. You'd have shorter stories to tell and fewer pictures to put people in.' He stepped back into his office and closed the door, but instead of going straight to his desk as he normally did, he stood and stared out through the glass, briefcase in hand, expressionless – like something old and ugly in a museum display cabinet. The man was a freak; he belonged in a nuthouse. Gibbs decided to try and outstare him. After a few seconds he lost interest, and gave up.

PC Robbie Meakin appeared in the doorway of the CID room. 'There's a Mr and Mrs Bowskill waiting for you in the canteen, Sarge.'

'The canteen?' Stepford sounded disappointed. It was as close to angry as he ever got.

'Best I could do, sorry. All the rooms are taken.'

'You could always book a room down the road, at the Blantyre,' Gibbs suggested. 'Talking of hotels.' Or was he supposed to call it 'Blantyre'? No, it said 'The Blantyre Hotel' on the front. He wondered how many nights at Blue Horizon he and Olivia could afford before all their money ran out. Quite a few, if she sold her two-thousand-quid dress.

He should ring her before saying anything to Stepford about Waterhouse's whereabouts; it was only fair to warn her. He had her number; Charlie must have given her his, and she'd texted him last week to say she was looking forward to 'witnessing' with him. In retrospect, now that Waterhouse's wedding was in the past, Gibbs realised he'd been looking forward to it as well. Without something to look forward to, what was the point of anything?

He decided not to ring Olivia straight away. It could wait an hour or so.

~

Where had he gone now? Charlie had assumed, when she'd booked Los Delfines, that it would be exciting and luxurious to live in an enormous house for a fortnight. It was turning out to be more frustrating than anything else. At home, when Simon disappeared and she went to look for him, she always found him within seconds. Here, it wasn't so easy; the last thing Charlie wanted to do was run round thirty rooms in this heat. 'Simon?' she called up the white marble staircase. Was he on the bog? Not for so long, surely – not without taking *Moby Dick* with him, and she'd just seen it by the pool. He couldn't be in bed; that was the last place he'd risk being found by her. In the kitchen, preparing lunch? Yesterday Charlie had complained about having to peel the shells off the prawns they'd bought from the supermarket down the road. Maybe Simon had decided to pre-peel them today, to save her the inconvenience. She laughed to herself. *As if.*

She adjusted her bikini top, and was heading for the kitchen when something caught her eye: a piece of paper on the sideboard with something written on it in capital letters. Had he gone out, left her a note? No, she'd have seen him while she was baking on her lounger; he'd have had to walk right past her.

She picked it up. It wasn't paper; it was Simon's plane ticket. On it, he'd written, '11 BENTLEY GROVE, CAMBRIDGE, CB2 9AW'. Charlie frowned. Whose address was that? Had he wanted her to find it, or was it a reminder to himself about something? Who did he know in Cambridge? No one, as far as she was aware.

She heard footsteps on the stairs.

'Did you call me?' Simon asked. 'I was on the roof terrace, looking at the face in the mountain. You should come up – you'll see it instantly.'

Was he still on about that? 'I don't care about not seeing the face.'

'I want you to see it,' Simon insisted. He started back up the stairs.

'What's 11 Bentley Grove, Cambridge?'

'Hm?'

'CB2 9AW.'

Simon looked confused. 'What are you talking about?'

'This.' Charlie waved the plane ticket at him.

'Let's have a look.' He moved closer. Stared at it, then at her. 'I've no idea,' he said. 'Is that your ticket from the aeroplane?'

'No. It's yours,' she told him. 'Mine's out by the pool – I've been using it as a bookmark. You stuffed yours in your pocket when we boarded the plane – I saw you. At some point between Friday night and now, you must have taken it out, written this address on it, and left it there on the sideboard.' How could he not remember?

He was shaking his head. 'No. I didn't. Did you?'

'Did I?' Charlie laughed. 'Well, obviously I didn't, or I wouldn't be asking you why you did.'

Simon looked unconvinced. He looked the way he looked when he was interviewing a suspect, Charlie realised uncomfortably: guarded. Distant. 'Who lives at 11 Bentley Grove?' he asked.

'Simon, this is the most insane conversation we've ever had – and, let's face it, there's stiff competition. I know nothing about that address. *You* do, because you wrote it down, so why don't you tell me who lives there?'

'Cambridge. You used to teach at Cambridge.'

'Don't *dare* to sound suspicious! Tell me what's going on, or I'll—'

'I didn't write this, Charlie. I don't know anyone in Cambridge.' He didn't look guarded any more; he looked angry. 'What the fuck's going on? You heard me coming downstairs and you knew you couldn't get to it in time to hide it, so you dreamed up some stupid elaborate double bluff – you decided to accuse me of writing it. Clever. But you must know it's not going to work. I *know* I didn't write it, remember? Which only leaves you. Unless you want to bring Domingo into this – maybe he wrote it.'

'Hey, hey!' Charlie held up her hands. 'Simon, this is crazy. Calm down, okay? I didn't write it. Domingo didn't write it

– he can hardly speak English. *You* wrote it. You must have done.'

'Except that I didn't.' The expression on his face chilled her. 'If something's going on that I don't know about, you're better off telling me now. However bad it is.'

Charlie burst into tears. She could feel the panic starting to churn in her stomach, goosebumps all over her skin. If you told the truth and weren't believed by the person who mattered most, what were you supposed to do next? 'I didn't write it!' she shouted in his face. 'All right, if you say you didn't either, I believe you – you ought to believe me too.'

'You want me to search the house for intruders with blue-ink pens in their hands?' Simon asked coldly. 'Or would I be better off searching your handbag for a blue pen?'

'Search my . . . ?'

'The ink would be a perfect match, I reckon.'

Oh, God, make this stop. How could Charlie put an end to it, before it spiralled out of control? She did have a blue pen in her bag, and if Simon found it . . . But she hadn't done it. And he was just as capable of taking a pen from her bag as she was. If he knew precisely which pen had written those words . . . No, she couldn't let herself think like that. They had to trust each other. 'Domingo must have written it,' she said. 'English or no English – he must have . . . I don't know, taken a message from someone – maybe from the owners, maybe they're English. Maybe they live in Cambridge, or they're staying there or something.' Was it possible? It had to be, if Simon was telling the truth.

'Find him. Ask him.'

'You find him and fucking ask him,' Charlie snapped. 'And if he says it wasn't him, then he's fucking lying!'

'You're shaking,' said Simon, walking towards her. She steeled herself for another verbal assault, but all he did was pat her arm and . . . was that a grin on his face? 'All right, game over,' he said. 'I wrote it.'

'Pardon?' Charlie felt as if she'd been turned to stone.

'I wrote it, and left it there for you to find.'

Words that made sense. And yet didn't make sense.

'Are you . . . *experimenting* on me?'

'I knew I'd have to spend the rest of the day grovelling, and that's what I'll do.' Simon smiled, proud of himself. He had it all worked out.

'This is something to do with work, isn't it? It's our honeymoon, and you're fucking working! I *knew* something was on your mind.'

'It's not exactly work,' he said. 'You can tell me later what thoughts are and aren't permissible on a honeymoon, but I need to ask you while it's fresh in your mind . . .'

'It'll be fresh in my mind in twenty years' time, Simon.' *Like all the times you've hurt me in the past: fresh as a field of daisies, one flower for each wound.*

'Did you believe me? That I hadn't written it? Did you start to wonder if there was any way you might have done it and not remembered?'

Charlie shuddered; the adrenaline was still coursing round her body. 'I hate you,' she said. 'You scared me.'

'You believed me, but only because you were desperate for me to believe you,' said Simon. 'You offered me a deal: reciprocal immunity from doubt. Which might have worked, thanks to Domingo. He's the only other person here, and he means nothing to us. If he'd said he hadn't written it, we could have dismissed him as a liar and it wouldn't have mattered to us, because we have no relationship with him. What if Domingo wasn't here, though? If you knew you hadn't done it, and I kept swearing I hadn't either, what would you have thought? Would you have started to wonder if you were going mad? Would that have been preferable to concluding I was a liar – one you couldn't force the truth out of?'

'You'd better tell me, right now, what all this is about,' Charlie said shakily. 'I'm not spending the rest of our honeymoon—'

'Relax,' said Simon. 'I was always going to tell you.'

'Then why not just tell me – at the airport, on the plane? Why drag it out, why torture me? I *knew* you had something on your mind. You denied it. You *are* a liar.' Was she making too big a deal of this? Should she laugh it off?

Simon was trying to. 'I thought I'd make you wait a bit,' he teased her. 'Build up suspense, get you really interested . . .'

'I see – so the same principle you apply to our sex life, then?'

The smile vanished from his face.

7

Monday 19 July 2010

Kit holds my hand under the table as Sam Kombothekra turns the laptop round to face us. I flinch; I don't want to see that room again. 'Don't worry,' says Sam, as I turn away and lean into Kit. 'You're not going to see anything unpleasant – only an ordinary lounge that you've seen before, with nothing in it that shouldn't be there. But I do need you to look. I need to show you something.'

'Do we have to do this here?' I ask. It doesn't feel right. Sam should have come to Melrose Cottage again, if this is the best alternative he can offer. We're in a canteen the size of a school assembly hall, hemmed in on all sides by the sound of trays clattering, dishwashers whirring, loud conversations on both sides of the serving hatch, as well as across it – two elderly scarecrow-like dinner-ladies, if that's what they're called, giggling uncontrollably at a joke made by a young, shiny-faced policeman in uniform. Along one wall there's a row of arcade-style machines, flashing their lights and bleeping.

I feel invisible. My throat is already sore from shouting to make myself heard; the combination of the intense heat in here and the sausage and egg smell is making me nauseous.

'Connie?' Sam says reasonably. Everyone is oh-so-reasonable, apart from me. 'Look at the picture.'

Do you want only part of the truth, or do you want all of it? What if it was all or nothing?

I force myself to look at the laptop's screen. There it is again: 11 Bentley Grove's lounge. No dead woman on the floor, no blood. Sam leans over and points to the corner of the room, by the bay window. 'Do you see that circle, on the carpet?'

I nod.

'I don't see it,' says Kit.

'A very faint brown curved line – almost a circle, but incomplete,' says Sam. 'Within it, the carpet's a slightly different colour – see?'

'The line, yes,' Kit says. 'Just. The colour looks the same to me, inside and out.'

'It's darker inside the ring,' I say.

'That's right.' Sam nods. 'The mark was made by a Christmas tree.'

'A Christmas tree?' Is he joking? I wipe sweat from my upper lip.

Sam lowers the lid of the laptop, looks at me.

Just say it, whatever it is. Tell me how you've managed to prove I'm wrong and mad and stupid.

'Cambridge police have been very cooperative,' he says. 'Far more so than I expected. Thanks to their efforts, I hope I'll be able to allay your concerns.'

I hear Kit's relieved sigh. Resentment hardens inside me. How can he do that, before he's heard anything, as if it's all over? Any minute now he'll whip out his BlackBerry and start muttering about having to get back to work.

'The owner of 11 Bentley Grove is a Dr Selina Gane.'

So that's her name. Sam has found out more useful information in forty-eight hours than I have in six months.

'She's an oncologist, works at Addenbrooke's hospital.'

'Know it well,' says Kit. 'I did my undergraduate degree at

Cambridge. Addenbrooke's relieved me of a putrid appendix, about an hour before it would have killed me.'

Kit's undergraduate degree is his only degree. He could have said, 'my degree', except then Sam Kombothekra wouldn't have assumed it was one of many.

If the University of Cambridge offered an MA course in Thinking the Worst of People, I'd graduate with distinction.

'Dr Gane bought the house in 2007, from a family called the Beaters. They bought number 11 from the developers when it was first built in 2002. Bentley Grove didn't exist before then. The Beaters' sale of the property to Dr Gane was handled by a local estate agent called Lorraine Turner. Lorraine is also the agent marketing the property now, coincidentally.'

'Not coincidentally at all,' Kit corrects him. 'If you want to sell your house, why not put it on with the person you know sold it successfully last time – to you? That's what I'd do, if I were selling Melrose Cottage.'

'*You* wouldn't be selling Melrose Cottage,' I can't help saying. '*We* would be selling it.' I want to apologise to Sam for Kit's interruption; I hate it when he shows off.

'Cambridge police spoke to Lorraine Turner yesterday. I spoke to her on the phone this morning. I think you'll be reassured when I tell you what she told me. In December 2006, the Beaters decided to put 11 Bentley Grove on the market – they wanted to move out to the countryside.'

Why, for God's sake?

'The day they made their decision was also the day Mrs Beater sent Mr Beater out to buy a Christmas tree.'

'Shall I get us each a mug of cocoa?' says Kit. 'This sounds like the beginning of a bedtime story.'

'You'll see why it's relevant shortly,' Sam tells him.

In other words, don't interrupt again.

'She wasn't in when he got back, and so wasn't able to remind him to put something down to protect the carpet before setting the tree down on it, in its pot. The pot had holes in the bottom, the earth in it was wet . . .'

'What a fool.' Kit laughs. 'I bet Beater wife gave Beater husband a tongue-lashing he'll never forget.'

'I'd say that's likely.' Sam smiles.

Why is everyone having a good time here except me? I can't take this seriously, any of it – all this trivia about Christmas trees and people who mean nothing to me; at the same time, I can't see anything to laugh about. My mind fills with a disgusting image: scratching my face until the skin comes off, until there's nothing left but a red-raw featureless bulb where my head used to be.

'When Lorraine Turner turned up to value the house, the first thing Mrs Beater showed her was the damaged lounge carpet. She had a lengthy moan about her husband's incompetence: "Typical useless man – the very day we decide to try and sell the house . . ." Et cetera. You get the idea. Mrs Beater hired a professional carpet cleaner, but the stain refused to disappear completely. A brown ring-like mark was left that couldn't be shifted.'

Sam turns from Kit to me. 'Last Monday, Lorraine went to value 11 Bentley Grove for Dr Gane. Three and a half years after she first set foot in the house, the stain was still there. She made a joke about it, apparently, then regretted it because Dr Gane seemed to take it the wrong way – as if Lorraine was implying she was slovenly, not having replaced the previous owners' ruined carpet. Lorraine said it was a bit awkward.'

Am I expected to feel sorry for an estate agent I've never met? Kit is chuckling: the perfect audience.

'She filmed the house and garden for the virtual tour, took photos to put in the brochure and on the agency's website,' Sam goes on. 'One was of the lounge, with the Christmas tree mark on the carpet clearly visible – that's the photograph we've just looked at.'

'So what?' I say, more rudely than I intended. 'What does any of this prove? What's it got to do with the dead woman I saw?'

'Connie,' Kit mutters.

'It's okay,' Sam tells him. He feels sorry for him, I think. *Can't be easy, being married to a mad woman.* 'This Saturday afternoon just gone, so nearly twelve hours after you saw the dead woman on the virtual tour, Lorraine Turner showed a young couple round 11 Bentley Grove. She told them the Christmas tree story, showed them the mark. It was the same mark, Connie – Lorraine says she'd swear to it. The rest of the carpet was immaculate. No blood.' He waits for this to sink in. 'Do you see what I'm saying?'

'You're saying it means that the carpet can't ever have had blood on it. Are you sure that's true? I've washed clothes with bloodstains on them, and the blood's completely disappeared.'

'Connie, do you really have to . . . ?' Kit tries to shut me up.

I talk over him. 'It's easy to get rid of blood: cold water, soap . . .'

'Believe me, if someone had bled to death on a beige carpet, you'd see a mark,' says Sam. 'However much soap and cold water and Vanish was applied afterwards.'

I run my hands through my unbrushed hair, fighting the urge to lie down on the sticky canteen floor, close my eyes and give up.

'Connie, when you saw the woman's body, was that mark there in the corner of the room, in the same photograph?' Sam asks. 'The Christmas tree mark?'

'I don't know.' *No. I don't think it was*. 'I didn't notice it, but . . .' I cast around for a likely explanation. 'Maybe the photograph of the dead woman was taken years ago, before Mr Beater put his Christmas tree down on that spot. Have you thought of that?'

Sam nods. 'You described a map on the wall – do you remember?'

'Of course I remember. Why wouldn't I? Saturday was only two days ago. I'm not senile.'

He pulls a notebook out of his shirt pocket, opens it and starts to read. '"Comitatus Cantabrigiensis Vernacule Cambridgeshire, 1646. Jansson, Johannes." Otherwise known as Janssonius.' He looks up. 'I don't suppose you've heard of him?'

'Is he a friend of the Beaters?' I say snidely. I can't help it.

'He was a famous Dutch cartographer – a map-maker. The framed map above Selina Gane's fireplace is a Janssonius original, worth a packet. Lorraine Turner admired it when she went to value the house for Dr Gane. Oh, and you mentioned the crests – they're the crests of the Cambridge colleges: Trinity, St John's . . .'

'Don't miss out the best one,' says Kit. 'King's.'

'Don't you get enough opportunities to boast to your adoring minions in London?' I snap at him. 'Do you have to turn this into a boast-fest too?'

'The empty crest was left empty deliberately – so that whoever bought the map could fill in their own family crest,' Sam continues as if I haven't just lashed out at my husband.

'Dr Gane told Lorraine all about it. It's one of her treasured possessions, understandably. Apparently it was a house-warming present from her parents when she moved to Cambridge from Dorchester, where she'd lived previously.'

Lucky her. Some people get antique Dutch maps, others get revolting home-made tapestries. Evidently Selina Gane's mother has better taste than mine. I dread to think what the Monk family crest might look like, if we had one. A picture of Thorrold House's kitchen; generations of provincial nobodies chained to a knackered old Aga.

Sam's eyes meet mine. I know what he's going to ask me.

'Connie, when you saw the dead woman on the virtual tour, did you also see the map? Did you see both things in the room at the same time, in the same picture?'

'Yes. That doesn't prove I imagined the woman's body,' I add quickly, afraid that it does. I need time to work out what this means, without Kit and Sam watching me.

'Doesn't it?' says Sam. 'Assuming you're right, when was the photograph of the dead woman taken? Before Selina Gane bought 11 Bentley Grove? Then what's her map doing up on the wall? After she bought the house? In which case, the blood would have ruined the carpet and she – or someone – would have had to replace it. And we know, thanks to Lorraine Turner, that that hasn't happened, because the mark from the Beaters' Christmas tree is still there.'

'Come on, Con, you can't argue with that,' says Kit, keen to hurry things along.

'Can't I?' *Can I? Plausibly?* Why do I want to, so badly? Why aren't I happy to be proved wrong? 'You can cut carpet, presumably,' I say in a monotone. 'If there was a line across the room where one section of beige carpet finished and another one of exactly the same colour started, would Lorraine Turner have noticed? Did you ask her?'

'This is ridiculous,' Kit mutters. 'Next you'll say what if Selina Gane laid another beige carpet over her original one, murdered someone, then removed the blood-soaked carpet and found the one underneath still in tip-top condition, miraculously unstained.'

'That's one definition of ridiculous, I agree,' I fire back at him. 'Another is pretending something didn't happen when you know it did – disbelieving your own eyes.' I turn to Sam. 'What are Cambridge police planning to do?'

His face tells me everything I need to know. I open my mouth to protest, but I've lost my grip on the words I was going to use. Everything has blurred. Sam is a fuzzy pink blob.

'Con?' I hear Kit say. His voice sounds as if it's coming from the other side of the world. 'Do you feel faint?'

My mind is shrinking, floating in pieces; I can't feel parts of my body. Can't speak.

'Shall I get her a drink?' someone says – Sam, I think.

'Water,' I try to say.

You're supposed to put your head between your knees – Kit is always trying to make me do that – but I feel better if I straighten my back and do nothing but inhale and exhale until it passes. Alice says it's okay to do that. 'Listen to your body,' she says. 'It's telling you what it needs.'

Gradually, I feel myself reassemble, as if someone has knitted me together again. *Thank God*. Every time this happens, I wonder if I will make it back. When my vision straightens out, I see Sam queuing at the serving hatch.

'Why doesn't he push to the front?' says Kit. 'You need water more urgently than that greasy-haired guy needs that fry-up.'

'I'm not sure water's going to help,' I say.

'If Kombo-whatsit had offered us a drink in the first place, you'd have been fine. It's sweltering in here – you're probably dehydrated. What's the point of meeting in a canteen if you don't even get a drink?'

'Alice thinks the dizzy spells are stress-related,' I say. I've told him this before.

'Great. It's my fault, then, like everything else.'

'I didn't mean that.'

'Connie, listen to me.' Kit takes both my hands in his. 'This is a turning point in our lives. Or it could be, if you'll let it.'

'You mean if I forget about the dead body I saw on Roundthehouses – if I agree to pretend I imagined it.'

'You *did* imagine it, sweetheart. Come on, you must see that you can't have it both ways: if stress can make you faint and have dizzy spells, it can also make you see things that aren't there at one in the morning, surely, when you're exhausted.'

He's right.

'Imagining things doesn't make you a freak, Con. You're talking to the man who once imagined that loads of blades of grass turned into a gigantic grass monster and attacked his feet – remember?'

'You were pissed out of your head. And stoned.' Reluctantly, I smile at the memory. A few weeks after we first met, Kit woke me up in the middle of the night, weeping and demanding that I examine his shoelaces, insisting they were frayed and full of holes from the grass monster's assault. It took me nearly an hour to persuade him that there was no monster and his shoelaces were intact. The next morning, he declared marijuana the root of all evil. He hasn't touched it since.

'I've been lying to you,' I tell him. 'I've been going to

Cambridge. Nearly every Friday.' I look down at the white Formica table, wishing I could sink into it and disappear.

Kit says nothing. He must hate me.

'I go by train,' I say, keen to continue with my confession now that I've started. 'The first couple of times I drove, but then Mum asked me why my car wasn't in the driveway two Fridays running, when I was supposedly at home working. I couldn't think what to say, until it occurred to me to tell her to mind her own business.'

'That must have gone down well,' says Kit. To my relief, he doesn't sound angry.

'After that, I decided to get the train, which takes twice as long. There's no direct train – you have to change at King's Cross. Once, I . . . I only just got back before you. We were both on the 17.10 from London to Rawndesley. You didn't see me, but I saw you. It was the scariest journey of my life; I knew I wouldn't be able to lie – if you'd spotted me, I'd have blurted it all out. When you got off at Rawndesley, you were talking on your BlackBerry. I hung back, waiting to see if you'd stay on the platform to finish the call. Luckily for me, you didn't. You headed for the car park. As soon as you'd gone, I made a dash for the taxi rank. I got home about two minutes before you. Another time, I—'

'Connie.' Kit squeezes my hand. 'I don't care about train timetables. I care about you, and us, and . . . what this means. *Why* have you been going to Cambridge nearly every Friday? What do you do when you're there?'

I risk a quick glance at him, see nothing but unhappiness and incomprehension. 'You can't guess? I look for you.'

'For *me*? But I'm in London on Fridays. You know that.'

'Sometimes I sit on the bench at the Trumpington Road end

of Bentley Grove and watch number 11 for hours, waiting for you to open the front door.'

'Jesus.' Kit covers his face with his hands. 'I knew it was bad. I had no idea it was this bad.'

'Sometimes I stand at the other end, behind a tree, waiting for you to drive up. Which you never do. Sometimes I wander round the city centre hoping to see you with her – in a café, or walking out of the Fitzwilliam Museum.'

'Her?' says Kit. 'Who is Her?'

'Selina Gane. Though I only found out her name today, when Sam told us. Sometimes I stand in the car park at Addenbrooke's and—' I stop suddenly. *Selina Gane, Selina Gane* . . . My throat closes tight as I make the connection. How could it have taken me so long? Instantly, I regret trusting Kit, telling him everything I've just told him. 'Show me your diary.' I say.

'What?'

'Don't pretend you haven't got it with you. You always have it.'

'I wasn't going to pretend. Connie, what is it? You look as if you've seen a ghost.'

'Give it to me.' I hold out my hand.

He pulls his diary out of his pocket, red in the face, and passes it to me. I flick through the pages. I know it was May, but I can't remember the exact date. There it is. I spread it open on the table, so that we can both see the evidence. '13 May 2010 – 3 p.m. SG.'

Kit groans. 'This is your big revelation? Proof that Selina Gane and I must be playing house together at 11 Bentley Grove behind your back? SG is Stephen Gilligan, a lawyer at London Allied Capital. I met him at three o'clock on 13 May, at the office in London. Ring Joanne Biss, his PA, and ask her.' He hands me his BlackBerry. 'Now, so that you'll know I haven't had a chance to ask her to lie for me.'

'You know I'm not going to ring anybody.'

'You can't risk being proved wrong, can you?' Kit leans in front of me, forcing me to look at him. 'You'd rather cling to your suspicions, the imaginary world you've constructed.'

'I didn't imagine what happened in January, and I didn't imagine that woman's body,' I say shakily.

'You went through my diary. Of all the low fucking . . .' Kit grabs my arms, pulls me towards him. His fingernails dig into my flesh. 'I don't know any Selina Gane,' he says in a fierce whisper. He doesn't want anyone to notice his anger – only me. 'I haven't been to Cambridge since the last time I went there with you, in 2003. I've never set foot inside 11 Bentley Grove. I'm not leading a double life, Connie – I'm leading a very lonely, very unhappy married life with a wife I hardly know any more.' He lets go of me when he sees Sam coming back with my water. All that time in the queue and it's a small glass, only half full. If that's what counts as a glass of water around here, I should have asked for seven. There's a dry burn in my throat, as if I've been screaming for a year.

'Connie? Is everything okay?'

'No,' says Kit. 'Things are far from okay. I'm going to work.'

Once he's gone, once I've composed myself, I say, 'We had a row. I expect I don't need to tell you that. You're a detective, after all.'

Sam taps his fingers on the table-top, as if he's playing the piano. 'What aren't you telling me?' he says.

~

'What aren't *you* telling *me*?' I fire the question back at him. 'You could have told me about the stain on the carpet over the phone. You must be busy, and yet here you are – wasting time on me and my silly story. Why?'

Sam looks caught out. 'Lorraine Turner told me something that bothered me,' he says.

I lean forward, my heart racing.

'Selina Gane's no longer living at 11 Bentley Grove. Immediately after putting the house on the market, she moved into the D— into a nearby hotel.'

I make a mental note to find out which Cambridge hotels have names that begin with D. Or maybe it was 'Du'. The Duchess? The Duxford? Isn't there a place near Cambridge called Duxford?

'Why would anyone do that?' I say.

Sam looks away. We're both thinking the same thing, or at least I think we are. He doesn't want to be the one to say it.

Fortunately, I have no such reservations. 'You'd do it if you knew someone had been murdered in your house. Or if you'd murdered that person yourself.'

'Yes,' Sam agrees. 'You would. But, Connie, you must see that—'

'I know: it doesn't prove anything. Do Cambridge police know?'

'I'm not sure. Probably not. Lorraine Turner happened to mention it to me when we were talking about the map – she was worried about something so valuable being left in an empty house – a house empty of people, I mean. Most of Dr Gane's belongings are still there, Lorraine says. Her furniture, books, CDs . . .'

'Did she tell Lorraine why she was moving out?'

'No. And Lorraine didn't ask. She didn't feel it was her place.'

I gulp my water down in one mouthful. 'You've got to tell Cambridge police,' I say.

'It won't make a difference.'

'If they analyse the carpet, they might find traces of blood, or DNA.'

'They won't do anything, Connie. There's no proof. Selina Gane moving out of her house is odd, I agree, but people behave strangely all the time. The guy I've been dealing with, DC Grint – he was satisfied with what Lorraine told him.'

'Then he's a crap detective! Lorraine's the person who took the pictures for the virtual tour, isn't she? She's the last person whose word he ought to rely on. Has he checked with the Beaters, or Selina Gane? What if the Christmas tree story's a lie?'

'Listen to what you're saying and think what it means,' says Sam. 'Lorraine Turner would have to be a psychotic killer who murders her victims in houses she's trying to sell, then posts photographs of their dead bodies on the internet. Does that sound likely to you?'

'Why victims, plural? Maybe there's only one victim: the woman I saw. And you could say that about any crime, in that disbelieving tone, make it sound implausible. "What, so he dissolved all his victims in a bath full of acid?" "What, so he hacked up young men's bodies and stored them in his freezer?" '

'Do you read a lot of true crime stuff?' Sam asks.

I can't help laughing. 'None,' I tell him. 'Everyone knows those stories. They're common knowledge. What are you suggesting, that I'm some kind of morbid blood-thirsty freak? What if Lorraine Turner's the freak, or Selina Gane, or both of them? Why does it have to be me?'

Because you're the one yelling at the top of your voice in a crowded canteen, idiot.

'I've answered your question,' Sam says calmly. 'Are you going to answer mine?'

How does he know I'm keeping something back? Because Kit and I had a fight? He can't have heard the details; he was too far away.

'I spoke to Alice Bean,' he says.

I try not to let my anger show. Alice is mine; sometimes I feel as if she's all I've got, the only person I can rely on to have my best interests at heart. How dare Sam poke around in my life? Why didn't Alice tell me she'd spoken to him?

'You told me Alice advised you to contact Simon Waterhouse, but you didn't speak to her in the early hours of Saturday morning, did you? You didn't tell her about seeing the woman's body.'

'I saw her later on Saturday and told her then.'

Sam waits.

'You're right,' I say. 'I hadn't told her on Saturday morning, when I spoke to you.'

'So she must have suggested you contact Simon about something else.'

I say nothing.

'I'd be very interested to hear what that something else was.'

'It's not really something else. I mean, it is, but . . . it's connected. 11 Bentley Grove is the connection.' I take a deep breath. 'Do you remember the snow we had in January?'

Sam nods. 'I was worried it was never going to end,' he says. 'I thought it was the beginning of the new ice age that the climate change scientists keep predicting.'

'On 6 January, I went to Combingham to buy ten big sacks

of coal. Kit loves real fires and we'd run out, and he couldn't go – he was in London. If you're about to ask why I didn't go to the nearest garage, Kit won't let us buy coal from anyone but Gummy in Combingham. That's not his name, but it's what everyone calls him. I'm a bit scared of him, and having teeth isn't his strong point, but Kit insists his coal is the best. I don't know or care enough about coal to argue with him.'

Sam is smiling, and he shouldn't be. This isn't a happy story.

'I took Kit's car because it's better in snow than mine – it's a four-wheel drive. I'd never been to Gummy's before, not on my own, and my sense of direction's hopeless, so I used the SatNav in Kit's car.'

'He didn't drive to London, then?' says Sam.

'He never does. Usually he parks at Rawndesley station, but it was too icy first thing that morning to drive anywhere apart from on the main roads. The gritters hadn't been out yet. Kit walked all the way down to the Rawndesley Road and caught the bus to the station.'

I wish he'd driven. I wish his car had been in the station car park that day instead of sitting outside our house, looking so much safer and more appealing than mine.

'I bought the coal. I probably could have found my way home, but I didn't want to go wrong, so I decided I'd play it safe and use the SatNav again. I pressed "Home".' I take a deep breath. 'The first thing I noticed was the driving time: two hours and seventeen minutes. Then I noticed the address.'

Sam knows. I can see from his face that he knows.

'As far as Kit's SatNav was concerned, "Home" was 11 Bentley Grove in Cambridge. Not Melrose Cottage in Little Holling, Silsford.' I start crying; I can't help it. 'I'm sorry. I just can't . . . I can't believe that six months later I'm still telling this story without knowing what it means.'

'Why didn't you tell me this on Saturday morning?' Sam asks.

'I didn't think you'd believe me about the woman's body if I told you everything. If you knew I was obsessed with 11 Bentley Grove already . . .'

'Were you?'

Is there any point in my denying it? 'Yes. Totally.'

'Because Kit had put it in his SatNav as his home address?'

I nod.

'And you wanted to know why. Did you ask him?'

'The second he walked through the door. He claimed not to know what I was talking about. He denied it, completely denied it. He said he'd never programmed in any home address – not ours, and not an address in Cambridge that he'd never heard of. We had a huge row – it went on for hours. I didn't believe him.'

'That's understandable,' says Sam.

'He'd bought the SatNav new – who else could have programmed in the address apart from him? I said that, and he said, "It's obvious, isn't it? You must have done it." I couldn't believe it. Why would I do something like that? And if I had, why would I accuse him of doing it?'

'Try to calm down, Connie.' Sam reaches over, pats my arm. 'Would you like another drink?'

I'd like another life – any life but this one, anyone's problems as long as they aren't mine.

'Water, please,' I say, wiping my eyes. 'Can you ask them to fill it to the top this time?'

He returns a few minutes later with a tall, full glass. I take a gulp that makes my chest ache.

'Did you suspect Kit had another family in Cambridge?' Sam asks.

'That was the first thing that sprang to mind, yes. Bigamy.' It's the first time I've said the word out loud. Even with Alice, I skirt around it. 'It sounds melodramatic, but it happens, doesn't it? Men really do commit bigamy.'

'They do,' says Sam. 'Some women do too, I guess. Did you talk to Kit about your suspicions?'

'He denied it – flat out denied it, everything. He's been denying it for six months. I didn't believe him, and that became another thing to fight about – the inequality. I didn't trust him as much as he trusted me.'

'So he believed you when you said you didn't do it?'

'He moved on to accusing my family – my mum, Fran, Anton. Reminded me of all the times one or other of them had been round when his SatNav was lying around in the house.'

'Who are Fran and Anton?' Sam asks.

'My sister and her partner.'

'Was Kit right? Could a member of your family have programmed in the address?'

'They could have, but they didn't. I know my family inside out. My dad's terrified of anything modern and gadgety – he refuses to acknowledge the existence of iPods and E-readers – even DVD players are too much for him. There's no way he'd go anywhere near a SatNav. Fran and Anton aren't imaginative enough or devious enough. My mother can be both, but . . . trust me, she wouldn't have put that address into Kit's SatNav.'

She'd rather swallow fire. I've seen her stiffen and change the subject when anything with a Cambridge connection comes up in conversation: the boat race, Stephen Hawking and his black hole theory. She doesn't even like me to hear Oxford mentioned, or any university, in case it makes me think of Cambridge. At first I thought she was worried about upsetting me, but then I realised her motivation was more selfish than that: she wants me to forget that Cambridge exists, that Kit and I were ever thinking of moving there. Her greatest fear is that I will one day leave Little Holling.

Mine is that I won't.

'Kit programmed in the address,' I tell Sam. 'He must have. That's what I think at the moment, anyway. That's what I've thought a thousand times, and then I accuse him again and he persuades me again that he's not lying about anything, and he's so . . . *convincing*. I want to believe him so much, I end up wondering if maybe I did it, then wiped the memory from my mind. Maybe I did. How do I know? Maybe I programmed 11 Bentley Grove into Kit's SatNav, and hallucinated a body that wasn't there. Maybe I'm some kind of deranged lunatic.' I shrug, embarrassed suddenly by how strange and pathetic my story must sound. 'This is what my life's been like since January,' I say. 'Round and round: believing, not believing, questioning my sanity, getting nowhere. Not much fun.'

'For you or for Kit,' says Sam. Does that mean he believes Kit's telling the truth?

'He even tried to say once that maybe someone in the shop he bought it from had programmed in the address.' I thought I'd finished, but I can't leave it alone. 'He wanted us to go down there together, ask all the staff.'

'Why didn't you?' Sam asks.

'Because it was bullshit,' I say angrily. 'I wasn't prepared to let him play games with me. I nearly agreed, but then I had a flash of clarity. I have those, sometimes, where it dawns on me that I don't need to torment myself speculating, wondering. I *know* the truth: it wasn't anyone in the shop, or me, or a member of my family. It was Kit. I know he did it.' As soon as I'm out of here, I'm going to ring London Allied Capital and ask to speak to Stephen Gilligan's secretary. Maybe he had a meeting with Kit at 3 p.m. on 13 May; maybe he didn't. I need to know.

'For six months, Kit's been telling you that he didn't programme in that address,' says Sam. 'What makes you so sure he did?'

Sure? I wonder who he's talking about. Will I ever again be sure of anything?

'Three things,' I say. Exhaustion sweeps over me; it's hard to summon the energy to speak. 'One: it's his SatNav. He had no reason to think I'd be using it, no reason to think I'd find out.' I shrug. 'The simplest explanation is usually the right one. Two: when I first asked him about it, before he had a chance to arrange his face into a puzzled expression, I saw something in his eyes, something . . . I don't know how to describe it. It was only there for a split second: guilt, shame, embarrassment, fear. He looked like someone who'd been caught. If you're about to ask me could I have imagined it, sometimes I think yes, I must have. Other times I'm certain I didn't.' I want to tell Sam how frightening it is to have the narrative of your life shift and lurch and change its contours every time you look closely at it, but I'm not sure any words can accurately describe it. Could Sam even begin to understand what it's like to inhabit such an unstable reality? He strikes me as a man firmly embedded in a consistent world, one that retains its shape and meaning from one day to the next.

I feel as if I have two lives: one created by hope and one by fear. And if both are creations, why should I believe in either?

I have no idea what the facts of my life would look like if I stripped away the emotions.

Better not to say any of this to Sam. I've caused him enough bother already without drawing him into a debate on the nature of reality.

You think too much, Con. Fran's been telling me that since we were teenagers.

'What's the third thing?' Sam asks.

'Pardon?'

'The third reason you're sure Kit programmed in the address.'

I'm going to have to tell him – peel away another layer, go back even further. I have to, if I want him to understand. It's all linked. What happened in the early hours of Saturday morning can't be separated from what happened in January; what happened in January is connected to what happened in 2003. If I want Sam to help me, I have to be willing to tell him all of it, just as I told Simon Waterhouse.

'Cambridge,' I say. 'I'm sure because 11 Bentley Grove is in Cambridge.'

8

17/07/2010

Olivia Zailer flicked through her diary, sighing loudly at the sight of each new page. She'd made too many appointments for the next few weeks, most of which she knew she would at some point cancel. Lunch with Etta from *MUST* magazine to discuss a column about famous books and which meals they would be, in the unlikely event of their being turned into food – *Wuthering Heights* equals Yorkshire Pudding was the example Etta had given; aerobic walking on Hampstead Heath with Sabina, Olivia's personal trainer; tea at the British Library with Kurt Vogel, who wanted her to judge an Anglo-German journalism prize in which all the entrants would be between the ages of eleven and thirteen.

Olivia wondered if she was the only person in the world who, with great gusto in the moment, made plans with almost everyone she came into contact with, knowing full well that she would email to cancel in due course. Why was it so hard to say straight out, 'I'm sorry, Kurt, but no, I can't be a judge'? Why did it feel so right to say, 'Oh, God, I'd *love* to,' and then sneak in the 'can't' bit later on? Olivia would have liked to ask Charlie; she knew no one else who'd be willing to discuss it with her. Dom certainly wouldn't. She suspected it had something to do with being eager to please others, but even more eager to please herself.

Her mobile phone rang, and she picked it up, determined not to make an arrangement with whoever it was, even an arrangement she wanted to make and would not cancel. She needed to purge her diary of all the fake appointments before she made any more real ones.

'It's me. Chris Gibbs.'

'Hello, Chris Gibbs. Oh, my God, that proves it! A watched pot really does never boil. You're only you because I was expecting you to be Kurt Vogel from the Dortmund British–German Society. All the times I was expecting it to be you, it wasn't – and now here you are.'

'Have you still got a spare key for Charlie's place?'

'Why, has something happened?' Olivia was immediately anxious.

'Not as far as I know.'

'Then why do you need a key?'

'I thought it'd be a good place to meet,' said Gibbs.

'You and me?'

'No, you, me, Waterhouse and Charlie, when they get back. For their wedding reunion evening.'

What the hell was she supposed to say to that? 'Wouldn't that be . . . a bit awkward?'

She heard a snort. 'Joking,' said Gibbs. 'Yeah, you and me. I haven't seen you for . . .' There was silence as he worked it out. '. . . about forty-four hours. I'm thinking of making it my new mobilising grievance.'

'You usually don't see me for forty-four hours,' Olivia reminded him. 'You've spent most of your life not seeing me, and you've been fine.'

He made a joke, a whole joke. And he's quoting me. Again.

'That's a matter of opinion,' said Gibbs.

She couldn't meet him at Charlie's house. Have sex in the bed Charlie shared with Simon? It didn't bear thinking about. She reached for a pen and wrote 'Olivia Gibbs' next to where it said 'Name' in her diary, on the personal details page. It looked good, well balanced: the roundness of the two capitals, O and G . . .

Should she scribble over it? She'd wanted to know how it would feel to write it, that was all. She ought to cross it out now. On the other hand, Dom would never look, not even if someone held the diary in front of his nose. The great thing about Dom, from a deceiving him point of view, was that he was interested in almost nothing.

'What do you reckon?' said Gibbs.

'No. Absolutely not.' If only she could be so forceful with Etta from *MUST* magazine.

Olivia had no willpower, and thought people who had it and used it on themselves were weird. Luckily, she had fear and anxiety in abundance. She couldn't have agreed to what Gibbs was proposing without feeling as if she'd crossed a line she was terrified of crossing, even with the safety net of possible future cancellation in place.

'All right then, a hotel,' he said.

'What about your work? What about Debbie?' She turned to the 'Notes' section at the back of her diary and wrote 'Olivia Gibbs' again, in neater handwriting. She wrote it underneath in capital letters.

'My problem, not yours,' said Gibbs. 'If you don't want to come to Spilling, I'll come to London.'

'If you want a . . . a girlfriend, you should find one closer to home,' Olivia told him, praying he wouldn't take her advice. *Why give it, then?*

'Why should I?' said Gibbs. 'There are only two people I've ever met who don't bore me: Simon Waterhouse and you. I don't want to shag Waterhouse – that leaves you.'

'I thought I did bore you,' Olivia felt obliged to point out, in case he'd forgotten. 'You said I was like a colour supplement.'

'I didn't mean it. I didn't know what to make of you, that's all.'

She heard a crunch. Was he eating an apple? 'That Los Delfines place,' he said. For a worrying moment, Olivia feared he was about to suggest they meet and have sex at Charlie and Simon's honeymoon villa. 'I need to tell Stepford that's where Waterhouse is. Something's come up.'

'What? No way, Chris. If you tell him, I'll . . .' She couldn't think of anything to threaten him with. 'What's come up?'

More crunching. Then, 'You let me tell Stepford, I'll tell you what's come up.'

'No! You're *not* going to ruin Charlie's honeymoon by telling Sam where they are so that he can drag Simon home. I'm feeling sick just thinking about it.'

'He won't have to come home – Stepford wants a quick chat with him, that's all. I'll give him the caretaker's number from the website – Domino's Pizza, or whatever he's called. Stepford'll ring, it'll all be over in five minutes – Waterhouse can go back to his deckchair.'

Olivia made a screaming face at the phone. 'How important is it, exactly?' She couldn't resist adding, 'Luxury villas have sun loungers, not deckchairs.'

'A murder might be involved.'

'Oh, fuck. Fuck, fuck, fuck. *Why* did I tell you where they are?'

'You really don't want me to say anything?'

'How can you not, if someone's been murdered?'

'Whoever it is'll still be dead in two weeks' time, when Waterhouse gets back,' said Gibbs.

Olivia could hear the shrug in his voice. 'What kind of attitude is that?' she snapped. 'Are you trying to impress me by being a maverick? If so, that's not how it works. Tearing up the rule book and going it alone is cool. Not caring about the random slaying of innocent civilians is just plain unacceptable.'

'I don't even know for sure anyone's been killed. You're fucking with my plan.'

'Sorry?'

'You were supposed to beg me not to say anything,' Gibbs explained. 'I was going to end up agreeing, on the condition that you agreed to meet me.'

'Of course you were,' said Olivia. 'If you haven't got a bunch of flowers to hand, there's always blackmail.'

Silence.

She hoped she hadn't offended him, though there was no doubt that he deserved to be roundly offended. Eventually he said, 'Talking to you's different to talking to other people. With other people, I say what I mean, they say what they mean. With you, it's like . . . I don't know whether I'm being a bastard, pretending to be a bastard, or reading out some lines from a play I don't understand.'

'It's called pre-sex banter.'

'Right.' A pause. 'I'll make sure not to call it a deckchair, then,' Gibbs said.

Olivia sighed. That was the second joke he'd made – in his entire life, probably. How could she say no? 'You come to London,' she said. 'I'll pay for the hotel. That way we'll both be . . . contributing something.' Given the choice between expending energy and spending money, Olivia opted for the latter every time.

'I'm setting off n—' said Gibbs, ending the call before he'd finished saying 'now'.

Olivia stared down at her never-to-be married name in her diary, all the different versions of it. She swore under her breath when she realised what she'd done: she'd left out her own surname, after all the fuss she'd made about changing her name to Dom's, her insistence that she must be Zailer-Lund instead of simply Lund, because of . . . she couldn't remember the reason she'd given him.

Was she less than a hundred per cent sure about committing herself to Dom?

If she was marrying someone else – not necessarily Chris Gibbs, but . . . well, she might as well use him as a random example, even though the idea was utterly ludicrous, they had nothing in common, he was obviously a deckchair sort of person – would she feel differently?

Olivia told herself firmly that she wouldn't. Her diary seemed to think otherwise.

~

Subject: 11 Bentley Grove, CB2 9AW
From: Ian Grint (iadgrint@cambs.police.uk)
Sent: 19 July 2010 00:10:53
To: Sam Kombothekra (s.kombothekra@culvervalley.police.uk)

Sam,

I keep ringing you and keep getting told you're in the canteen. And your mobile's going straight to voicemail. Can you pull your nose out of the trough and ring me? Soon would be good.

Cheers.

Ian (Grint)

POLICE EXHIBIT REF: CB13345/432/22IG

Important - You will need this to tax your car. Please keep it in a safe place.

Wheel Women
Wayman Court, Newmarket Road,
Cambridge, CB5 9TL

Date of issue: 08/11/2009

This Certificate is evidence that you have insurance to comply with the law. It is not valid if changed in any way. For full details of your insurance cover, please also see your Car Insurance Schedule and your Policy Booklet.

Certificate of Motor Insurance

Certificate and Policy number:	26615881
Registration Mark of vehicle:	MM02 OXY
Name of Policyholder:	Elise Gilpatrick
Insurance commencement date:	06/11/2009 at 00:00 hours
Date of insurance expiry:	06/11/2010 at 00:00 hours
Persons or classes of persons entitled to drive:	Elise Gilpatrick, Donal Gilpatrick

(providing the person driving holds a licence to drive the vehicle or has held and is not disqualified from holding or obtaining such a licence)

The policyholder, Elise Gilpatrick, may also drive with the owner's permission a motor car that they do not own and that is not hired or leased to them under a hire purchase or leasing arrangement.

Limitations as to use: Social, domestic and pleasure purposes

I hereby certify that the policy to which this Certificate relates satisfies the requirements of the relevant law applicable in Great Britain, Northern Ireland, the Isle of Man, the Island of Jersey, the Island of Guernsey and the Island of Alderney.

Rosemary Vincent

Rosemary Vincent, Authorised signatory

9

Monday 19 July 2010

I start to tell Sam Kombothekra about the first row Kit and I ever had. It was about Cambridge. We'd been together for nearly a month.

Kit didn't mean to start a fight; he was trying to pay me a compliment. Technically I was probably the one who started the row, though it didn't feel that way at the time. We were walking back from Thorrold House to Kit's rented two-bedroom flat in Rawndesley; we'd been to Mum and Dad's for lunch. It was about the fifth or sixth time Kit had met my family. It took him nine years to pluck up the courage to ask if he might sometimes be excused from the several visits a week that he could see were required of me.

My father, wanting to impress Kit, had suggested opening a particular bottle of wine that had been given to him two years previously by a grateful Monk & Sons customer. I know nothing about wine, and neither does Dad, but the customer had led him to believe that there was something special about this bottle – it was either very old or very valuable or both. Neither of my parents could recall the precise details, but whatever the customer had told them had been sufficient to impress on them the foolhardiness of opening the wine and drinking it, so instead they had consigned it to a safe place – so safe that when Dad decided that the arrival of a well-spoken

Oxbridge-educated potential son-in-law at his dinner table was an occasion that merited the unleashing of the antique wine's magic powers, neither he nor Mum could remember where they'd put it. Kit tried to tell them it didn't matter, that he'd prefer water or apple juice, as he was driving, but Dad insisted that the special bottle must be found, which meant that Mum had to leave her food to go cold while she ransacked first the cellar and then the house. The rest of us followed Dad's lead and carried on eating. 'If you don't tuck in while it's piping hot, Val'll have your guts for garters,' Dad told Kit, who felt uncomfortable starting without Mum. Fran, Anton and I were used to it. Dad often decides he needs Mum to go and get something for him just as she's about to sit down to eat. I think he looks at the food on her plate, panics slightly about how long it's going to be before she's next available to attend to him, and decides he might as well get his most pressing requests in early.

As we ate, we heard loud panting and a series of small groans coming from beyond the kitchen; Mum wanted us to know exactly what it was costing her to search for the sacred plonk. I could see that Kit was tense, feeling responsible even though he wasn't. Then Mum called out, 'Oh, for heaven's sake! Cotton-wool brain strikes again. I know where I put it.' We listened as a door creaked open. It was a creak Fran and I knew as well as we knew each other; it had been part of Thorrold House's soundtrack since we were children. Dad laughed and said to Kit, 'The cupboard under the stairs – I don't know why she didn't look there straight away. That's where I'd have started. It's the obvious place.'

'Pity you didn't share that insight with Mum,' Fran said pointedly. 'You'd have saved her about half an hour of her life

– her *only* life.' I remember wondering if she was angry because Dad was fawning over Kit and ignoring Anton, who wasn't Oxbridge-educated, whose parents lived in a static caravan on the outskirts of Combingham.

A few seconds later, there was a thud and a stifled scream. The special wine wasn't all Mum had found in the cupboard under the stairs. We all rushed out into the hall. She was on her hands and knees, leaning over a cardboard box. Inside was a lumpy black mess, part solid but mainly liquid. The smell was overpowering; it made me gag. 'What's that when it's at home?' Dad asked, bending to pick up the hallowed bottle, which, in her shock, Mum had dropped.

'I think it must have been a cabbage,' she said. 'I remember putting a cabbage in there ages ago, in a box . . .'

'Well, it's not a cabbage any more,' said Dad, elbowing Kit in the ribs as if to say, 'Another hilarious episode in the life of the Monk family!'

'I'll get rid of it for you, Val,' said Anton. He moved my mother to one side like a bomb-disposal expert preparing to secure the scene.

'Anton to the rescue,' said Dad for Kit's benefit, as if Kit might not understand what was going on; subtitles might be required. 'There's no one better in a crisis.'

'Yup,' Fran muttered. 'When it comes to disposing of decaying vegetables, no one can touch him.'

I looked at Kit, dreading the disgust I was sure I'd see on his face. He grinned at me and widened his eyes in a secret signal, as if to say, 'We'll talk about this later.' I smiled at him, grateful because he'd made me feel like a fellow outsider, not part of the Thorrold House madness. Not implicated.

We all watched as Anton opened the front door and carried

the box containing the former cabbage outside. 'Right.' Dad clapped his hands together. 'Back to what matters: food and wine.'

We ate our cold lasagne – which Dad kept insisting was still 'piping hot' and Mum kept threatening to heat up in the microwave – drank the wine, which was nice but nothing spectacular, then drank some ordinary wine when the overhyped stuff had run out. Dad carped at Mum for dropping the bottle on the carpet, rotten cabbage or no rotten cabbage, because 'it could easily have smashed', even though it hadn't. Kit tried not to let Dad fill his glass again and again, Dad bored me and Fran and shocked Kit with his views on drinking and driving: 'As far as I'm concerned, if you can't drive responsibly when you've had a few, you're not fit to drive at all. A good driver's a good driver, tipsy or sober.'

Then, apropos nothing, Mum burst into tears and ran from the room. Taken aback, we listened to her weeping as she ran upstairs. Dad turned to Fran. 'What's the matter with her? Too much vino, do you think?'

'Dunno,' said Fran. 'Why don't you make her drive up and down the A1 for a few hours? If she crashes, she's pissed. If she doesn't, she isn't. Or is it the other way round, according to you?'

'Go and check on her,' said Dad. 'One of you. Connie?'

I stared down at my plate, resolutely ignoring him. Fran sighed and went off in search of Mum.

Dad said, 'We'll have a nice cup of tea in a minute, and pudding – apple and rhubarb crumble, I think it is.' He meant that we would have both when Mum came downstairs. I bit back the urge to say to Kit, 'My dad might suck up to you and force his best wine down you, but he will never, ever make you a cup of tea, no matter how many years you spend sitting at his kitchen table, no matter how thirsty you are.'

At that moment, it struck me as a form of cruelty: to know and supposedly love someone – your own daughter – and yet never to have offered them a cup of tea or coffee in thirty-four years, unless it was with the certainty that someone else would make it.

Fran reappeared, looking annoyed. 'She says she'll be down in a minute. She's upset about the cabbage.'

'Why, for goodness' sake?' Dad was impatient.

Fran shrugged. 'I couldn't get much out of her. You want more information, ask her yourself.'

A few minutes later, Mum swept into the kitchen wearing newly applied make-up and started talking with manic cheeriness about crumble and custard. The rotten cabbage wasn't mentioned again.

Two hours later, after pudding and tea, we were able to escape. As diplomatically as possible, Kit fielded Dad's attempts to insist that he drive home despite having had four large glasses of wine. He left his car outside Thorrold House – he completely agreed with Dad about drink-driving, of course he did, but there was the fuddy-duddy traffic police to consider – and we walked back to Rawndesley, which took an hour and a half. We hardly noticed; we were busy discussing my family.

'Fran kept savaging your dad, and he didn't respond at all,' said Kit, animated and full of life now that we were free. 'He didn't even notice. It was hilarious. She's like a Culver Valley Dorothy Parker. If I spoke to my dad like that, even once, he'd cut me out of his will.' Kit was still on reasonable terms with his parents at that point.

'Who's Dorothy Parker?' I asked.

Kit laughed; he obviously assumed I was joking.

'No, really,' I said. 'Who is she?'

'A famous funny person,' said Kit. '"When it comes to disposing of decaying vegetables, no one can touch him." Those are the very words Dorothy Parker would have used, I reckon. Your dad didn't get it at all – that Fran was taking the piss out of him for damning Anton with the faintest of faint praise: "There's no one better in a crisis." True, as long as all that's needed to resolve the crisis is for someone to carry some decomposing food to the bin. That was the only time your dad acknowledged Anton's existence all afternoon, he was so busy ingratiating himself with me. No wonder Fran was pissed off.'

'I'm sorry about the smelly cabbage,' I said solemnly, and we both burst into yelps of laughter. It was a cold February day – getting on for night – and it had started to rain, which made us laugh even more: thanks to Dad and his special wine, we were going to get soaked.

'It's obvious why your mum got so upset about the artist formerly known as cabbage,' said Kit, trying to keep a straight face.

'She can't stand any kind of waste,' I told him. 'That's twenty pence she could have saved last year.'

'She was mortified that it had happened in front of me. If only she'd said so, I could have reassured her that I couldn't care less. Far be it from me to think badly of someone who keeps rancid liquefied vegetable matter in a . . .' He couldn't say any more; he was laughing too much.

Once we'd composed ourselves, I said, 'It's not that, what you said. Yes, she'll have been embarrassed, but that wasn't why she had that weird meltdown. Appearances are important to Mum, but control is her God. She works so hard to be in control of every aspect of her life and world, and most of the time she succeeds. Time stands still for her, the world shrinks to the size of Thorrold House's kitchen, the universe's energy flow stops in its tracks – it knows better than to argue with Val Monk. And then she finds a cabbage that's been there for months if not years – that's been, unbeknownst to her, turning all squelchy and stinky and black, and she had no idea. And then it makes an unscheduled appearance one afternoon when she's got guests. She tries to move on and pretend it hasn't bothered her, but she can't get past it. The cabbage is evidence she can't ignore – evidence that she's not in charge. The forces of death and decay are on the march, they're the ones running the show. They're inside the building, and not even my sensible organised mother, with her "recipes for the week" notebook and her meticulously filled-in birthdays calendar, can keep them at bay.'

Kit was staring at me. He wasn't laughing any more.

'Sorry,' I said. 'When I drink too much, I talk too much.'

'I could listen to you talking for the rest of my life,' he said.

'Really? In that case, you're wrong about Fran too.'

'She's not the Culver Valley's answer to Dorothy Parker?'

'She wasn't having a go at Dad, though she'd probably pretend she was if I asked her about it. *She* was the one damning Anton with faint praise. She loves him, don't get me wrong, but I think sometimes she wishes he . . . I don't know, had a bit more to him.'

'Why didn't you go to university?' Kit asked me.

The sudden change of subject surprised me. 'I told you: none of my friends were going, and Mum and Dad had offered me a well-paid job at the shop.'

'You're incredibly bright and perceptive, Connie. You could

be a lot more than your parents' book-keeper if you wanted to. You could go far – really far. Further than Little Holling, Silsford.' He stopped walking and made me stop too. It struck me as wonderfully romantic that he'd bring us to a standstill in the rain in order to tell me I was brilliant and full of potential.

'My teachers at school almost got down on their knees and begged me to think about university, but . . . I was suspicious of it, I suppose. Still am. Why spend three years being ordered to read certain books by people who think they know more than you do, when you can choose for yourself what you want to read and educate yourself without anyone's help – and without paying for it?'

Kit brushed a droplet of rain off my face. 'That's exactly the sort of philistine thinking I'd expect from someone whose education was prematurely curtailed at the age of eighteen.'

'Sixteen,' I told him. 'I didn't do A-levels either.'

'Bloody hell,' he said. 'Next you'll tell me you were raised by wolves.'

'Do you know how many books I read last year? A hundred and two. I write them all down in a little notebook—'

'You should go to university,' Kit talked over me. 'Now, as a mature student. Connie, you'd love it, I know you would. Cambridge was the best thing that ever happened to me – without a shadow of a doubt, the best three years of my life. I . . .' He stopped.

'What? Kit?'

I noticed that he wasn't looking at me any more. He was looking past me, or through me, seeing another time and another place. He turned away from me, as if he didn't want my presence to interfere with whatever he was remembering. Then he must have realised what he'd done, because he made a concerted effort to bring himself back. I saw that look in his eyes, the same one I saw ten years later, in January, when I asked him why 11 Bentley Grove was programmed into his SatNav as his home address: guilt, fear, shame. He'd been caught out. He tried to make a joke of it. 'The second best thing that ever happened to me,' he said quickly, reddening. 'You're the best thing, Con.'

'Who was she?' I asked.

'No one. That wasn't . . . No one.'

'You had no girlfriends at uni?'

'I had lots, but no one significant.'

The week before, I had asked him how many times he'd been in love before me, and he'd dodged the question, saying things like, 'What do you mean by *in* love?' and 'What kind of love are you talking about?', while his eyes darted around the room and refused to meet mine.

'Kit, I saw your face when you said Cambridge was the best three years of your life. You were remembering being in love.'

'No, I wasn't.'

I knew he was lying, or I thought I did. Something inside me darkened and curdled; I decided to become the bitch I can be so effortlessly when I'm feeling miserable. 'So you were thinking about lectures and tutorials, were you, with that wistful expression on your face? Dreaming of essay notes?'

'Connie, you're being ridiculous.'

'Was she your lecturer? Your lecturer's wife? Wife of the master of the college?'

Kit denied it and denied it. I kept up my inquisition all the way back to his flat – was it a man? Was it someone underage: the college master's not-quite-sixteen-year-old daughter? I refused to share a bed with Kit that night, threw a completely undignified tantrum, threatened to end our relationship unless he told me the truth. Then, seeing that he wasn't going to, I scaled down my threat: he didn't have to tell me the truth, but he had to admit that there was something he didn't want to tell me, to reassure me that I wasn't mad and hadn't imagined the fervour I'd seen in his eyes, or the guilt. Eventually he admitted that he might have looked a bit sheepish, but it was only irritation with himself for having been so stupid as to give me the impression – mistaken, he assured me – that his university education was more important to him than I was.

I wanted to believe him. I decided to believe him.

The next time the subject of Cambridge came up between us was in 2003, three years later. I'd moved into Kit's Rawndesley flat by then, and Mum had taken to chirping, 'Hello, stranger,' when I turned up for work each morning. I ignored her, and left my defence to Fran: 'For Christ's sake, Mum! Rawndesley's twenty-five minutes by car. You see Connie *every day*.'

All my life, I had assumed that my family was crippled by a disease that affected no one else, of which the chief symptom was extremely narrow horizons. Then one day Kit and I were on our way out for a meal and we bumped into some neighbours, a couple who lived in the flat next to ours, Guy and Melanie. At the time, Kit worked with Guy at Deloitte; it was Guy who had told him there was a duplex apartment available in his building with a great view of the river. While the men talked shop, Melanie looked me up and down and interrogated me: what did I do, was my hair naturally so dark, where was I from? When I said Little Holling in Silsford, she nodded as if she'd been proved right. 'I could tell from your voice that you weren't from round here,' she said.

Later, at Isola Bella, the better of Rawndesley's two Italian restaurants, I told Kit how much Melanie's remark had depressed me. 'How can Silsford not count as "round here" when you're in Rawndesley?' I complained. 'Culver Valley people are so parochial. I thought it was just my parents, but it's not. Even in Rawndesley, which is supposed to be a city . . .'

'It is a city,' Kit pointed out.

'Not a proper one. It's not cosmopolitan and buzzy, like London. It's got no . . . vibe. Most people who live here don't choose it. Either they were born here and aren't imaginative enough to leave, or they're like me – born and bred in Spilling or Silsford, and so sheltered and insular that the prospect of moving thirty miles down the road to the metropolis that is Rawndesley feels as exciting as moving to Manhattan, or something – until you get there, that is. Or people move here because they have no choice, because they get jobs that—'

'Like me, you mean?' Kit grinned.

Strangely, I hadn't thought of him. 'Why *did* you come here?' I asked him. 'From *Cambridge*, of all places – I bet that's a buzzy, vibrant city.' It was the first time Cambridge had been mentioned by either of us since the big fight.

'It is,' said Kit. 'It's a beautiful city, too, unlike Rawndesley.'

'So why leave it and move to the stifling Culver Valley?'

'If I hadn't, I wouldn't have met you,' Kit said. 'Connie, there's something I need to ask you. That's why I suggested going out for dinner.'

I sat up straight. 'Will I marry you? Is that it?' I must have looked excited.

'That's not it, no, but since you've brought it up . . . Will you?'

'Let me think about it. Okay, I've thought about it. Yes.'

'Excellent.' Kit nodded, frowning.

'You look worried,' I said. 'You're supposed to look blissfully in love.'

'I am blissfully in love.' He smiled, but there was a shadow behind his eyes. 'I'm also worried. It's a massive coincidence, but I need to talk to you about my job, and . . . well, about Cambridge.'

I held my breath, thinking he was about to entrust me with the story he'd refused to tell me three years earlier. Instead, he started talking about Deloitte, telling me there was an opportunity for him to lead a new team at the Cambridge branch, doing new, exciting work, how good the promotion prospects would be if he agreed. My heart started to pound. Kit's words were coming faster and faster; I couldn't take in the details, and some of what he was saying made no sense to me – phrases like 'client-facing' and 'granularity' – but I got the gist. Kit's firm wanted him to relocate to Cambridge, which meant that I, as the person who'd just agreed to marry him, even if I did kind of ask myself, had a chance to escape from my family and from the Culver Valley.

'You've got to say yes,' I hissed at Kit as the waiter arrived with our tiramisus. 'We've got to get out of here. When did they ask you?'

'Two days ago.'

'Two days? You should have told me straight away. What if they've changed their minds?'

Kit covered my hand with his. 'They won't change their minds, Con.'

'How do you know?' I demanded, panicking.

'They're one of the UK's leading accountancy firms, not a bunch of hysterical teenagers. They've made their offer – an extremely generous offer – and now they're waiting to hear from me.'

'Ring them now,' I ordered.

'Now? It's quarter past nine.'

'What, they'll be asleep? Of course they won't be! If I were one of the UK's leading granulated client-facing accountancy firms, I'd stay up till ten thirty to watch *Newsnight*.'

'Con, slow down,' Kit said, taken aback by my desperation. 'Don't you want to think about it first? Give it some time, mull it over?'

'No. Why, do you?' What if Kit didn't want to move? He'd lived in several different places already: he was born in Birmingham, then moved to Swindon when he was ten, Bracknell at fifteen. Then Cambridge for university, then Rawndesley. He wasn't trapped in the way that I was; he wouldn't necessarily share my urgent need to escape.

'The job's an improvement, no question,' he said. 'And you're right, Cambridge is a great city. And Rawndesley . . . isn't. But . . . are you sure, Con? I almost didn't bother mentioning it. Yesterday I was on the point of turning it down without even asking you. I didn't think you'd be willing to leave your family, you're all so . . .'

'Unhealthily co-dependent?' I suggested.

'What about your job?' Kit asked.

'I'll get another one. I'll do anything – mow lawns, clean offices. Ask Deloitte if they need a cleaner.'

By the time we left the restaurant, Rawndesley already felt like somewhere we used to live. We were ghosts, haunting our old life, living the hope of a new one.

I told Mum, Dad, Fran and Anton the next day. I was afraid they'd find some way to stop me, even though Kit had done his best to reassure me that this wasn't possible, that I was a free agent.

A long silence followed my announcement. I watched Mum's and Dad's faces rearrange themselves around the shock, feeling as if I'd just unloaded seven tons of invisible psychic rubble in the middle of the room and crushed the breath out of everyone present.

Fran was the first to respond. 'Cambridge? You've never even been there. You might hate it.'

'It's the daftest plan I've ever heard,' Dad said dismissively, wafting my words away with a shake of his newspaper. 'Think how long it'll take you to drive to work every morning. Two hours each way, it'll be, at least.'

I explained that I would be leaving Monk & Sons, that Kit and I planned to get married, that Deloitte had made him an offer he'd be crazy to turn down. Mum looked stricken. 'But Kit's got a job *here*,' she said, her voice unsteady. All of a sudden, because we were proposing to move to Cambridge, Rawndesley had become 'here', not 'there'. '*You've* got a job here,' Mum said. 'If you move to Cambridge you'll be unemployed.'

'I'll find something,' I told her.

'What? What will you find, exactly?'

'I don't know, Mum. I can't see into the future. Maybe I'll do a . . . course at the university.' I didn't dare to use the word 'degree'.

'A course is all very well, but it isn't a job,' said Mum. 'It won't pay the bills.'

Fran, Anton and Dad were all watching her, waiting to see how she was going to fend off the impending calamity. 'Well,' she said eventually, turning away. 'I suppose it's good news for Kit, anyway – a promotion. Our loss is his gain.'

In Mum's personal dramatisation of the situation, Kit was

the winner, she, Dad and Fran were the losers, and I was nowhere to be found.

'Congratulations on getting engaged,' said Anton.

'I thought you thought marriage was old-fashioned and too much hassle,' Fran snapped at him. She didn't congratulate me. Neither did Mum or Dad.

~

First thing the next morning, I leaped out of bed and ran to the bathroom to be sick. Kit asked me if I could be pregnant, but I knew I wasn't. 'It's purely psychological,' I told him. 'It's my body's reaction to my family's reaction to us moving. Don't worry, it'll pass.'

It didn't. Kit and I got into the routine of going to Cambridge every Saturday to look at houses. We both wanted to buy rather than rent – Kit because rent was money down the drain, and me to bind myself legally to a place that wasn't Little Holling, to make it less likely that I'd ever go back. Each time we went house-hunting, Kit had to stop the car at least once so that I could throw up by the side of the road. 'I'm not sure about this, Con,' he kept saying. 'You were fine before we decided to move. We can't live in Cambridge if you're allergic to your parents' disapproval.' He tried to make a joke of it: 'I don't want you turning into a bedridden Victorian-esque neurotic, all white lace nightgowns and smelling salts.'

'I'll get past this,' I told him firmly. 'It's just a phase. I'll be fine.' My hair had started to fall out, but it wasn't obvious yet. I was trying to hide it from Kit.

We found a beautiful house: 17 Pardoner Lane – a three-storey, high-ceilinged Victorian townhouse with original fireplaces in all the reception rooms and bedrooms, black railings outside, steps up to the front door and a roof terrace with a panoramic view of the city. Inside, it was beautifully decorated, gleaming, with a new kitchen and new bathrooms. Kit adored it the moment he set eyes on it. 'This is it,' he muttered to me, so that the estate agent wouldn't hear.

It was the most expensive house we'd seen, by some distance, and the biggest. 'How come we can afford it?' I asked him, suspicious. It seemed too good to be true.

'There's no garden, and it's attached to a school on one side,' he said.

I remembered the sign we'd seen on the building next door. 'The Beth Dutton Centre's a school?'

'Not exactly,' said Kit. 'I checked. It's the sixth-form part of a private school that takes a maximum of fourteen students per year-group, so there'll be no more than twenty-eight kids in it at any given time. They might chain their bikes to our railings, but I'm sure they'll be civilised. Most things in Cambridge are civilised.'

'What about the bell?' I said. 'Won't it ring after every lesson? That might be annoying – we'd be able to hear it through the wall.'

Kit raised his eyebrows. 'I thought you wanted buzzy urban vibrancy? We can move to Little Holling, next door to your folks, if you want to hear nothing but flowers growing and the occasional squeak of someone polishing their Aga.'

'No, you're right,' I said. 'I do love the house.'

'Think of all the space. You'll be able to have a dedicated darkened Victorian sick-room all to yourself.'

'I suppose we'd be able to ask the Beth Dutton people to turn down the volume of the bell, if it was a problem.'

'The bell won't be a problem.' Kit sighed. 'Your fear is the only problem.'

I knew he was right, and that there was only one way to solve it: I had to do what I was afraid of doing, and prove to myself that the world wouldn't end. Mum and Dad would come round, given time; I could visit them regularly. Them coming to stay with us in Cambridge was less feasible. Three years previously, Mum had been to Guildford to visit a friend. She'd had a panic attack on her second day there, and Dad had been summoned to fetch her home. Since then, Silsford town centre was the furthest she'd travelled.

'So, what are we doing?' Kit asked me. We were sitting in his car outside Cambridge Property Shop's offices on Hills Road. 'Are we buying this house or not?'

'Definitely,' I said.

We cancelled the rest of the viewings we'd arranged for that day. Kit made an offer for 17 Pardoner Lane, and the estate agent told him she'd get back to him as soon as she'd had a chance to speak to the vendor.

The next morning I woke up to find that I couldn't move one side of my face. My right eye wouldn't squeeze closed – the most I could do was draw the top eyelid down like a blind and leave it resting there – and when I stuck out my tongue, it went to the left instead of straight ahead. Kit was worried I'd had a stroke, but I assured him it wasn't that. 'It's what you said yesterday,' I told him. 'Stress. Fear. Just ignore it – that's what I'm planning to do.' Fortunately, it wasn't immediately obvious to anyone who saw my face. Kit was far more worried about it than I was. I promised him that as soon as we'd moved and settled in to what we were both now calling 'our' house, my symptoms would disappear. 'You don't understand me like I do,' I kept telling him.

'This is my brainwashed subconscious's desperate last-ditch attempt to make sure I spend the rest of my life worshipping the Fear God. I have to resist it. I don't care if my leg falls off, if I go blind, if I turn into a dung beetle – we're buying that house.'

The estate agent took a while to get back to Kit. When she finally did, after avoiding his calls and ignoring his messages for four days, she told him that another buyer was interested in 17 Pardoner Lane, and had offered more money than we had, more even than the asking price. 'We can go higher,' Kit told me, pacing up and down the lounge of our Rawndesley flat. 'What we can't do is go higher, *and* still be able to go out for meals, go on holiday . . .'

'Then let's not buy it,' I said. After the initial plunge of disappointment, I felt a knot start to loosen inside me.

'I'm willing to make sacrifices and tighten belts if you are,' said Kit. 'We eat out a lot, and half the time the food's disappointing.'

'That's because the restaurants we go to are in Rawndesley. In Cambridge the food will be better. Everything'll be better.'

'So we can eat out once every couple of months, instead of once a week,' said Kit. 'Any sacrifices we have to make, it'll be worth it, Con. We won't fall in love with another house, not in the same way. I'm going to ring and offer another five grand.' Five grand more than the other interested party had offered, he meant, which would be an extra twenty grand on top of our original offer.

'No.' I intercepted him on his way to the phone. 'I don't want this move to be any scarier than it already is. Let's look for a cheaper house, one we're sure we can afford.'

'What are you talking about?' Kit was angry. 'You'd give up on 17 Pardoner Lane that easily? I thought you loved it.'

'I do, but . . .' I stopped when Kit pointed at me.

'Your face,' he said. 'It's gone back to normal.'

He was right. I hadn't even noticed. Tentatively, I touched my eyebrow, then my cheek. I stuck out my tongue. 'Perfectly straight,' said Kit. 'Whatever it was, it's gone. Two seconds of you thinking you're off the hook, and it went.' He shook his head. 'Unbelievable.'

'It can't be that,' I protested. 'Even if we don't buy that house, we're still moving to Cambridge.'

'In theory,' said Kit. 'You can handle the theory. The reality – offering on a house, having that offer accepted, so that this move might actually happen – that has you paralysed with terror, literally.'

I had nothing but contempt for the woman he was describing. The idea that she was me made me so angry I wanted to gouge my own eyes out. 'Ring the estate agent,' I said. 'Go *ten* grand higher, and I swear to you, I'll be fine – absolutely fine. I won't have morning sickness, my face won't freeze . . .'

'How do you know?' Kit asked.

'Because I've decided. All that's over. I'm sick of being . . . defective. From now on, my will is reinforced steel, and it's going to spend every minute of every day kicking the shit out of my scared-child alter ego. Trust me – I'll be fine.'

Kit stared at me for a long time. 'All right,' he said. 'But I'm not upping the ante by ten grand when there's no need to. For all we know, five might do the trick.' He phoned the estate agent, who said she would get back to him.

The next day I was in the office at Monk & Sons when Kit turned up unexpectedly. 'Why aren't you at work?' I asked him, then gasped. 'Have we got it? Have we got the house?' I wasn't aware of any fear this time; there was no 'but' in my mind; I wanted 17 Pardoner Lane, pure and simple. I was excited, more excited than I've ever been.

'The vendor accepted our offer,' said Kit. I tried to throw my arms round his neck, but he stopped me. 'And then I withdrew it,' he said.

'Withdrew what?' I didn't understand.

'The offer. We're not moving, Con. I'm sorry, but . . . we can't.'

'Why not?' Tears pricked my eyes. *No. This couldn't happen, not now.* 'Have Deloitte . . .'

'It's nothing to do with Deloitte. I'm worried that if we go ahead with this, you'll . . . I don't know, have some kind of breakdown.'

'Kit, I'm absolutely—'

'You're *not* fine, Con. Last night you were shouting in your sleep.'

'No, I wasn't. What was I saying?'

He avoided looking at me. 'Your hair's been falling out and you've been trying to hide it,' he said. 'And . . . knowing the way your parents feel about us moving, I don't think we'd enjoy it. It's hard to live with the knowledge that you've made someone else miserable, especially when those someones are your mum and dad.'

'That is such bollocks!' I hissed at him, leaning over to slam the office door so that no customers overheard. '*I* wouldn't be making them miserable – they'd be making themselves miserable because they're too *stupid* to realise that having a daughter move a hundred and fifty miles away isn't a terrible disaster! I'd rather they were happy about it, of course I would, but there's no way I'm taking responsibility for them not being!'

'I agree, you shouldn't,' said Kit. 'I also know you would.

You'd feel bad. It'd ruin things. We'd always have this ... shadow hanging over us.'

I was sobbing by this point, horrified by what I was hearing, yet afraid it was the truth. If I moved, would there always be a voice in my head whispering that I had deserted my family?

'I've been thinking,' said Kit. 'There are ways of achieving what we want that don't involve moving away.'

I wondered if he'd lost his mind. Moving away was what we wanted, wasn't it? It was the only thing we wanted: to live in Cambridge. How could we achieve that from our flat in Rawndesley?

'We could buy a house instead of renting – not in ugly Rawndesley, but in Spilling, or Hamblesford, or—'

'*Spilling?*' I wanted to pull his head off his neck and kick it across the room. Did someone slit his skull open in the night and steal his brain? 'Old ladies who play bridge and join the Rotary Club live in Spilling! I'm young, Kit – I want to have a proper life in a place that's got something going for it. I can't believe you're saying this!'

Kit's eyes hardened. 'All kinds of people live everywhere, Connie. You can't generalise. Do you think there won't be bridge-playing old ladies in Cambridge?'

'Yes, maybe – among the masses of students and ... other exciting people.' I knew I sounded like a naïve country bumpkin; that was precisely the problem I was attempting to address with this move. 'In Cambridge the stuffy old people can do their worst, and they still won't be able to stifle the place with their boringness, because there's a constant influx of new, interesting people, because of the university. I thought you wanted me to do a degree?'

Kit fell silent, turned away. After a few seconds, he said

quietly, 'I'd *love* you to do a
hard.'

'But what? You don't think I'n
think Cambridge University would h

He spun round. 'You think that's wh
they'd have you in a hearbeat. I'd move
you in a heartbeat if I thought you'd be able t
He shook his head.

'What did I say last night?' I asked him.

'What?'

'Last night – you said I was shouting in my sleep. That's what's made you change your mind, isn't it? Yesterday we were fine – we were buying 17 Pardoner Lane, at whatever price, outbidding the other buyer even if it meant eating nothing but cold porridge for two years. Remember? What did I yell in my sleep last night that made you want to forget all that and give up? Kit?'

He rubbed the bridge of his nose with his index finger and thumb. 'You said, "Don't make me go." ' He emphasised the word 'make'. I understood why, and that it was his emphasis, not mine. Deep down, I wanted to stay put, he thought, and if we moved and I was unhappy I would hold him responsible, because he'd started the whole thing, with his too-good-to-refuse job offer from Deloitte. 'You kept repeating it,' he told me. 'You were begging me, Connie. Your eyes were open, but you didn't respond when I . . . You don't remember?'

I shook my head. Something inside me switched off. Kit and my subconscious were colluding against me. There was nothing I could do in the face of that sort of opposition. 'What about Deloitte?' I said dully. 'Your promotion.'

'I'm going to leave Deloitte,' said Kit. He smiled. 'I told you:

readjusting. We both need to get out of a rut
thing to get excited about, even if that thing's
ge. So we're going to set up our own business. You
rk part-time for your parents if you want, but mainly
working with me. You need more independence from
family – being there eight hours a day five days a week is
much. Your mum and dad need to see that you're capable of doing something that wasn't originally their idea, or your dad's dad's dad's idea. That'll help them to see you for what you are: a bright, capable, independent woman.'

I opened my mouth to tell him he couldn't decide all this without consulting me, but he was too quick, and was already describing the next strand of his plan. 'We'll find a house we love – *really* love, even more than 17 Pardoner Lane. That won't be hard. That's one thing places like Spilling and Silsford have got over Cambridge – more unusual houses, more variety. In Cambridge almost everything's a brick-built terrace.'

'I love 17 Pardoner Lane,' I said pointlessly. Now, for the first time and with startling clarity, it hit me that it was the perfect house, the only house I wanted, now that I was being told I couldn't have it.

'You'll love the house we buy in the Culver Valley, I promise you,' said Kit. 'If you don't, we won't buy it. But you will. And then, once our business is a runaway success, and we've got pots of money, and you've shown your parents that you can manage on your own, without the almost non-existent salary they pay you . . .'

'I thought I'd still be working for them part-time,' I said. My leaving Monk & Sons altogether would bother Mum as much as the move to Cambridge would have.

'At first, if you want to.' Kit nodded. 'But once our business really takes off, once we're clearing so much from it that, really, it'd be ridiculous for you to still be earning seven hundred quid a month or whatever it'd be as Monk & Sons' part-time book-keeper, then you'll just have to tell your parents you've got better things to do – say, "I'm sorry, Dad, but if I wanted to do voluntary work, I'd sign up with the Red Cross." '

I couldn't help laughing. 'So what's this hugely profitable business of ours going to be?' I asked.

'Haven't a clue,' Kit said cheerfully, relieved that I was looking and sounding happier. 'I'll think of something, though, and it'll be good, whatever it is. And, in five years' time, we can talk about moving to Cambridge again, maybe, or somewhere else – London, Oxford, Brighton – and you'll find you won't be half as scared then as you are now, because you'll already be well on the way to' – he mimed peeling something away from something else – 'extricating yourself.'

'That's why Melrose Cottage is so beautiful,' I tell Sam Kombothekra, whose eyes look glassy from listening to me for so long. He's probably drawing the conclusion round about now that no sane person would make such a melodrama of a simple plan to relocate to another part of the country. *Therefore I must be insane, and likely to hallucinate dead women in pools of blood on my computer screen.* 'Melrose Cottage is the name of our house in Little Holling,' I add, in case he didn't notice the sign on the door.

'It's certainly chocolate-box perfect,' he agrees.

'It had to be. To make up for . . . everything.' It's seven years since Kit and I had that conversation in the office at Monk & Sons. He hasn't mentioned the possibility of moving to Cambridge or London or Brighton again, not even once. London would certainly be out of the running; now that he works there several days a week, he's started to bring home stories of how hellish it is: litter-strewn, noisy, grey. It's the sort of thing my mum, who has never been to London, says, but it depresses me more when it comes from Kit, who's supposed to be my ally in the struggle for freedom.

The Christmas after we moved into Melrose Cottage, Kit bought me the '4/100' King's College Chapel print. 'I thought we should have a picture to remind us of Cambridge, since we're not going to be living there,' he said. I couldn't see it as anything but a symbol of my defeat; it ruined my Christmas. The laughing woman on the chapel steps seemed to be laughing at me.

'In January, when I found that address in Kit's SatNav, I started to wonder about . . . well, about his sudden change of mind,' I tell Sam. 'He made out it was because he was worried about my stress levels, but what if it wasn't that at all? What if the reason he wanted to move to Cambridge in the first place was because he had a girlfriend there?' *Selina Gane*. 'And then they split up – they had a huge row, and she dumped him – and that's why he changed his tune. And then, at some point later on, one of them contacted the other and they got back together, but this time, instead of suggesting to me that we move, Kit had a better idea: to set up home with her at 11 Bentley Grove, while keeping me in Little Holling, safely out of the way. He loves Melrose Cottage – he did exactly what he set out to do in 2003: found a house he loved even more than 17 Pardoner Lane. He'd never give it up if he didn't have to. A couple of weeks ago he commissioned a local portrait artist to paint it, as if it were a person or something.'

Isn't that how you feel about it too?

I don't dare to admit that I'm on the verge of starting to

hate my own home, even though it's lovely and has done nothing wrong.

'Kit wants both, like a lot of men,' I say angrily. 'Two lives. Me and Melrose Cottage in one compartment, Selina Gane and Cambridge in the other. And he doesn't care what I want. I'd still like to move. He doesn't even ask me any more. He assumes I'm happy with things as they are, but why would I be?' I snap at Sam, who, like Melrose Cottage, has done nothing wrong.

'You don't know that Kit's involved with Selina Gane,' he says.

'You don't know that he isn't.'

And now there's nothing else you can say, is there? Nothing more to be said, nothing you can do, no way of knowing. Welcome to my world.

'Did you tell Simon Waterhouse all this?' Sam asks.

Talking to Simon was easier than talking to Sam, much easier. I felt less like a freak. Simon wasn't repelled by the strangeness of my story. Sam is, though he's doing his best to hide his discomfort. I had the impression, somehow, when I talked to Simon, that strangeness was his element. He nodded at things I said that would have provoked incredulity in most people, and seemed puzzled by the more ordinary details, asking questions that had no obvious bearing on anything. He kept asking me about Kit's parents, when and why he broke off contact with them.

I didn't tell Simon everything. Not wanting to admit to anything that might be illegal, I didn't mention my stalking habit, my Cambridge Fridays. I didn't tell him I sometimes followed Selina Gane to work, walking behind her, or that she'd turned on me once, in the hospital reception area, asked if she'd seen me somewhere before.

'No,' I'd said quickly, mortified. 'I don't think so.'

'Do you live on Bentley Grove?' she'd asked. She must have seen me there, maybe more than once.

I'd lied again, pretended I had friends who lived there.

I didn't tell Simon that, only a fortnight after the hospital incident, I bumped into Selina again – by chance, in town. I'd decided nothing was going to happen at 11 Bentley Grove that day, so had walked into the city to get something to eat. I was about to plump for Brown's on Trumpington Street when I saw her walking ahead of me. I knew it was her; I'd parked my car at the cul-de-sac end of Bentley Grove and watched her leave the house that morning, and she was wearing the same clothes: green denim jacket, black trousers, high-heeled boots. It was her, and she hadn't seen me. I felt unreasonably annoyed that she wasn't at Addenbrooke's, when I'd been certain that was where she was headed this morning, where she would spend her whole day.

I followed her along King's Parade and onto Trinity Street. When she went into a clothes shop, I hung around outside. She was in there for ages – so long that I started to worry that my eyes had misled me. Perhaps I'd lost her and was standing outside the wrong shop while she hurried away somewhere else, leaving me behind.

After I'd waited nearly an hour, my frustration made me do something so stupid, I still have trouble believing I did it. I walked into the shop. I was so sure I wouldn't find her in there, but there she was. She and the woman behind the till stared at me with the same angry, triumphant look in their eyes; I knew without anyone saying anything that they were friends. 'What's going on?' Selina Gane demanded. 'Who are you, and why are you following me? Don't even think about denying it, or I'll call the police.'

My legs nearly gave way. I stared wildly at her, not knowing what to say. I noticed that she wasn't wearing a wedding ring, which made me feel better about nothing.

'Lock the door,' she said to her friend. Then, to me, 'I'm getting an answer from you – whatever I have to do.'

Before her friend had a chance to move from behind the till, I ran for the door, and was out and tearing down Trinity Street like a hunted animal in fear for its life. I ran for what felt like miles. When I finally dared to stop and turn round, I saw that there was no one there, or at least no one with any interest in me, and burst into tears of relief. I'd got away. She didn't know who I was. It only occurred to me the following day that I might have said, calmly, 'My name's Connie Bowskill. I'm Kit Bowskill's wife.' How would she have reacted? Blank incomprehension, or shock? Did she know Kit? Did she know that he was married?

I didn't find out her name on that day either. I only found it out this morning, when Sam Kombothekra told me.

'Connie?'

'Mm?'

'Did you tell Simon Waterhouse?'

'Yes,' I say. 'I told him everything I've told you.'

'What did he say?' Sam asks.

10

19/07/2010

'I asked her if there was any possibility that she programmed the address into her husband's SatNav herself,' Simon told Charlie. They were sitting at the large wooden table on one side of the swimming pool – Simon under an umbrella and Charlie in the full glare of the sun. She knew it was bad for her, but she loved it: the way it burned its glow into her skin and made her feel as if her brain was dissolving, so that she had no choice but to hurl herself into the pool.

On the lunch front, the unthinkable was happening: Simon was peeling prawns and handing them to her, one by one; that was how guilty she'd made him feel. She was no longer hungry, but she wanted him to keep peeling. He didn't seem to mind, which irritated her a little, but then he'd only done eight prawns so far and she reckoned she could eat about fifty, even if she did end up being sick afterwards. She was confident he'd be fuming and swearing before she was ready to let him off the hook.

'Why would she programme the address in herself, then accuse her husband of doing it?' she asked Simon.

'Because she genuinely believes he did it. If she's erased the memory of *herself* doing it, and then she finds it there – well, he must have done it, mustn't he? And she wants to know why. Why's he putting this unknown Cambridge address into his SatNav as "home"?'

'Bollocks,' said Charlie. 'People's brains don't erase memories. Why that address, anyway? Your post-traumatic memory-wipe hypothesis would make more sense if the address she'd found in the SatNav had been 17 Pardoner Lane.'

'Unless 11 Bentley Grove has equal significance for her,' said Simon. 'Which it might. If she's traumatised enough to delete the memory of putting it into the SatNav, who's to say she wouldn't delete *all* her memories connected to the house? So that, when she sees the address, it means nothing to her.'

Charlie groaned. 'Here's what happened: the husband, Kit, programmed in the address. The simplest solution and all that.'

Simon held up a peeled prawn and stared at it. 'Occam's Razor? It's a myth,' he said. 'If you think back over the last few years of our working life . . .'

'Connie Bowskill isn't work, so don't pretend she is,' said Charlie. 'She's your latest fucked-up hobby. And *our* working life doesn't exist. I left CID years ago. I have my own paid job working for the police, in addition to being your unpaid reality-check provider.'

'All right, then, *my* working life,' Simon said impatiently. 'Nothing I've ever had to deal with has been straightforward. Nothing's ever what it looks like, nothing's predictable.' He sighed. 'Maybe the simplest solution's the winner every time when I'm not around, but it's never worked for me.'

'The husband's the one who was a student at Cambridge,' said Charlie. 'He was the one who suggested moving there in 2003, and the address was programmed into *his* SatNav, in *his* car. I'd think exactly what Connie Bowskill thought: that he must have another wife and family at 11 Bentley Grove—'

'He hasn't,' Simon cut her off. 'I went to Cambridge, called round at the house. The owner's a woman called Selina Gane, a doctor. Late forties, no kids, lives alone. I asked her if she knew a Kit Bowskill. She said the name meant nothing to her. She wasn't wearing a wedding ring, so . . .'

'When was this?' Charlie snatched the prawn from his hand. 'When did you *call round* at 11 Bentley Grove?'

'Few weeks ago. I took a couple of days off.'

'You told me you were buying a new suit and shoes for the wedding.'

'I did that as well.'

'In Cambridge?'

He knew he'd been caught out.

'You told me you'd bought both at Remmick's in Spilling.'

'Only because I didn't want to tell you I'd been in Cambridge. You'd have asked why. It'd all have come out, and I didn't want to tell you then. I wanted to tell you now.'

'I'm not hungry any more,' Charlie said, when he tried to hand her another prawn. 'You saved it up, to tell me on our honeymoon?'

He nodded. 'I planned the whole thing – writing the address down somewhere for you to find, denying I wrote it . . . the whole thing.' For about two seconds, he tried to look contrite. When he saw Charlie trying not to laugh, he smiled, and she saw that he was still pleased with himself for staging his reconstruction so successfully. 'We've never spent two weeks alone together before,' he said. 'I was worried we'd run out of things to talk about.'

'Trust me, that'll never happen. So, is she attractive?'

'Who? Connie Bowskill or Selina Gane?'

'Both.'

'I don't know. You always ask me that.'

'No, I don't,' Charlie protested automatically.

'You even asked it about the face in the mountain. Look.' He pointed. 'You can see it from here, surely?'

Charlie wondered if this was another of his circuitous games. Perhaps Connie Bowskill wasn't the only damsel in distress he had on the go at the moment. Maybe there was some other woman whose husband had claimed he'd seen a face in a mountain, one that she couldn't see however hard she tried. Maybe she'd ended up drowing him in a Spanish swimming pool.

'Selina Gane's what most men would call attractive, I reckon. Shiny blonde hair, decent face, bobbly figure.'

'*Bobbly?*'

'You know.' Simon did an outline with his hands.

Charlie narrowed her eyes at him. 'More commonly known as "hourglass",' she said. 'She's in her late forties, did you say?'

'Around that. She's rich, as well.'

'How old's Connie Bowskill?'

'Thirty-four.'

'Attractive? For God's sake, Simon, there's nothing embarrassing about saying whether someone's attractive or not!'

'Skinny, dark. You'd say she was very pretty.'

'Oh, I'd say that, would I? How do you know Selina Gane's rich?'

'The way she looked,' said Simon. 'Her clothes, everything. Loaded, I'd say.'

'So, if Kit Bowskill's involved with Connie and Selina, he's got it sewn up all ways, hasn't he? One dark, one blonde; one skinny, one bobbly; one older, one younger; one rich, one not so rich. Maybe he's like Sellers – as long as she's female, she's his type.'

'He's not involved with both of them,' said Simon. 'I spoke to a few of the neighbours while I was at Bentley Grove, asked them about anyone they'd seen coming and going from number 11 . . .'

'I assume you asked in your professional capacity, even though your being there had nothing to do with work?' Charlie said snidely, knowing Simon wouldn't have allowed ethical considerations to get in his way. His own take on whether something was right or wrong was all he ever cared about; the general consensus of opinion was irrelevant to him. He and Charlie had that in common; in his shoes, she'd have abused her power in exactly the same way.

'I checked with the Land Registry. 11 Bentley Grove's listed in Selina Gane's name only – no mention of Kit Bowskill. I also showed the next-door neighbours on both sides a photo of Bowskill that I'd got from Connie. One of them said he didn't look familiar, she'd never seen him before. Told me she'd only ever seen various women and an elderly couple visiting number 11. The other neighbour, a bent-double guy who looked about two hundred and had the longest name I've ever heard – Professor Sir Basil Lambert-Wall – he said the same about the visitors: lots of women, a couple he described as middle-aged, but I reckon they and the other neighbour's elderly couple are one and the same – Selina Gane's parents, probably. Lambert-Wall took one look at the picture of Kit Bowskill and said, "Of course I recognise him. He installed my new burglar alarm." '

'Alzheimer's?' Charlie asked.

'I don't think so,' said Simon. 'Mentally, he seemed as sharp as a twenty-year-old, even though he was leaning on a stick twice the width of his body. I didn't want to dismiss what he'd told me just because he was an antique, so off I went to Safesound Alarms in Trumpington . . .'

'Where they'd never clapped eyes on Kit Bowskill before, or heard of him,' Charlie summed up.

'No. They hadn't.'

'So the old man made a mistake.'

'He seemed sure,' Simon said doggedly. He sighed. 'You're right. Despite his spectacular name, he must have got it wrong. What would Kit Bowskill be doing fitting burglar alarms?'

'If I were as mad as you, I might say that if he's got two lives running concurrently, with a wife and a home in each, then he might have a job in each – data-system blah blah in Silsford, burglar alarm fitter in Cambridge. Maybe there's a strong anti-cop culture at Safesound Alarms, so they automatically deny everything when the police turn up.' Seeing Simon's worried frown, Charlie slapped his arm. 'I'm kidding. I hope you told Connie Bowskill her husband's in the clear.'

'Not yet. I didn't want to get her hopes up. Just because none of the neighbours have seen him at the house doesn't mean he hasn't been there. Maybe he and Selina Gane are careful. No.' Simon did this when he was in obsessive mode: disagreed with himself out loud. 'They're not romantically involved. They can't be. So what's he doing programming her address into his SatNav as "home"?'

'Why can't they be romantically involved?' Charlie asked.

She watched as Simon realised what he'd said, that he'd sounded a bit too certain. He looked trapped.

'I'm sorry, did you not want to tell me the whole story now?' she asked. 'Are you saving the punch-line for week two?'

'Something strange happened when I was talking to Selina Gane,' Simon said.

'Even stranger, you mean. The whole thing is strange.'

'I showed her the photo, and drew a blank. She's not a good

liar – I found that out about ten seconds later – so I'm pretty sure her lack of response to the picture was genuine. Kit Bowskill's face meant nothing to her. Then I put the photo away and asked her if she knew the name. "No," she said. "Who is she? I've never heard of her." '

'Fair enough.' Charlie yawned. 'Kit could be a woman just as easily as a man.' The heat was having a sedative effect on her. How did anyone manage to work in this climate? If I lived in Spain, I'd have to be a cat, she thought.

'When I told Selina Gane that Kit Bowskill was a man, something happened to her face,' said Simon.

Charlie couldn't resist. 'Did you see a mountain in it?'

'She was surprised – shocked, even. There was this . . . I don't know how to describe it – this outbreak in her eyes of "No, that can't be right". I watched her readjust her assumptions. When I asked her about it, she clammed up, but she couldn't have made it more obvious she was lying if she'd tried.'

'That is strange,' Charlie agreed. 'So . . .' For a second, she couldn't get her head round it. No one should have to think so hard on holiday. 'She didn't know his face, and she didn't know his name. So . . .' Eventually, her sun-frazzled brain came up with the question it had been fumbling for. 'So why was she so certain Kit Bowskill was a woman?'

~

When Sam got back to the CID room, there was no sign of Sellers or Gibbs. Proust wasn't in his office either.

Sam checked his emails. He had seven new ones, five of which looked as if they could safely be ignored; the other two were from DC Ian Grint and Olivia Zailer, Charlie's sister. Sam opened the one from Grint, who'd been trying and failing to get hold of him. Sam wasn't sure he had the energy to ring him back after his exhausting session with Connie Bowskill; he felt like an unpaid shrink – another meeting like that and he'd need to see a shrink himself. Grint had probably called with a current phone number for the Beaters, the couple who had owned 11 Bentley Grove before Selina Gane; Sam had requested it at one point, thinking he might ask them about the Christmas tree stain on their carpet. He smiled to himself. Grint probably thought he was crazy; Sam wouldn't have blamed him if he did.

The email from Olivia contained a string of confusing instructions, double negatives and veiled non-specific accusations – 'I'm not saying you should or you shouldn't . . .', 'please don't, or rather, only do if you feel you have to . . .', 'after I'd mulled it over, I decided I just couldn't not give you the number . . .', 'clearly no one else was going to tell you . . .' – and provided Sam with a means of reaching Simon, which put him in a position he'd have given anything not to be in. Unforgivable to disturb someone on their honeymoon, even with a quick phone call. Which, Sam had to admit, wouldn't be especially quick. There was so much he wanted to ask Simon, and tell him, he wasn't sure he'd know where to begin; the honeymoon would be over by the time he'd filled him in, and Charlie would be marching towards the CID room to bash Sam unconscious with a heavy suitcase.

The phone on his desk started to ring. Sam prayed for it to be Simon: bored, killing time while Charlie had a nap, calling in the hope of a long chat.

It was Ian Grint. He launched in without preamble. 'Looks like your lady's telling the truth. I've had a woman turn up this morning, saw exactly the same thing. Do you believe in synchronicity? I never have, but I might have to start.'

'That's . . .' What was it? Sam didn't know. He wasn't sure what he'd expected to happen, but it certainly wasn't this.

'Same description,' said Grint. 'Of the woman and the room. Framed map, coffee table, the works. Woman: slim, petite, green and lilac patterned dress, dark messy hair fanned out around her head, large pool of blood, darker around the stomach. The timings coincide too. They must have pressed the virtual tour button within seconds of each other. Probably the only two people in the country who did, as it was past one in the morning.'

'Maybe not,' said Sam. 'Maybe other people are on their way to you – or aren't, because they're not sure how to prove they saw it.'

'It disappeared from the website almost immediately after the two known sightings, there's no doubt about that,' said Grint. 'Jackie Napier – that's the lady here – she says she shut the tour down, then started it up again and the body wasn't there. That's exactly what happened to your Mrs Bowskill, right?'

'It is,' Sam told him.

'How soon can you and she get down here?' Grint asked.

'Me and . . . me and Connie Bowskill?' He'd extricated himself from her barely controlled hysteria less than five minutes ago, and had no desire to seek her out in the near future. She'd ordered a taxi to pick her up, since her husband had taken the car and left her without a means of transport. She was probably long gone by now. As for dropping everything and heading for Cambridge, Sam could imagine Proust's reaction. 'I'm not sure I can.'

'Oh, you can, believe me.' Grint's chuckle made it clear that he was unamused. Sam heard the underlying seriousness, the hint of threat. 'There's quite a bit more to it, and I can't go into it over the phone – you need to hear it for yourself. We've got a mess on our hands, the like of which you've never seen before. I know I haven't. I need you both here, you and her.'

A few seconds later, Sam was sprinting along the corridor, in case Connie Bowskill was still waiting in the nick car park for a cab that hadn't yet arrived.

POLICE EXHIBIT REF: CB13345/432/23IG

Dear Elise, Donal, Riordan and Tilly

Just a quick note, very belatedly, to say thanks SO much for that fab weekend! It was just what we needed after a hellishly stressful few months — a real tonic! Cambridge is every bit as beautiful as you described, and we can't wait to come and stay again! On the way home, we asked the kids what was their favourite part of the weekend and they said, 'All of it' — which pretty much sums up how we all feel. That punting trip down the river was sublime: the beautiful college buildings, the sun . . . Oh, by the way, we think we might have solved the mystery of that punt we bashed into under the bridge: 'Step to Heaven'. A mate of ours here was a student at Trinity College, and he says they have their own punts, and each one is named after something that's one of three — there's a song called 'Three Steps to Heaven', isn't there? Gene Vincent, or was it Eddie Cochrane? Anyway, we've been trying to work out what the other Trinity punts must be called: Musketeer? Blind Mouse? Wise Man? Let us know if you see any of those on the Cam (or the Granta, for that matter!).

Your house is a stunner — we're so jealous! Does it feel like home yet, or do you still feel like you're playing house? I remember you said that about the last place too, and felt as if someone might snatch it away from you when you weren't looking! Relax, it's yours! Meanwhile, I wish someone'd snatch our dilapidated hovel — and preferably sort the leaky roof out while they're at it! Anyway, thanks again for making us feel so welcome!

Leigh, Jules, Hamish and Ava

PS. Jules insists that one of the Trinity punts must be called 'Lion on a Shirt', but I think that's probably stretching it a bit!

11

Monday 19 July 2010

I walk out into the heat, stop as the dizziness takes hold. I close my eyes and lean against the police station wall, propping myself up to make sure I don't end up on the ground. A car horn beeps. I can't tell how far away it is. It's probably my taxi. I ought to look, but I know better than to risk it when my mind is breaking up into clumps of woolly grey. I won't open my eyes until I'm certain the world will look normal again. The worst thing about these attacks is the visual distortion. If I keep my eyes open, it's terrifying – like falling further and further back inside my head, being dragged by an internal current away from my eyes, which stay fixed where they are as I recede into the depths.

'Connie!' The car horn again. I recognise the voice, but can't identify it. I'm still resting against the wall with my eyes closed when I feel a hand on my arm. 'Connie, are you okay?'

My sister. Fran.

'Just a bit light-headed,' I manage to say. 'I'll be all right in a minute. What are you doing here? How did you know . . . ?'

'I rang Kit when your phone went straight to voicemail. He told me you'd need a lift home.'

Because I made him angry, and he left me stranded.

'I'm not taking you home yet, though. Get in the car.'

Not taking me home? *Where, then?* I open my eyes. Fran's

Range Rover is parked half in and half out of the disabled space closest to the building. The driver and passenger doors are hanging open. It makes me think of a film I saw when I was little about a magic car that could fly; its doors were its wings.

Fran's wearing the faded jeans and orange and white striped rugby shirt that I think of as her non-work uniform. Sometimes, when I'm at her house and see them drying on the clothes rack, I think about stealing them and throwing them away, though there's nothing particularly wrong with them.

'I've ordered a cab,' I say. 'I ought to wait.'

'Forget the cab. I've called Diane in on her day off to cover for me because I need to talk to you – now. Like it or not, you're coming with me.'

'Where?'

'The tea rooms at Silsford Castle. We're going to have a cup of tea and a chat.' Fran sounds grimly determined. Nothing about her tone suggests that any of it will be fun.

I allow her to push me into her car. It smells of a mixture of crisps and Johnson's aloe-scented baby-wipes, which she still uses all the time, even though Benji is five and there is currently no baby in her branch of the family. I'm aware that I have no right to find this irritating. Fran gets in on the driver's side, dumps her bag in my lap and sets off without bothering to fasten her seatbelt.

'Why Silsford Castle?' I ask. 'Why not somewhere that's on our way home?'

'Home? Where's that, then?' Fran turns to look at me, to check her words have shocked me as they were intended to.

'What?' I snap. A stab of fear makes my gut twist. 'What do you mean?'

She shakes her head as if to say 'forget it'. 'Is your phone still switched off?' she asks.

'No. I turned it on when I—'

'Turn it off. Don't ask why, just do it. I don't want any interruptions.'

I obey the order, aware that I probably ought to protest; that would be most people's response. Does it say something bad about me that I find it soothing to be told what to do, so I don't have to think for myself?

Why did Fran ask me where home was?

'You need to go back to the doctor,' she says as we leave Spilling town centre behind.

'What's the point? He can't find anything wrong with me.'

'He can't be looking very hard,' she mutters.

We drive the rest of the way in silence. As Fran pulls into one of five disabled parking spaces on the cobbles outside Silsford Castle, I can't stop myself from saying, 'You're not allowed to park here.'

'I don't care about allowed. And I'm okay with it ethically because I've got you with me,' she says. 'If walking out of the police station and nearly collapsing for no reason doesn't count as a disability, I don't know what does.'

I hate her for saying it, for making me panic about what will happen when I get out of the Range Rover. Will the dizziness strike again? What if I don't have enough time to get to something I can lean against?

Fran hasn't asked me how it went with the police. She must know why I was there.

I'm fine when I step out of the car into the sunny afternoon. Therefore it can't be going from inside to outside that sets me off, and it can't be standing up when I've been sitting for a while. All I've managed to establish, after months of monitoring myself, is that I can have a dizzy attack at any time, in any circumstances – there's no way of predicting it. *Or avoiding it.*

The tea rooms at Silsford Castle smell of cinnamon, ginger biscuits and roses, as they have since I was a child. The waitresses' aprons haven't changed either – they're still pale blue, frilly-edged, spotted with tiny pink roses. Without asking me what I'd like, Fran orders two cups of Lavender Earl Grey, then heads for the round table in the corner by the window, the same table Mum always made a beeline for when she brought us here as kids for what she called our 'weekend treat', after our Saturday morning trips to the library.

Right, then, girls – shall we get out our library books and read one while we have our chocolate fudge cake?

'Why am I here?' I ask Fran.

She narrows her eyes, peering at me. 'Is it Benji?' she says. 'It must be.'

'Is what Benji?'

'The reason you're pissed off with me.'

'I'm not.'

'If you don't want to babysit every Tuesday night, you don't have to – just say the word. Tell you the truth, Anton and I don't like it any more than you do. It's like you've got a timeshare in our son. Often we want to do things as a family on a Tuesday and we can't – it's carved in stone that you have to have Benji, or that's how it feels sometimes.' Fran sighs. 'Loads of times I've nearly rung you and asked if it'd be okay for us to keep him just this once, and I've chickened out, in case you'd be offended. Which is ridiculous. Why am I scared to be honest with you? I never used to be.' I'm not sure if it's herself she's angry with, or me.

A timeshare in our son. She didn't think up that phrase

today. She and Anton have been bitching about me and Kit – probably as much as we've been bitching about them.

Mum was the one who said, after the first time I babysat for Benji, 'Maybe it could be a regular thing. You and Kit could have him every Tuesday, overnight – give Fran and Anton a break, and give you a chance to get to know him properly, not to mention a bit of practice for when you have your own.' It didn't matter what Fran or I thought; Mum wanted it to happen, so it happened.

This can't be why Fran has brought me here, to talk about babysitting. 'I don't care,' I tell her. 'I'm happy to have Benji every Tuesday, some Tuesdays, no Tuesdays – whatever you want. You and Anton decide.'

Fran shakes her head, as if there was a right thing to say and what I've just said wasn't it. Sometimes I feel as if, more and more, I'm speaking a different language from the rest of my family; translation in either direction adds a dollop of provocation, a patina of offence, that wasn't present in the original.

'That house in Cambridge, 11 Bentley Grove – you're not buying it, are you?'

Why does she sound triumphant, as if she's caught me out? I open my mouth to remind her that I can't afford a 1.2-million-pound house, but she talks over me: 'You're *selling* it.'

'What?'

'Come on, Connie, don't bullshit me. It's your house. You own it, you and Kit. You're the ones who've put it up for sale.'

This has to be one of the more absurd things that's been said to me in my life so far. It almost cheers me up. I start to laugh, then stop when I see the waitress heading our way with a serving-trolley. As she lays out saucers, cups, spoons, tea strainer, milk jug and sugar, I can feel Fran's impatience radiating across the table; she wants an answer.

'Well?' she says, as soon as the waitress has retreated.

'That's the maddest thing I've ever heard. Where did you get that idea from?'

'Don't lie to me, Con. I don't know how the dead woman face down in a pool of blood fits into the story – I'm not convinced you didn't make her up, though I can't think why you'd—'

'Will you shut up and listen?' I snap. 'I didn't make anything up – I saw what I told you I saw. Do you think it's my idea of fun, spending the whole morning at the police station for no reason? I don't care if you believe me or not – it's the truth. I don't own 11 Bentley Grove. A doctor called Selina Gane does. Ask the police if you don't believe me.'

'Then why were you looking at it on Roundthehouses in the middle of the night, if you don't own it already and you can't afford to buy it?' Fran asks. 'Don't pretend you were just browsing. There's a link between that house and you and Kit.'

'How can you know that?' *Damn*. Have I just admitted she's right? She seems to think so, if the gleam of triumph in her eye is anything to go by. Why aren't I a better liar? 'All of a sudden, you're interested in 11 Bentley Grove,' I say bitterly. It's easier to be angry with Fran than with myself. 'On Saturday you didn't give a shit. I asked you if you thought I'd imagined what I saw – do you remember what you said? "I don't know. Not necessarily. Maybe." That was it – the sum total of your response, before you turned your attention back to Benji's supper.'

Fran pours cups of tea for us both. I wait for her to defend herself but all she does is shrug. 'What should I have said? I didn't know what I thought – how am I supposed to know whether you saw a dead woman on Roundthehouses or not? Mum and Dad were both kicking off in their different ways – I figured you had enough to deal with from them, so I took a back seat.' She puts down the teapot and looks at me. 'Soon as I'd put Benji to bed that night, I logged onto Roundthehouses myself. While you were stewing about my lack of interest, and slagging me off to Kit for sure, I was looking at photos of 11 Bentley Grove. I did nothing else all evening, even though the pictures didn't change. That's how uninterested I was.'

Something made her connect the house with me and Kit. It's an effort to swallow the tea that's in my mouth. 'What did you see?' I ask, my voice cracking. 'Tell me.' Why didn't I see it, whatever it was? I spent hours looking.

'You're pathetic, Connie,' Fran says matter-of-factly, ignoring my question. 'You sit there thinking the worst of everyone, harbouring your secret grudges and resentments, blowing stupid things up into huge problems and dwelling on them endlessly, making sure never to say a word about what's bothering you so that no one has the chance to explain that they're not quite as bad as you've decided they are.'

'What did you see, Fran?'

'You flinch every time Mum opens her mouth, as if she's the devil in oven gloves. Yes, she can be annoying, but you should do what I do: tell her to get a grip and then move on, forget it. Same with Dad. Tell all of us to piss off if you want to, but be upfront about it, for God's sake.'

She's clever, Fran. She makes everything sound so manageable and normal. Listening to her, I could almost believe that the Monk family was an entirely harmless organisation, that its members were allowed to leave Little Holling as and when they pleased, and would suffer no adverse effects if they chose to exercise that freedom.

'Tell me what you saw,' I say again.

'You tell me first,' Fran says, leaning towards me across the table. 'Everything. 11 Bentley Grove – what's the deal? For fuck's sake, Con, are we sisters or strangers? Let me know, because I can be either. It's your choice.'

'Yes. It is, isn't it?' She expects me to refuse. I'm going to surprise her. She asked to know everything, so everything is what I'll give her: not only the bare facts, but all the tiny permutations of possibility, all the ways in which I've changed my mind and then changed it back, sometimes ten or twelve times a day. As I talk, I begin to enjoy myself. I know from my own experience of the last six miserable months that this story I'm telling offers no narrative satisfaction whatsoever, only a series of insoluble problems. Let Fran be as confused as I am; let her be drawn into the nightmare that never ends. I wonder if she can hear the sadistic relish in my voice as I make sure not to spare her one single detail.

When I finish, finally, she doesn't look as confused as I hoped she would. She doesn't look surprised, or shocked. 'So did you ring him?' she says.

'Who?'

'Stephen Gilligan – the SG that Kit was supposed to have had a meeting with on 13 May. Did you ring his secretary, Joanne Thingummy?'

'Joanne Biss. No. I was going to, in the taxi on the way home, but then you turned up, and I . . .'

Fran isn't listening. She has whipped out her mobile phone, and is already asking for a number for London Allied Capital's Canary Wharf office. I close my eyes and wait, thinking about what Alice said: that I don't really want to know the truth about Kit. Is she right? Would I have phoned Stephen Gilligan, if it had been left to me? Was that why I had a dizzy attack as soon as I left the police station, so that I could avoid making the call?

'Joanne Biss, please,' says Fran. 'That's fine. I'm happy to wait.'

'I would have rung,' I tell her. 'When I got home.' She flashes me a sceptical look. I can imagine exactly what she's thinking. 'Why should I waste money on a private detective when I can stake out Kit's Limehouse flat myself, for free?' I say defensively.

'Have you?' Fran asks.

'I've driven there in the evening two or three times, sat outside in the dark. Kit never closes the lounge curtains, and the flat's on the ground floor. I ring him from the car park outside, pretending I'm calling from home. I watch him through the window, drinking red wine while he talks to me – the same kind he drinks at home. There's never been anyone else there with him.' *And when he smiles, it's the same affectionate smile I see on his face when he knows I'm watching*. I can't bring myself to share this fact with my sister; it's important to me, and I don't trust her with it.

'Two or three times doesn't prove anything,' she says dismissively.

'I've spent hours waiting in my car on Bentley Grove for him to come out of number 11. He never does.' Why am I trying to convince Fran that everything's okay when I know it isn't?

She raises a hand to silence me and presses her phone to her ear. I listen as she introduces herself to Joanne Biss as a new member of Nulli staff, and asks about the meeting between

Kit and Stephen Gilligan on Thursday 13 May – did it go ahead as planned, or was it cancelled? She says nothing about why she wants to know, but her voice exudes the confidence and entitlement of a person who feels no need to explain herself. I would never have been able to pull off that particular tone; I'd have sounded nervous and fraudulent, and would have been quizzed about why I needed information about a meeting from two months ago. A few seconds later, Fran thanks Joanne Biss and says goodbye.

'Kit was telling the truth,' she says, laying her phone down on the table. She sounds disappointed. 'He and Stephen Gilligan met on Thursday 13 May at three o'clock.'

It's as if a dark mass of cloud has lifted.

'Kit could have rung Joanne Biss and told her what to say,' Fran points out. 'He's had ample time. Even if he didn't, even if the SG in his diary *is* Stephen Gilligan, it doesn't mean he isn't having an affair with this Selina Gane woman.'

'It means he might not be,' I say, feeling more optimistic than I have for a long time. 'There's nothing to connect him with her – nothing at all – apart from her address in his SatNav as "home". And maybe he wasn't the one who put it there. Maybe someone else did it.' *Go on. Say it.* 'You might have done it. Or Anton.' It's hard to evict suspicion once it's made a home inside you; much easier to change its focus than to banish it altogether.

'I'm not going to bother responding to that,' says Fran impatiently. 'Me or Anton,' she mutters. 'Why would we?'

Because you're jealous. Because we've got more money; because Kit's successful and Anton isn't.

'Why are you so quick to think the worst of Kit?' I press on with my attack, before it occurs to Fran to point out my hypocrisy. 'Why don't you tell me whatever it is you've got to tell me?' Wouldn't she have told me already, if it was something real? Is she clever enough and devious enough to dream up an elaborate plan to ruin my marriage and destroy my sanity, a plan so intricate and manipulative that I can't even begin to guess what it might be?

For fuck's sake, Connie – she's your sister. You've known her all your life. Get a grip.

Fran couldn't have made a woman's dead body appear on my computer screen. She can't have any connection with 11 Bentley Grove. She's never been to Cambridge; she never goes anywhere apart from Monk & Sons, Benji's school, the supermarket and Mum and Dad's.

'You can't have looked at the photos of 11 Bentley Grove more carefully than I did,' I say shakily. 'There's no trace of Kit in those pictures, and nothing that links him to Selina Gane. Nothing. It's not even his sort of house. Kit would never call a place like that "home" – a modern, characterless box surrounded by clones of itself, other modern characterless—'

'Grow up, Connie, will you?' Fran snaps. 'If he's got the hots for the woman *in* the house, he won't give a toss about its lack of cornicing and ceiling roses. Have you forgotten what it's like to fall in love?' She smirks to herself. 'I almost have, but not quite. I can tell you right now: if I fell head over heels for someone, I'd live anywhere with them. I'd live in an ex-council flat in Brixton, or somewhere equally grim – those hideous high-rises.' She wrinkles her nose in distaste.

I nearly laugh. Most people from Brixton would consider themselves unfortunate if they had to spend even half an hour in Little Holling. In a quarter of that time they'd have sampled everything it had to offer, and would be wondering why its inhabitants weren't fleeing its deathly green quiet and making for the nearest noisy city at a hundred miles an hour.

'*Anyone* could have programmed that address into Kit's SatNav,' I tell Fran. 'Someone in the shop, like he said.' Do I believe what I'm saying, or have I abandoned everything apart from the desire to be the winner here? If Fran was sticking up for Kit, would I be insisting he was a cheat and a liar? 'Unless you can prove he's been lying to me—'

'I can't,' Fran cuts in. 'Look, I thought I saw something on the Roundthehouses website, that's all. Maybe I'm wrong, I don't know. I can't help noticing that you're in no hurry to find out what it is.'

'This isn't denial, Fran. This is me coming to my senses – trying to save my marriage, which I've spent the last six months tearing apart with accusations and doubt.' I sniff back tears. 'I've been torturing Kit – that's no exaggeration, believe me. Interrogating him constantly, turning away from him in bed . . . He's been so patient and understanding – anyone else would have left me by now. Know what I did the other day? I got home from the shop and he was in the bathroom with the door locked. He never locks the door. I made him open it. He refused at first, said he was in the bath, but I knew he wasn't. I'd heard him walking around. I insisted. Said I'd leave him if he didn't let me in immediately. I thought maybe he'd gone in there to phone her – Selina Gane, though I didn't know her name then. When he unlocked the door and opened it, I expected to see him holding his mobile and looking guilty, or trying to flush it down the loo or something. I thought, this is it, finally – I'll grab his phone and find her name and number, and then I'll have my proof. I've looked at his phone before and found nothing, but I thought maybe this time . . .' I stop. It's difficult to describe a state of mind that now seems so alien. It's as if I'm reporting on the behaviour of someone else, a lunatic.

'My heart was beating so fast I thought it was going to explode. Then I saw the words "Happy Birthday" on a roll of wrapping paper next to Kit's feet, and a Chongololo carrier bag. Scissors and sellotape . . .' I cover my face with my hands. 'Poor sod was trying to wrap my birthday present, not a mobile phone in sight. He was doing something nice for me, and I wrecked it. My suspicion fucked it up, like it's fucking up everything. I'd have been furious if someone did that to me, but Kit wasn't. He tried to make me feel better – insisted that I hadn't ruined anything, that my present would still be a surprise. "All you know is that it's from Chongololo," he said, "and you don't even know that. The bag might be a decoy. You don't know there are clothes in it." '

'For God's sake, stop punishing yourself,' Fran says. 'Let me show you what I saw on Roundthehouses. Once you've seen it, if you want to trust Kit, that's up to you. Come on.' She stands up.

Automatically, I do the same. 'Where are we going?'

'Next door, to the library. We can get on the internet there.'

This is good, I tell myself as we head down the spiral stone staircase and out of the castle. This is a test, and I'm going to pass. Let Fran play her trump card, whatever it is. I know there's nothing in those Roundthehouses pictures of 11 Bentley Grove that implicates Kit, so I've nothing to fear.

I can't believe Fran's so ready to think the worst of him. How dare she?

Back in our glass house with our big bag of stones, are we?

'Talking of Chongololo, where's your pink coat?' she asks, as we walk across the cobbles to the library.

'Coat? It's warm, in case you hadn't noticed.'

'Where is it?'

'I've no idea. In my wardrobe, probably.'

'It's bright pink, Con. If it was in your wardrobe, you'd see it every day – it'd leap out at you.'

'Maybe it's hanging up on the pegs near the back door. Why?'

'I want to borrow it,' Fran says.

'In July?'

'You haven't worn it in ages,' she persists, not looking at me. 'Maybe you've thrown it away.'

'No, I wouldn't have . . . Oh, I know where it is – in Kit's car, behind the back seats, tucked in behind the headrests. It's been there for about two years. I'll dig it out for you if you really want it. I thought you hated pink.'

There's a stiff expression on Fran's face as we walk into the library. I want to ask her more questions, but she's busy trying to attract the attention of a librarian. To the right of the main doors, four grey rectangular tables have been pushed together to make a big square. Around it, twenty-odd middle-aged and elderly women and one young man with the tiniest beard I've ever seen are drinking bright orange tea out of Styrofoam cups and interrupting each other. It must be a reading group meeting; the table is covered with plastic-backed copies of a book called *If Nobody Speaks of Remarkable Things*.

I would love to join a reading group, but not one in Silsford. Brixton, maybe.

The children's section is full of mothers begging their giggling, squealing toddlers to calm down. When Mum used to bring me and Fran here, we were silent from the moment we walked in until the moment we left. We communicated by pointing and nodding, terrified that the librarians would throw us out if we opened our mouths. Mum must have told us that they would. I remember hearing other children whispering enthusiastically about which Enid Blyton books they'd already read and which they hadn't; I always wondered why they weren't as intimidated as I was.

Fran beckons me over. Knowing I'm about to see 11 Bentley Grove again, I have to force myself to move towards the monitor. For one insane moment, I imagine that Selina Gane will appear from behind a bookshelf and catch me in the act of virtual spying: *Why are you still looking at my house? Why can't you leave me alone?*

I stand behind Fran, steeling myself, waiting for her to click on the virtual tour button. Instead, she goes for the button next to it: Street View. She clicks again to enlarge the picture of the road when it appears, so that it fills the screen. It's ever so slightly blurred, as if the photograph was taken from a moving vehicle. 'That's not number 11,' I say. 'That's the other side, and further down – number 20 or something.' There are white lines and arrow symbols superimposed on the picture, for moving up and down the street. They're covering up the house number, but I'm pretty certain it's 20. Conformist and cloned as they are, the houses on Bentley Grove would only look identical to someone who hadn't spent nearly every Friday for the past six months in their company; I know the lining on every curtain, the beaded trim on every blind.

'So let's turn it round and find number 11,' says Fran, manoeuvring the mouse. I watch as Bentley Grove begins to rotate.

A spinning road, a spinning lounge. A spinning dead woman in a pool of blood.

I grip the back of Fran's chair and order myself not to feel dizzy, not now. To my surprise and relief, it works.

Now we're facing the right way. 'Along a bit to the left,' I tell Fran, though she doesn't need my directions; she must have rehearsed this at home. She clicks on a white arrow and we're transported to number 9. The front door is open. There's a blur of fuzzy white hair and red towelling dressing gown in the doorway: the tiny, bent-backed old man who lives there. He's holding his walking stick. I don't think he could manage more than a couple of steps without it. I've seen him often, in the flesh – or what's left of it, given that he looks about a hundred and fifty. He is for ever hobbling from his house to his various recycling bins, which stand in a Stonehenge-like circle in the middle of his front garden. Without exception, all the other Bentley Grove residents keep their bins in their garages.

I wait for Fran to press the white arrow again, to move us further on, but she doesn't. She turns and looks up at me. 'That's number 9,' I say. 'Not number 11.'

'Forget the house. Look at the car pulling away from the kerb. The number plate's been blurred out, annoyingly, but even so . . .'

A sour taste fills my mouth. I want to tell Fran she's being ridiculous, but I can't speak; I need all my energy to push away the panic and horror that's rushing at me. *No. She's wrong.*

'Soon as I saw it, I thought, "They've been to view that house. I bet they've made an offer." Then I remembered you solemnly promising Mum and Dad that you weren't buying it, and I wondered if that was because you owned it already. You were selling it – that was why you were so interested in this particular house. I admit, I got carried away. I decided you and Kit had been secretly millionaires for years, hiding it from the rest of us.' Fran's tone is airy and flippant. Is she enjoying this? 'Course, if it was your house, you'd have parked on the drive, not on the street. I don't know why that didn't occur to me. The houses on Bentley Grove have big driveways. Kit could have parked right outside number 11's front door, but he wouldn't, would he?'

Tell her. Tell her she's talking rubbish, that you don't want to hear any more.

'Not if he wasn't supposed to be there,' Fran goes on, firing words at me too fast. 'He wouldn't want anyone to make the connection between him and Selina Gane. Whereas if he parks on the pavement, outside the house next door . . .'

'There's no connection,' I manage to say before the mental blurring sets in, curling the corners of my thoughts inward. I close my eyes, welcome the descent into mindlessness. *Make it go away, all of it.* As the smudgy grey spreads over me and pulls me down, I realise it's no good; it hasn't worked. I've brought with me the thing I most wanted to leave behind: an image of Kit's car on Bentley Grove, pulling away from the kerb, with my pink Chongololo coat clearly visible through the rear windscreen, tucked behind the headrests of the back seats.

12

19/7/2010

Charlie couldn't believe it. Here was Domingo, hurrying towards her across the grass, holding his clenched fist to his ear in a gesture that could only mean one thing. Exactly as she'd imagined it, except in her anticipated worst-case scenario, it had been day, not night. She should never have told Liv where they were going and trusted her to keep it to herself. Still, better for it to happen now, while Charlie was alone. Simon had gone for a walk. She could deal with this before he got back, make it clear to Sam or Proust or whoever it was that Simon was unavailable, no matter what had happened – however urgent, however unforeseen or unusual. *Even if every last inhabitant of Spilling has been butchered in his or her bed.* Charlie savoured the grimness of the possibility.

She wouldn't tell Simon about the call, and she'd sweet-talk Domingo into not mentioning it either. This was her honeymoon, for Christ's sake, even if her newly acquired spouse had insisted on going out on his own tonight, leaving her to cry and chain-smoke on the terrace alone, staring resentfully at a dark hump of mountain that might or might not have a face. *For a walk.* Who went for a walk at ten in the evening, with no particular destination in mind? Who said to their wife, on their honeymoon, 'Don't take this the wrong way, but I'd rather you didn't come with me'? What kind of man had Charlie married? She suspected she'd spend the rest of her life struggling to answer that question.

'Simon, that is you?' Domingo shouted from the other side of the swimming pool. Charlie had switched off the terrace lights, not wanting to be illuminated with tears pouring down her face even if there was no one around to see her.

'It's me,' she said quietly, half hoping he wouldn't hear. She wondered what the caretaker would say if she offered to give him a blow job, and smiled at the absurdity of the idea.

'Telephone. England.' Domingo gestured towards his wooden cabin. 'You ring on my house, I have number.'

Might Simon's mother have carked it? Unlikely; Charlie had a strong hunch that Kathleen would still be flexing her neuroses in thirty years' time, still sucking the life out of all those close to her in her uniquely spindly way. Charlie had always been scathing about hunches – her own and other people's, Simon's especially – but in the light of her phone-call-from-England premonition having materialised so reliably, she decided that perhaps now was the time to start trusting her instincts.

She stubbed out her cigarette, wiped her face with her hands and stood up. She was halfway down the steps before she changed her mind. 'Fuck it,' she muttered under her breath. Why should she have to make all the effort? She was fed up of trying to force things into the right shape; it was someone else's turn to make sure nothing fell apart. 'Simon's not here, he's gone out,' she yelled across the pool. That was all she needed to say. If Domingo wanted to come back in an hour and give Simon a message or a number to ring, that was up to him. If Simon wanted to spend the rest of the honeymoon on the phone to Sam Kombothekra or the Snowman, if he wanted to catch the next available flight home and scuttle back to work instead of staying in Spain in a beautiful villa with Charlie . . . well, luckily someone had invented a wonderful thing called divorce.

'You phone, no Simon,' said Domingo. 'Sister Olivia. You come now, you phone on my house. She much upset, crying.'

Charlie had already started to run. All her thoughts – divorcing Simon, loving him, hating him – had fallen away, leaving only one word in her mind: cancer. Olivia had survived the disease years ago, but Charlie had always secretly feared it might come back, no matter how many times her sister had assured her that wasn't the way it worked. 'If it doesn't come back within five years, then, officially, it can't ever come back,' Liv had insisted. 'If I'm unlucky enough to get cancer again, it'll be a new cancer – not the return of the old one.'

Liv wouldn't ring unless it was serious, not after hearing Charlie describe what she'd do to anyone foolish enough to intrude on her and Simon's privacy. *Tell nobody where we are – nobody – unless it's life or death. Or someone determined to give us a very large amount of money.*

Life or death. Had she made this happen, by using those words?

Somehow, she made it into Domingo's wooden lodge. He had to punch in the number for her and put the phone in her hand. He touched her shoulder briefly before leaving her alone, closing the door behind him. No doubt in his mind that the news would be bad; no doubt in Charlie's either.

'Liv? Is that you?' All she could hear was sobbing.

'Char?'

'Calm down. Tell me.'

'I think I've messed up my life.'

'What's wrong? What's happened?'

'I'm going to have to leave Dom. I've slept with someone else. More than once. Don't be angry with me for ringing. I *had* to talk to you – I feel as if I'm going mad. Do you think I might be?'

Charlie rubbed her swollen eyes and sank into the nearest chair – a round wicker thing, like a large tilted picnic basket on legs, covered with a blue and red tartan wool throw. She waited for her heartbeat to catch up with her brain. Terror still had her in its grip – a monster that needed to be wrestled into submission. *A monster you created yourself, out of nothing. Needlessly.* Had she done the same thing with Simon's walk? He'd tried his best to convince her that it was nothing to do with not wanting to spend time with her. 'I'm not used to never being alone,' he'd said. 'I only need half an hour, maybe an hour – then I'll be back.' Was that unreasonable? 'I'll probably even miss you while I'm gone,' he'd added grudgingly, eyes down, as if the admission had been extracted from him under duress.

'Here's the deal,' Charlie said, once she was calm enough to speak. 'I'll talk to you for five minutes – only because I'm relieved. I thought you were going to tell me Mum and Dad had dropped dead on the golf course.' *I thought you were dying. I thought my marriage might be over.*

'You've never liked Dom. You must be doubly relieved.'

'Do you want to waste your five minutes on a fight?'

Silence.

'How's the honeymoon?' Liv asked eventually.

'Fine, until you phoned. Well, fine-ish.'

'Why "ish"?'

Charlie lowered her voice. 'We've had sex a grand total of once.'

'Is that so bad? It's only Monday.'

Charlie had given this some thought. If it happened again tonight, then it wouldn't be so bad. If not, that'd be two consecutive nights without – how could that be anything but a disaster? If Simon didn't make a move when they went to bed later, Charlie didn't think she'd be able to put a brave face on it as she had last night, when he'd turned his back on her and been asleep within seconds. Was that why she was so jumpy, so ready to assume the worst? Today had more pressure on it than an ordinary Monday should have to bear.

'It's as if he thinks we shouldn't be doing it,' she said tearfully. 'He . . . avoids me afterwards, like we've done something shameful. He's lying there right next to me, but he's avoiding me.' Charlie sighed. 'It's hard to explain.'

'Simon's weird in all areas, not just sex,' said Liv, as if this somehow made things better. She sounded a lot less distraught than she had a minute ago. Charlie wouldn't have put it past her sister to feign a wrecked life when all she really wanted was to gossip. 'You've been sleeping together for a while, living together for even longer – it changes things. I *never* want to have sex with Dom any more. I've got this little trick—'

'Please don't tell me about it,' Charlie cut in.

'What? No, it's not a sexual thing, it's psychological. If Dom starts angling in, if I only don't want to a little bit, I make a point of letting him. That way, when I *massively* don't want to, when I'm desperate to finish whatever book I'm reading and it really can't wait, I'm off the hook – I can say no with a clear conscience, knowing there's no way he can accuse me of never saying yes.'

Charlie stared at the phone. Was it something to do with this being a long-distance conversation? Would she understand her sister better if they were in the same country? She tried not to picture Dom angling in.

'. . . isn't that I don't find him attractive – I do. But . . . I don't know, we've done it so many times.'

And now you're doing it with someone else as well.

'Has Simon got worse since the wedding?' Liv asked. 'Is the shag rate in decline? Too early to tell, I suppose.'

Charlie sighed. *Tastefully put.* 'Look, I don't really want to talk about it, and I especially don't want to whisper about it in a Spanish caretaker's hut. Tell me about leaving Dom.'

'I *can't* leave him.'

'Who's your new man?'

'I can't leave Dom, Char. It would destroy him. He has no idea that it would, but it would. And if I leave him for this . . . other person – not that he's asked me to, not that we have *anything* in common – I'll soon be equally bored of having sex with *him*, won't I? Even if it doesn't feel that way at the moment. So I might as well stay with Dom and cheat on him discreetly until my fling becomes as boring as my main relationship. Not that Dom himself is boring – just the sex. Which isn't to say it's *bad*.'

Charlie couldn't bring herself to attempt a response.

'What do you think?' Liv asked anxiously.

'You don't want to know.'

'I'm bound to get bored of New Sex Man, once the novelty wears off. Don't you think?'

'I'm bored of talking about him, if that helps,' said Charlie. *New Sex Man*. He was probably a weedy vegan arts journalist or some pompous writer Olivia's paper had sent her to interview.

'It's inevitable.' Liv sniffed. Charlie heard her blow her nose.

'It's a law of nature. Every grand passion shags itself into tedium, given time.'

'How uplifting,' said Charlie. 'Talking of time, yours is up.'

'Wait – there's one more thing I wanted to ask you, just quickly. Simon won't mind that I phoned, will he?'

'He won't know,' Charlie told her. 'He's gone for a walk.'

'On his own?' Olivia's indignation could be heard all the way from London. 'Why didn't he take you with him?'

'What's your question, Liv?'

'I just asked it: will Simon mind that I phoned? I don't think he'd mind. Would you mind if he had a very quick phone conversation with . . . someone, anyone? From home, or . . . work?'

Charlie swallowed the scream that was clogging her throat. 'Sam wants to talk to Simon, does he?'

'Don't go mad. I haven't told him where you are, but . . . could Simon maybe ring him? I don't know the details, but I think someone might have been murdered.'

'So? That's like interrupting a postman on his honeymoon because someone wants to send a parcel to their gran. You can tell Sam from me that he's a gutless fuckhead, using you to pass on his messages.'

'Don't be mean about Sam – he's sweet. And he hasn't asked me to pass on anything – I haven't spoken to him for months. Look, whoever's been murdered, I think it might be someone Simon knows. Or knew. Oh, I don't know!'

Someone Simon knew? Immediately, Charlie thought of Alice Fancourt. *Not her, anyone but her*. Charlie didn't know if Simon ever thought about her these days – the subject, like so many others, was well and truly embargoed – but she knew as surely as she knew her own name that if Alice had been murdered, Simon would start to obsess about her again.

Charlie could feel her brain struggling to fight off the intense heat and the red wine. Something didn't add up. Something fairly obvious, once you thought about it. 'If you haven't spoken to Sam, how do you . . .' She stopped, unable to find the missing words as the answer hit her like a lead ball in the chest. How many men had Liv had time to meet, since Friday? 'New Sex Man,' she said, as neutrally as possible. 'Who is he, Liv?'

'Don't be angry,' Liv sounded terrified.

'He's Chris Gibbs, isn't he?'

'I didn't plan it. I didn't mean for—'

'End it.'

'Oh, God, don't *say* that! You've no idea how—'

'End. It. That's not a suggestion, it's a fucking order. You stupid *fuck*!'

Charlie dropped the phone on the table, ran out into the hot night, and collided with Domingo. She'd completely forgotten about him. She might forget him again, one day, but she would never forget his wooden hut, his phone, his splintery picnic-basket chair with its red and blue blanket. She would think of all those things whenever she thought about betrayal, from now on. And she thought about betrayal a lot.

'Sister okay?' Domingo asked.

'No, she's not,' Charlie told him. 'She's a stupid cunt.'

13

Tuesday 20 July 2010

'Tell them,' I say to Kit. 'Forget about my feelings, forget about trying not to hurt me. Say what you really think. How can you stand to sit there and listen to me tell lies about you, if that's what I'm doing?'

We're at Parkside police station in Cambridge, in a room with yellow walls, a blue linoleum floor and one large square window that's covered with some kind of chicken-wire grid. *So that no one can throw themselves out*. Sam Kombothekra is sitting on our side of the table, between Kit and me. That surprised me; I thought he'd sit opposite, with DC Grint. Is a detective from Spilling still a detective when he's in Cambridge? Does Sam have any power in this room, or is he here today only as our chauffeur, our silent chaperone?

Kit looks at Grint. 'I've never been to Bentley Grove – never walked there, never driven there, never parked there.' He shrugs. 'What else can I say? Plenty of people drive black saloon cars.' There are two red grooves on his neck where he cut himself shaving this morning, and blue-ish shadows under his eyes; neither of us slept last night, knowing we had this ordeal to get through today. Neither of us combed our hair before leaving for Cambridge. What must Grint think of us? He did his best not to react when I explained about my bruises and the lump above my eye, but I can tell he finds me disgusting, and he can't have much respect for Kit. What kind of idiot would marry a woman who blacks out and bangs her head on library tables? I feel defensive on behalf of us both; I want to tell Grint that we're better people than he thinks we are.

I want it to be true.

You don't remember knocking your head on that table. What else don't you remember?

'The pink blur in the black car on Street View isn't the same pink as Connie's coat,' says Kit. 'It's deeper – more like red.'

'Connie says it's the same pink,' Grint counters.

Kit nods. He heard me say it.

'Why are you nodding?' I snap at him. 'You don't think it's the same pink. Why don't you argue?'

'What's the point?' Kit keeps his eyes on Grint. 'Aren't there things you can do to the Street View picture to unblur the car registration? That's the only way to prove if it's my car or not. Maybe you could see who's driving it.'

'He means me,' I say.

'Time and money,' says Grint. 'If you were a suspect in a serious crime, if we needed to prove your car had been parked on Bentley Grove, we'd look into enhancing the image. Has a crime been committed, Mr Bowskill? To your knowledge?'

'Not . . . No.' Kit lowers his eyes.

I can't stand this any more. 'He was going to say, "Not by me." Weren't you? I don't know why you won't admit it! I know what you're thinking.'

'Mr Bowskill? Mrs Bowskill seems to think you have something to tell us.'

Kit presses his fingers into his eyes. I realise I've never seen him cry, not once since we first met. Is that unusual? Do most men cry?

'Just because it's crossed my mind doesn't mean I believe it! I *don't* believe it.'

'He thinks I may have murdered a woman,' I translate, for the benefit of Grint and Sam. 'In the lounge at 11 Bentley Grove.'

'Is she right?' Grint asks Kit. 'Is that what you think?'

'Something's changed, that's all I know.' Kit stares down at his hands. 'Yesterday morning, DS Kombothekra told us there was no reason to worry about anything. Then suddenly we're summoned here. Suddenly you're interested in us – in the colour of Connie's coat, in where I did or didn't park my car . . . Doesn't take a genius to work out what's going on.'

'What conclusion would that genius draw?' Grint asks, rubbing his index finger along his silver tie-pin. He's tall and lanky, with bad scars on his chin from years-old acne. His voice doesn't suit him. It's too heavy and deep, the wrong sound for a skinny man to make.

'You believe in Connie's dead woman,' Kit says. 'Something's happened to make you believe she's real. You wouldn't waste all this time on us otherwise.'

'And how does that change things for you? If she's real.'

'How did my wife know she was dead?' Kit asks Grint angrily, as if all this is his fault. 'There was no body on that virtual tour, I can promise you that. I looked at it seconds after Connie did, and there was nothing: an ordinary lounge, nothing more, nothing less. No dead woman, no blood. At the time I thought Con must have been seeing things – she was tired, stressed . . .'

'She was stressed as a result of having found 11 Bentley Grove programmed into your SatNav as your home address? Correct?'

'That's what I thought at the time, yes.'

Grint leans across the table. 'And now you think?'

Kit groans. 'I don't know why you're asking me. I don't *know* anything.'

'But you suspect.'

'He suspects I'm a killer,' I say helpfully.

'Connie could have programmed the address in herself,' says Kit, refusing to look at me. He must be grateful Sam's sitting between us, even if Sam himself looks anything but glad to be where he is. Who can blame him? I wonder if ours is the worst marriage he's ever seen in action.

'I didn't programme it in,' Kit says. 'Connie must have done it. I've been kidding myself that it might have been someone else – someone in the shop that sold me the SatNav.' He laughs bitterly. 'I suppose we believe what we want to believe, don't we?'

Some of us do. Others fail, however hard we try.

'Connie's been a mess. For months,' Kit mutters.

Go on. Don't stop now. In a way, it will be a relief to hear him say it. At least then I'll have something concrete to fight against.

'There was no dead woman on the Roundthehouses website. Maybe Connie saw her in the flesh. In that house, in the lounge. Connie could have parked my car on Bentley Grove. She often drives my car, she's in Cambridge all the time . . .'

'I've never driven there in your car,' I tell him. 'Not once.'

'Ask her,' Kit urges Grint. 'Make her tell you the truth – she won't tell me.'

Ask away, DC Grint. As many questions as you want, and I'll tell you no lies.

'Why do you think Connie goes to Cambridge?' Grint stays focused on Kit.

'She told you why. Don't you listen? Why don't you tell us what's happened, what you know about this dead woman? Is there a dead woman?'

'Why does Connie go to Cambridge so often? She doesn't live there, she doesn't work there . . .'

Kit slumps in his chair. 'Like she said before: she's looking for me.'

'*She* said that, yes, but what do you say? She claims she's trying to catch you out in an adulterous relationship. She claims she found 11 Bentley Grove as the home address in your SatNav – she says you programmed it in. If *she* programmed it in, as you're suggesting, then surely she would know you *didn't*. Why, then, would she hang around 11 Bentley Grove waiting for you to emerge on the arm of your bit on the side? Does that make any sense to you, Mr Bowskill?'

Kit says nothing.

'Or did she put the address into your SatNav *because* she suspected you were having an affair with the woman that lived there? Was it her way of saying, "The game's up"?'

'Kit?' Sam prompts.

'I don't know. I don't know why! I don't know anything.' Kit makes a choking sound, covers his mouth with his fist. 'Look, Connie's not evil, she's . . . I love her.'

I can't help jumping slightly, as the word 'evil' joins us in the room. *Like a gust of cold air.*

'Shall I take over?' I say briskly, trying to sound as impartial as I can. The only way to get through this is to be objective. Grint needs to know what Kit and I both think. Then maybe we can make some progress. 'Kit thinks I murdered a woman. Or maybe I didn't murder her – maybe it was manslaughter or self-defence, since I'm not evil. Either way, I'm so guilty and traumatised, I try to block it out. I succeed in banishing 11 Bentley Grove and the dead woman from my conscious mind, but my subconscious isn't so compliant. The guilt erupts, and causes trouble for me. Like Kit says, I'm a mess – that's definitely true, that's the one thing we agree on. I programme the address of the house where the murder took place into his SatNav. Maybe, deep down, I want to be caught and punished.'

'Connie, stop,' Sam mutters, shifting in his seat. He really shouldn't work for the police if he can't cope with tense, unpleasant situations.

I ignore him and continue with my story. 'When the house comes up for sale, the part of me that knows the truth is terrified that whoever buys it will find evidence of my crime. That's why I stay up all night looking at it on Roundthehouses, staring at the pictures of every room. The dead woman and the blood are long gone – I'd have made sure to remove all traces – but I'm paranoid, and, in my panic, I imagine I can see the crime scene exactly as it was: the body, the blood—'

'Hold on a second,' Grint interrupts. 'If you're looking at the house to check there are no traces of the murder you committed, then you haven't repressed the memory, have you? You know what you've done.'

'No, I don't,' I say, impatient because he's missing the point and it's so obvious. 'I only know it subliminally. I've blocked it out: the murder, putting the address into the SatNav – everything. As far as I'm aware, Kit must have programmed in the address. But he denies it, so, understandably, I'm suspicious. I start going to Cambridge nearly every Friday, trying to catch him red-handed.' I flinch as an image of bloodstained hands fills my head. *Streaked with red past the wrists, down to the elbows.*

'Are you okay?' Sam asks me. 'Would you like some water?'

'No. I'm fine,' I lie. 'One day – the Friday just gone – I see that 11 Bentley Grove has sprouted a "For Sale" sign in its garden. That night, I'm determined to have a nosy at the pictures on a property website, to see if I can spot anything that belongs to Kit in any of the rooms. I find nothing – not a scrap of proof. I almost go to bed feeling reassured: everything's under control. Up until this point, I've successfully repressed my awareness of what I've done, but having the pictures of the house there on the screen in front of me is too much – the memory flares up, and I see the . . .' I stop, swallow. 'I see the death scene, as clearly as if it were on the website. I don't realise it's a mental projection; I believe I've seen it on my computer.'

Kit is openly crying now.

'I'm only saying what I know you're thinking,' I tell him.

'Let me see if I've got this right,' says Grint. 'You kill a woman, and manage to conceal the memory from yourself, so that most of the time you have no idea you've done it. There are only two occasions when your guilty subconscious breaks the surface: once when you programme the address into the SatNav, and then again when you see a dead body that isn't there on the Roundthehouses website.'

'That's what Kit thinks, yes.'

Grint pushes his chair away from the table, leans back. He kicks the heel of one shoe against the toe of the other. 'So, when you look at 11 Bentley Grove on Roundthehouses, on a superficial level you're looking for evidence of your husband's presence in the house. Simultaneously, without allowing yourself to acknowledge it, you're actually looking for any evidence you might have left behind that could link you to the murder you committed.'

I force a smile. 'Absurd, isn't it?'

'Who is she, then, this dead lady? Why did you kill her?'

'I didn't. Kit thinks I did. I'm hoping you're going to tell him that the scenario I've just described is the biggest load of rubbish you've ever heard.'

Grint drums his fingers on the arm of his chair. 'Post-traumatic memory loss is a handy fictional device, but I've never come across it in real life,' he says, after a short pause. 'Though I've met a fair few low-lifes pretending to be afflicted with it.'

'What do you think?' I ask Sam.

'You keep saying all this is what Kit believes . . .'

'Oh, he believes it – look at him! Have you heard him deny it? Or rather, it's what he wants us all to *think* he believes. Most of all, he wants *me* to think he believes it – don't you? You want me to be terrified that I've lost control of my own mind – that I might have killed someone and buried the memory so deep that I don't know I've done it!'

Kit covers his face with his hands. 'Can somebody make this stop?' he murmurs.

'I think we should . . .' Sam tries to come to Kit's rescue, but Grint raises a finger to silence him. So it's Grint and me versus Sam and Kit, is it? Two of us want to hear the worst; two of us don't.

'Course, Kit would tell you I've got a powerful subconscious,' I say with false brightness. As concisely as possible, but omitting none of the gory details, I tell Grint about my hair loss, the vomiting, the facial paralysis – how my assorted symptoms sabotaged our escape to Cambridge in 2003. 'I've regretted not moving ever since. I've got a bit of a thing about Cambridge. I've built it up in my mind to be this . . . civilised beautiful paradise, unreachable for the likes of me. Even being here, in a police station – I can't say I'm enjoying it, but I'd rather be under suspicion of murder here than anywhere else.' Silently, I congratulate myself on a fine performance; the person I'm pretending to be is shielding me from the pain I would otherwise be feeling. If Grint's a competent detective, he should be able to distinguish between insanity, eccentricity and a sense of humour.

'I'll take that as a compliment,' he says.

'Cambridge, for me, it's like . . . the one that got away, if that makes sense. Kit calls it my "land of lost content". It's a quote from a poem.'

'A E Housman,' Grint smiles. '"Into my heart an air that kills/From yon far country blows:/What are those blue remembered hills,/What spires, what farms are those?/That is the land of lost content,/I see it shining plain/The happy highways where I went/And cannot come again." '

I start to laugh. I can't stop.

'Connie.' Sam puts his hand on my arm.

'What's funny?' Grint asks me.

'Only in Cambridge would the cops quote poetry at you. You're reinforcing all my preconceived ideas.'

'Will you shut up?' Kit snaps at me, looking at me for the first time since we got here. 'You're embarrassing yourself.'

I turn on him. 'I'm scaring you, you mean. I've seen through you, and you hate me for it. Look at you – you can barely be bothered to keep up the pretence any more! You've told so many lies, you're running out of energy. Little inconsistencies are creeping in – if I drove to Bentley Grove in your car, then that's my pink coat in the back window, isn't it? Why say it's a different pink?'

'Mrs Bowskill—' Grint tries to cut in.

I raise my voice to block him, wanting only to hurt Kit, to inflict the deepest wound that I can. 'Do you honestly think you can make me believe I'm suffering from some kind of multiple personality disorder, that Subconscious Me might have committed a crime that Conscious Me knows nothing about? It's fucking ludicrous! How stupid do you think I am, exactly? *You're* the one who should be embarrassed! Even on its own terms, it doesn't work. If I was suppressing the memory of having killed a woman, surely it'd come back to me now, when we're all discussing the possibility in great detail?'

Grint rises to his feet. 'Why don't I tell you why you're here?' he says.

I hear a long sigh. I'm not sure if it came from Kit or Sam.

'I've got a woman called Jackie Napier in an interview room one floor down. That name mean anything to either of you?'

'No,' I say. Kit shakes his head. Maybe making him hate me is the way forward; when he no longer cares that he might destroy me, perhaps he'll tell me the truth.

'Jackie logged onto the Roundthehouses website at almost exactly the same time you did, early hours of Saturday morning.' Grint watches me, waits for a reaction. I try to keep up, to process what he's saying. As far as I'm concerned, there are only four people in my nightmare: me, Kit, Selina Gane and the dead woman. There's no Jackie. 'She brought up the page for 11 Bentley Grove,' Grint goes on. 'Like you, she clicked on the virtual tour button. Guess what she saw?'

Bile fills my throat. I press my mouth shut, afraid I'm going to be sick.

'She saw what you saw, Connie,' says Sam. He sounds relieved, as if he's been wanting to tell me this for a long time.

'Her description was interchangeable with yours,' Grint says.

'Copious amounts of blood on the carpet, dark woman in a patterned dress, face down, hair fanned out around her head, as if she'd fallen. But d'you know what struck me most? She said – and so did you, from what Sam here tells me – that the blood was darkest next to the woman's stomach.'

I close my eyes and see it all again. 'You should have told us straight away,' I manage to say.

'D'you think?' says Grint. 'I disagree. If I'd told you when you first walked in here, I'd have been telling strangers.'

What's that supposed to mean?

'Jackie couldn't stand to look at it, she said. She shut down the tour, went to pour herself a large G&T. She thought about phoning her best mate, but didn't want to wake her up. Ten minutes later, once she'd calmed down a bit, she went and looked again. Second time round, there was no woman's body.'

'So . . .' Kit's sitting up straight now. 'If this Jackie woman saw what Connie saw . . .'

'There's more.' Grint walks over to the window, loops his fingers around the wire grid. 'I spoke to someone at Roundthehouses. The virtual tour of 11 Bentley Grove's nothing to do with them – it's the agent selling the property that provides all the material – photos, tours, room dimensions, everything.'

'Lorraine Turner,' I say, remembering her name from Sam's story about the previous owners and their Christmas tree, the stain on the carpet.

'Right.' Grint smiles. He looks inappropriately happy. I hope it's only his power over us all that he's enjoying, not the prospect of a woman dead from a stomach wound. 'Lorraine Turner's the agent selling 11 Bentley Grove, but she has nothing to do with the IT side of things. How much do you know about computer hacking?'

'There's nothing about computers that Kit doesn't know,' I say.

'I'm not a hacker.'

'But you understand how hacking works.' It's not so much a rhetorical question as a statement of fact. Grint turns to me. 'Do you?'

'Not a clue.'

'Then I'll ditch the technical waffle and keep it simple. One of the estate agent's IT guys rang me back about half an hour before you got here. Someone hacked into their website just before 1 a.m. on Saturday. Looks like they substituted one virtual tour for another – the one with the woman's body for the official version.'

'That makes no sense,' says Kit, grey-faced. 'When I looked, there was no dead body, no blood.'

'At 1.23 a.m., the hacker did his stuff again,' says Grint. 'Or *her* stuff, I suppose I should say, since it could have been either. The original tour was reinstated.'

'It wasn't as late as 1.23 when I looked,' says Kit. 'I remember seeing the time on the computer, thinking "What the fuck am I doing up so late?" It was 1.20, exactly. And I didn't hit the virtual tour button again – I looked at Connie's tour, the one she'd started. It was on a repeating loop. Why didn't I see what she saw?' Kit's eyes dart round the room, not settling on anything or anyone.

'It's obvious, isn't it?' I say. 'In the hacker's version, he arranged it so that the picture of the dead woman only came up once in every twenty loops, or once in every fifty.' Haven't I explained this already? Why has Kit chosen to forget?

'Would that be possible?' Grint asks him. *Because Kit's the computer expert here, or because Grint thinks he's the one who tampered with the virtual tour?*

'Anything's possible.' Kit shrugs. He lets out a long, slow breath. 'So I guess that's me off the hook. Think about it, Connie. Where was I, just before 1 a.m.? In bed, next to you. I was reading – you were asleep. Pretending to be asleep,' he corrects himself. 'Where was I at 1.23 a.m.? Back in bed – awake and wishing I wasn't. Wondering whether to put up with your paranoid delusions for another six months, or pack a bag and get the hell out first thing in the morning.'

He's right. I see Grint register the look of defeat on my face. He must think I want my husband to be guilty of computer hacking, or bigamy.

Or murder.

What I want – all I want – is to understand. *To know*. At this precise moment, I don't care what the explanation is, as long as there is one. If Kit didn't hack into the estate agent's website . . .

'What are you doing about this?' I ask Grint. 'Have you got – forensic people looking at the carpet? Have you interviewed Selina Gane?'

He ignores my questions, points his finger first at me, then at Kit. With his thumb raised, it looks as if he's miming a gun. 'Don't go anywhere. Sam and I are going to talk to Jackie Napier, then we'll be back.' Sam leaps up, on cue. I don't think he realised his presence would be required, but he's not going to quibble; he's going to follow the leader.

As soon as they've gone, I stand up and head for the door.

'Con, wait . . .' Kit reaches out his hand.

'No,' I tell him. 'I won't wait. I've waited too long already.'

~

Outside the police station, I run. My head pounds, too full of blood, as I turn a corner, then another, then another. The pavement tilts. I blink, breathe in as much air as I can. My legs feel wobbly, unconnected to the rest of me. I sink down in a heap on the pavement, prop myself up against a wall. A woman walks past with two small boys behind her, both on push-along scooters that look like strange, angular dogs. One of them says, 'Mummy, why's that lady sitting on the road?' I must look deranged, clutching my bag to my chest – as if I'm afraid someone's going to mug me.

When you know there's a threat, but you don't know where it's coming from, it makes sense to be scared of everything. I don't suppose the boys' well-turned-out mother has ever bothered to explain that to them.

Once I've got my breath back, I pull out my phone, ring 118118, and ask for the names of any hotels in Cambridge that begin with 'D' or 'Du'. Sam said yesterday that Selina Gane was staying in a hotel; there has to be a good chance she'll still be there. She wanted to talk to me once before, and I ran away. Maybe if I hadn't, I'd have found out the truth a lot sooner.

'There's the Doubletree by Hilton Garden House hotel on Granta Place. Is that the one you want?'

It could be.

'It's the only hotel listed in central Cambridge that begins with "D".'

'Put me through,' I say. *She won't be there. She'll be at work.* I stay on the line. Even if she's out, I want to find out if it's the right hotel.

Why? Are you planning to pay her a visit?

I listen to the automated voice's instructions: 1 for meetings and events, 2 for group reservations, 3 for hotel bedroom prices and individual reservations, 4 for directions and any other enquiries. I press 4 and get through to a human being, a woman. She sounds French. I ask if there's a Dr Selina Gane staying at the hotel, expecting a one-word answer: yes or no.

'Putting you through now,' says the receptionist. My heart starts to race. I will myself not to black out again. The only thing stopping me from pressing the end-call button is my certainty that Selina Gane won't be in her room at two thirty on a Tuesday afternoon. She might have recorded her own voicemail greeting; some hotels I've stayed in allow you to do that. I wait, wondering if I'm about to hear her voice. Wondering what it might say.

Please leave a message after the tone, and, yes, I am having an affair with your husband.

'Hello?'

Oh, God. Fuck, fuck, fuck. What do I do now?

You want to talk to her, don't you?

'Is that Selina Gane?'

'Speaking.'

I can't do this. Can't. *Have to.*

'It's me. Connie Bowskill. I'm the one who's been . . .' I stop. What have I been doing, exactly? 'I'm the woman who—'

'I know who you are,' she cuts me off. 'How did you find out where I'm staying? How did you get a key to my house?'

'I haven't—'

'Leave me alone! You're sick! I don't know what's wrong with you, or what your game is, and I don't want to know. I'm phoning the police.'

There's a click, then the line goes dead.

I start to shiver, suddenly ice-cold in the pit of my stomach. When I try to subdue the shaking, it gets worse. My first impulse is to ring Sam, to get to the police before Selina Gane does and tell them it's not true – I haven't got a key to her house, I don't know what she's talking about. I can't think straight. If the dead woman was real, am I about to be accused of her murder? How can that be, when I've done nothing, when I know nothing? Maybe Selina Gane's not lying deliberately; maybe it's a mistake. I need to explain . . .

No. Think, Connie. If you ring Sam, he'll persuade you to go back to the police station, back to Grint. And Grint won't take you where you want to go.

I need to get into that house. It's the only way. I've looked at the pictures again and again and I still can't bring to mind the missing detail, the shadow that moves out of sight whenever I try to focus on it. I need to be there in person – stand in that lounge myself, however much I don't want to, however sick I feel at the prospect. Maybe then the missing piece will slot into place.

I wish I did have a key to 11 Bentley Grove. If I did, I wouldn't need to make the call I'm about to make. I fumble in my bag, pull out an old Sainsbury's receipt. There's a phone number written on the back of it: 0843 315 6792. I saw it on Grint's computer screen about an hour and a half ago, wondered why I hadn't noticed it before on Roundthehouses: the number to ring to arrange a viewing of 11 Bentley Grove, or to ask for further information. While Grint, Sam and Kit were busy staring at the blurred black car, I excused myself to go to the bathroom and wrote it down.

I key in the number and press dial.

'Connie!'

Kit is sprinting towards me. There's no time to run away. I curl into a ball, wrap my arm around my knees and tighten my grip on my phone. He's not going to stop me from doing this.

'Thank God. I thought you'd—'

'Quiet.'

'Who are you phoning?'

'I *said* be quiet.' *Pick up. Pick up.*

'Who are you phoning, Connie?'

'Lorraine Turner,' I say, my voice hard. 'She's got a house to sell. I'm going to arrange a viewing.'

Kit hisses an obscenity under his breath, shakes his head. I try to hear only the ringing, preferring it to the sound of my husband's disgust. *Pick up. Please.*

'You think they're going to be showing people round? A woman gets murdered there, and the police don't think to tell the agent to hold off on viewings? What the fuck's wrong with you? Look at you, crouched on the pavement like a . . . Do you actually have any idea what you're doing?'

He's right. I didn't think. Of course Grint will have told them not to show anyone round 11 Bentley Grove; it must be full of police. 'You don't know anything,' I say, keeping my phone clamped to my ear. I won't give up, not while Kit's watching me.

The ringing stops. Someone's picked up. A woman's voice says, 'Lasting damage.'

I can't speak. The breath in my throat has set, turned to concrete.

'Lasting damage,' she repeats, louder this time. Sing-song. As if she's taunting me.

Do you actually have any idea what you're doing?

Lasting damage. Lasting damage. Lasting damage.

I cry out, throw my phone into the road. I don't want it anywhere near me.

'Con, what's wrong?' Kit crouches down beside me. 'What happened?'

'She said . . .' I shake my head. It can't be true. *It must be*. I heard it, twice. 'She said, "Lasting damage", the woman who answered the phone. Why would she say that to me?'

I see my confusion reflected in Kit's eyes: blank incomprehension. Then he breathes in sharply and his face changes. 'She didn't say, "Lasting damage", Connie. She said, "Lancing Damisz" – it's the name of the agency.'

I wrap my arms around myself, rocking back and forth to make it go away. 'She said, "Lasting damage".' I know what I heard.

'Connie . . . Connie! Lancing Damisz is the estate agent that's selling 11 Bentley Grove. It's the company Lorraine Turner works for: Lancing Damisz.'

Lasting damage. Lancing Damisz. I'm not sure how many times Kit says the name before I allow myself to hear it. 'How do you know? How do you know what the estate agent's called?'

He closes his eyes, waits a few seconds before answering. 'I can't believe you *don't* know. The logo's on the Roundthehouses page. Just above where it says, "11 Bentley Grove, Cambridge". Can't you picture it? We've just spent half an hour staring at it, with Grint and Sam. All in upper case, with the D hanging off the L, looped over it. I noticed it because it's an unusual name. I thought, "They must be new – there was no Lancing Damisz in 2003, when we were looking at houses." '

The D hanging off the L. Yes: navy blue letters. I didn't take in the name because I wasn't interested in which estate agent was selling 11 Bentley Grove; I was too busy looking for my husband in the photographs.

'Are . . . are you sure?' I ask Kit. How could I not know the name? I've phoned the estate agent before – last Friday, when

I first saw the 'For Sale' sign in the garden. I asked if anyone was available immediately to show me round. No one was.

'Ring them back.' Kit glances at my shattered phone lying in pieces in the road, then tries to pass me his. 'Don't take the word of someone you don't trust.'

'No, I . . .'

'Ring them!' He waves it in my face. 'Prove it to yourself. Maybe then you'll realise you need help – proper medical help, not some crappy quack homeopath who knows a gullible idiot when she sees one.'

What about you, Kit? Do you know a gullible idiot when you see one?

I find the Sainsbury's receipt again, key in the number. Drops of water fall on the phone's screen. Tears. I wipe them away.

This time someone answers after only one ring. 'Lancing Damisz.'

It's the same voice, same woman. *Same words*. How could I have misheard it? I pass the phone back to Kit, who is waiting for me to admit my mistake and apologise.

What's the point? What's the point of Kit and me saying anything to one another, when neither of us can be trusted?

14

20/7/2010

'It was only two days,' Jackie Napier answered Sam's question with her eyes on Ian Grint. 'Two days isn't a long time. I saw it on Saturday, and I phoned the police first thing Monday morning. I explained to you why.'

'Could you explain it to me?' Sam asked. Jackie tore her eyes away from Grint to scowl at him. She had taken out one of her gold sleeper earrings and was using the end of it to scrape underneath her pink-painted fingernails. Odd behaviour for someone so well turned out, Sam thought; the immaculate presentation and the rather unsavoury public grooming seemed to contradict one another. Jackie's make-up looked as if it had been applied by a professional, and her bobbed dark hair had been styled with architectural precision. Sam didn't see how it was possible to achieve that rigid triangular look – not without scaffolding and an RSJ, at any rate.

He couldn't pin down Jackie's age in the way that he could most people's – she might have been anything from twenty to forty-five. She had a round childlike face, but her bare legs were covered with a tracery of prominent blue veins, like a much older woman's. Or maybe it had nothing to do with age. If Sam's wife Kate were here, she would say, 'The legs might not be her fault, but the skirt is. Trousers were invented for a reason.' Or words to that effect. Strange things offended

Kate, things Sam didn't give a toss about: people wearing clothes that didn't suit them, clocks in public places that showed the wrong time, houses with brown window-frames, hot-air hand dryers.

Sam had the impression that Jackie Napier had been expecting Grint to take the lead, and resented this hijacking of proceedings by a newcomer who wasn't even local, but Grint had decided Sam should direct the interview and had so far contributed nothing. He was sitting in the far corner of the room, using a radiator as a footstool. Sam thought his disaffected schoolboy posture was inappropriate, and would have preferred him to put his feet on the floor, but he had no illusions about who was in charge. Wherever I go, someone else turns out to be in charge, he thought. It worried him only indirectly: he spent a lot of time wondering if he ought to try to assert himself more, and always ended up concluding that he'd rather not have power over others, not if he could help it. What he would have liked was for those with power to behave as he would if he were them.

'I'm not criticising you,' he told Jackie. 'You've given us some very useful information, and, as you say, two days isn't a long time.'

'No, it isn't. What am I supposed to do, ring the police and say, "Excuse me, but I saw a dead body on a property website, except now it's disappeared?" Who's to say it was ever there at all? No one would have believed me. I'd have looked like an idiot.'

'And yet you did come forward,' Sam pointed out.

'Well, I couldn't just leave it, could I? I mean, maybe I imagined it, maybe it was never there at all, but I've still got to tell someone, haven't I? What if I didn't imagine it? I worried about it till it did my head in, asked all my mates – waste of time, they all gave me different advice. Some said, "Don't be daft, you couldn't have seen it", some said, "You've got to tell someone". Most just laughed at me, to be honest. It wasn't funny, you know,' she said indignantly, as if Sam had said it was. 'Monday morning, I woke up and thought, this is going to bug me if I don't get it off my chest. It shouldn't be my responsibility, should it? No one pays me to worry about people getting murdered. So I rang the police.' Her accent sounded like Essex to Sam, but perhaps it was Cambridge. Was there such a thing? he wondered. If so, it wasn't one of the better known regional accents, like Brummie or Scouse.

'You did the right thing,' he said.

Jackie nodded. 'I'll swear to you right now: I didn't imagine it. That's just not me, I'm not an imagination sort of person. Do you know what I mean?'

Sam did. Jackie Napier was about as different from Connie Bowskill as it was possible to be. They were at opposite ends of the scale. *With a dead woman lying in her own blood smack bang in the middle of the space between them.*

'Two things about me . . .' Jackie counted them off on her fingers. 'One: I'm as loyal as they come. If I'm on your side, I'm on your side for keeps. Two: I live in the real world, not fantasy land. I don't get ideas, I don't kid myself about my life, pretend it's better than it is: I prefer to see things how they really are.'

Did she mean she didn't get ideas above her station? Sam wondered. Fancy, far-fetched ideas? Or ideas, period? She'd given him one: maybe he could garnish his deficiencies with a bit of inverted boasting. He imagined himself saying to Proust, 'Two things about me, sir: I avoid confrontation wherever I can, and I let my DCs run rings around me.' That would go down well – about as well as Sam's having devoted today to helping Ian Grint with his maybe-real-and-maybe-not murder, as if he had no cases of his own to attend to.

'What time was it when you saw the woman's body on Roundthehouses?' he asked Jackie.

'I told DC Grint: about quarter past, twenty past one.'

And Grint could have told Sam. But Sam was glad he hadn't, now that he'd got this far, now that Jackie was looking at him, finally, and no longer grimaced at everything he said. When, earlier, he'd asked to be debriefed, Grint had chuckled and said, 'Too much effort, not enough time.' Sam had walked into the interview room knowing only Jackie's name, and that she claimed to have seen what Connie Bowskill had seen. As a result, he was experiencing her first-hand, undistorted by whatever conclusions Grint had drawn based on his prior meetings with her.

Grint was right: it was a better way to do it. Sam wasn't fooled by the outward flippancy; Grint cared about 11 Bentley Grove's disappearing dead woman. When you were in the presence of someone who really cared about something – above and beyond professional conscientiousness – you could feel it in everything they said and did. In Grint's company, Sam had that feeling – as if there was adrenaline in the air, in the walls, in the furniture – and he knew he wasn't the one generating it. Grint's like Simon Waterhouse, he thought. He'd have put money on the two detectives hating one another.

'Do you normally go on the internet late at night?' he asked Jackie.

'Lord, no. I'm a nine-o'-clock-to-bed person, me. I was jet-lagged. I got back from holiday last Thursday, and I'm never right for a few days afterwards, if it's long-distance.'

'Where did you go on holiday?'

'Matakana in New Zealand. You've never heard of it, have you?'

Sam had, but he pretended he hadn't, guessing that Jackie would enjoy enlightening him.

'My sister lives there. It's a pretty little place. She runs a café. Well, it's an art gallery, really – but they do cake and coffee and stuff. It doesn't know what it is – it'd make more money if it did. I always say, it's great for a holiday, Matakana, but you wouldn't want to live there.'

Same wondered how often Jackie had said this in the presence of her sister, while enjoying her hospitality.

'Do you mind my asking what you do for a living?'

Jackie jerked her head in Grint's direction. 'Hasn't he told you anything?'

'It's helpful for me to hear it from you,' Sam told her.

'I'm an estate agent. I work for Lancing Damisz. We're the ones selling the house where the body was, 11 Bentley Grove. Why do you think I was looking on Roundthehouses?' She frowned. 'Are you one of those people who hates estate agents?'

'No, I . . .' Sam heard a scraping sound, and turned; Grint had chosen this moment to adjust the position of his chair. *An estate agent*. That was the last thing Sam had expected, as Grint well knew; it explained the hint of a smile on his face.

'When I couldn't sleep Friday night, I thought I'd have a look at what had come on the market while I was away,' said Jackie. 'I knew 11 Bentley Grove'd be there – I knew she was selling it, the doctor that owns it, Dr Gane. I'd have dealt with the sale myself, only I was due to go to New Zealand, so I handed it over to Lorraine – my colleague, Lorraine Turner?'

'So . . .' Sam felt as if he was lagging behind. 'Sorry, you might have to clarify something for me: you said you were looking at Roundthehouses to see what had come up for sale while you were out of the country . . .'

'That's right. To see what had sold, too, and what was under offer. Keep an eye on our competition, check they weren't selling more than us. The property market's strong in Cambridge. The downturn didn't hit us as badly as it did some places, and things are really picking up now. Any house or flat in the city centre that comes on for less than about six hundred grand gets snapped up within days, unless it's a huge refurb job or on a busy road. It's a supply and—'

'Sorry, if I can just stop you there.' Sam smiled to compensate for the intrusion. 'So essentially you were trying to get up to speed before you went back to work.'

'Yeah. See, the thing about me is, I love my work – it's a vocation more than a career for me. I even miss it when I go away. There's no job I'd rather do, and that's the God's honest truth.'

'I think that might answer the question I was about to ask.' *The question I'd have asked some time ago, if you weren't quite so keen on the sound of your own voice.* 'Why did you play the virtual tour of 11 Bentley Grove? I suppose you need to see a house's interior to know whether it's fairly priced,' Sam answered his own question, imagining how he might feel if selling homes were his passion in life.

'You do.' Jackie nodded enthusiastically. 'Too right you do. Still, I'd already seen inside Dr Gane's house, twice. I looked at the virtual tour because I was curious to see if she'd moved out like she said she was going to. Just being nosy, really. She told me she wouldn't be able to stay there after what had happened, said she'd have to go to a hotel. I said to her, "That'll cost you a bomb – staying in a hotel till you've sold, and bought somewhere else." She'd gone and done it, though – I could tell from the tour. She'd left most of her stuff in the house, but there was no toothbrush, toothpaste or loo roll in the bathroom, no pile of books or water glass on her bedside table.' Jackie tapped the side of her nose. 'I've got an instinct, when it comes to houses – and the people that live in them.'

And the people that die in them?

'I remember thinking, "She's only done it – moved into a hotel, at God knows what cost. Silly woman!" And then the picture of the lounge came up, and I saw that body lying there, all that blood . . .' Jackie shuddered. 'I don't want to see anything like that again, thank you very much.'

'You said, "After what had happened". I need you to start from the beginning, I'm afraid.' Sam could feel Grint watching him.

Jackie laughed scornfully. 'That's a bit of a tall order. Like I said to DC Grint, I don't know what the hell's going on, so how do I know when it began?' Bored with picking her nails, she slotted her earring back through the hole in her ear.

'Start with the phone call on 30 June,' Grint told her. If Sam had been a different sort of person – if he'd been Giles Proust, for example – he might have turned round and said, *DC Grint! So glad you could join us.*

Jackie sighed heavily. 'I was at work. I answered the phone,' she recited in a bored, 'been there, done that' voice. 'It was a woman. She told me her name was Selina Gane – *Dr* Selina Gane. She made a point of saying that. Normally people don't – normally we ask. So, like, if you rang me and said your name was Sam . . .' Jackie wrinkled her nose. 'What's your surname again?'

'Kombothekra.'

'So you'd say your name was Sam Kombothekra and we'd say, "Is that Mr, Doctor or Professor?" Or, if you were a woman, we'd say, "Is that Miss, Mrs, Doctor or Professor?" We don't ask about "Ms" – not allowed, orders from on high. The whole traditional image thing.' Jackie mimed quote marks. 'I've got a real bee in my bonnet about it, actually. I'm a Ms – so are most of my colleagues. But Cambridge is Cambridge – a lot of people here don't realise that change is going to happen to them whether they like it or not.'

'Phone call,' Grint intoned from the back of the room. '30 June.'

'Yeah, so I got this call, Dr Selina Gane she said her name was. Wanted to put her house on the market, 11 Bentley Grove, so I arranged a meeting with her for later that same day at the house. She seemed nice – there was nothing about her that made me suspicious. I looked round, measured up, talked to her about commission, marketing, we agreed an asking price. I took some photos for the brochure . . .'

'You took the photos?' Sam asked. 'When I spoke to Lorraine Turner, she told me she took them.'

'Yeah, that's because I deleted mine,' said Jackie, as if this ought to have been obvious.

'Lorraine took the pictures that ended up in the brochure and on the website,' Grint contributed from his ringside seat. 'But let's not leap ahead. Go on, Jackie.'

'The woman – the one who said she was Selina Gane – she told me she'd pop into the office the next day, to proofread the draft brochure, which she did. She made a few changes, and I said, great, thanks, I'll send a copy of the brochure when it's ready. She said not to bother – she didn't need one. She gave me a spare key, told me to arrange viewings whenever I wanted, let myself in and out. She was going away, she said. I told her I'd ring her to let her know when I was coming, as a courtesy, but she said, no, there was no need.'

Sam was having trouble concentrating. He knew something was on its way that he wouldn't be able to predict if he tried for a million years. Would Simon know where Jackie's story was heading, if he were here? Would he already have a theory? Sam was straining to pay attention to every word, and his awareness of the effort he was making was interfering with his ability to listen. Grint's looming background presence wasn't helping.

'By the time the brochures were done, I'd already rung round a few of the buyers on our priority list,' Jackie went on. 'Anyone I thought might be interested. Not university people – they all want historical buildings and period features, and there's not much of that on Bentley Grove. Luckily the science park and Addenbrooke's lot don't care – they want square footage, shiny and new, big gardens. I had a family who were gagging to be shown round, the Frenches – they were the first ones I rang, to be honest. I knew they'd be perfect for 11 Bentley Grove.'

Odd way to look at it, thought Sam. A house needed to be right for its inhabitants, surely, not the other way round.

'When I turned up at the house with the Frenches, I let myself in and walked into this woman I'd never seen before. Except I had – I'd seen a photo of her, a passport photo. She looked terrified, as if she thought I was going to attack her, or something. She asked who I was, what was I doing in her house, how come I had a key? She went white in the face – honest to God, I thought she was going to pass out. I asked her who *she* was. She said she was Selina Gane – well, she *was* Selina Gane, I know that now – but she wasn't the woman *I* knew as Selina Gane.' Jackie patted the nape of her neck, as if to emphasise her own identity. 'She had no idea what I was on about. Some bloody woman had only gone and put her house on the market without telling her.'

~

Charlie was taking photographs. As many as she could, of as much as she could: of the pool from every angle, her favourite trees and plants in the gardens, her and Simon's bedroom. *Otherwise known as the site of only one shag*. He'd put his arm round her in bed last night – in that way of his, stiff with significance and awkward invitation – but she'd been too upset about Liv and Gibbs, then more upset still because Simon hadn't seemed to mind her not wanting to.

She took one picture each of all the empty bedrooms they hadn't used, a few of the lounge, kitchen, dining room, the various sun terraces. God, she loved this place. How was it possible to love a place when you'd been nothing but miserable there? In the same way that it was possible to love a person with whom you were miserable, she guessed.

Grudgingly, she included in her photo-shoot the annoying mountain that doggedly refused to show its face to anyone but Simon. She had asked Domingo about it this morning; he hadn't been able to see it either. From his evident bewilderment, she'd concluded that no other guest had ever mentioned it. Yet again, Simon was the special one. Charlie still hadn't ruled out the possibility that he was pretending to see something that wasn't there: another of his twisted thought-experiments.

Was she going to take a photograph of Domingo's wooden

lodge? Yes, why not? For the sake of completeness, she ought to have one. If she ever spoke to her sister again, she could show her the picture and say, 'That's where I was when I found out you were screwing Chris Gibbs.'

As she approached, she heard Simon's voice. He'd been talking to Sam for nearly an hour. They were going to have to offer Domingo a contribution towards his phone bill. Charlie listened outside the open door: something to do with Roundthehouses, the property website. And a murder, or a death. Connie Bowskill was involved; Simon had mentioned her name a couple of times at the beginning of the conversation, before Charlie had given up trying to understand what was going on and gone to find her camera.

She photographed the hut from every angle. Leaning into the dark, stuffy room that smelled of Domingo's woody aftershave, she pushed Simon to one side so that she could get a shot of the wicker chair through the open door, the blue and red blanket draped over it.

That's where I was sitting when you ruined my honeymoon, you selfish bitch.

'I'll try to get Sam later,' Simon was saying. 'I'll have to go to Puerto Banus, find another phone to ring him from. I feel under pressure here, with the caretaker waiting to get his gaff back. Can't really concentrate. What? There are no other rooms, only this one and the bog. For as long as I'm on his phone, he has to stand outside.'

Get Sam later? Charlie frowned. Sam was the person Simon had said he was phoning. Had he rung somebody else afterwards? The Snowman? No; the rigid hatred was missing from his voice, so it couldn't be Proust. Colin Sellers, then. It had to be.

Simon grunted goodbye. He didn't put the phone down straight away. Charlie took a photo of him tapping it against his chin, mouthing words to himself – that was always a sign that his obsession levels were soaring, well on their way to being off the graph. 'Smile, you nutter,' she said.

'I thought you weren't taking any photos till the last day.'

She laughed. 'You think this isn't our last day? Don't kid yourself.'

Simon took the camera from her hand. 'What are you talking about?'

'You want to go home.'

'No, I don't.'

'It'll be a few hours before you admit it to yourself, a few more while you pluck up the courage to tell me we're going.'

'That's crap. We're going nowhere.'

'Sellers just told you something about a dead woman. You want to be there, where the action is. Where the rigor mortis is, rather.'

'I want to be here. With you.'

Charlie couldn't allow his reassurances to penetrate her wall of resentment. It would hurt too much if she believed him and then he went back on it. 'Why wouldn't you want to go home?' she said angrily. 'Your friend Connie witnessed a murder and wants to tell you all about it. What a coincidence that she just happened to stumble across the body. Is the dead woman her husband's girlfriend, by any chance?'

'Nobody knows anything.' Simon sighed. 'Least of all you. Connie Bowskill saw a dead body lying face down on a bloodstained carpet on the Roundthehouses website. In one of the interior shots of 11 Bentley Grove – the house her husband had in his SatNav as "home".'

Charlie stared at him. 'You're serious, aren't you? You're actually serious.'

'Friday night, this happened – early hours of Saturday morning.'

'Simon, Roundthehouses is a property website,' Charlie spelled it out as if for a child or a fool. 'There aren't any dead bodies on it, only houses for sale. And for rent – let's not forget the lettings side of the operation. Apartments, maisonettes . . . no dead women. Did Sellers . . .' Charlie stopped, shook her head. 'It's a wind-up, isn't it? He's probably been planning it for months.'

'I haven't spoken to Sellers. That was Gibbs on the phone.'

Gibbs. Charlie felt as if an invisible hand was closing around her throat, gripping tightly so as to let nothing out. Probably a good thing if it was; sensible of the human body to put a system in place to prevent a person from screaming all the way through their honeymoon.

It was Chris Gibbs who, four years ago, had uttered the words that had brought Charlie's world to a standstill. He and only he had seen the look on her face as she realised what she'd done, as her life began to unravel – in public, in broad daylight, in the fucking nick of all places. Perhaps Gibbs had thought nothing of it, unaware that he was witnessing the destruction of the thing Charlie held most dear: her sense of herself as someone who was worth something. It hadn't been Gibbs' fault; all he'd done was provide her with information she'd asked for and that he'd found for her. Logically, she knew he'd done nothing wrong, but she held it against him all the same. He'd been front row and centre, spectator at the scene of her humiliation.

'You said you were going to ring Sam.'

'His phone's switched off.' Simon leaned forward to see

Charlie's face. 'What? Don't look like that. I didn't say anything about Olivia. You heard the conversation – it was about Connie Bowskill. Gibbs and I don't have personal conversations.'

Everybody and you don't have personal conversations.

'You spend an hour on the phone to Gibbs chatting about made-up dead bodies on property websites, and you don't think to mention that he and my traitor of a sister have done their best to wreck our wedding and honeymoon?'

Simon slotted Domingo's phone back into its base. 'They can't wreck anything,' he said. 'Apart from their own relationships, and that's their lookout.'

'You've changed your tune! Last night you said you'd always think of our wedding day as the day that—'

'No, *you* said that. And you told me I felt the same way – let down, implicated . . .'

'Well, don't you? It was *our* wedding day. They had no right to make it anything else.'

Simon pushed past Charlie, out into the sunlight. 'Anything that's ours, the only people who can fuck it up are you and me. If you don't want your honeymoon ruined, stop talking about going home early.'

'That's . . . you're confusing two things that have nothing to do with each other!'

'Am I?' Simon pushed a hanging tree out of his way. Orange petals fell on Charlie; she brushed them off her face.

'Last night you said you'd lost all respect for both of them.' She was running to catch up with him. 'Was that a lie? Have you forgiven them already?'

'It's not up to me to forgive or not forgive. Yeah, I think less of them. Gibbs is married, Liv's supposed to be getting married. They shouldn't have done it.'

'You didn't sound like you thought less of Gibbs, before, on the phone. You sounded the same as you always sound.'

'Does he need to know what I think?' Simon sat down on the steps of the swimming pool, put his bare feet in the water up to his ankles. 'Doesn't stop me from thinking it.'

Charlie pressed her eyes shut. Nothing she said would make a difference. Simon and Gibbs would go on as if nothing had happened – talking about work, slagging off Proust, drinking together in the Brown Cow. What had she expected, that Simon would take a stand? Refuse to speak to Gibbs until he apologised and promised to leave Liv alone?

Like everyone at Spilling nick, Gibbs knew what had happened at Sellers' fortieth birthday party. He knew Simon and Charlie had been in a bedroom together, that Simon had changed his mind and made a run for it, leaving the door wide open and Charlie naked on the floor. Stacey, Sellers' wife, had been outside on the landing with three of her friends; she'd seen everything. Charlie had laughed off all references to the incident at work, and had mentioned it to nobody outside work. Liv knew nothing about it. *Yet.*

'I don't believe in collective responsibility,' Simon said. 'Gibbs is the one cheating on Debbie. He's met Liv plenty of times before. How many times have they been at the Brown Cow with us, without Debbie or that tosser Dom Lund? It could have happened any time – didn't need us getting married to make it happen.'

'And if Debbie finds out we knew, and didn't tell her?'

Simon looked up, shielding his eyes from the sun with his hand. 'Why would we tell her? It's none of our business.'

It was like trying to explain the way planet Earth worked to an extra-terrestrial. Charlie took a deep breath. 'Liv's my sister. If this gets out, people are going to assume I'm on her side.'

'Then you can tell them what you told me last night: that you never want to see her fat treacherous slut face again.'

'I said that?'

'I was convinced,' said Simon. 'I can't see anyone doubting you.'

Charlie hated being reminded that she'd said that about her own sister. But whose fault was it? Who had made her say it? 'Debbie's popular,' she worried aloud. 'All her friends are police wives – Meakin's wife, Zlosnik's, Ed Butler's – Debbie's a central part of that . . . network. She and Lizzie Proust go to the same Aquafit class at Waterfront. If it was Stacey Sellers, I wouldn't worry so much – everyone thinks she's a bitch. And *she's* not having IVF, *she* hasn't had a million tragic miscarriages. Did you see that "Good Luck" card that was doing the rounds, before Debbie had her first . . . hormone thingy?'

Simon nodded. 'Couldn't squeeze my signature on, there were so many.'

Charlie wrapped her arms round herself, feeling shaky. 'Everyone at work's going to hate me, Simon. I've been through that once—'

'The only person who hated you four years ago was you.'

'I seem to remember the tabloids offering their support,' Charlie said bitterly. 'I can't cope with it again, Simon – I can't cope with being the bad guy everyone's pointing at.'

'Charlie, the *Sun* and the *Mail* don't give a shit about Debbie's IVF.'

'What if Debbie finds out, and she and Gibbs split up, and Liv becomes the new Mrs Gibbs? Mrs Zailer-Gibbs, with her double-barrelled fucking pretentious . . .'

'You're working yourself up into a state for no reason.'

'I'll leave work and there she'll be, waiting in the car park to pick him up after his shift. There'll be no getting away from her. She might move to Spilling.' Charlie shuddered. 'You think none of this has occurred to her? This thing with Gibbs, she's done it deliberately.'

'I hope so,' said Simon. 'Fucking Gibbs by accident'd be traumatic for anyone.'

'She's always preferred my world to hers – hovering on the sidelines, waiting for me to invite her in. She saw her chance and she took it – now she's *in*. All she needs to do is eliminate Debbie. She doesn't need me any more for access.'

No response.

'Say something!' Charlie snapped.

Simon was staring into the water.

Charlie thought about the last thing he'd said. He'd never used the word 'fucking' in a sexual context before. Never.

'Simon?'

'Sorry, what?'

'You're not listening to me.'

'I know what I'd be hearing if I was: someone who's addicted to suffering. Who'll go to any lengths to create opportunities to feel bad, and make other people feel bad.'

Charlie tried to push him into the swimming pool. He grabbed her wrists to stop her. She gave up; he was far stronger. A few seconds later, it was as if it had never happened. She sat down on the steps beside him. 'You're not listening because you're thinking about bonkers Connie Bowskill, with her stupid SatNav and dead body stories,' she said. 'You might as well be in Spilling.'

'I've got a theory.'

Charlie groaned.

'Not about Connie Bowskill – about you. *You're* the one who wants to go back. You want Liv to find out via your mum and dad that we sacked it after four days. That way the symbolism's clear: one day she rings up, next day the honeymoon's dead – unambiguous. A romantic dream in tatters, a high-concept disaster . . .'

'Oh, shut up!'

'A lifetime of guilt for your sister.'

'Can I ask you something?' Charlie's voice was brittle. 'Why did you marry me if you think I'm such a bitch?'

Simon looked surprised. 'I don't,' he said. 'You're human, that's all. We all have shitty thoughts, we all do shitty things.'

Charlie wanted him to say that there was a clear distinction between her shittiness and Liv's, that Liv's was a hundred times worse. From many years of experience, she knew that the thing you wanted Simon Waterhouse to say was never the thing he said.

His eyes narrowed. He squinted at Charlie, as if he was concentrating on memorising her face. 'Categories of people – that's where we start. You post the image of a dead body on a website, you're either the killer . . .'

'I don't believe this,' Charlie muttered. She walked down the steps of the pool into the water and started to swim. Her dress clung to her; her sandals were like bricks tied to her feet.

Simon stood up and walked along the side, keeping pace with her. 'If you're not the killer or an accomplice, who are you? The person whose house it is? Course, the owner might *be* the killer. The estate agent selling the house? I can't see how that would work, can you? Or maybe someone interested in buying. Nothing better for lowering the price than blood and guts all over the living room floor.'

'Fuck off, Simon, fuck off, and thrice fuck off.'

'If you're the killer and you post a picture of the body online, you're advertising your work. If you're not the killer—'

'There's no dead body apart from in Connie Bowskill's mind,' Charlie shouted over him.

'Didn't I tell you?' said Simon. 'Someone else saw it too, and contacted Cambridge police.'

'*What?*' Charlie stopped swimming. 'Who? Connie Bowskill's best friend? Her mum?' It had to be a lie.

'If you're not the killer, were you there when it happened? Were you watching? Hiding? Did you know it was going to happen? Were you waiting with a camera? Or did you only come along afterwards and find the body?'

Charlie hauled herself out of the pool. Now she was weighed down by the water trapped in her clothes; moving quickly in the heat was even harder.

'Where are you going?' Simon asked her.

'Where am I going?' she echoed his question. 'Where could Charlie be going?' Let the speculator speculate, she thought, hurrying towards Domingo's wooden house. She was going to ring the airline, find out how soon they could fly home.

~

Sam understood, finally, something Grint had said in passing earlier: that he'd asked Lorraine Turner for the names, addresses and phone numbers of everyone she'd shown round 11 Bentley Grove so far, as well as anyone who'd enquired about it, even if they hadn't followed up with a viewing. Sam had put it down to thoroughness, a desire to cover all bases, but he saw now that it had been more than that. The woman who had assumed Selina Gane's identity and put her house on the market without her permission might have decided to pose as a prospective buyer. The psychology was consistent. This was someone with form for gaining entry under false pretences, someone who was known to have lied about who she was. Sam could see that it might amuse her to deceive yet another member of Lancing Damisz staff.

And then? What would the woman who wasn't Selina Gane do next? Make an offer? Buy the house? Was that the aim, all along? It was pointless speculating, Sam decided, with so few solid facts available.

'Couldn't make it up, could you?' Jackie was chatting to him now as if they were old friends. 'There was me standing there like a lemon, and the poor Frenches, who'd have bought that house, guaranteed, except I had to tell them it wasn't for sale after all, it was a mistake. Embarrassed doesn't even begin to cover it! The Frenches were gutted. It's the worst part of my job, having to deal with the emotional fallout when things go wrong. It must be the same with your job.'

It was a pity Jackie Napier wasn't more intelligent; a cleverer person would have known which parts of the story were important and which weren't. Sam had an awful feeling he would shortly be hearing all about Jackie's saving of the day – the even better house she found for the Frenches, with its sunnier garden and superior garaging facilities – if he didn't take active steps to avoid it.

'I need to clarify this,' he said. 'You're saying the woman you met at 11 Bentley Grove the first time you went there wasn't Selina Gane? The woman who told you she wanted to sell the house, the one who proofread the brochure and gave you a key?'

'She was nothing like Dr Gane,' Jackie said angrily.

'So the real Selina Gane was the one you met when you turned up with the Frenches a few days later?'

'Exactly a week later,' said Grint. 'Wednesday 7 July.'

'I should have known as soon as I saw that bloody passport photo,' said Jackie, tight-lipped. 'Selina Gane's blonde and pretty. The other woman was dark and . . . sort of severe-looking, but you don't think, do you? Someone shows you a passport photo and says, "I used to dye my hair blonde," you believe them, don't you? You don't think, "I wonder if they're pretending to be someone else." I had no reason to be suspicious of her. She had a key to the house, for God's sake – she was *in* the house when I went to meet her there. Of course I assumed it was her passport and her house – who wouldn't? Who puts someone else's house up for sale? I mean, why would anyone do that?'

Why would anyone put a photograph of a murder victim on a property website?

'How did you come to see the passport?' Sam opted to ask an easier question.

'We have to see ID for anyone whose house we're selling. So we know they're who they say they are.' If Jackie was aware of the irony, she was hiding it well.

'You say she was dark, the woman who wasn't Selina Gane. What was her body shape – small, tall, fat, thin?'

'Small and thin. Petite.'

Sam felt something click into place in his mind before he realised why. Then it came to him: petite. Connie Bowskill had used the same word. A dark-haired petite woman . . .

Some bloody woman had only gone and put her house on the market without telling her. That's what Jackie had said.

Some bloody woman . . .

'Jackie, the woman you saw on the virtual tour, lying face down – could she have been the woman who met you at 11 Bentley Grove and pretended to be Selina Gane?'

Jackie frowned. 'No. I don't think so, no. The dead woman – you could see the backs of her legs. She had darker skin. The woman I met was pale. And she had a wedding ring on, but a really thin one – not much thicker than a ring-pull from a can. The dead woman was wearing a thick wedding ring.'

'You're sure?' Sam asked.

Jackie tapped her finger against one of her earrings – the same one she'd used to pick her nails. 'I always notice jewellery,' she said proudly.

Even when there's a butchered woman in the same photograph, competing for your attention? Sam noticed that Jackie wasn't wearing a wedding ring herself, and felt sorry for the unfortunate man who might one day put one on her finger.

'The real Selina Gane doesn't wear a wedding ring,' Jackie added. 'She's not married. I think she might be the other way – it was just a feeling I got.'

Pale skin. Thin wedding ring. Sam turned to look at Grint, saw that he was hunched and frowning. Connie Bowskill was petite, with pale skin and a very thin wedding ring. Sam shivered involuntarily. Why would Connie Bowskill pretend to be Selina Gane and put 11 Bentley Grove up for sale? Because she thought Selina was living there with Kit? Sam didn't like that as an explanation – the logic of it was too hazy. It was hardly the first thing you'd think to do in that situation. If Connie was the dark woman Jackie met at 11 Bentley Grove, how did she get hold of a key?

Grint had stood up, and was making his way across the room, hobbling. 'Foot's gone to sleep,' he said. 'Jackie, do you reckon you'd know her face if you saw her again, the woman who impersonated Selina Gane?'

'Definitely. I'm good with faces.'

Sam thought that was debatable, given that she'd fallen for the passport photo. When he looked up, he found her staring at him, her face frozen in a mask of dislike. It gave him a shock; what had he done wrong?

'You think I should have known it wasn't her, from the passport. Don't you? How stupid must I be, that I didn't clock it was a picture of someone else? She'd thought of that. "I used to dye my hair blonde," she said. "It suited me too. Admit it, I look better there than in real life. Most people's passport photos make them look like serial killers – mine makes me look like a film star. Sadly, the reality falls way short." '

'That was what she said?'

'Not exactly that,' said Jackie. 'I don't remember her exact words. It was over a month ago. But she gave me some flannel about not looking like her photo. She definitely said the serial-killer-film-star bit. Oh, she was clever. She knew all she had to do was talk about people not looking like they do in their passports. If she made me think about all those other people, she wouldn't have to convince me – I'd do all the work myself. It's one of those things everyone says, isn't it? "He looks nothing like his passport photo, I'm surprised he's ever allowed back into the country." '

Sam had to concede she had a point.

'What if we were to introduce you – here, today – to the woman who passed herself off as Selina Gane?' Grint asked Jackie.

'I'd ask her what the hell she was playing at.'

Grint nodded. 'I'll ask her the very same. Between us, we might get an explanation out of her.'

Sam didn't like what he was hearing. Jackie hadn't yet identified Connie as the woman she'd met; why was Grint acting as if she had, offering her his support? Was it a tactic? If he seriously planned to put Jackie and Connie in a room together, Sam didn't want to be there too. Plus, there was something else worrying him, something that wasn't any of the things he knew he was worried about. He'd suddenly become aware of a dragging anxiety beneath the surface of his thoughts. What was it? It hadn't been there a moment ago.

'I'd like to hear the end of Jackie's story,' he said. 'There you were at 11 Bentley Grove, with the Frenches and a frightened, confused Dr Gane – what happened?'

'The Frenches scurried off home to ring my boss and complain.' Jackie rolled her eyes. 'Ungrateful sods – nothing like giving someone the benefit of the doubt, is there? They assumed I'd cocked up. I haven't spoken to them since. I wouldn't.'

So, no superior garaging and sunnier gardens for the Frenches, Sam thought, not if Jackie could help it. Hadn't she described herself as loyal, at the beginning of the interview? In Sam's experience, people who extolled their own loyalty often sought to impose reciprocity, by coercion if necessary. Almost always, there was an unspoken caveat: *but if you cross me, or let me down . . .*

'I was left standing there like a spare part, with Selina Gane threatening to ring the police. I managed to calm her down, at least enough to explain what had happened. She was in a state – who wouldn't be? So was I, to be honest. I mean, it wasn't like anything bad had happened to me, but it freaks you out a bit, thinking you've been tricked by some weirdo and you don't even know why. What I don't get is, what was the point of it all, from the dark-haired woman's point of view?

She must have known what'd happen: I'd turn up to show people round the house, and I'd meet the real Dr Gane. Eventually that was bound to happen, wasn't it?'

Sam wondered if the point had been to scare Selina Gane out of her senses. To make her think, 'If my lover's wife is capable of this, what else might she be capable of?'

'I don't suppose Selina Gane said anything about who the dark woman might be?'

'She wasn't making much sense. At first when I asked her who'd do a thing like that, she said, "I know who did it." I waited for her to say more, but she started yapping on about changing the locks. She grabbed the *Yellow Pages* and started looking up locksmiths, and then she threw the book on the floor, burst into tears and said how could she stay in the house after this? "If she can get a copy of my front door key once, she can do it again," she said. I told her she ought to contact the police.'

'She took your advice,' said Grint. He aimed his next comment at Sam. 'She made a statement on Thursday 8 July. In it, she said that she was aware of a dark-haired woman who'd been following her – she had no idea who she was, but this woman had been hanging around, behaving oddly. From her statement, there was no way of us working out who this person was, but then . . .' Grint turned back to Jackie. 'There have been some developments, recently.'

Grint couldn't have known about this statement yesterday morning, Sam thought, or else he would have sounded far more interested than he had the first time Sam had spoken to him about 11 Bentley Grove and Connie Bowskill's disappearing dead woman.

'I had to ask her,' said Jackie. 'I wanted to know who she

thought had done it. She said, "I don't know who she is." But a few minutes before, she'd said she *did* know who it was. She mustn't have wanted to talk about it.'

Grint and Sam exchanged a look. Grint said, 'I think what she meant was that she suspected the woman who'd been following her was responsible – she knew she had a stalker, but didn't know the stalker's identity.'

'Right,' said Jackie. 'Yeah, I suppose so. I didn't think of that.'

'So you threw the brochures in the bin, took 11 Bentley Grove off the website . . .' said Sam.

'Deleted the photos I'd taken, explained to my boss what had happened.' Jackie sounded bitter. 'I got a right bollocking for not checking the passport properly.' She gave Sam a look that said, *I know whose side you're on*. 'Then, just before I went to New Zealand, I got a call from Dr Gane – the real Dr Gane. I checked.'

Sam wondered how rigorous the checking process had been, over the telephone. *Are you really Selina Gane this time? Yes. Oh, okay, great.*

'I recognised her voice,' Jackie snapped at him.

'Fair enough,' Sam said evenly.

'She rang me because she said I'd been kind and understanding, that day with the Frenches.' There was an unmistakeable '*So there*' on Jackie's face, as if Sam had called her essential goodness into question. 'She wanted to sell her house, wanted me to take care of it. Said the house didn't feel like hers any more. I could see where she was coming from – I'd have felt the same way in her shoes, to be honest. She said, "If that woman got in once, she might have got in a hundred times. I can't live here knowing she's violated my space. She might have slept in my bed, spent nights here while I've been away." I told her I couldn't deal with it, I was off on holiday, and I'd ask Lorraine to ring her. She was okay with that – she knew Lorraine, from when she bought the house – it was Lorraine that sold it to her. Lorraine went round, took new photos . . .'

'Hold on,' Sam stopped her. 'When I spoke to Lorraine Turner, she said nothing about anyone impersonating Selina Gane and putting her house up for sale without her knowledge.'

'I didn't tell her,' said Jackie. 'Dr Gane asked me not to.'

'She didn't want anyone to know what had happened who didn't need to,' Grint told Sam. 'She found it distressing and embarrassing, didn't want people asking her about it.'

Sam was still thinking about Lorraine Turner, whose relationship with 11 Bentley Grove went further back than Selina's, Jackie's, Connie's. Lorraine had sold 11 Bentley Grove to Selina on behalf of the Christmas tree couple, Mr and Mrs Beater. Did she also sell the house *to* the Beaters, when it was first built, or had the developers done that themselves?

'I told Lorraine she'd have to meet Dr Gane at Addenbrooke's or at her hotel to collect the key,' Jackie went on. 'I was thinking, "Don't bother asking her to meet you at Bentley Grove – she won't go near the place." She said to me she wasn't going back to that house ever again.'

Grint was moving towards the door of the interview room. 'Let's go and meet Selina Gane's stalker, shall we?' he said. Jackie rose to her feet. A more sensitive person might have been nervous, Sam thought; he certainly was. He tried to imagine Connie Bowskill admitting it, and couldn't. Couldn't imagine her denying it either – how could she, if Jackie pointed the finger in no uncertain terms? As Connie had said herself, it was difficult to maintain a state of denial when what you were trying to deny was laid out before you and you were forced to confront it head-on.

If it was *denial*. It occurred to Sam that Connie might be cannier than she seemed. How good an actress was she? Her painful-to-watch attack on her husband had been inconsistent, lurching from one accusation to another; Sam had put this down to confusion and panic at the time, but now he wasn't so sure. At first Connie had seemed convinced that Kit thought she was a killer, and terrified that he might be right. She'd wanted Grint to say that for her to have killed a woman and then repressed the memory was impossible – she'd virtually put the words in his mouth. Then she'd changed tack: Kit didn't really think she'd killed anybody, but he wanted her to think that was what he believed – wanted to plant in her mind the fear that she might have committed a murder of which she now had no memory.

Listening, Sam had wondered how she could harbour these two suspicions simultaneously. He'd concluded that she was most afraid of not being in control of her own behaviour; she preferred to think that her husband was a monster.

After talking to Jackie Napier, Sam had a different theory. It was no accident that he'd been left wondering which of the two it was: Kit the liar, Kit the killer, messing with his wife's head in the hope that he could make her collude in his framing of her for a crime she didn't commit – or Connie the unfortunate victim of a mental breakdown whose psychological disintegration was so severe that she couldn't be held responsible for her actions. It was no accident that a choice had been set up between these two possibilities and no other. Sam's attention, and Grint's, had been skilfully diverted away from a third possibility: that Connie had knowingly and deliberately killed a woman. That the anguished on-the-edge persona she presented to the world was a carefully constructed lie.

Sam was torn. Part of him would have liked to take Grint to one side and ask him what was happening on the forensic front, what Selina Gane had said when Grint had interviewed her, as Sam assumed he must have. He'd have liked to know if the former owners of the house, Mr and Mrs Beater, had identified the stain on the carpet as being the same one made by their Christmas tree, or if Grint was content to take Lorraine Turner's word for it. Sam wouldn't have been; a couple of times he'd opened his mouth to tell Grint as much, then changed his mind. Not his patch, not his problem.

It was time to extricate himself and return to his own far duller caseload. The more he discussed 11 Bentley Grove's disappearing dead woman with Grint, the deeper he'd be drawn in. Interviewing Jackie Napier had been a step too far; he should have refused. *Why didn't you, then?* his wife Kate would say – the most pointless question ever to be formulated, and one Kate asked regularly.

I didn't because I didn't.

As he followed Grint and Jackie up a narrow flight of grey stairs, Sam admitted to himself that he had no choice but to put Grint in touch with Simon, who, if nothing else, would be able to confirm that Connie had told the truth about the conversations she'd had with him. Simon would have formed an impression of her character, positive or negative. He wouldn't be afraid to take a position, or several: reliable or dishonest, crazy or sane, victim or victim-maker. *Good or evil.* Simon dealt in larger concepts than Sam felt comfortable with, and trusted his own judgement; he was the help Grint needed. *Someone who didn't constantly equivocate.* It often seemed to

Sam that, while most people's minds were like manifestos, foregrounding their beliefs and commitments, his own was more of a suggestion box, with every side of every argument stuffed into it, all clamouring for attention, each demanding equal consideration; Sam's only role was to sort through the competing claims as impartially as possible. Maybe that was why he felt tired nearly all the time.

He'd have to contact Simon in Spain and warn him that Grint would be in touch; it was only fair. *Great.* Offhand, Sam couldn't think of anything he wanted to do less than interrupt a honeymoon, especially not one that belonged to Charlie Zailer. Charlie wasn't known for her forgiving nature.

Sam got a shock when Grint opened the interview room door and he saw the Bowskills. Both seemed out of breath. Connie looked as if she'd been crying non-stop for the whole time she'd been alone with her husband. There were grey streaks on her trousers that hadn't been there before. What the hell had happened? An unpleasant, sour smell hung in the air, one Sam could neither describe to himself, nor match to anything he'd smelled before.

'Sam?' Connie's voice was thick. Her eyes were on Jackie Napier, but there was nothing to suggest she recognised her. 'What's going on? Is this the woman who saw what I saw?'

If she's lying, Sam thought, then by now the lie is as necessary for her survival as her heart and lungs are; she'll cling to it no matter what, because she can't envisage a life without it. Most of the liars Sam's work brought him into contact with favoured the disposable variety – they'd put a story together and trot it out in the hope that it might net them a lighter sentence, but they knew they were talking rubbish; that was how they defined it to themselves. They weren't emotionally attached to their invented scenarios; when you pointed out to them that you could prove they weren't where they said they were at a particular time, they normally shrugged and said, 'Worth a try, wasn't it?'

Sam steeled himself for confrontation. He sensed a powerful latent aggression in Jackie Napier, always on the lookout for a legitimate outlet. That she would lay into Connie Bowskill, verbally if not physically, seemed beyond doubt. So why the delay? Why was she staring at the Bowskills, saying nothing?

Jackie turned to Grint, her mouth a knot of impatience. 'Who's *this*?' She gestured towards Connie.

Grint took a second or two to answer. 'This isn't the woman who showed you Selina Gane's passport?'

'I did *what*?' said Connie.

'What the fuck are you talking about?' Kit turned to Sam. 'What does he mean?'

'No,' Jackie Napier said irritably. 'I don't know where you got her from, but you can put her back. I've never seen her before in my life.'

POLICE EXHIBIT REF: CB13345/432/24IG

CAVENDISH LODGE PRIMARY SCHOOL

Date: 13.07.06 **Name:** Riordan Gilpatrick

Form: Lower Kindergarten
Average Age: 3 years 4 months
Age: 3 years 8 months

COMMUNICATIONS, LANGUAGE, LITERACY

Riordan has made good progress this year with language. Always clear and fluent in his speech, he has good recall and enjoys story time. He recognises all the Letterland characters and their sounds and is now building words from their individual sounds.

MATHEMATICAL DEVELOPMENT

Riordan recognises numbers up to 9 and counts to 18. He can complete a 6-piece jigsaw, recognise colours and geometric shapes and sort for colour and size. Riordan enjoys playing number games and joining in songs.

KNOWLEDGE AND UNDERSTANDING OF THE WORLD

Riordan shows interest in the world about him and likes to join in the discussions we have. He enjoys planting seeds and bulbs, baking, looking at the day's weather for our weather chart and learning about topics such as Farms, Life Cycles and 'People Who Help Us'.

PHYSICAL DEVELOPMENT

Riordan's fine motor skills are excellent. He draws some lovely pictures and handles pencil or paintbrush with skill. He can thread beads and use scissors and he traces his letters carefully. Gross motor skills are also very good: he runs and jumps, enjoys pushing the prams, and likes to join in playground games.

CREATIVE DEVELOPMENT

Riordan just loves to dress up and role play in the Home Corner with his friends! He also likes to use his imagination with the small world toys. He is always eager to sit at our creative table and paint, draw lovely detailed pictures or make collages.

PERSONAL, SOCIAL AND EMOTIONAL DEVELOPMENT

Riordan has settled well into his first year at school and made lots of friends. He socialises well and is caring towards his friends. He is a pleasure to have in the class: we shall miss him when he moves up to Kindergarten next year! I am sure he will enjoy being in Kindergarten. Well done, Riordan!

Form Teacher: Teresa Allsopp

15

Friday 23 July 2010

'Nothing?' Mum looks at Dad with a plea in her eyes, as if she expects him to spring into action to correct the injustice. 'What do you mean, they're doing nothing?'

Kit and I are prepared. We knew the reaction we'd get. We foresaw the horrified gasp, the quiver of outrage in the voice. We predicted Dad's reaction too, which we've not had yet, but we're fully covered on that front, because we prophesied the time delay. Mum is the instant responder of the two of them, spewing out her panic in gusts of self-righteous accusation. It will be ten minutes – fifteen at the outside – before Dad contributes anything to the discussion. Until then, he will sit with his head bent forward and his hands laced together, trying to come to terms with yet more unwelcome evidence that life does not always behave in the way Val and Geoff Monk believe it ought to.

Anton will continue to lie across my living room rug, propped up on one arm, talking mainly to Benji about their current favourite subject: a collection of fictional aliens called things like Humungosaur and Echo-Echo. Fran's a multitasker; while making sure Benji doesn't demolish Melrose Cottage, she will aim regular half-grumpy, half-jokey criticisms at Mum and Dad as a way of shielding them from the larger, more devastating criticism they deserve.

In the company of my family, Kit and I are psychics who never get it wrong. The predictability of the Monks ought to be a welcome relief after everything we've been through. Predictably, it isn't.

'From what we can gather, there's a disagreement internally,' Kit tells Mum. No one would guess from listening to him how miserable and lost he feels. Whenever my parents are around, he plays the role of their brilliant, strong, capable son-in-law; he told me once that he enjoys it – it's the person he'd like to be. 'Ian Grint doesn't want to let it go, but he's being leaned on. Heavily, or that's the impression we're getting from Sam Kombothekra.'

'But Connie saw that . . . that terrible thing! Another woman saw it too. How can the police just go on as if nothing's happened? There must be something they can do.' Anyone listening who wasn't an expert on the way Mum's mind works might think she had forgotten that she didn't believe me at first. That's what most people would do: say one thing, then, when they were proved wrong, say another and choose to forget that at one time they were on the wrong side. Not Val Monk; no ordinary ego-preserving self-deception for her. She explained to me and Kit on Tuesday night, when we were too exhausted from our day with Grint to argue with her, that she had nothing to rebuke herself for: she was right not to have believed me at first because nobody knew about Jackie Napier at that stage, and, without her corroboration, what I was saying couldn't possibly have been true. Later, once we were alone, Kit said to me, 'So, to summarise your mum's position: she was as right not to believe you then as she is right to believe you now. Even though if it's true now, it must have been true then as well.' We laughed about it – actually laughed – and I thought how strange it was that in the middle of all the misery and uncertainty and fear, after a day spent being questioned by detectives who didn't like or trust either of us, Kit and I were still able to glean some comfort from our old favourite hobby of ripping my mum to pieces.

'It's the lack of forensic evidence that's the problem,' Kit explains to her now. 'They've gone over every inch of 11 Bentley Grove, taken up the carpets, the floorboards – essentially, they dismantled the house and sent the various parts off for analysis, and they found nothing. Well, no, they found more than nothing,' Kit corrects himself. 'They found nothing in a way that means something.'

'Twenty billion's more than nothing, isn't it, Daddy?' Benji asks Anton, tapping him on the leg with a grey plastic alien toy.

'Anything's more than nothing, mate.' If things were normal between Kit and me, I would look at him now and send a silent message: *Could this be the most profound thing Anton's ever said?*

'Sam told us there are two different kinds of non-result, in forensic terms,' Kit goes on. 'The conclusive and the inconclusive.'

Still with us, Anton?

'What's that supposed to mean?' Mum says impatiently.

'You can find nothing at the site of a possible crime and still not know if a crime's been committed there or not. Or, as in this case, you can find no forensic evidence and say beyond doubt that a particular crime *wasn't* committed there. Sam says there's no way there could have been the amount of blood in that house that both Connie and Jackie Napier saw without it leaving forensic . . . detritus behind. Since it didn't . . .' Kit shrugs. 'The police have nothing to work with. Forensically, they have to conclude no one was killed there. They've got one estate agent and two former owners of the house swearing blind that the carpet in the lounge now is the same one that's been there for years, since before the present owner moved in. They've spoken to the neighbours, who told them not much, apart from that Bentley Grove's a lovely quiet street. No known missing persons fit the description Connie and Jackie Napier gave them, and there's no body. What can they do?'

'They're the police,' says Mum, tight-lipped. 'There must be something – an angle they haven't thought of, something else they can pursue.'

'Kit's trying to explain to you that there isn't,' Fran tells her. I wonder if it bothers her that she's sticking up for a man she believes to be a liar with a secret life. She hasn't said anything about the conversation we had on Monday – not to Mum and Dad, not to Anton. They don't know about the address in Kit's SatNav, or his car on Street View. I didn't ask her not to tell anyone; it's her choice that we should all keep playing Happy Snappy Families. She's playing her role as willingly as Kit's playing his.

And you, Connie? Why don't you say something? Why don't you tell everyone your husband might be a murderer?

'Ian Grint's no fool, Val,' Kit tries to soothe Mum. 'He knows Connie and this Jackie person are telling the truth. Sam thinks his bosses know it too, but look at it from their point of view. If a murder *has* been committed, they've got no body, no suspects, no evidence apart from two witness statements and no way to take it forward. Completely hamstrung, aren't they? It's not so bad for Grint – he's only a DC, the buck doesn't stop with him. His DI's the one who's got everything to gain by saying, "This isn't a crime, it might just be a prank – let's assume it is, and forget all about it." '

'A *prank*?' Mum appeals to Dad again. 'Did you hear that, Geoff? Killing someone is a joke, now, is it? Leaving them bleeding on a carpet . . .'

'Mum, for God's sake.' Fran makes a face that suggests mental impairment. 'Kit's saying that the police think there *was* no killing – the prank was getting someone to lie down in a load of red paint, or tomato ketchup . . .'

'I know the difference between blood and paint,' I say.

'What sort of prank is that?' Mum demands. 'It's not very funny, is it? What woman in her right mind would ruin a lovely dress by lying in paint?'

'Sam and Grint both think the prank theory's as daft as we all think it is,' says Kit. 'Someone higher up the Cambridge police ladder suggested it when they found out that whoever hacked into the website and changed the virtual tour changed it back again half an hour later. I don't really understand why that's significant, and I'm not sure Sam and Ian Grint do either, but there's not a lot any of us can do. The decision's been made.'

'And you're just going to sit back and do nothing?' Mum stares at me in horror. 'Pretend it never happened? What about your responsibility to that poor woman, whoever she is?'

'What can Connie do?' Kit asks.

'I could apply for a job as Chief Constable of Cambridgeshire police,' I suggest.

'Where's the cake, Daddy?' Benji asks Anton. 'When are we going to give Connie her presents?'

I have no idea what he's talking about. Then I remember that this is supposed to be my birthday party. Today is my birthday. Like all Monk family celebrations, it began at 5.45 p.m. and will finish at 7.15 p.m., so that Benji can be in bed by 8.

'First thing Monday morning, Kit, you phone the police,' says Dad. *Welcome to the conversation.* 'You tell them you think it's a disgrace – you want answers and you want them now. You want to know what they're planning to do, and they'd damn well better be planning to do something.'

'That's right.' Mum nods her support.

'If they mess you around, you threaten to go to the press. If they still don't pull their finger out, you put your money where your mouth is. The minute it hits the local papers, the minute Cambridge residents know about this and start to panic, there'll be nowhere for DC Ian Grint and his chums to hide.'

'Dad, *what* are you talking about?' Fran laughs. 'Local residents won't start to panic. You make it sound as if there's a maniac on a killing spree, roaming the streets of Cambridge. Would you panic, if you heard that someone had been killed in Little Holling, if you had no reason to think *you* were in danger?'

'That would never happen,' Mum says. 'That's why we live in Little Holling – because it's safe and no one's likely to murder us in our homes.'

'Cambridge isn't exactly Rwanda, is it, and someone seems to have been murdered there,' Fran fires back at her.

'Cambridge is a city, with . . . people from all over the place living in it. No one knows anyone in a city, there's no sense of community. Nothing like what Connie saw would happen here, and if it did, the police would investigate it properly.'

'Define "here".' Fran looks to me for support. I look away. I can't risk getting into any kind of argument with Mum, in case I get carried away and accidentally mention that if ever a murder is committed in Little Holling, it will very likely be of her, by me. 'Cambridge isn't that far away. I'm sure it's got quite a low murder rate, because people who live there are generally quite intelligent and have better things to do than kill each other. Whereas in the Culver Valley . . .'

'The Culver Valley's one of the safest places in England,' Dad says.

'Are you kidding me? Anton, tell him! Don't you two *read* the local papers? In Spilling and Silsford in the last few years, there have been . . .' Fran stops. Benji is tugging at her arm. 'Yes, darling? What?'

'What's a murder? Is it when someone dies, when they're a hundred?'

'Now look what you've done!' Mum wails at Fran. 'Poor little Benji. It's nothing for you to worry about, angel. We all go to heaven when we die and it's lovely in heaven – isn't it, Grandad?'

'*Angel?*' Fran looks ready to pounce. I don't think I've seen her this angry before. 'We're on earth at the moment, Mother, not in heaven, and his name's Benji.'

'First thing Monday morning, Kit.' Dad wags his finger. 'You let that DC Ian Grint have it right between the eyes.'

I have to get away from them all. I mumble something about tea and cake, and force myself to leave the room at a normal pace, instead of running, which is what I want to do. In the kitchen, I close the door and lean against it. How long can I get away with staying in here? For ever?

The sound of knocking interrupts my fantasy. *Kit.* It must be – I can hear Mum, Dad and Fran still arguing in the lounge. I don't want to let him in, but as his co-conspirator I have no choice. He might have something important to say about the maintenance of the lie that we're presenting to my family this afternoon: our fake happy marriage.

'You okay?' he asks me.

'No. You?'

'Just about staying afloat. Let's get on with the tea and cake, and then maybe we can get rid of them early.'

'They'll leave at exactly seven fifteen, whatever we do or don't do,' I say. Kit ought to know better than to hope something different might happen. 'Dad and Anton'll go straight to the pub for their Friday night pint, and Mum'll be busy for at least half an hour helping Fran put Benji to bed. I'll drive you to the station at seven twenty-five – that way I can be back by the time they all resurface. If any of them bothers looking, they'll see both our cars and assume we're both here.'

Kit nods. I fill the kettle and switch it on, take the shop-bought birthday cake out of the bread bin. I chose the most expensive one in the supermarket, as if that could make up for anything. I load cups, saucers and teaspoons onto a tray, fill the milk jug with milk, scrape the discoloured granules off the surface of the sugar so that Mum won't recoil when she looks into the bowl. Last but not least, a plastic lidded beaker full of apple juice for Benji, the only five-year-old in the world who still drinks out of a baby cup.

Kit's pulling clean cake plates out of the dishwasher. 'Tomorrow I'll spend the day at Mum and Dad's,' I tell him. He holds out a large serrated knife for me to take. 'If I'm there, none of them will come here. I'll tell them you're at home working.'

'This is insane, Con. Why can't we tell them the truth? Our current project's coming to a head in London, I'm needed there full-time, so I've decided to stay at the flat for the foreseeable future.'

I take the knife from him. 'That isn't the truth, Kit.'

'You know what I mean,' he says impatiently, as if I'm splitting hairs. 'Not the *truth* truth, but . . . can't we tell them something closer to it, so that we don't have to pretend I'm living here when I'm not?' I watch him make up his mind to say more, and know what's coming. 'Or we could make our lie true: you could let me move back in.'

'Don't.' I push him away, not daring to meet his eyes in case it's obvious from mine how much I miss him. He moved out on Wednesday. For the last two nights I've lain awake crying, unable to sleep, using all my willpower to stop myself from ringing him and begging him to come home. I thought of myself as a good person until all this happened, but I understand now that I'm not. I could so easily lose my grip on what's right, turn to Kit and say, 'You know what? I don't care if you've been seeing someone behind my back. I don't care if you're a liar or even a killer – I'm going to love you and stay with you anyway, because the alternative is too soul-destroying and too much effort.'

'We're going to have to do it, aren't we?' Kit closes his eyes. 'The full performance: sing happy birthday, open presents, blow out candles, "For she's a jolly good fellow", hugs and kisses all round . . .' I see the shudder pass through his body.

'Of course we are. Isn't that what's happened every year since you've known me? My family don't know this year's any different.'

'Connie, we've got a choice.' He moves towards me. I ought to stop him. 'We can put all this behind us, go back to how we were. Imagine neither of us had a past, imagine today was the first day of our lives.'

'We wouldn't be married. We'd be strangers.' If I don't turn myself against him quickly, I might never be able to. 'I agree, that might be preferable,' I say. 'At the moment we're strangers who *are* married.'

'What are you two up to?' Mum throws open the kitchen door without bothering to knock. 'What are you talking about? Not the police still, I hope. This is supposed to be a celebration. Geoff's right, Kit – you'll ring this Ian Grint fellow on Monday, and it'll all be sorted out one way or the other.'

'I'm sure it will,' Kit says expressionlessly.

One way or the other. Which two ways does she have in mind? I wonder. Scientists could kidnap my mother and replace her with a robot that looked exactly like her, and no one would notice as long as they made sure to programme enough clichés into the machine's vocabulary: *one way or the other, now look what you've done, what's that supposed to mean?*

I do the only thing that might make the rest of this so-called party bearable: I go back to the lounge and start a conversation with Anton about fitness. I tell him I'm fed up of being skinny, ask what I can do to build up muscle tone without ending up looking like an action woman with hard bulgy arms. I don't listen to his answer, but thankfully it's long and detailed, and saves me having to talk to anyone else. Dad and Fran argue on the other side of the room about whether anybody who moves to a city is signalling his or her willingness to be viciously assaulted on a regular basis, and Benji throws plastic aliens up in the air, trying to hit the ceiling and often succeeding.

Between them, Mum and Kit arrange my presents in a heap on the rug – another Monk family ritual performed on all gift-worthy occasions. Everyone takes their turn to pick a present out of the pile and hand it to its recipient. The picking must be done in order of age: Benji, Fran, me, Anton, Kit, Mum, Dad, then back to Benji again if there are still more parcels to be distributed. The system is not without its flaws: when it's my birthday and my turn to pick, obviously I know that I'll end up giving whichever present I select to myself. For years, Dad has been lobbying for change: if the occasion is a birthday rather than Christmas, the person whose birthday it is should be excluded from the picking. Mum is violently opposed to a reform along these lines, and has so far succeeded in blocking it.

The whole pantomime makes me want to shoot myself in the head.

This year, Benji has bought me a lavender bag in the shape of a heart. I give him a thank you cuddle and he tries to wriggle free. 'When people die, when they're a hundred, their hearts stop beating,' he says. 'Don't they, Daddy?'

Mum and Dad give me what they always give me – and Fran, Kit and Anton – and have done ever since we've had homes of our own, for our birthdays, Christmas and Easter: a Monk & Sons voucher for £100. I plaster a smile to my face, kiss them both, feign gratitude.

Kit's parents used to be good at presents. I assume they still are, even if they no longer buy them for us. I always loved the things they gave me: spa day vouchers, tickets to the opera, membership of wine and chocolate clubs. Kit was never impressed. 'Anyone can buy stuff like that,' he said. 'They're corporate client gifts, from people with plenty of money who don't care.' Even before he cut his parents off, he didn't seem to like them much. I couldn't understand it. 'I'd give anything to have parents who were normal, interesting people,' I told him, impressed by the way that Nigel and Barbara Bowskill, who lived in Bracknell, often drove into London to go to the theatre or to an art exhibition.

When Simon Waterhouse asked me why Kit had disowned his mum and dad, I told him what Kit had told me: that in

2003, when I was having my mini nervous breakdown at the prospect of leaving Little Holling, when my hair was falling out and my face was paralysed and I was vomiting all the time, Kit's parents had told him that he was on his own with his problems and could expect no help or support from them – they were too busy setting up their new business.

I couldn't imagine either Nigel or Barbara being so uncaring, but when I said that to Kit, he snapped at me that I hadn't been there and he had, and I'd have to take his word for it: his parents didn't give a toss about me, or about him, so why bother having anything further to do with them?

I thought I'd given Simon an answer to his question, but he looked dissatisfied. He asked me if there was anything else I could tell him, anything at all, on the subject of Kit and his parents. I said there wasn't. It was true, strictly speaking. What would have been the point of saying that I'd always wondered if Kit deliberately misinterpreted or magnified something more innocuous that Nigel and Barbara had said, wanting an excuse to cut them out of his life? I decided it was probably unfair of me to suspect him of framing them in this way, so I said nothing about it to Simon.

'Go on, Connie – everyone's waiting.' Mum's voice drags me back to the party I'd rather not be part of. There's a parcel in my lap, wrapped in 'Happy Birthday' paper: my present from Kit. Only he, Fran and I know that I've seen it before, that it contains a Chongololo carrier bag. All three of us are thinking about me nearly spoiling Kit's thoughtful birthday surprise – or at least I am. *Me in the doorway, Kit hovering over the scissors and the Sellotape, trying to look as if he isn't hurt by my lack of trust.* I see it like a still from a film that means nothing to me; I feel no remorse, no regret. Guilt gets boring after a while; you end up deciding it must be someone else's fault, not yours.

I don't want this present, whatever it is, but I must pretend I do. Mum claps her hands together and says, 'Ooh, I can't wait to see it! Kit's got such good taste!' I make fake enthusiastic noises as I tear off the paper, thinking that at some point I will have to tell Mum and Dad that Kit has moved out, that I could save myself weeks or months of lying by telling them now. Why don't I? Am I naïve enough to hope, in spite of everything, that the trouble between us will blow over?

What did Kit say? *We could make our lie true.*

I drop the wrapping paper on the floor, open the Chongololo bag and pull out a blue dress.

'Hold it up,' says Mum. 'We all want to see it, don't we, Geoff?'

'Dad wouldn't know a Chongololo dress from a watering can, Mum,' says Fran.

And he never answers you when you ask him a direct question. Haven't you noticed, in all the years you've been married to him? He speaks to you only when it suits him, not in response to any need of yours.

I stand up, shake out the dress so that Mum can see it. It isn't only blue, there's pink in it too. A pattern. Wavy lines.

Wavy lines, short fluted sleeves . . .

No. No, no, no.

Darkness creeps in from the edges of my vision, towards the centre. 'Are you okay, Con?' I hear Fran say.

'What's wrong, Connie?' Mum's voice distorts on its way to me. By the time they reach me the words are stretched out and twisting, like the lines on the dress.

I have to do something to push away the dizziness. So far,

I haven't had an attack in front of Mum, and I can't allow it to happen now. In 2003, in a moment of weakness, I confessed to her about my hair loss and vomiting, the facial paralysis. I never told anyone, not even Kit, but I found it frightening the way she latched on to my new invalid status. It gave her a story to tell herself, one she liked: I made myself ill by pretending I wanted to move to Cambridge when, deep down, I didn't – I was only saying I did to please Kit. Now I was suffering for my stupidity, and she was going to nurse me back to health. The moral of the story? No member of the Monk family must ever think about leaving Little Holling.

'Connie?' Through the haze, I hear Kit say my name, but there's no connection between my brain and my voice, so I can't answer.

Don't give in to the greyness. Keep thinking. Grasp a thought and focus all your energy on it, before it dissolves and leaves you floating in darkness. You didn't tell Kit because you didn't want to admit it to yourself, did you? It's one thing to bitch about your mother being a paranoid control freak, quite another to say . . . Go on, say it. It's the truth, isn't it? You know it is. She was glad you were ill; she thought you deserved it.

She'd rather you were sick than free.

The clouds in my head start to clear. When my vision returns to normal, I see that Fran and Kit are both poised to spring out of their chairs and catch me, but they needn't worry. The dizziness has gone, and it won't be back. Nor will my lies, any of them – not the ones I tell myself, and not the ones I tell other people. I'm sick of poisoning myself with dishonesty.

I throw the dress at Kit. 'This is the dress the dead woman was wearing,' I say.

Mum, Dad and Fran all start to protest loudly. I hear

'... blue and pink ... ridiculous ... strain of all this police ... can't be ...'

'It's the dress she was wearing,' I repeat, keeping my eyes on Kit. 'You know it is. That's why you bought it for me – part of your plan to destroy me.' Mum makes the sort of noise a horse under attack might make. I ignore her. 'I'm supposed to go properly mad now, am I?' I spit the words at Kit. 'Fall apart? Because you can't possibly have bought me the same dress for my birthday that a murdered woman was wearing in a picture I saw on Roundthehouses, so I must be insane, I must be losing it – is that about right?'

'Why's Auntie Connie upset, Daddy?' Benji asks.

'Connie, think about what you're saying.' Kit's face is pale. With his eyes, he gestures towards Mum as if to say, *Do you really want to do this in front of her?*

I couldn't care less any more. I'll say what I have to say, whoever happens to be listening, whether it's Mum, Dad, the Pope or the Queen of England.

'You said the dress you saw was green and mauve.' Kit's eyes are on me, but his words aren't for my benefit; he wants our audience to hear that he has proof of my inconsistency, and therefore my madness. 'This dress is blue and pink.'

'You *did* say green and lilac, Con,' Fran weighs in on his side.

I pick up my bag. As I leave the room, Mum calls after me, 'I don't know what you think you'll achieve by running away!'

I've already achieved it. I'm gone.

~

'The design was exactly the same,' I tell Alice. 'There must have been a green and lilac version and a blue and pink version.'

It's my second emergency appointment in less than a week. Last time, I was worried in case she minded my imposing on her. Today, when I turned up as she was about to leave work for the day, I didn't apologise or give her a choice. I told her she had to see me.

'The woman who was murdered at 11 Bentley Grove was wearing a dress from a small, independent boutique that makes all its own clothes and has only one branch – in Silsford.' I pause to allow the significance of this to impress itself on Alice.

'Let's zoom out a little.' She makes the shape of a camera with her hands, pulls them back towards her body. 'Leaving the dress aside for a moment . . .'

'Even Fran believes Kit, and she thinks he's a liar,' I blurt out. 'She told me the other day that any doctor who said there was nothing wrong with me can't have been looking very hard.'

'Forget Fran,' says Alice. 'I want us to talk about you and Kit. Nobody else is important. You say Kit's trying to make you doubt your own sanity. Why would he do that?'

I open my mouth, then find I have nothing to say, no answer. I play it all back in my head: finding the address in the SatNav, Kit denying all knowledge of it; the virtual tour of 11 Bentley Grove, the woman's body, the police, Jackie Napier seeing the body too; Fran looking on Street View and spotting Kit's car; me unwrapping my birthday present from Kit and finding that dress.

I recognise nearly all the characters in the story: guarded, intelligent Simon Waterhouse; kind and modest Sam Kombothekra; practical, insensitive Fran; Selina Gane, angry and frightened. I can even find adjectives for Jackie Napier, whom I saw for only five minutes: sanctimonious, superior, charmless. And the dead woman on the carpet: she was dead, drained of blood, still. Those were her defining characteristics. There's only one person I can't bring into focus, however hard I try.

'Connie?' Alice prompts me.

'I have no idea who or what Kit is,' I say eventually. 'It's as if he isn't a person at all, just a . . . an image, or a hologram. A collection of behaviours.'

'You mean you don't trust him.'

'No.' It's hard to describe something that's missing. An absence only has a clear shape when it was once a presence, when you know what's gone. 'I don't trust him, but that's not what I'm saying. When I'm with him, I don't sense a . . . a person there, under the skin.' I shrug. 'I can't explain it any better than that, but . . . this isn't new. It didn't start with me finding 11 Bentley Grove in his SatNav. I've known it for years, I just haven't allowed myself to admit it.'

Alice is waiting for me to say more.

'When Kit was a student in Cambridge, he fell in love with someone. He sort of let it slip, but when I asked him about it he clammed up and denied it. He's always resented his parents, but would never tell me why. He pretended he didn't, but I could see that he did – I heard it in his voice whenever he spoke to them. Then he disowned them altogether, and I'm pretty sure he lied about the real reason.'

'And then came the SatNav, his car on Street View, the woman's body, the dress,' says Alice. She twists her swivel chair round to face the window. 'Connie, I wouldn't normally say something like this to a patient, but I'm going to say it to you: I think you're right not to trust Kit. I have no idea what he's done, but I think you need to stay away from him.'

'I can't. Selina Gane won't speak to me, and the police have said they aren't taking it any further. The only way I'll find out what's going on is if I can persuade Kit to tell me the truth. What?'

Is that pity in her eyes?

'You don't think I'll ever find out, do you? You think I should give up.'

'I know you're not going to.' She smiles at me. 'I wouldn't either, if I were you.'

'Before all this happened, I was like Kit,' I tell her. 'I wasn't real either. Now I have a characteristic: I'm the woman who won't give up.'

'You weren't real?'

I'm not sure it's something I can explain, but I have to try, however crazy it sounds. 'In 2003, when Kit and I were looking at houses in Cambridge, I felt . . . non-existent.'

Alice waits for me to elaborate.

'Most people have a type of house they prefer: townhouse in the centre of a city, stone cottage in the middle of nowhere. Some people always buy new-builds, some would only ever consider a house that's more than a hundred years old. The house you choose says something about the sort of person you are. When Kit took me to see a cottage in a village called Lode, just outside Cambridge, I thought, "Yes, I could be a rural cottage sort of person." Then he took me to a penthouse flat on a main road in the city centre, and I thought, "This could be me – maybe I'm a townie at heart." I didn't know myself at all, or what I wanted. After three or four viewings, I started to panic that I didn't have an identity. I was transparent – I saw through myself and there was nothing there. I thought, "I could live in any of these places. I can't say about any of them that they're 'me' or 'not me'. Maybe I don't have a personality." '

Alice leans back in her chair. It creaks. 'You were open-minded. Kit took you to see lots of beautiful houses, and you liked them all in different ways. Perfectly understandable, and nothing to worry about. Perhaps each house spoke to a different aspect of your character.'

'No.' I wave away her reassuring words. 'Yes, it was silly of me to panic about not knowing what sort of house I wanted, of course it was, but I *did* panic – that's what's worrying. Each time I saw a house and wasn't instantly sure if it was "me", I felt more and more unreal. As if any self that I might once have had was draining away, drop by drop.' I chew on my thumbnail, afraid that I'm admitting too much and will somehow be made to suffer for it. 'And then we found this amazing house, 17 Pardoner Lane – the best of the bunch by far, I can see that now – and I was in such a state, I had no idea whether I loved it or hated it. Kit adored it. I pretended to – don't know how convincing I was. I felt like I was falling apart. All I wanted was to be able to say, "Yes, this house is absolutely me" and . . . know what that *meant*.'

Alice bends down, reaches into the open brown suitcase under her desk. It's where she keeps her remedies; the inside of the case is divided into tiny square compartments, each one containing a small brown glass bottle. 'You were anxious and depressed, overwhelmed by your family's unreasonable expectations,' she says, picking up one bottle, then another, reading the labels. 'That sense of your self diminishing came from trying to stifle your own needs for your parents' sake, because they found them inconvenient. It had nothing to do with being flexible about what sort of house you wanted to buy, I promise you.' She has found the remedy she was looking for. *For extra, extra mad people*.

I want to say more about the house I should have fallen in

love with, but was too neurotic to see clearly. I need to confess to all of it: how I set out to ruin things, chipped away at Kit's conviction with my paranoia. '17 Pardoner Lane was next to a school building – the Beth Dutton Centre,' I tell Alice. 'I lost sleep – whole nights – over the bell. How ridiculous is that?'

'The bell?'

'The school bell. What if it rang between lessons and was too loud? The noise might drive us mad, and we'd never be able to sell up and move on because we'd have to be honest with prospective buyers – we couldn't lie about a thing like that. Kit said, "If the bell's too loud, we'll ask them to turn the volume down." He laughed at me for worrying about something so stupid. He laughed again when I got cold feet a few days later for an equally ridiculous reason: the house had no name.'

'I'm giving you a different remedy this time,' says Alice. 'Anhalonium. Because of what you said about feeling as if you were transparent and having no personality.'

'I'd never lived anywhere that didn't have a name,' I say, not listening to her. 'Still haven't. First I lived at Thorrold House with Mum and Dad, then I moved in with Kit. His flat in Rawndesley was number 10, but the building had a name: Martland Tower. Anyway, that was different. Neither of us thought of the flat as home – it was temporary, a stop-gap. Now I live in Melrose Cottage, Fran and Anton's house is Thatchers . . . In Little Holling, all the houses have names. It's what I'm used to. When Kit was so keen on 17 Pardoner Lane, and I tried to imagine myself living in a house that was just a number, it seemed . . . wrong, somehow. Too impersonal. It scared me.'

Alice is nodding. 'Change is incredibly scary,' she says. She always sticks up for me. I'm not sure it's what I need, not any more. It might do me more good to hear her say, 'Yes, Connie. That's really mad. You need to stop thinking in this crazy way.'

'One night I woke Kit up at four in the morning,' I tell her. 'He was asleep, and I kept shaking him. I think I must have been hysterical. I hadn't slept all night, and I'd worked myself into a state. Kit stared at me as if I was a maniac – I can still remember how shocked he looked. I told him we couldn't buy 17 Pardoner Lane unless we gave it a name – I couldn't live in a house with no name. I wanted us to look on the web, find out if it was possible to give a house a name if it didn't have one already. You know, officially.'

Alice smiles, as if there is something understandable or endearing about my insanity.

'Kit saw I wasn't going to calm down or let him get any sleep until he'd come up with a solution to the problem I'd invented, so he said, "Come on, then – let's go and investigate." He soon found enough on the internet to convince me there was no need to worry: we could give number 17 a name if we wanted to. It's easy – all you have to do is write to the Post Office. He said, "How about The Nuthouse?" '

'You must have been hurt,' says Alice.

'Not at all. I started laughing – thought it was the best joke I'd ever heard. I was so relieved that everything was going to be okay – Kit would get the house he loved, and I'd be able to make it feel like home by naming it. Course, on one level I must have known I'd now have to come up with some other obstacle . . .' I shake my head in disgust. 'I wonder what it would have been: that I didn't like the doorknob, or the letter-box. My hysteria would have attached itself to some other random thing, given half a chance, but I didn't see that then. Kit was relieved too. We were almost . . . I don't know, it was like we were celebrating. We didn't go straight back to bed – we stayed up looking at house name websites on the internet, laughing at the ridiculous suggestions: Costa Fortuna, Wits End. Apparently names like that are really popular – that's what the website said. I found it hard to believe, but Kit said he could imagine some of his colleagues calling their houses things like that. "It's a common affliction, thinking you're funny when you're not," he said. "Wits End. Might as well call your house, 'I'm a Dullard'." I asked him what he wanted to call ours.'

'What did he say?'

'Oh, loads of stupid things – things he knew were stupid, to wind me up. I don't think he tried too hard – he knew it wasn't up to him. The name needed to be perfect, and it had to come from me – something that would say "this is home" and make all my anxiety go away. Kit started talking rubbish. "I've got an idea," he said. "Let's call it the Death Button Centre. Do you think the people at the Beth Dutton Centre'd be pissed off? Or the postman?" I told him not to be ridiculous. Should've known that'd only make him worse.' The memory, absent from my mind for so many years, is suddenly more vivid than reality. I can see myself clearly, sitting at the desk in the Martland Tower flat, Kit kneeling down beside me, both of us in our pyjamas. We only had one computer chair in those days. I was howling with laughter, so loud I could hardly hear Kit's voice, tears pouring down my face. 'He pretended he was deadly serious, said, "It's growing on me the more I think about it: the Death Button Centre. We could get a plaque made for the front door. No, I know, even better – let's call it 17 Pardoner Lane . . ." ' The words evaporate in my mouth as new fear surges through my body. *What? What is it?*

The Death Button Centre. The Death Button Centre . . .

I stand up, stumble, steady myself against the wall.

'Connie? What's wrong?'

I know what I saw – the missing detail that I haven't been able to bring to mind until now. *Yes*. It was there. It was definitely there, in the picture with the dead woman and the blood. But not in the photograph of the lounge, the one without the woman, the one I would see if I looked at the tour of 11 Bentley Grove now. In that picture, it's missing. 'I've got to go,' I tell Alice. I grab my bag and run, ignoring her pleas for me to stay, leaving behind the bottle of remedy she has prepared for me that's standing on the corner of her desk.

POLICE EXHIBIT REF: CB13345/432/25IG

VOLCANO

by Tilly Gilpatrick, 20 April 2010

Very hot lava
Over all the land
Like a big hot wet blanket
Covering the world in
Ash
Nobody can fly home from their holiday
Orange hot lava!

Super work, Tilly! Some lovely images!

No, it's an appalling poem, even for a five-year-old.
This is a good poem:

When first my way to fair I took
Few pence in purse had I,
And long I used to stand and look
At things I could not buy.

Now times are altered: if I care
To buy a thing, I can;
The pence are here and here's the fair,
But where's the lost young man?

- To think that two and two are four
And neither five nor three,
The heart of man has long been sore
And long 'tis like to be.

16

23/7/2010

Ian Grint was early. Simon had guessed he might be; he'd sensed the detective's anger within seconds of meeting him, the impatience of a man who needs to prove people wrong, and quickly. Grint headed for the bar, making a pint-lifting gesture at Simon, who nodded. Actually, he hadn't needed as much time as both he and Grint had thought he would. He'd finished reading everything half an hour ago, and had gone for a stroll. The pub Grint had chosen, the Live and Let Live, was in a residential area, so Simon hadn't seen any of the historical college buildings that Charlie had told him he had to see because they were so beautiful, only houses and another small pub: the Six Bells.

Walking around, Simon had drawn the conclusion that Cambridge was a more imaginative place than Spilling. More tolerant too. The front door colours had surprised him: yellow, orange, lilac, pink, bright turquoise. Evidently the inhabitants of Cambridge believed that all shades were eligible for consideration; in Spilling most people opted for something sombre and dignified: black, dark red, dark green. Simon doubted there was a single orange door in the whole of the Culver Valley.

The names of the pubs in Spilling were stodgily traditional: the Brown Cow, the Star, the Wheatsheaf, the Crown. Never in a million years would a Culver Valley landlord choose to call his establishment the Live and Let Live. Live and Carp About Anyone Who Doesn't Live the Way You Live, perhaps – the Live and Carp for short. The Liv and Chris Gibbs, Simon thought surreally – that was one pub Charlie wouldn't be setting foot in.

He moved the papers off the table, put them down on the chair next to him as Grint approached with their pints. 'I hope none of my esteemed colleagues has been in here and spied those over your shoulder,' he said. 'Much as I'd love to get sacked at the moment, I probably ought to try not to. Don't think my wife would appreciate it.' The word 'esteemed' was loaded with sarcasm.

'I'm going to disappoint you,' Simon told him. 'I haven't found much. Nothing you could put in front of your DI and say, "This is a new angle, a way of taking things forward." '

'You've found something, though?'

'Something and nothing. The statements Kit and Connie Bowskill signed – did you take them separately or were they—'

'Separately.' Grint took a swig of his beer, wiped his mouth with the back of his hand. 'The official statements, they were both alone with me. Later I put them in a room together and took them over it all again, brought Sam Kombo in as well. I wanted to see how they changed in each other's company, if at all.'

'Did they?'

'Not in any way you couldn't predict. He looked more uncomfortable when she was there, but so would I have done, in his shoes – she was spitting accusations at him left, right and centre. She was a bit more high-octane in front of him than on her own, but only marginally.'

Simon sorted through the pile of papers, looking for Connie

and Kit Bowskill's official police statements. 'When you interviewed them separately, did you spot anything odd?'

Grint laughed. 'You mean, apart from everything about them?'

'Factual contradictions.'

'Where do you want me to start? He's convinced she must have programmed the address into his SatNav, she says he did it. He reckons she might be a psycho killer, she thinks he's the psycho. They're each ready to suspect the other one of murder on the basis of a picture and not much else – a picture he didn't even see.' Grint shakes his head. 'Bizarre doesn't begin to cover it.'

'There's a smaller point of disagreement between them that might be significant.' Simon passed the two statements to Grint. 'The house they nearly bought in Cambridge in 2003. In Connie Bowskill's statement, she gave the address as 17 Pardoner Lane. In Kit's, it's 18 Pardoner Lane.'

Grint frowned. Stared as Simon pointed out the relevant paragraphs. 'Can't believe I missed it,' he said eventually. 'Still, at a distance of seven years, it's an easy mistake for one of them to have made. I doubt it means anything.'

Simon disagreed. 'They both mention that the house was next to a school called the Beth Dutton Centre. Both go into detail about why this particular house appealed to them: original Victorian fireplaces, original iron railings outside . . .' Simon shrugged. 'Whichever one got it wrong, I can't see why they'd remember all that and not the number of the house.'

'I forget trivial stuff all the time,' said Grint. 'Don't you?'

Simon never forgot anything. He dodged the question. 'Connie Bowskill's phone's going straight to voicemail – I must have tried her fifty times since I got back from Spain. I never spoke to the husband, so I didn't have his number. Your files did, though, so I made use of it.' He waited for Grint to remonstrate with him. When it didn't happen, he volunteered more information. 'He's agreed to meet me this evening at eight.'

'Where?' Grint asked.

Not your business. Simon told himself to stop being a tosser. Grint had a right to know.

'In a pub – the Maypole. I was going to ask you for directions.'

Grint made a dismissive noise. 'The Maypole,' he muttered, as if even the name offended him. 'I won't be coming with you, in that case.'

I didn't ask you to. Simon was better at talking to one person alone than he was in a group, even a small one.

'You can ring me later, tell me if you get anything worthwhile out of him,' said Grint. 'If not, I'm going to have to stop pretending I'm a superhero. I'll make the guv happy by following orders and pretending nothing ever happened – not much else I can do, is there?'

He was disappointed, Simon realised. Sam had talked up Simon's talents, and Grint had expected him to come up with a plan of action, to see something in the files he'd given him that wasn't there to be seen. Simon was the one who had turned out not to be a superhero.

'According to Kit Bowskill, Connie's phone's broken,' he said. 'She threw it into a main road.'

'Yeah, I can see her doing that.' Grint looked at his watch. 'You've got just over an hour to kill. Fancy grabbing a curry? You can tell me your unlikely theories and I'll tell you mine. I've always found it's the shit ideas that lead to the good ones.'

Simon felt uncomfortable eating with people he didn't know well. He and Grint weren't friends. Why did they need to have a meal together? What was the point? 'I wasn't thinking about food,' he said. He was thinking about Pardoner Lane, that it couldn't be too far from where he was now. He had time to find it, see whether the Beth Dutton Centre was next to number 17 or number 18. A small discrepancy, true, but there was no reason to think it wasn't important all the same.

No reason to mention his plans or his thoughts to Ian Grint, either.

~

'Do you remember that night in the Brown Cow a couple of years ago, when you nearly got into a fight?' Olivia asked Gibbs. They were in bed together at the Malmaison hotel in London. They'd tried a few hotels this week, but this one was Olivia's favourite. The walls and floors were dark – reds, browns, purples, black in places; it was like walking into the inside of a human heart. Liv had told Gibbs her theory several times: the hotel must have been decorated with secret passion in mind.

'I've nearly got into lots of fights.'

'This one was with a man who said you'd nicked his mate's chair after he'd said it was taken. You said he'd told you it *wasn't* taken.'

Gibbs shook his head. 'Don't remember.'

'But you remember seeing me at the Brown Cow?'

He gave her an odd look. 'All the time.'

'What did you think?'

'Think?'

'When you saw me.'

'I don't know. "There's Charlie's sister with the posh voice and the massive tits." What did you think when you saw me?'

'I didn't think this would happen, not in a million years. Did you?'

'No.'

'Don't you think that's odd?'

'What?'

'That neither of us had a clue we'd end up . . . where we are.'

'Not really,' said Gibbs. 'How could we know what was going to happen before it happened?'

'But I mean, we didn't even think we *wanted* it to happen.'

'So? It was still going to happen.'

'What do you mean?' Olivia pushed him off her. 'Do you think that's true? That it was *going to happen*, even then, before we had a clue?'

Gibbs thought about it. 'It happened,' he said. 'Before it happened, it was going to happen.'

'You think us ending up here together was inevitable?'

'It is now,' said Gibbs.

'Yes, but I mean . . .' Olivia wondered how best to put the question. 'Before Charlie and Simon's wedding, might we either have got together or not got together, or did the possibility that we wouldn't get together never exist at all?'

'Second one,' said Gibbs.

'Really?' Liv tried to keep the excitement out of her voice. 'There was never any possibility that we wouldn't have an affair – that's what you really think? So you believe in destiny? You think free will's an illusion?'

'You're doing it again.'

'What?'

'Whatever I say, you change it into something I don't understand, then tell me that's what I said. There's no point me saying anything. You write my lines, I don't care.'

'*I'm* the one who doesn't understand,' Liv groaned. 'Explain!'

Gibbs stared up at the ceiling. 'When something happens, you can look back and say it was always going to happen – because it did. There's no other choice, once it's happened.'

'I can't work out if you're saying something romantic or not.'

He shrugged. 'Not deliberately. Just stating a fact.'

'Okay, then – what do you think about the future?'

'Full of sex.'

'With me?' Olivia asked.

'No, with Ant and fucking Dec. Obviously with you.'

'I don't think Debbie'd see it as obvious.'

'Don't talk about Debbie.'

'Dom wouldn't either.'

'Or him.'

'What's in their future? Dom's and Debbie's?'

'Not us,' said Gibbs.

~

'I used to come here all the time as a student,' Kit Bowskill told Simon. 'Loved the place. Ever since, I've had a thing about tucked-away pubs down side streets. Never on main roads. A pub on a main road's all wrong.' He smiled, took a swig of his Guinness. 'Sorry. I'm rambling.'

'I'd have come to Silsford,' Simon told him, sensing his nervousness. 'Or London. Did you have a reason for wanting to meet here?'

'Like I said: I love the Maypole.'

Simon kept his eyes on him. Eventually Bowskill flushed and looked away, loosening the knot of his tie. 'I'm a hopeless liar, as you can see. I was coming to Cambridge tonight anyway. To meet Connie.'

'She's here?'

'I don't know if she's here now, but she told me to meet her at nine thirty.'

'Where?'

Bowskill looked apologetic. 'I told her I was meeting you, that you've been trying to get in touch with her. She doesn't want to speak to you.'

'Why not?'

'She's angry with you for going away without telling her. She went to you for help and you didn't help her.'

Evidently Simon failed to conceal his annoyance, because Bowskill said, 'I wouldn't take it personally. Con's angry with everyone at the moment – feels the whole world's let her down.'

At the table next to them, three middle-aged men with loud voices were talking about a scholarship – someone had been awarded one who didn't deserve it; someone who had deserved it hadn't got it. One of the men was angry about this; Simon tried to block out his words, concentrate on Bowskill's.

'The house you and Connie nearly bought in 2003,' he said.

'18 Pardoner Lane?'

'That was the address?'

Bowskill nodded.

'Connie doesn't think so.'

'What do you mean?'

'She told Sam and Ian Grint that it was number 17. 17 Pardoner Lane.'

'She's misremembered, in that case,' said Bowskill. 'It was number 18.'

'Why would she get it wrong?'

'Why does anyone get anything wrong? If I sat here and

listed everything Connie's been wrong about in the last six months, we'd still be here next Tuesday.'

Simon nodded. 'You must be pretty angry with her.'

'I'm not allowed to be, am I? I wish I could believe she'd deliberately set out to ruin both our lives – then at least I'd be able to hate her. As it is, I'm living in an anonymous box in London, surrounded by lots of other suits in their anonymous boxes, banished from the home I've spent years creating – from scratch, almost. Melrose Cottage was a wreck when we bought it. It wasn't Connie who sanded the floors, tiled the fireplaces, landscaped the garden – it was me. And now she's booted me out. Yeah, I'd love to be angry with her, but it's not her that's doing all this, it's . . . I don't know, something that's got into her, some madness. She hasn't got a clue what she's doing from one minute to the next. She's not Connie any more – that's the worst thing about all this.' Bowskill blinked away tears, no doubt hoping Simon hadn't noticed them.

'I've just come from Pardoner Lane. The house you didn't buy in 2003 was number 18.'

'So you believe me?'

A question Simon was keen to avoid answering, especially now that Bowskill was looking more confident. Believing had nothing to do with it; Simon had checked the facts for himself. His confidence was in his own findings, not in Kit Bowskill. Still, he had other more personal questions he wanted to ask, and it wouldn't do any harm to go as far as he could down the feel-good route. '18 Pardoner Lane's next door to the Beth Dutton Centre, so there's no argument,' he said. 'You're right and Connie's wrong. About the house number, anyway. She got everything else right: the iron railings, the Victorian architecture, the sash windows. Number 17's on the other side of the road.'

Its owners, a friendly middle-aged couple, had invited Simon in for a coffee and looked disappointed when he'd said there was no need, he only had one quick question for them. They had bought the house brand new in 2001, since which time it had never been on the market. Yes, they remembered number 18 going up for sale in 2003. It was snapped up within weeks, they told Simon, and the same thing happened when it came up for sale again last year. 'We considered buying it, actually – both times. It's got more kerb-appeal than ours and bigger rooms. Unfortunately, that was reflected in the price. And when we thought about it, it seemed crazy to move across the road – though it doesn't make sense really, that, does it? It's like when you go out for a meal and someone orders the thing you want and you think, "Oh, well, I can't have that now that she's having it", and you end up ordering something you don't like half as much!'

Simon had nodded, bemused. He tended to avoid restaurants, but still, he felt he ought to have known what 17 Pardoner Lane's owner was talking about, and he didn't. He spent too much of his time nodding at things that made no sense to him, for politeness' sake.

'I need to ask you a personal question,' he told Bowskill.

'Fire away.'

'Your parents.'

The reaction was unmistakeable: instant resentment. Of Simon, for having asked, or of Mr and Mrs Bowskill senior? Simon couldn't tell. He knew a little bit about them, thanks to Connie. Their names were Nigel and Barbara and they lived in Bracknell, Berkshire. They ran their own business: something to do with making lasers which were used for fingerprinting.

Bowskill had regained his composure. 'Let me guess,' he

said. 'Connie told you I'm no longer in contact with them. I take it she told you why?'

'She told me she'd never really understood why.'

'That's bu—' Bowskill caught hold of his anger. A strained smile replaced his scowl. 'That's simply not true. Connie knows perfectly well what happened.'

'Do you mind telling me?' Simon asked.

'I can't see why you'd care. What's it got to do with anything?'

'Just interested.' Simon tried to make it sound incidental. No reason to tell Bowskill it was the main reason he'd wanted to meet him. 'As someone whose own parents are on the trying side . . .'

'But if you hit rock-bottom, they'd be there for you, wouldn't they?' said Bowskill. 'In an emergency, they'd do whatever it took – they'd look after you.'

Simon had never thought about it. In her younger days, throughout his childhood, his mother had stifled him with her nurturing, treated him as if he was made of glass and might break if he did anything rash like go round to a friend's house. Now, it was hard to imagine Kathleen looking after anybody. She'd lost her air of authority a long time ago. Although she was only sixty-one and had no health problems, she moved and spoke like a frail old relic shuffling ever closer to annihilation. Simon had often imagined meeting her as a stranger, what he'd think of her. Asked to guess her age and story, he'd have said eighty for sure, and at some stage she must have been mugged at knife-point by teenage thugs and lost the will to live.

He opened his mouth to say that in the direst of emergencies he would go to a whole range of people – including complete strangers – before he would involve his mother, but Bowskill was on a roll. 'What parents wouldn't help their child? I haven't got siblings, so it's not as if there's any competition for their attention. I wasn't asking them to donate their kidneys.'

'What happened?' Simon asked.

'Connie was disintegrating. Physically and mentally – shouting in her sleep, nightmares, her hair was falling out. I was properly worried about her. I thought . . . well, she didn't, so it's not tempting fate to say it: I thought she might do something stupid.'

Simon nodded. *Properly worried about her*. As opposed to pretending to worry about her? Was that what Bowskill was doing this time round?

'Mum and Dad made it clear I could expect no help from them.'

'Did you ask for their help?'

'Oh, yes. There was nothing ambiguous about it. I asked, they said no.'

'What did you want them to do, exactly?'

'Has Connie told you about her parents?' Bowskill asked. 'That they brainwash her and browbeat her, cripple her thought processes so that she can't think for herself?'

Simon shook his head. 'She mentioned them being difficult. About you moving to Cambridge.'

Bowskill laughed. 'Understatement isn't usually Connie's strong point,' he said. 'Nice to know she's expanding her repertoire.'

'So what happened?' Simon asked. 'With your parents?'

'Connie needed to get away from her family, especially her mother. I don't know why I'm talking in the past tense – she still does. I was hoping Mum would act as a mother figure, just temporarily – you know, boost her confidence, tell her she could have the life she wanted, achieve whatever she set out to achieve. I told her myself until I was sick of the sound of my own voice, but it had no effect. I'm only one person, and I'm not a parent, I'm an equal. No matter what I said, I wasn't enough to replace Connie's family, however bad for her they were – and she knew perfectly well the harm they were doing her, it wasn't as if she couldn't see it. But . . . she was scared to go against her mum, who didn't want her to move to Cambridge. It was hopeless. I knew I'd never lure her away from her family unless I had . . . well, something more than myself to offer her. She and Mum had always got on well, Mum and Dad claimed to love her like their own daughter, but . . . when it came to it, when I asked them to rally round and *be* a family for Connie, they said, "No thanks, we'd rather not get involved." '

'Do you think they were wary of encouraging her to go against her own parents?' Simon asked. 'They didn't want to interfere?'

'No,' said Bowskill flatly. 'Nothing to do with that. They don't give a shit about Val and Geoff Monk, only about themselves. They didn't want to put themselves out, simple as that. Started spluttering about the need to stand on one's own two feet, dependency not being good for people . . . It was disgusting, frankly – a complete abnegation of responsibility. I'd never do that to my child, if I had one. I looked at them and thought, "Who are you? Why am I bothering with you?" That was it – I haven't spoken to them since.'

'Sounds rough,' said Simon. He tried to produce a cheerless expression to match Bowskill's, hide his satisfaction. He'd had a theory, and although he hadn't yet been proved right, everything Bowskill had just said indicated that he soon would be.

17

Friday 23 July 2010

'Connie.'

Don't look pleased to see me. You won't be, once you've heard what I've got to say.

'Thanks for coming.' *He's not your husband. He's a stranger. This is a business meeting.*

I try to pass Kit a menu but he pushes it away. He smells of beer. We're in the restaurant at the Doubletree by Hilton Garden House, Selina Gane's hotel and now mine too. I checked in an hour ago.

'Not hungry?' I say. 'I'm not either.' It seems a shame. The food would probably be good. The lime green and purple velvet upholstery looks expensive. It makes me think of the dead woman's dress; the colours are the same.

I put the menus down on the table, pour us both some water.

'Don't play games,' Kit says. 'Why are we here?' He's still on his feet, poised for flight, unwilling to commit to a conversation with me without knowing what its subject will be.

'I'm staying here.' I don't tell him that Selina Gane is too. Of course, he might know that already.

'You're . . .' His breathing speeds up, like someone running. I wonder if he's thinking about escape. How hard is it for him to stay where he is? 'You walk out of your own birthday party without any explanation . . .'

'The birthday party *was* the explanation. That and the dress you bought me.'

'I swear to God, Con . . .'

'Forget it,' I say. 'I don't care. I need to talk to you about something else. Sit down. Sit.'

Reluctantly, he lowers himself into a chair across the table from me. He looks as unrelaxed as I've ever seen a person look – shoulders hunched, jaw rigid, red in the face. 'We ought to discuss work,' he says.

'Go ahead.' This is a business meeting, after all. You can't invite your husband to a business meeting and then tell him he can't talk about work.

'You're Nulli's business and financial director. All the strategy originates with you, all the planning . . . You're the one who makes sure everyone gets paid. I can slog my guts out, my team can do the same, but we're wasting our time if you're not doing your bit.'

'Agreed,' I say.

'If you don't keep on top of things, Nulli falls apart.'

'And you don't think I'm keeping on top of things?'

'Are you?'

'I haven't been, no,' I admit. 'Not since I saw that woman's body on Roundthehouses. But it's been less than a week. The company's not going to crumble to dust because I've neglected the paperwork for a week. Anyway, all this is irrelevant. This time next year, Nulli's unlikely to exist.'

The colour drains from Kit's face. 'What are you talking about?'

'You're bright, you're determined,' I say briskly, deciding I ought to offer him some compensation for losing both his wife and his business. 'You'll start another company without me. I'm sure it'll do very well.'

Kit's mouth and eyes start to move – random twitches, uncoordinated. He doesn't think this can be happening to him. I know how he feels.

'How can you . . . ?'

I'm sorry. I don't love you any less than I did before all this happened. I trust you less, like you less, am more willing to cause you pain, but the love hasn't changed. I wouldn't have thought that was possible – would you, Kit?

I resist the urge to explain, knowing it wouldn't help.

'How can you calmly sit there and announce your intention to destroy everything we've got?' Kit's voice is hollow, hoarse. 'Our marriage, our company . . .'

'I need you to read something.' I pull the letter out of my bag and pass it across the table to him. 'I wanted you to see it before Selina Gane does. Once you've approved it, I'll push it under her door. She's staying here too. Did you know that?'

Kit shakes his head slowly, his eyes wide, fixed on my handwritten words.

I expected it to be hard, but it was the easiest letter I've ever written. I assumed, for the purposes of the exercise, that Selina Gane was innocent, and I explained everything, or at least as much as I could explain: finding her address in Kit's SatNav, my suspicions and fears, how they led me to wait outside her house and follow her, how in retrospect I wish I'd been more upfront about it, spoken to her directly. That's what she'll want if she's as frightened and baffled as I am, I thought: a straightforward letter of clarification and apology, one innocent person to another.

I didn't waste time worrying about what to include and what to leave out; I was generous with information, telling her far more than she needed to know – even that I was staying at the Garden House, though in a room nowhere near hers. 'I'm sorry if that makes you feel as if I'm stalking you all over again,' I wrote. 'I'm really not. I chose this hotel because its name was in my mind, because I rang you here. In an ideal world, I'd have been tactful and chosen another hotel, but I'm exhausted and my energy levels are well into the red, so I didn't.'

Reading snatches of the letter upside down, as Kit reads it, I decide that I did a good job of making myself sound sane. If I were Selina Gane, I would agree to meet and talk to me.

Kit drops the pages on the table. He raises his head slowly, as if he can hardly bear to drag his eyes up to meet mine.

'Well?' I say.

'You're offering to buy her house.'

'Yes.'

'Have you gone mad? Even more mad? You're offering the asking price – 1.2 million pounds. You can't afford—'

'Your information's out of date,' I tell him. 'As of today, the asking price is a million. She must be pretty desperate to sell if she's discounting it after only a week, don't you think?'

Kit puts his head in his hands. 'So you're offering her more money, when she's asking for less – all of it money you don't have and wouldn't be able to borrow. I don't understand, Connie. Help me out here.'

'Or you could help me out,' I say evenly. 'All I want, now, is to know the truth. I don't care what it is. I really mean that. However bad it is, even if it's worse than I can possibly imagine. I don't care about our marriage . . .'

'Thanks a lot.'

'. . . I don't care if you've killed someone – on your own or with Selina Gane's help. I won't even go to the police – that's how much I don't care. I only care about myself – *my* need to know what exactly happened to *my* life.'

'Stop.'

'I'm sorry if I'm upsetting you,' I say. 'I just want you to realise that this can be easy: you can just tell me. Tell me what's going on, Kit. Then I won't have to shove this letter under Selina Gane's hotel room door . . .'

'Connie.' He grabs my hands across the table.

'Tell me!'

I see something shift in his eyes: fear, awareness, calculation. Mainly fear, I think. 'Oh, God, Con . . . I don't know how to . . .'

I wait, afraid to move a muscle in case he changes his mind. Am I going to hear the truth, finally?

'How can I convince you?' he says in a harder voice. 'I don't know anything. I haven't done anything.'

No. You didn't imagine it. There was a chance, and now it's gone. He chose not to take it.

'You don't believe me, do you?' he says.

'No, I don't.' The sinking heaviness inside me is so overpowering that for a few seconds I can't speak. *What did you expect, a full confession?* 'All right, then,' I say eventually. 'If you won't tell me the truth, I'll have to find it out for myself. Hence this letter.'

'*Hence?*' Kit's laugh shocks me. How can one short sound contain so much rage? 'Sorry, are you implying a logical connection? How does sharing all the details of our misery with a stranger and offering to buy a house you can't afford take you closer to the truth?'

'Maybe it won't.'

'What do you achieve, with this?' He hits the letter with the back of his hand.

'Probably nothing. I'm not doing it because I think it's a brilliant idea and bound to work.' If I wasn't so exhausted, I would try harder to make him see how far I've drifted, in the past six days, from the realm of winning possibilities and positive options. 'I'm doing it because it's the only idea I have – the only way I can think of to take things forward, now that the police have said they're not going to do anything.'

A waiter approaches. Kit holds out a hand to repel him, like a lollipop man stopping traffic. 'We don't want anything apart from to be left alone,' he snaps. Some businessmen at a nearby table turn to stare at us. One raises his eyebrows.

'I know two things for sure,' I say calmly, sticking to my planned script. '11 Bentley Grove was in your SatNav as "Home". A woman was murdered there, in the lounge. I can't explain those two things. You say you can't either. So. If I want to get to the truth, I need to find out a lot more about that house than I know at the moment.' I shrug. 'Buying it's the only plan I can come up with. Don't bother to tell me how unlikely it is to work – I know that already. I also know that when you buy a house, you find out all sorts of things about it that you wouldn't have known otherwise: there's a musty smell in the airing cupboard, a safe under the bedroom floorboards . . .'

'Connie, you can't afford to buy 11 Bentley Grove.'

'Yes, I can. Or, rather, *we* can. I need your help and you're going to give it to me. If you don't, I'll start divorce proceedings tomorrow. Or Monday – as soon as I can. I'll also walk away from Nulli without a backward glance, and refuse to sell you my half of the business. I'll be your worst nightmare: an equal partner who contributes nothing. I know exactly how to make your life hell and run Nulli into the ground. Don't make the mistake of thinking I wouldn't do it.'

I've never heard a silence so loud. Other people in the restaurant are talking – I can see their mouths moving – but the sound is drowned out by the vast blackness in my head, Kit's horrified wordless stare.

Two or three minutes pass, the two of us frozen in place. Then Kit says, 'What have you turned into?'

'Someone who fights her corner,' I tell him. 'So, are you going to help me?'

'How?'

'All you'll need to do is sign forms as and when I tell you to.'

'I don't get to hear the financial master plan?'

What harm can it do to tell him?

I take a gulp from my water glass, suddenly nervous, as if my maths teacher is about to mark my homework. 'As things stand, you're right – we can't afford to buy 11 Bentley Grove. We haven't sold our house – it isn't even on the market. Even if we put it on tomorrow, it's unlikely we'd have a firm buyer in time. Now that 11 Bentley Grove's asking price is down to a million, it'll be sold within days. It's being marketed as a bargain – price reduced for a quick sale. And it's in one of the best parts of Cambridge. If I had to guess, I'd say a deal will have been done by the end of Monday.'

'Can I inject a bit of realism into this fantasy?' Kit says. 'Even if we could magic up a buyer, the most we'd get for Mellers is three hundred grand. We still wouldn't be able to afford it.'

'With our incomes and Nulli's profits, we could get a mortgage for somewhere between eight hundred and nine hundred thousand, I think. Not from the Halifax or NatWest . . .'

'Then who?'

'There are plenty of private banks who'd like nothing more than to lend us a shedload of money in exchange for us transferring our business and personal accounts over to them. We're exactly the sort of clients they'd want to attract. Think of Nulli's profits in the last two years – they've rocketed. I'll need to beef up projected profits for this year and next by equivalent amounts, so that the bank looks at the figures and thinks, "Great, no risk," but that's easy enough to do. The bank'd get Nulli and 11 Bentley Grove as security – I can't see why they'd turn us down.'

Kit says nothing. At least he's listening. I wasn't sure he would. I thought that by this point I might be talking to an empty lime green chair.

'You've read the letter,' I say steadily, working my way through my prepared speech. 'You've seen that I'm offering Selina Gane 1.2 million, the original asking price. I've done that for two reasons. One: she doesn't want to see or speak to me. An extra two hundred grand that she wasn't counting on getting might prove to be the incentive she needs. Two: once word gets round that 11 Bentley Grove is now going for a million, it'll attract so much interest, there'll probably be people bidding against each other. Once that happens, the price will start to rise again. Unless Selina Gane's a naïve idiot, she'll know this. If I want to put in a successful pre-emptive bid, I need to make sure it takes into account that demand might force the price up. Realistically, I reckon the top bid in that situation might be 1.1 million.'

'So why not offer that?' Kit asks, his voice stony. I tell myself this is progress: he is engaging with the possibility, at least. Asking sensible questions.

'I thought about it,' I tell him. 'But the combination of Selina Gane's antipathy towards me and the possibility that she might end up getting 1.1 million anyway might make her more inclined to tell me to get stuffed. 1.2 million is an offer she'd be truly crazy to refuse – I don't see how she could.'

And she'll know things about the house that no one else knows – about what's hidden there and what's disappeared, what was there once and has been taken away. A woman's body, the death button . . .

I could ring Lancing Damisz and give a false name, ask Lorraine Turner to show me round 11 Bentley Grove, but what's the point? Even a well-informed estate agent would only know a fraction of what the owner knows.

Offering Selina Gane more than a million pounds seems a good way of persuading her to talk to me.

'Are you listening to yourself?' Kit hisses, leaning across the table as if greater proximity to his hostility is likely to make me change my mind. 'An offer she'd be truly crazy to refuse? It's an offer you'd be truly crazy to make! Even if we could borrow nine hundred thousand from some private bank . . .'

'How would we afford the monthly payments?' I have anticipated every question he might ask, all possible objections. 'I've done some very rough calculations. Borrowing on an interest-only basis, and if we pour in ninety per cent of our salaries and all our personal savings, we could afford to make the payments for two to three years, depending on certain variables. After that, I don't know. Maybe we'll be rich by then from some new business venture, or . . .'

No. Stop.

I promised myself I wouldn't lie in order to make this easier, for Kit or for me.

There's not going to be a new business. There's no 'we', not any more.

'When we can no longer make the payments, 11 Bentley Grove will be repossessed,' I tell Kit. 'It's inevitable, and it doesn't worry me. If I haven't found out what I need to know in two years, the chances are I'll never find out. At that point, I'd have to think about giving up.'

'You're proposing this plan *knowing* it's going to lead to bankruptcy?'

'There's no point in having money if you're not willing to spend it on the things that matter. I assume that if I was literally penniless, the government would have to provide me with somewhere to live – a room in a B&B, a council flat, benefits. I wouldn't starve.'

'Your figures don't add up,' says Kit, a triumphant sneer on his face. He ought to know better. When have my figures ever not added up? Hysteria bubbles up inside me. *My life might be falling apart but my accounting skills have survived intact. Yippee.* 'You're talking about borrowing nine hundred grand, but this letter's offering 1.2 million.' Kit hits it again with the back of his hand. 'Where's the missing three hundred grand going to come from?'

'The sale of Melrose Cottage,' I tell him. 'You talked about magicking up a buyer? That's exactly what I've done. A firm buyer who won't let us down, so that we can make a deal with Selina Gane straight away and know it won't fall through.'

'Who? You're talking crap! You haven't had time to find anyone. The house isn't even on the market! Your mum and dad aren't going to help you bankrupt yourself, that's for sure – they'd drop dead from a unanimous heart attack if they heard what I've just heard. Fran and Anton haven't got any money. Who's your buyer, Connie? You're fucking delusional!'

'We're going to sell Melrose Cottage to ourselves. To Nulli.'

No reaction.

I press on. 'Nulli has a hundred and fifty grand in its account at the moment, give or take. Legally, it's a separate entity from you and me, even though we own it. It can borrow money in its own right. This is how it works: Nulli buys Melrose for three hundred grand. I don't know, maybe it could even pay a bit over the odds – three hundred and twenty, say, or three hundred and fifty. Yes, come to think of it, I think Nulli might be so impressed with our high-spec interior, it won't be able to resist offering an extra fifty grand to see off the competition. The surveyor will be told that's the price the vendor and buyer agreed on, and won't think to question it – three hundred and fifty grand isn't unthinkable for our house, with all the work we've done to it.'

'The work *I've* done,' Kit mutters.

I'm not going to argue with him. It's a fair point. 'Nulli puts down a hundred grand toward Melrose, borrows two hundred and fifty,' I say. 'The fifty grand left in the company account would then cover the stamp duty on Melrose, legal costs, everything – there might even be some left over for salaries.' *You have to laugh, don't you, Kit? Or else you cry.* 'Soon as Nulli owns Melrose, it puts it up for sale. Shouldn't take too long to sell. Someone I went to school with will buy it, or one of Mum and Dad's friends who wants to downsize now that their kids have left home. Meanwhile, we'll have got a lump sum from selling our house – we'll have three hundred and fifty grand in cash. We put down three hundred towards 11 Bentley Grove and borrow nine hundred. 'No,' I correct myself. 'Sorry. We put down two ninety, borrow nine hundred and ten. The sixty we don't put down from the sale of Melrose covers stamp duty, which'll be colossal, and legal costs. Soon as Melrose sells to a genuine buyer, Nulli gets two hundred and ninety grand back, and ends up only sixty grand out of pocket. And it won't really be out of pocket at all, because it's us and we're it – we'll have made use of that sixty grand already. Apart from anything else, it's a brilliant way of getting a huge amount of money out of the company tax-free.'

Kit says nothing, doesn't even blink. Perhaps he's dead; I've shocked the life out of him.

'At first I thought Nulli could buy 11 Bentley Grove, but that wouldn't work,' I say. 'I need to move in, live there – I won't find out anything if I'm not there. If Nulli owns the house and I live there, it becomes a taxable benefit in kind. Plus, a private bank wouldn't lend Nulli anywhere near as much as it'd lend us, and it'd charge twice as much interest – the terms for commercial loans are much tougher than for personal mortgages. This way round, it's perfect. Nulli buys Melrose, which we're no longer living in, so it isn't a taxable benefit – it's an investment. We feed the bank some crap about maybe renting it out.'

'Shut up!' Kit bellows. 'I don't want to hear any more, just . . . stop.'

Obediently, I wait in silence for him to be ready to tear me to pieces. He's not an impulsive person, Kit. He'll want to rehearse his attack first.

Everyone in the restaurant is watching us and trying to pretend they're not. I consider making a public announcement: *Don't bother with the subtlety. We're beyond caring what anybody thinks of us.*

Suddenly, desperately, I want a Kir Royale. This is a Kir Royale sort of place. Why would anybody want to drink anything else, in this lime and purple velvet room with its soft lighting and river views?

I can't ask for a Kir Royale. It wouldn't be right. *Inappropriate. Crazy Connie.*

'Do you have any idea how *fucked up* this is?' Kit says after a few minutes. He's lowered his voice to a whisper; perhaps he does care about making a good impression, even now. I remind myself that I know nothing about him, nothing that matters. 'You say, "We'll have made use of that sixty grand already," as if there's a profit in this for us! Yeah, we'll have made use of the sixty grand – hooray. We'll have used it to buy a house we'll lose within two to five years because we can't afford it. And Nulli, that we've taken so long to build up and poured all our effort and energy into – Nulli'll go down the tubes. By the time the sale of Melrose Cottage to a legitimate buyer completes, we'll have had, what? Two, three months of not being able to pay anybody?'

'You're right,' I cut him off. 'Nulli will be a casualty of the plan, almost certainly. And we'll lose both houses, Melrose Cottage and 11 Bentley Grove. On the plus side, if 11 Bentley Grove is repossessed, we might get some equity out of it, depending on what the bank sells it for. And when Nulli sells Melrose, even if it's in the process of folding by then, that's three hundred grand that'll come back to us, minus the costs associated with going bankrupt.'

'We'll be left with nothing,' says Kit, his voice leaden with misery. 'That's the one thing all people who go bankrupt have in common. Use your brain, for fuck's sake.'

'I think you're being too pessimistic,' I tell him. 'We'll get something out of it. Remember, there are two houses to sell to generate funds.' *Time to be generous. Incentivise him.* 'You can have all of it,' I say. 'Everything we're left with at the end of all this. I meant what I said: I don't care if I end up poor and homeless.' A voice in my head – my mother's, probably – says, *It's all very well saying you don't care. You* should *care.*

But I don't.

'I need to know the truth,' I tell Kit. 'I may never find out, but if I do, this is how it's going to happen. This plan is the beginning of me maybe getting some answers to my questions.'

1.2 million pounds. The most expensive answer in the history of the world.

'If I say no, you're going to divorce me, right?' Kit says.

I nod.

'What happens to our marriage if I say yes?'

'That depends. If I find out the truth, and the truth is that you're not a liar, not a murderer . . .' I shrug. 'Maybe we can find a way back, but . . .' I stop. It's not fair to offer him false hope, even if it would further my cause. 'I think our marriage is probably over either way,' I say.

'It's what your average dimwit-on-the-street would call a "no-brainer".' Kit's smile is shaky. 'If my choice is between definitely losing the woman I love and only probably losing her, I'm going to have to opt for only probably.' He stands up. 'I'll sign anything you want me to sign. Just say the word. You know where to find me.'

18

23/7/2010

'I need you to do something for me.'

'Hello to you too.' Charlie made a rude face at the phone. 'I'm fine, thanks for asking. Where are you?'

'Get hold of Alice Fancourt, arrange to see her as soon as you can. Alice Bean, sorry – she's dropped the Fancourt. Find out when she last saw Connie Bowskill and what—'

'Who-oa, hang on a minute.' This was the sort of conversation that demanded the accompaniment of a glass of wine: cold, white, bone dry. Charlie hit the pause button on the remote control, hauled herself up off the sofa and pulled the lounge curtains closed, or as near to closed as they'd go. They didn't quite meet in the middle; she'd made a pig's ear of hanging them. Liv had said, 'Take them down and rehang them, then – properly', but as far as Charlie was concerned, curtains fell into the category of things that only got one chance. So did sisters.

She would never have admitted it to anybody, but she was pleased to be home – queen once more of a small, badly decorated terraced house, no longer an outsider in paradise. 'Connie Bowskill knows Alice?' she said, swallowing a yawn.

'Alice is her homeopath,' said Simon. 'I need to know when she last saw her, what Connie said, if she's got any idea where Connie is now.'

'At the risk of sounding selfish, what does that list of needs have to do with me? I was watching a DVD.' So far it was brilliant. *Orphan*. It featured a psychotic adoptee protagonist called Esther who seemed intent on killing all her siblings. Charlie identified with her hugely, though she suspected that wasn't the reaction the director had been hoping for.

'I can't talk to Alice, can I?' Simon said impatiently.

'You both have mouths and ears, last time I checked. You mean you don't want to talk to her.' Charlie poured herself a glass of wine, glad he wasn't there in person to see her smile. The smile faded as it occurred to her that his not wanting to speak to Alice could be interpreted in a range of ways: dislike, embarrassment, an aversion to revisiting the past. Any of those would be okay, Charlie thought, putting the wine back in the fridge. *Searing unrequited love – the kind that knows it would be magnified to greater agony by confrontation with its object*. No. Ridiculous. It was clear from his tone that Alice was a means to an end. Connie Bowskill was the one he was interested in now. And no, Charlie told herself firmly – not in that way.

'I don't want to talk to Alice, no,' said Simon.

Neither did Charlie, but she knew what would happen if she refused: he would overcome his reluctance and do what he had to do to get the information he wanted. This was her opportunity to prevent a reunion. 'Fine, I'll do it. Where are you?'

'In Cambridge still.'

'Are you coming home?'

'No. I'm going to Bracknell to talk to Kit Bowskill's parents.'

'Now? It'll be midnight by the time you get there.'

'They're expecting me first thing in the morning. I'll camp in my car outside their house.' Anticipating her objection, he said, 'There's no point me coming back just to spend a few hours in bed. I wouldn't sleep anyway.'

As if there was nothing to do in bed apart from sleep.

'So . . .' He was going too fast for her. 'Kit Bowskill gave you his parents' phone number?' Why would he do that? Why would Simon ask for it?

'Directory Enquiries did. There was only one Bowskill in Bracknell – N for Nigel.'

'But . . . you met Kit Bowskill?'

'Yeah. Asked him three times what caused the rift between him and his folks. First two times he dodged the question. It was his third answer that convinced me he's hiding something that matters. He gave me what sounded on the face of it like a full answer, but it was all psycho-babble – used a lot of words to distract me, so I wouldn't notice he was telling me nothing. He said his mum and dad wouldn't "rally round", wouldn't be a family to Connie when she needed them. That could mean almost anything.'

'Might he have decided it was none of your business?' Charlie asked. She could understand Kit Bowskill's disinclination to discuss a traumatically severed relationship with a brusque detective he'd never met before.

'No. He was scared.' After a pause, Simon added, 'He's the bad guy. Don't ask me to prove it because I can't. Yet.'

'You don't even know there is a bad guy.'

'He told me Connie doesn't want to speak to me – she's angry with me for going away without telling her. Does that sound likely?'

'Yes,' said Charlie. 'I was angry with you earlier, when you set off to Cambridge without telling me. I could have come with you.'

'What if he's killed her too, and that's the reason she isn't answering her phone?'

'Pure invention, Simon.'

'How many people do you know who cut their parents out of their lives?'

'You're obsessed with Kit Bowskill's bloody parents,' Charlie grumbled.

'From now on, it's my guiding principle: any time I've got two people saying different things and I don't know which to believe, if one of them's disowned the two people who brought them into this world, I'm going to believe the other one.'

'That's . . . really absurd.' Charlie laughed and took a sip of her drink.

'No, it's not.'

'Wow – what a convincing argument.'

'Every day of my life I think about my mum dying – every single day. I think about how free I'd feel. And then I realise she'll probably live for another thirty years.'

Charlie waited. Counted the seconds: one, two, three, four, five, six . . .

'The point is, I wouldn't ever say to her, "Sorry, you're out of my life," ' Simon went on. 'Anyone with a heart knows how it'd make any parent feel to hear those words, anyone with the ability to empathise even a *fraction* . . .' The breathing in between the words was louder than the words. Simon wouldn't have been willing to have this conversation in person, Charlie guessed; only the distance made it possible for him. 'No child should ever renounce its parents, not without a rock-solid reason,' he said. 'Not unless it's life or death.'

Charlie wasn't sure she agreed, but she made a noise that would allow Simon to think she did. 'If Kit Bowskill doesn't want to tell you what happened, chances are his mum and dad won't either,' she said.

'Risk I have to take.'

Accept it, Zailer: he's not coming home.

Charlie carried her wine through to the lounge and flopped down on the sofa. Psychotic orphan Esther, fixed in place, scowled at her from the TV screen. 'Even if the parents tell you what the rift was about, so what?' she said. 'How can it have anything to do with Connie seeing a dead woman on a property website? Assuming she saw any such thing. I'm still not convinced – I don't care how many independent witnesses have come forward.' Her camera was sitting on the sofa arm beside her. She put down her drink and picked it up. Since getting back from Spain, she'd kept it with her all the time – next to her side of the bed while she slept, on the bathroom windowsill while she was in the bath. She was addicted to looking at her photos of Los Delfines.

'Independent,' said Simon. 'Interesting choice of word.'

'Sorry?' Charlie was staring at a tiny sweaty Domingo, leaning against the trunk of the upside-down lily tree.

'Two people see the dead woman's body on Roundthehouses: Connie Bowskill and Jackie Napier. No one else. Does it seem likely to you that the only two people to see this dead body on the website – for the brief half hour that it's up there, before it's replaced – happen to be these two people? Think of all the millions that might have seen it.'

'*Likely?*' Charlie made a 'silent scream' face. 'Simon, we left likely behind several light years ago. None of this is likely. I still think it's some kind of . . . bizarre practical joke. There's absolutely no evidence – proper evidence, I'm talking about – that anyone's been killed, hurt, anything. Oh, my God!'

'What? What's wrong?'

'It's hideous. It's fucking hideous!'

'What is?'

'The face! In the mountain. It's so obvious now that I can see it: eyes, nose, mouth.' Charlie pressed the zoom button on her camera. 'I asked you if it was attractive – why didn't you tell me it was a complete minger? It looks like Jabba the Hut from *Star Wars*.'

'What do you mean, you can see it?' Simon sounded irritated. 'You're at home.'

'On my camera.'

'There's no way a photograph could—'

'It's that panoramic one, the one I took from the top terrace. Pool, barbecue, gardens, mountain – complete with ugly face.'

'The face I saw wouldn't show up in a photograph,' said Simon.

'Simon, I'm looking at a face here. How many faces can one mountain have?'

'You can't tell anything from a picture,' he said curtly.

'Did the face you saw look like Jabba the Hut from *Star Wars*?'

There was a pause. Then Simon said, 'If you didn't see it first-hand, you can't claim to have seen it – not on the basis of a tiny photo.'

'To whom can I not claim that?' Charlie teased him. 'The Board of Mountain Face Classification? What does it matter if I see it too? Does it make you less special?'

'No.' He sounded confused by her question. 'I wanted you to see it, but you didn't. Seeing it in a photograph's not the same.'

'No, it's different. But I can still see it.'

'Not in the mountain.'

Charlie held the phone at a distance and blew a raspberry

into it – a long, loud one. When she put it next to her ear again, Simon was talking so quickly that she couldn't follow what he was saying. Something about someone called Basil. 'Slow down,' she told him. 'I missed the beginning of that. Start again.'

'Basil Lambert-Wall,' he said breathlessly. 'Professor Sir, the one who lives on Bentley Grove, Selina Gane's next-door neighbour. He said he'd seen Kit Bowskill before, remember, when I showed him a photo? Said Bowskill had fitted a burglar alarm for him?'

Charlie remembered. 'And then you went to the burglar alarm company, who said they didn't recognise Bowskill and he didn't work there.'

'You tell me you've seen a face in a mountain when you haven't – you've seen it in a photograph.' Simon's words collided with one another, as they always did when he was excited. 'Why do you make that mistake? Because you associate the photograph with the mountain – it's such a strong association in your mind that you confuse the one with the other.'

Charlie opened her mouth to protest, but it was clear he wasn't stopping.

'Basil Lambert-Wall was wrong about Bowskill being the guy that fitted his burglar alarm – we know that. But what if he was right about seeing him? What if seeing Kit Bowskill is strongly associated in his mind with the day he got a new burglar alarm? What if something *else* happened that same day, and the professor's confusing the two things? Think about it – it's got to be! Why else would he be so sure Kit Bowskill had fitted his alarm when he hadn't?'

Because he's old and doddery and just plain wrong? Charlie didn't bother to say it out loud. When Simon was like this, there was no point talking to him.

She heard a click, then the line went dead. *Dismissed*. It was Professor Sir Basil's turn to have his evening interrupted, poor old sod. It struck Charlie as odd that she knew what was about to happen to him and he had no idea. She hoped he wasn't asleep.

Sighing, she pressed play on the remote control and stretched out on the sofa to watch the rest of her film. Alice Fancourt could wait until tomorrow. If Simon could have a guiding principle, Charlie could too: people who ended phone calls without saying goodbye didn't deserve to have their errands attended to immediately.

~

'Sam.' Kate Kombothekra took the phone out of her husband's hands and put it down on the coffee table between them. She was wearing her yellow pyjamas, holding a roll of cling-film in one hand. 'I need your attention for five seconds. Think you can manage it?'

'Sorry.'

'Did you remember to get paper for the printer?'

'No. Sorry. I'll do it tomorrow.'

'Did you ring the council?'

'Was I supposed to?'

'Yes. To ask about skip hire, get some quotes . . .'

'Oh, right. No. Sorry.'

Kate sighed. 'All right, just one more question, and only because I'm desperate to hear a "yes": would it be fair to assume that you've neglected to do all four things you promised you'd do today?'

'That was Connie Bowskill on the phone,' Sam told her. 'She wants me to ask Grint for Jackie Napier's number.' Not an unreasonable request, in the circumstances.

'Oh, not this again!' Kate whacked the cling-film rhythmically against the palm of her left hand in what would surely have qualified as a threatening gesture had the weapon been less innocuously domestic. 'Forget Connie Bowskill. Come and help me get the boys' stuff ready for tomorrow. I've nearly finished the packed lunches – if you could dig out their big rucksacks from the cellar. The camouflagey ones, you know.' Kate performed a mime: a seated person springing up from a chair and breaking into a run.

Sam didn't move. 'She's staying at the Garden House,' he said. 'Same hotel as Selina Gane.' He wasn't sure why the idea of the two women in such close proximity disturbed him. Was he worried Connie might do something? No. She wasn't violent. Desperate, though. Much of the violence Sam had encountered over the years had been born of desperation.

He was fighting the urge to ring Grint and tell him to go to the hotel. And do what, once he got there? It was crazy. So was not wanting Connie to talk to Jackie Napier. Sam didn't like to think of himself as a control freak – the sort of person who made decisions on other people's behalf and justified it on the grounds that it was for their own good. He could easily have told Connie that Jackie worked for Lancing Damisz, that there was no need for him to bother Grint – Connie could contact Jackie via her work if she wanted to speak to her. It was natural that Connie should want to be put in touch with the only person in the world who would believe her for sure, the woman who'd seen exactly what she'd seen. In her shoes, Sam would also want to compare notes, go over details. So why were his instincts telling him to do everything he could to keep the two women apart?

He couldn't stop thinking about something Jackie Napier

had said when he'd interviewed her, about the woman who pretended to be Selina Gane and put 11 Bentley Grove on the market. *She knew all she had to do was talk about people not looking like they do in their passports. If she made me think about all those other people, she wouldn't have to convince me – I'd do all the work myself. It's one of those things everyone says, isn't it? "He looks nothing like his passport photo, I'm surprised he's ever allowed back into the country."*

Had Sam misremembered? No, he was fairly sure that was what she'd said.

He opened his mouth to ask Kate if he was imagining problems that didn't exist, but she had already left the room.

~

'Pick a number between one and thirty-nine.'

'Sixteen,' said Simon. His and Charlie's wedding anniversary.

Professor Sir Basil Lambert-Wall dragged his index finger along the books on the shelf closest to him, counting them off one by one. When he got to the sixteenth, he worked it loose from the row, hooked his walking stick over the back of the nearest chair and proceeded to try and take hold of the bulky hardback with both hands. Simon stepped forward to help, regretting the sentimentality that had led him to pick what was undoubtedly the heaviest book on the shelf – *The Whisperers*, it was called. The subtitle was *Private Life in Stalin's Russia*.

'Stay where you are!' the professor barked. His voice was large and powerful for a man so small. 'I can manage perfectly well.' He made a series of huffing noises as he circumnavigated the chair and sat down in it. More huffing as he adjusted the book on his lap.

Simon watched the effort, trying not to wince, hoping

Lambert-Wall's tiny wrists wouldn't snap. He berated himself for not having guessed what the old man had in mind; if he had, he'd have gone for skinny number fifteen, *Maxims of La Rochefoucauld*. There was no shortage of books to choose from: every wall was covered. There were shelves above the door, above and below both windows – all full. In between the two armchairs and the sofa were three piles of magazines. One was topped with an issue of *The Economist*, another with something called *PN Review*. The third was supporting two empty mugs. Simon couldn't see the name of the journal beneath them; it had a picture of the Statue of Liberty in one corner.

'You chose well,' said the professor once he'd got his breath back. '*The Whisperers* is an unusually excellent book. Now, pick a number between one and six hundred and fifty-six.' He flicked through the pages.

'You're sure I'm not keeping you up?' Simon asked. It was the red towelling dressing gown that was making him feel guilty, the grey striped pyjamas, the sallow tubes of calf protruding from the brown slippers. Didn't necessarily mean bedtime, though; Lambert-Wall had been wearing the same outfit last time Simon had called round, at midday.

'It's not even ten o'clock,' said the old man, making Simon feel like a fussy over-protective parent. 'I sleep between four and nine. And I write between eleven and a quarter to four, so as long as we'll be finished by eleven . . . ?' He glanced towards the digital clock on the windowsill, then raised his eyebrows at Simon, who nodded. 'Good. So – a number?'

'Eleven.'

The professor laughed. 'Page eleven it is. And now . . . a number between one and thirty-four, please.'

'Twenty-two.' Charlie's birthday.

'Excellent. And finally, a number between one and . . . thirty-four.'

'Twelve.' Simon's birthday. He didn't see how his choices could reveal anything about him that he wouldn't want a stranger to know.

'Ah. Sorry.' The professor frowned. 'You can't have the twelfth word on the twenty-second line, I'm afraid. It's "Trotsky". Proper nouns are not eligible.'

'I'll go for eleven again,' said Simon, too curious to be impatient. What was the point of this game?

'You've chosen the word "life".' Lambert-Wall smiled. 'A very impressive result – the best in a long while.' He slapped the book shut, placed it on the beige carpet by his feet. Simon thought about Selina Gane's beige carpet next door, with the Christmas tree stain in one corner. Had the developers fitted all the houses with the same carpet when they'd built them? From the outside, they had a generic look: one design, multiplied by thirty-odd. Simon found himself staring at the three magazine towers in front of him. Imagined moving them to reveal three round scarlet stains, each the shape of a human head. He told himself to get a grip.

Basil Lambert-Wall had hauled himself out of his chair and was hobbling, without the help of his stick, towards a free-standing desk in front of the window that had many paperweights on it but no loose paper. When he arrived at his destination, he picked up a lidless pen and wrote something in a notebook that lay open. His back to Simon, he said, 'You're a man of discernment and a force for good in the world. And you had a question you wanted to ask me. Please go ahead.'

Simon was confused. Had the professor struggled over to his desk in order to record the outcome of his peculiar test?

Simon would have liked to study the contents of the notebook in detail. As always when someone paid him a compliment, he was tempted to argue. 'Life' had been his second choice. He'd picked 'Trotsky' first time round – an enthusiastic mass murderer. What did that say about him? On what grounds were proper nouns disqualified?

'The day you had your new burglar alarm fitted – Tuesday 29 June.'

'How do you know that was the date?' the professor asked.

'You told me, last time we spoke. Safesound Alarms confirmed it.'

'You checked up on me?'

'I check everything,' Simon told him. 'Always.'

'If I told you a precise date, that means I must have looked it up in my diary.'

'You did.'

'Then there was no need to check.' Lambert-Wall lowered himself into his chair, then rose again to adjust his dressing gown.

Simon waited until he was settled. 'Never mind the date. I want you to think back to that day. You had your new alarm fitted. Was there anything else going on that you remember, anything that happened at roughly the same time?'

'Yes.' The old man blinked several times in quick succession. It was disconcerting to watch – as if someone was messing around with his eyelid controls. 'I read an exceptional book – *People of the Lie* by M Scott Peck. It offers the best definition of human evil that I've ever come across.'

Simon pictured a two-word text, the two words being 'Giles' and 'Proust'. 'Anything else?' he asked.

'Yes. I ate something called a "tian" for my lunch. I had and still have no idea what a tian is, but it tasted delicious. It was cylindrical. I liked the look of it in the shop, so I thought I'd give it a try. Oh, I went to the shop, of course – the supermarket.'

'On the day your burglar alarm was fitted?'

Lambert-Wall nodded. 'My daughter took me, in the morning, to Waitrose. She takes me every Tuesday morning. She'd like me to shop online, but I resist.'

Simon nodded. This was getting him nowhere. 'So you read *People of the Lie*, had lunch, went shopping . . .'

'Yes, though not in that order. I napped in the afternoon, as I always do – one o'clock to four o'clock. Oh, and one of my neighbours was rude to me, which spoilt what would otherwise have been a rather pleasant day.'

'Which neighbour?'

The professor pointed towards the window. 'One of the men who lives in the house opposite,' he said. 'He's usually the soul of politeness, which was why I was surprised. He and his wife had bought new curtains, and they were carrying them into the house. She'd had to lower the back seats of her car to fit them all in. I wandered over to have a chat, intending to make a remark on the subject of the coincidence – new curtains, new burglar alarm. Not terribly compelling, I grant you, but no doubt it would have led on to matters of greater interest. His reaction was entirely uncalled for.'

'What did he do?'

'He shouted at me. "Not now! Can't you see we're busy?" Then he said to his wife, "Get rid of him, will you?" and went into the house carrying an armful of curtains. Most unattractive they were too, from what I could see through the plastic wrapping.'

Simon's skin had started to prickle. This had to be it: a

normally polite man, suddenly rude and offensive. Kit Bowskill? Except that it didn't make sense. Assuming it existed, Bowskill's illicit connection was with 11 Bentley Grove. That was the address his wife had found in his SatNav, the house she'd been looking at on Roundthehouses when she'd seen the dead body. Number 11 Bentley Grove was next door to Basil Lambert-Wall's house, not opposite.

'His wife was terribly apologetic,' the old man went on. 'She must have said sorry twenty times. "Ignore him," she said. "It's not you, it's the two hours we've just spent at the curtain warehouse. Never again!" You'd think after spending all that time that they'd put the new curtains up, but they still haven't.'

Simon produced a photograph from his pocket, the same one he'd shown Lambert-Wall last time, of Kit Bowskill. 'Is this face familiar?' he asked.

'Yes, that's him,' said the professor.

'The neighbour who was rude to you?'

'Yes.'

'From the house directly opposite?' Simon walked over to the window and pointed, to avoid ambiguity.

'That's right. You seem surprised.'

Kit Bowskill lived in Little Holling, Silsford. Kit Bowskill was Professor Sir Basil Lambert-Wall's neighbour, in Cambridge. How could both those statements be true?

'So . . . the man in the picture, he isn't the one from Safesound, who fitted your alarm?'

Lambert-Wall did his multiple blinking trick again. 'Why would the chap from across the road install my burglar alarm?'

Simon didn't have the heart to remind him of what he'd said last time they spoke. 'You described him as "one of the men who lives in the house opposite". Is there another?'

'Yes. Night Man.'

Simon tried not to show his surprise. Evidently he failed, because the professor laughed. 'I should explain: the man who was rude to me is Day Man. Those aren't their real names – I forgot those long ago, I'm afraid, if I ever knew them.'

'Tell me about Day Man and Night Man,' said Simon as neutrally as possible.

'Night Man is married to Night Woman and they have two children – a boy and a girl – but I never see any of them during the day, only in the evening. And Day Man is married to Day Woman. Well, I say "married to" – who knows what that means in this day and age? Perhaps they aren't married, but they're certainly a couple.'

'So all six of them live in the house – Night Man, Night Woman and their two children, and Day Man and Day Woman?'

'I don't know how they manage it,' said the professor. 'These houses aren't as big as they look from the outside – there's barely enough room in this one for me and my extended family.'

Another surprise. 'You have family living here with you?'

Lambert-Wall smiled, gestured around the room. 'I was referring to my books,' he said.

Simon asked his next question without knowing what he meant by it. 'Have you ever seen Mr and Mrs Night and Mr and Mrs Day together?' He couldn't think at the same time as talking to the old man, not properly. He had to hope his instincts were pushing him in the right direction.

'Now that you come to mention it, no, I haven't. Night Man and Night Woman are there in the evenings, as I said . . .'

'What about weekends?' Simon asked.

'Weekends I spend at my daughter's house in Horseheath. She returns me at ten o'clock on Sunday evening, which allows enough time for me to unpack and be at my writing desk by eleven.'

They were back to the number eleven.

'Anything else spring to mind?' Simon asked.

'Yes. All homes with a population of more than one have their hierarchies, and the house opposite is no exception. I'd hazard a guess that it belongs to Night Man and Night Woman. They and their children take precedence.'

'Why do you say that?' Simon didn't know anyone who bought curtains for a house owned by someone else.

'Their parking arrangements.' The professor smiled. 'Night Man and Night Woman park their cars in their garage. Day Man and Day Woman park on the street. They can't park on the drive – that would block the entrance to the garage. If Night Man and Night Woman came back during the day, they wouldn't be able to get their cars in. At all times, day or night, their parking rights are protected. Doesn't that suggest to you that they're the residents who take priority, and therefore probably the owners?'

'Either that, or . . .' Simon stopped. Would it be unprofessional to say more? He could see no reason why, tonight, he shouldn't do exactly as he pleased. This wasn't work; officially he was still on his honeymoon. 'Or Day Man and Day Woman aren't supposed to be there,' he said.

'What are you implying?' The professor leaned forward. For a second, Simon feared he'd leaned too far and was about to topple out of his chair.

'What if the Night family have no idea they're sharing their house with Mr and Mrs Day?' *Mr and Mrs Day. Kit Bowskill and . . . who?*

'Imposters, you mean? Intruders?' Lambert-Wall considered this in silence for a few seconds. 'No, I'm afraid you're wrong.'

'What makes you say that?'

'Day Man has a key to the house. Day Woman too. I've seen them letting themselves in, together and separately.'

Simon nodded. He thought about the sort of person who might have a key to a house, and about Lorraine Turner, an estate agent he'd never met. Sam hadn't met her either, though he'd spoken to her on the phone.

'Ah.' The professor held aloft the index finger of his right hand. 'I've remembered a name. Isn't it peculiar that one minute you're completely unaware of something, and the next it's as if a screen has been drawn back and there it is: information that must have been there all along?'

'A name?' Simon prompted.

'Yes. Day Woman is called Catriona. Though she told me nobody calls her that, which is rather a shame. The abbreviation of Christian names is a form of vandalism, don't you think?'

Simon knew, with a sick feeling in the pit of his stomach, what was coming. He also knew someone whose name was Catriona.

'Everyone she knows calls her Connie,' said the old man.

19

Saturday 24 July 2010

Selina Gane is standing outside her front door when I pull up in my car. A set of keys dangles from her right hand. In her black trousers and blue linen shirt, she could be an estate agent, ready for her meeting with a prospective buyer.

Isn't that what I am?

Her blonde hair is tied back from her face, which is serious. I wonder if she wears the same expression when she has to give bad news to patients. Or maybe she's not that sort of doctor; maybe she spends her days in a lab examining tissue samples, never coming into contact with their owners.

From her posture, I can see that she's tense. She's not looking forward to this.

Of course she isn't looking forward to it. Why would she be?

I wipe the sweat from my upper lip and get out of the car, remind myself that there's no reason to be nervous. I've already told her everything, in my letter. Today it's her turn to tell me what she knows. I can't believe she knows nothing at all. 11 Bentley Grove is her home.

Except that's not how it feels, as I walk up the lavender-bordered path towards her. Her isolated body language suggests she's found herself standing here, outside a house that has nothing to do with her, and she's not sure why. 'I didn't want to go inside alone,' she says, and I hear how much she wishes 11 Bentley Grove didn't belong to her.

'Thanks for agreeing to meet me,' I say.

She unlocks the front door. Eyes down, she indicates that I should go first. She would rather stay outside in the sun and fresh air, delay the moment of entry for as long as she can. That's when I know for sure: she's going to accept my offer.

She wants nothing to do with 11 Bentley Grove, and it's a violent want, not a mild preference. As we walk in together, she must feel as if she's breaking into a cordoned-off part of her past.

I'm stepping into my future, with no idea what it might contain.

I expected a bad atmosphere, but there's nothing. The inside of 11 Bentley Grove is light and airy. *Harmless*. But then it isn't houses that do harm, it's the people who live in them. I look around, aware of Selina Gane's presence behind me. I smell lavender. She hasn't closed the front door. I expect she will leave it open for as long as we're inside, not wanting to be shut in here.

Without waiting to be asked, I move in the direction of the lounge. I can't remember ever looking at the floorplan on Roundthehouses, but I must have, because I can see it in my mind, and I know where everything is. I know that the room where the dead woman lay is through this door to my right.

I don't need to go in. One glance tells me there's no blood, no body.

Were you really expecting it to be there? Waiting for you?

I see an expanse of unspoilt beige carpet, the edge of the coffee table, the one with the flowers trapped under its glass. The fireplace, the map above it . . . I knew all these things were real, but it's still strange to see them in front of me: like falling into a dream.

'I don't know your husband,' Selina Gane says. 'I've never known him, and I'm not having an affair with him.'

My letter can't have made much sense to her, then.

The stairs. I should have looked at the stairs first, and it worries me that I didn't. My mind is not working as it should; I'm too overwhelmed by being here. For six months I have thought about this house almost constantly. I have spent whole days standing outside it. Now that both its owner and the police have abandoned it, I've set myself the task of unearthing its hidden story.

No one cares about 11 Bentley Grove as much as I do. Is that why I feel as if it's already mine?

Selina Gane fills the silence by saying, 'I'm a doctor. I spend most of my waking hours trying to save lives. I've never killed anyone, and if I was going to, I wouldn't do it in my living room.'

I nod.

'Did your husband really have this address programmed into his SatNav as his home address?' she asks.

'Yes.' I run my hand along the banister. The top of the newel post is dark wood – a curved-edged cube of varnished brown.

'I need to ask you something,' I say. *I need to ask you about the death button*. 'In the picture of . . .'

Start again.

'Something about this staircase is different.' That's better – keep it vague. Don't tell her; let her tell you. 'It hasn't always looked like this, has it?' I pat the flat top of the wooden cube.

She looks confused. 'Yes. It's always looked exactly like that. What do you mean?'

'At one time it had a decorative bit on top that was white.

Sort of round, like . . . like a thick disc. Attached to the top here, but not as wide.' I pat the flat surface again.

'No.' She's shaking her head.

Yes. I saw it.

I try again. 'Like a big button. In the middle, here. White, or cream, maybe.'

'A button?' I watch as she makes a connection. She knows what I'm talking about. For a fraction of a second, when she opens her mouth, I imagine she will smile and say, 'Welcome to the Death Button Centre'. My heart stumbles, its rhythm changing with every beat – drawing out, then slamming in. I might run, if I knew who or what I was running from. What I told Alice once to make her feel sorry for me is true now, even if it wasn't then: I envy all those who know what threatens them, and can name it even if they can't escape it. Fear with nothing concrete to attach itself to is a hundred times worse than fear with a solid cause.

'Why are you asking about my staircase?' The flare of hostility in Selina Gane's voice is unmistakeable. It reminds me that she isn't obliged to tell me anything, and has every reason not to trust me.

'I'm sorry. I should have explained,' I say. 'The last thing either of us needs is more unanswered questions.'

'I won't argue with that,' she says.

'I saw it in the photograph, the same one that had the dead woman in it. On the virtual tour, when the lounge started to rotate . . .'

'Rotate?'

'The pictures on the virtual tour aren't stills,' I tell her. 'For each room, someone must have done a 360-degree turn with a camera in their hand, filming.'

Whoever filmed the lounge must have stood on the edge of the blood, just past where it stopped. He or she must have walked around it, holding the camera, careful not to tread in the wet redness . . .

I push the thought out of my mind.

'When the picture turned, the hall and the bottom of the stairs were visible through the open lounge door. This was visible.' I grip the newel post's curved cube head with both hands. 'It had a white section on the top – round and flat, not spherical. I definitely saw it. I didn't remember it at first, but I knew there was something missing, something else I'd seen apart from the woman and the blood. And then yesterday, I . . . I was talking to someone, and I said the word "button", and suddenly the image was absolutely clear in my mind.'

'That staircase has always looked the way it looks now,' Selina Gane insists.

She's lying.

'When I woke Kit up and he looked at the tour, the woman's body had disappeared and so had the white thing from here,' I say, still clinging on to the post, as if by touching it I can somehow enlist its physicality on my side of the argument. 'I spent the rest of the night opening the virtual tour, watching it again, closing it, opening it again. I must have done it two hundred times – open, look at the lounge, close – but I didn't see the woman's body or the blood again.' Feeling light-headed, I order myself to slow down, breathe. At first the air resists my effort and won't go into my lungs. I stop trying and exhale instead, to the pit of my stomach. *Empty*. Then I inhale slowly, steadily, and feel the oxygen rushing in – an emergency service to the rescue.

'I didn't see the white disc thing again either,' I say. 'It was in the picture of the dead woman, but not the other photo – not the one I've seen every time I've looked since that first time.'

Another memory rushes back to me: Mum, Fran, Benji and me at Bella Italia in Silsford. We went there for lunch last year, to celebrate the arrival of Benji's first grown-up tooth. The waitress gave Benji the activity pack they must give to all children: crayons, dot-to-dots, word searches, various games to keep him amused. There was a game that involved looking at two nearly identical pictures of a dog sitting under a tree, and trying to find the seven differences between them. The first three or four were pretty obvious, even to Benji. Between us, Fran, Mum and I identified the fifth and sixth differences, but none of us could spot the seventh. After nearly half an hour of tormenting ourselves, peering at the piece of paper endlessly, we admitted defeat and looked at the answers which were upside down at the bottom of the page. The seventh difference was so tiny that we would never have spotted it, no matter how many hours we'd wasted looking: one extra line on the tree's lowest leaf in picture two.

'There's a name for what you're describing,' Selina Gane says. 'It's called a mortgage button.'

'A what?'

She sighs. 'I need a drink. Come on.'

I follow her through to the kitchen I've seen so many times on the screen of my laptop. She pulls a tall stool away from the island at the centre of the room – the obligatory island, Kit called it – and indicates that I should sit there. 'Tea or whisky?' she asks.

'Tea, please.'

'I think I'm going to need both,' she says.

I wait in silence while she sorts out the drinks. The words

'mortgage button' turn around slowly in my mind. I examine them from every angle, but still don't understand them. How can something called a mortgage button exist? It sounds too unlikely.

Selina puts milk in my tea, no sugar. It's what I would have told her to do, if she'd asked me.

She doesn't sit, but leans against the sink with her back to the window, holding her whisky with both hands. 'It's an American tradition,' she says eventually. 'When you've paid off your mortgage and you own your house outright, you buy a mortgage button and fix it to the top of the newel post, dead centre – exactly where you said you saw it. You can get cheap plastic ones, wooden ones, engraved ones – even ones made of ivory, for those who want to broadcast their affluence and success to all visitors.' Her tone suggests a low opinion of such people. 'They look a bit like white draughts – you know, as in the game. In America it's called checkers.'

Mum and Dad used to play draughts when I was little, before they finally gave in to Fran's and my protests and bought a television – something every normal person in the country had done several years earlier. 'That's exactly what it looked like: an oversized draught.'

'Then I'm right,' says Selina. 'What you saw was a mortgage button. But there's never been one in this house.'

I can't hear even the faintest trace of an American accent. 'But you know what they are,' I say, hoping it doesn't sound too much like an accusation.

'My friend has one.' Selina's eyes slide away from me. 'She's from New England.' I feel as if a spotlight that was trained on me has been switched off; I'm no longer the focus of her thoughts. She chews the inside of her lip, staring at the shelf next to her – at a white mug that looks like bone china, with a design of red feathers. She reaches to pick it up, looks inside, then puts it back on the shelf. I hear a clinking sound. Whatever's in there, she wanted to check it was still there.

The white button? Having denied its existence, would she be so obvious?

'What aren't you telling me?' I ask. The same question I asked Sam Kombothekra a few days ago, the question I've asked Kit more than a thousand times since January. I ought to have a T-shirt made with those words printed on it.

'Nothing. Sorry,' she says, still looking worried. 'I was just thinking that I've been neglecting my friend recently – all my friends. Too busy with work.'

I nod, pretend I'm satisfied.

'Talking of mortgages, will you need one, to buy? Assuming I agree to sell you the house.'

I tell her I will, that I can sort it out quickly. I hope it's true. 'You won't get a better offer than mine,' I say.

'You're serious about this?'

'Very.'

'I won't ask why you want to,' she says. 'If you really saw what you say you saw . . .' She stops, shakes her head. 'I said I won't ask, so I won't. If you want the house, if this isn't the sickest of sick jokes, you can have it. The sooner I'm rid of it and it's nothing to do with me, the better.'

I can't help smiling. 'An unconventional sales pitch,' I say. 'When you say I can have it . . .'

'For 1.2 million,' she says quickly. 'That's what you offered.'

'Just checking you weren't proposing to give it to me for free.'

'I'll give you my solicitor's details – ask yours to make the offer official, as soon as possible.' She drains her glass, puts it down on the worktop. 'Would you like me to show you round? Or is that a waste of time? You don't care what the rooms look like, presumably. You want to buy the house because you think someone might have been murdered here – the same reason I want to sell it.'

I can't be bothered to defend myself. If she wants to think I'm doing this for ghoulish reasons, let her. 'I'd like to look round,' I say.

'Let's get it over with, then,' she says brusquely. 'I need to get out of here.'

As we go from room to room on the ground floor, she says nothing. Not a word. She hesitates for a few seconds by each door, as if afraid to open it and walk in. There's a conservatory that wasn't in the pictures on the website – plastic, not wood. Kit would hate it.

At the bottom of the stairs, Selina says, 'If you've got any questions, ask.'

'I already have,' I tell her.

'I mean about the house – the central heating, the burglar alarm . . .'

'I'm not interested in anything like that.'

I follow her upstairs. Standing in one room after another, I look around, pretending to pay attention, not really seeing what's in front of me. I'm still thinking about the china mug with the red feathers on it, the hard thing inside it that made a clinking noise.

As Selina leads the way into the bathroom, I say, 'Oh – hang on. I think I can hear my phone ringing in my bag – I'll just go and grab it.' Without waiting for her reaction, I turn and run down the stairs.

On the threshold of the kitchen, I freeze. Did I mention my mobile phone being broken, in the letter? No, I don't think I did. I told her to ring me in my hotel room, but I said nothing about having no mobile.

I move towards the red feather mug. My hand shakes as I lift it off the shelf and look inside. There's no white button or disc in there, only a set of keys attached to a yellow plastic fob. The hammering of my heart throbs in my ears. There's a label on the fob, words written in small handwriting. I pull it out very slowly, so that the keys don't knock against the side of the mug, and take a closer look.

I read it again and again, my eyes racing over the small print. It can't mean what I think it means. *It must.* Why else would Selina have looked at the mug when she did, picked it up to check the key was there? A loud roaring fills my head. My breathing speeds up. I can't control it; it's running away from me.

Oh, my God.

How could I not have known, all this time?

I think of what I told Alice, what Kit said about naming our Cambridge house: *It's growing on me the more I think about it – the Death Button Centre. We could get a plaque made for the front door. No, I know, even better – let's call it 17 Pardoner Lane.*

How could I have told Alice that he said that, and still not realised?

'Connie?' I hear Selina's footsteps above me.

'Coming,' I shout. I stuff the keys into my pocket, replace the empty mug on the shelf, and run back upstairs. 'I've got to go,' I say. 'I just . . .' No convenient lie springs to mind. 'Something's come up.' It's the best I can do. I have to get out of here before Selina realises I've taken the keys.

Why did you take them? What are you planning to do?

She frowns. 'You're still buying though, right?'

For a second, I'm afraid I'll laugh in her face. What would she say if I told her I don't need to pay over the odds for her house any more? *I'm so sorry, but I'm going to have to pass – I've managed to work out what's going on without bankrupting myself. Aren't you pleased for me, Doctor?*

Everything has changed. I no longer need to buy 11 Bentley Grove.

But I still want to. *Why?* asks my internal Alice. *Because it's in Cambridge*, I tell her, *and Cambridge is where I want to live. It's where I've wanted to live since 2003. And this house is for sale, and I've already offered to buy it, and no one was killed here – I was wrong about that. And . . . when I pressed 'Home' on the SatNav, this was the address that came up: 11 Bentley Grove.*

I can't work out whether my reasons are understandable or insane, and I don't much care.

'I'm still buying,' I tell Selina Gane. 'Don't worry, I won't let you down.' And then I run.

20

24/7/2010

'Thank you.' Alice Bean smiled as Charlie took the letter from her. 'Sam Kombothekra looked terrified when I tried to give it to him.'

'Men are cowards.' Charlie opened her bag, made sure Alice saw her putting the envelope safely inside. 'You could give Sam a note for the milkman and he'd worry about getting mixed up in a scandal.'

'My aim isn't to make trouble. The opposite. I care about Simon.'

'Then take this opportunity to help him.' Charlie reminded herself that she was here to extract information. It would have been too easy to say, 'Yeah, well, he wants nothing to do with you – why do you think I'm here?'

She'd suggested to Alice that they meet at Spillages café, but Alice had proposed the park instead. It had irritated Charlie at the time – she hated people who talked about being 'cooped up' and behaved as if it was obligatory to go and stand directly under the sun whenever it was out – but now she was glad to be in the open air, following the narrow tree-fringed footpath around the lake, listening as the birds overhead conducted a vigorous debate in a language she didn't understand. Walking alongside somebody, you didn't have to look at their face, or let them see yours. Sitting across a table from Alice would have been much harder.

Harder to resist the temptation to say, 'Oh, by the way – guess who got married last Friday?' Charlie had decided before ringing Alice that she wouldn't mention it. She knew that to tell her would lead to open hostility between them, even if she didn't know exactly how it would happen. Probably it would be her fault. In her official capacity as Simon's wife, she might feel obliged to say, 'Take your letter and stick it up your arse.'

She hoped she'd be glad later – proud, even – that she'd chosen the mature, non-confrontational path. She certainly wasn't enjoying it now, while it was happening; hostility, even if you went on to regret it later, was much more fun in the short term.

'I'll help if I can,' said Alice, 'but . . . can I ask you a question first?'

'Fire away.'

'Do you think Simon will ever forgive me?'

That was one Charlie could answer honestly. 'No idea,' she said. 'He might have forgiven you already. Or he might bear a grudge for ever. The only thing I can guarantee is that he'll never discuss it with anyone.' *Especially not me.*

Alice had stopped in front of a wooden bench by the edge of the lake, under a weeping willow. She brushed the trailing leaves off it and bent to read the writing on the gold plaque. 'I can never walk past one of these without reading it,' she told Charlie. 'I'd feel as if I was leaving someone to die alone. Look at this one – two brothers, both died on 29 April 2005. One was twenty-two and one twenty-four. How sad.'

'Car accident, probably,' Charlie said matter-of-factly. She didn't want to talk about sad things with Alice. With anyone. She imagined herself and Liv both dying on the same day as she reached into her bag for her cigarettes; getting one in her mouth and lit suddenly felt like an urgent need. She took a long drag. 'When I die, I want my park bench plaque to say, "She always meant to give that up." '

Alice laughed. 'That's good.'

'Simon's worried about Connie Bowskill.' *Time to stop pretending you're friends enjoying a nice day out.* With someone like Alice Bean, there was no such thing as small talk, in any case. So far she'd brought up forgiveness, lonely death, family tragedies – what subject would be next, the torture of small animals?

'I'm worried too.'

'Do you know where Connie is?' Charlie asked.

'No. She's not answering her landline or her mobile.'

'When did you last speak to her?'

'Much as I'd like to tell you, I'm not allowed to,' said Alice. 'Patient confidentiality.'

Charlie nodded. 'I understand that you have to respect Connie's privacy. I also know you're not averse to drafting a new set of ethical guidelines when someone might be in danger. You did it for your own sake, seven years ago. Isn't it worth relaxing your professional integrity to ensure Connie's safety?'

'I did it for my daughter's sake seven years ago,' Alice corrected her, apparently without resentment. 'And I don't know for sure that Connie's in danger, or that Simon can keep her safe, assuming she is.'

'But you think she might be in danger.' *You've been trying to convince yourself otherwise, and you've failed.*

'I was pretty shocked last time she came to see me,' Alice admitted. 'Having been one myself, I recognise a creature threatened with extinction when I meet one. There's a really harmful energy around Connie, trying to crush the life out of her. It's unmistakeable – being in a room with her has never been easy, but recently it's been a real challenge – just for me to stay there, to keep reminding myself that she's someone who needs my help. What I can't tell is whether the threat has an external origin, one that she's internalised, or whether the vicious energy's coming from Connie herself. It's not easy to distinguish the two – when people seek to destroy us, we often respond by making ourselves their accomplice, punishing ourselves on their behalf.'

'Any chance I could get some or all of that in layman's terms?' Charlie asked.

Alice stopped walking. 'My gut instinct tells me Connie might not survive. Either there's someone out there trying to obliterate her, or she's doing it to herself.'

'Who's your money on?'

Charlie didn't expect an answer, and was surprised when Alice said, 'The husband.'

'Kit?'

'Yesterday was Connie's birthday. His present to her was a dress: the same one she saw on the dead woman in the virtual tour picture – different colours, but the design was the same. I shouldn't be telling you any of this.'

'So you spoke to her yesterday,' said Charlie. Why was it that everything Connie Bowskill said – to Simon, Sam, Alice – required a such a gargantuan suspension of disbelief? *Because the woman's a pathological liar*. 'Apart from the dress, what did the two of you talk about?'

'Connie's fears, her unhappiness, her suspicions – same as usual. Our sessions are always hard-going, but . . . I've never been frightened for her before, but this time she said two things that . . . I don't know, this thing with the dresses really shook me. I had a nightmare last night – I knew it was a nightmare, even though everything in it really happened. I dreamed my session with Connie, exactly as it was: her sitting in my consulting room telling me that one dress was blue and pink, the other green and mauve.' Alice shuddered. 'Sometimes, all the evil seems to be packed into the smallest details.'

Charlie knew what she meant, and wished she didn't.

'I can't stop thinking about Kit – a man I've never met – taking two dresses up to the till, one for each of his women. One of them ends up dead on a carpet somewhere in Cambridge – what's going to happen to the other one?' Alice turned towards Charlie, put a hand on her arm. Her face was pale in contrast to her bright red lipstick. 'Where is she? Why isn't she answering either of her phones?'

'You said there were two things.' Charlie realised she was at an advantage, as the person who cared least. She also felt excluded. Simon was worried about Connie Bowskill; Alice was, if anything, even more worried. They could get together and have a panic party. Charlie was as convinced as she'd ever been that Crazy Connie was talking nonsense; she wouldn't be invited. 'What else did Connie say that scared you?' she asked Alice.

'It won't make sense out of context: "the Death Button Centre".'

Charlie laughed. 'The what?'

'I wasn't the only one who was scared. Something occurred to Connie when she said it – something she hadn't thought of before. I saw it dawn on her, whatever it was. Like she'd seen a ghost inside her head. She ran – literally, ran away.'

'The Death Button Centre?'

'Connie and Kit nearly moved to Cambridge in 2003. The house they were going to buy was next to a school building called the Beth Dutton Centre. Connie was stressed at the thought of leaving her family behind. She got it into her head that she couldn't live in a house that didn't have a name.'

'A name?'

'You know: The Beeches, The Poplars, Summerfields . . .'

'Right, I see,' said Charlie. Did she? No, not really. Not at all, in fact. 'Why couldn't she live in a house without a name?' Plenty of people did; most people.

'It was an excuse. Connie's lived in Little Holling all her life, and all the houses there have names – it's what she's used to. She was afraid of straying too far from the only place she'd ever known, and ashamed to admit it. She and Kit had found this house – the perfect house, or so she said – and she told him she wouldn't buy it unless they could give it a name. It was attached to the Beth Dutton Centre on one side, and Kit – as a joke – suggested calling it the Death Button Centre. He asked her if she thought it'd annoy the Beth Dutton Centre people, and the postman.'

Charlie turned away to hide her smile. Alice and Connie could find it terrifying if they wanted to; she reserved the right to find it amusing. 'So you think Connie realised something as she was telling you this? Something that frightened her enough to make her run?'

'I'm certain of it. I keep going over the conversation in my mind – there was nothing else that could have panicked her. It was the last thing she said before she left.'

'What exactly did she say, can you remember?'

'Only what I've already told you: that Kit wanted to call the house the Death Button Centre, or pretended to want to – it wasn't clear which. I assume he was joking. No one would really give a house that name, would they?'

Charlie didn't think there was anything about which you could safely say, 'No one would do it.' There was always some lunatic who would step forward to prove you wrong. After what Alice had been through – after what she herself had done – Charlie wondered how she could be so naïve.

'He said the name was growing on him the more he thought about it, suggested getting a plaque made for the front door.' Alice's eyes narrowed as she concentrated on the memory. 'I think that was the last thing Connie said before she . . . Oh, no, sorry. Kit suggested another name for the house, even sillier – 17 Pardoner Lane – but that wasn't what provoked Connie's fearful reaction.'

'How do you know?'

'It's hard to explain. You probably don't believe in energetic vibrations . . .'

'Probably not,' Charlie agreed.

Alice changed tack. 'Take my word for it: it was the Death Button Centre that frightened Connie – that horrible name. Who would dream up such a disturbing name for a house they loved and wanted to live in? Even as a joke, you wouldn't.'

Somehow, Charlie felt the shiver as it passed through Alice's body. How was that possible?

The Death Button Centre. *Press the button and someone dies.*

'17 Pardoner Lane was the address of the perfect house they didn't buy,' said Alice.

'So Kit wanted to stick with just the address?'

'No, he . . .' Alice looked up at the sky. 'Oh,' she said, sounding surprised at having interrupted herself. 'Maybe you're right. Maybe what he meant was, "Let's not call the house something daft – let's be sensible and call it by its address: 17 Pardoner

Lane." Though, I have to say, that wasn't my impression, from what Connie said.'

'You've lost me,' said Charlie.

'I thought she meant that Kit had leapt from the absurd to the even more absurd and suggested 17 Pardoner Lane as a *name* for the house – one that also happened to be its address. I thought the duplication was the joke.' Seeing the expression on Charlie's face, Alice looked embarrassed. 'I know – it's mad. But so is the Death Button Centre. Connie's often described Kit as funny, witty – maybe he's got a surreal sense of humour.'

'So letters would be addressed to 17 Pardoner Lane, 17 Pardoner Lane, Cambridge?' Charlie found herself smiling again. 'Sounds to me like he was taking the piss out of her.' The more Charlie thought about it, the more she liked the idea: giving a house its own address as a name was a bit like sticking two fingers up at everyone who took the business of house-naming too seriously. She decided to suggest it to Simon: 21 Chamberlain Street, 21 Chamberlain Street, Spilling. They could have labels printed. Simon's mother, who had no sense of humour, would be horrified, and, although nothing would be said in so many words, Simon and Charlie would be given to understand that the Lord shared her horror. It was nothing short of miraculous, the way God and Kathleen Waterhouse saw eye to eye on every issue.

Liv would think it was hilarious.

'I'm going to have to go.' Alice looked at her watch. 'I've got to take my daughter to a birthday party.'

'If you remember anything else, can you ring me?' said Charlie. Simon wasn't going to be happy. A joke about calling a house the Death Button Centre was unlikely to be the answer to anything. If Connie Bowskill was in a fragile emotional state, on a self-destruct mission, mightn't the word 'death' be enough to bring on an attack of paranoia? She had probably put two things together that weren't connected at all – a daft joke her husband made years ago, and the dead woman she'd seen on her computer screen, or claimed to have seen.

As she watched Alice walk away, Charlie felt something vibrate against her stomach. *Energy vibrations*. What crap. She pulled her mobile phone out of her bag. It was Sam Kombothekra. 'What are you doing?' he asked without preamble.

'Not much,' said Charlie. 'How about you?' Under normal circumstances, she would have told him, but she didn't want to say the name 'Alice' out loud in case Sam sensed her guilt down the phone. Not that she felt guilty; she simply recognised that she was. Or soon would be. On this occasion, her culpability didn't bother her. Tucking her phone under her chin, she used both hands to retrieve Alice's letter from her handbag.

'Where are you?' Sam asked.

Charlie laughed. 'Is your next question, "What colour underwear are you wearing?" '

'My next question is, where's Simon? I've been trying to ring him.'

'He's in Bracknell talking to Kit Bowskill's parents,' Charlie told him. How ludicrous that she felt proud: she knew where Simon was and Sam didn't.

'Can you meet me at the Brown Cow in fifteen minutes?'

'Should be okay. What's the problem?'

'I'll tell you when I see you.'

'I'll get there quicker with a hint to speed me on my way,' said Charlie. Her fingers traced the sealed flap of the envelope. Nothing good would come of opening it; Simon was unaware of its existence, and Charlie didn't want its contents in her own head any more than she wanted them in his. She ripped the envelope into small pieces, then smaller ones still, letting them fall at her feet.

'Jackie Napier,' said Sam. 'The problem is Jackie Napier.'

~

'You have to treat it as you would a bereavement,' Barbara Bowskill told Simon. 'You used to have a son, but you don't any more. You're in the same position as a mother whose son went to fight in Iraq and was killed by a bomb, or someone whose child died of cancer, or was murdered by a paedophile. You tell yourself there's nothing you can do – they're gone – and you stop hoping.' She looked like Simon's idea of what a bereavement counsellor ought to look like, though in reality they rarely did: frizzy dyed auburn hair, grey at the roots; an embroidered tunic over flared jeans, chunky wooden jewellery, sandals with fabric tops and heels made of rope and cork. And no real bereavement counsellor would advise pretending that one's child had been murdered by a paedophile when that child was alive and well and living in Silsford.

Not for the first time since he'd arrived, Simon had doubts about Kit Bowskill's mother. It wasn't only the paedophile remark. He found her smile unsettling, and was glad he'd only seen it twice – once when she'd opened the door to let him in, and then again when she'd handed him a mug of tea and he'd thanked her. It was intrusive, a violation of a smile – one that suggested extreme empathy, shared pain, yearning and a strong desire to devour the soul of its recipient. There was too much crinkling of the skin around the eyes, too much pursing of the lips, almost as if she was about to blow a kiss and start crying simultaneously.

Nigel Bowskill looked as if he belonged to a different world from his wife, in his grey suit trousers, green T-shirt and white trainers. 'It's too painful otherwise,' he explained. 'We can't spend the rest of our lives waiting for Kit to change his mind. He hasn't for seven years. Probably never will.'

'Why should he have that power over us?' Barbara sounded defensive, though no one had criticised her. There was something odd about the way this couple spoke, thought Simon – as if each disagreed violently with what the other had just said, though if you listened to the words rather than the tone, they appeared to be unanimous all the way down the line.

So far, Simon hadn't enjoyed being in their house: a detached beige-brick modern villa which, together with its built-on double garage, made an L-shape. He reminded himself that it didn't matter; this was unpaid work, not fun. Day eight of his honeymoon. He wished he'd brought Charlie with him, but knew that if by some miracle time were to rewind to yesterday, he would choose again to make the trip alone. 'It must be hard,' he said. 'Do you mind if I ask what caused the rift?'

'Kit didn't tell you?' Barbara rolled her eyes at her own foolishness. 'No, of course he didn't, because he couldn't, not without revealing something about himself that he didn't want you to know – that once he tried to do something and didn't succeed, shock horror. What you've got to understand about my son is that he's the most intensely private person you'll ever meet, as well as the proudest. Since he refuses to come to terms with his own fallibility, his pride is easily wounded – that's where the secrecy comes in, all in the good cause of saving face. There's no doubt in Kit's mind that the whole world is watching him, eagerly awaiting his downfall. He might seem relaxed and chatty on the surface, but don't be fooled – it's all image management.'

'He spent his whole childhood hiding from us,' said Nigel.

Automatically, Simon looked round the living room for possible hiding places, and saw none; there was nothing here to hide behind, only two leather sofas at right angles to one another, each one pushed up against a wall. The hall Simon had been ushered through had been the same, as had the kitchen he'd stood in, briefly, while Barbara made him a cup of tea. He'd never seen a less cluttered house. There were no shelves, no ornaments, no coats on pegs by the front door, no plants, no fruit bowls or clocks, no occasional tables. The house was like a film set, not yet fully installed. Where did Kit's parents keep all their things? Simon had asked them if they'd only just moved in, and been told that they'd lived in the house for twenty-six years.

'I don't mean he hid physically,' Barbara was saying. 'We always knew where he was. He never stayed out and left us worrying, like some of his friends did to their parents.'

'We thought we knew *who* he was, too,' said Nigel, whose face was his son's plus two and a half decades. 'A contented, polite, obedient boy – sailed through school, loads of mates.'

'He showed us what he knew we wanted to see,' Barbara blurted out, as if afraid her husband might get to the punchline first if she wasn't quick about it. 'All through his childhood, our son was his own spin doctor.'

'What was he trying to hide?' Simon asked. So far, the questioning had been all one way. If either of Kit Bowskill's parents wondered why a detective had invited himself to their house in order to ask about their son, they were keeping quiet about it. If only everyone Simon interviewed could share their lack of curiosity; he hated having to explain himself, even when the explanation was a good one.

'No guilty secrets,' said Nigel. 'Only himself.'

'His low opinion of himself,' Barbara amended. 'What he perceived as his weakness. Of course, we've only worked all this out in retrospect – we've been rather like detectives, you might say. We've spoken to his school friends, found out things we had no idea about at the time because Kit made sure to conceal them from us – the torture he inflicted on boys who won the prizes he thought he should have won, the bribes he offered those same boys once he'd come to his senses, so that they wouldn't say anything to their parents or teachers about who'd injured them.'

'He terrified the life out of all those who came within his orbit,' said Nigel.

Barbara smiled. 'In his absence, we've put together a psychological profile of him, the way you lot do with criminals. At the time, he had us completely fooled. Deliberately or not, he played on our egos. Nigel and I were happy, prosperous – we had a successful business. Of course we believed that our son was this blessed golden boy who never suffered a set-back, never got upset or angry, never admitted to having a problem.'

'His act was watertight.' The regret in Nigel's voice was laced with admiration, Simon thought. 'He couldn't bear for anybody to see that he was an ordinary human being who sometimes made a fool of himself – with highs and lows, just like the rest of us. Kit had to appear to be above all that – always in control, happy all the time . . .'

'Which meant that no one was allowed to know what mattered to him, or that he sometimes got upset, that he sometimes failed or wasn't the best at something.' Barbara's frenzied delivery made it hard to listen to her. Her eagerness to speak made her sound unbalanced. She seemed to find it unbearable when it was her husband's turn and she had to wait. 'All his life, Kit's worked on an image of perfection. *That's* the real reason he can't forgive us – for a few hours in 2003, the mask slipped and we saw him agitated and unhappy, having cocked up something that really mattered to him. It's himself he won't forgive, for allowing things to reach the point where he needed to come to us for help – nothing to do with us not giving him the fifty grand.'

'Fifty thousand pounds?' Simon asked. Was that what Kit had meant when he'd said his parents had failed to 'rally round'?

Nigel nodded. 'He needed it to buy a house.'

'I've still got the brochure somewhere, I think,' said Barbara. 'Kit brought it round to show us. When we wouldn't cooperate, he told us he didn't want the brochure, not if he couldn't have the house. "Why don't you tear it up, or burn it?" he said. "I expect you'd enjoy that." I think he thought that as soon as we looked at the pictures and saw how stunning it was, we'd hand over the money. And it *was* stunning, but . . . it wasn't worth the amount the vendor was asking Kit to pay on top, and we didn't think it would be fair on the people who thought they were buying it if Kit and Connie were to pull the rug out from under them all of a sudden. What kind of charlatan behaviour is that?'

'It was no way to treat them, and no way to treat us.' Nigel threw this out as a challenge, daring someone to disagree. He was gearing up to have the fight all over again, as if Kit were sitting here opposite him instead of Simon. 'Connie and Kit could easily have afforded a house in Cambridge that was more than adequate for their needs – there'll have been any number of places they could have bought. Why did they have to have this particular house, which was effectively already sold?

Because Kit was too proud to compromise, determined to hold out for the ideal?

'Kit saw no need to tell us why,' said Barbara. 'He behaved as though it was his God-given right to have that house, at whatever cost.'

'He had a damn nerve, telling us he wanted to waste fifty thousand pounds doing something immoral and expecting us to foot the bill. He didn't even ask for a loan, that was what got to me. Said nothing about paying the money back, just expected us to give it to him. When we said no, he turned vicious.'

Simon wanted to ask Nigel what he'd meant about the house already being sold, but he didn't want to interrupt. He could get the details later. 'Vicious how?' he asked instead.

'Oh, it all came out. Barbara and I had no standards – we didn't know the difference between a good thing and a bad thing, didn't know a beautiful house when we saw one, didn't understand the importance of beauty, didn't notice it when it was staring us in the face. Oh, and we didn't notice ugliness either, and didn't take the appropriate steps to avoid it – we'd only ever bought ugly houses.' Nigel tried to sound light-hearted as he reeled off the list of his son's insults, but Simon could hear the hurt in his voice.

'And of course we'd made Kit suffer, because he'd had to live in those ugly houses with us,' Barbara contributed. 'He said we were like animals, we didn't understand about aiming high and only accepting the best. What did we know about anything? We'd chosen to live in three awful, barbaric places one after another: first Birmingham, then Manchester, then Bracknell – all places that should be wiped off the face of the earth. How could we have made Kit live in them? How could we have lived in them ourselves?'

'From the moment Kit set foot in Cambridge, nowhere else was good enough,' said Nigel. 'We weren't good enough any more.'

'Though Kit was so skilled at concealment, we had no idea we'd gone down in his estimation – not until we wouldn't give him the money he thought it was his right to take, and he was angry enough to tell us that everything we'd ever done was wrong.'

'The list of our crimes was endless.' Nigel started to count them off on his fingers. 'We should have moved to Cambridge when Kit started at university – moved our home and our business – so that he wouldn't have to leave the city in the holidays and come back to Bracknell . . .'

'. . . which he described as "the death of hope". Imagine saying that about your home!'

'We should have helped him when he finished his degree and the only job he could get was in Rawndesley – should have offered to support him financially, so that he didn't have to move, didn't have to leave Cambridge.'

'At the time he'd told us he was thrilled with his new job in Rawndesley and really looking forward to a change of scene!'

'His usual tactic,' said Nigel. 'Pretending that what had happened was what he'd wanted all along, so that he could come out looking like the winner.'

'He was very convincing. Kit's always convincing.' Barbara stood up. 'Would you like to see his room?' she asked Simon. 'I've kept it exactly how he left it – like a dead child's room, everything just the same, and me the grieving mother, curator of the museum.' She let out a bark of laughter.

'Why would he want to see Kit's bedroom?' Nigel snapped. 'We don't even know why he's here. It's not as if Kit's missing and he's after leads.'

Simon, on his feet now, waited to be asked about the reason for his visit.

'He might be missing,' Barbara told her husband. 'We don't know, do we? Might even be dead. If he isn't, then he's of interest to the police for some other reason. Anyone who wants to understand Kit needs to see his bedroom.'

'We'd have been told if he was dead,' said Nigel. 'They'd have to tell us. Wouldn't you?'

Simon nodded. 'I'd like to see the room, if you don't mind showing me,' he said.

'The more the merrier,' said Barbara, her tone flirtatious. She stretched out her arms, inviting a non-existent crowd to join them. 'Though I warn you, I'm rusty. I haven't done my tour guide bit for a while.' Out came the voracious maudlin smile again; Simon tried not to recoil.

Nigel sighed. 'I won't be joining you,' he said.

'No one asked you to.' Barbara slapped down her response like a trump card.

Simon followed her out of the room. Halfway up the stairs, she stopped and turned to face him. 'You're probably wondering why we don't ask,' she said. 'For the sake of our emotional survival, we can't give in to our curiosity. It's much easier if we hear no news.'

'It must take a lot of discipline,' said Simon.

'Not really. No one likes to suffer unnecessarily, or at least I don't, and Nigel doesn't. Any new information about our ex-son would knock three days off our lives. Even the most insignificant detail – that Kit went to the shop and bought a newspaper this morning, that he wore a particular shirt yesterday. Even if that was all you told me, I'd be in bed tomorrow, unable to do anything. I don't want to have to think about him in the present tense – does that make sense?'

Simon hoped not, hoped it didn't make the sense he thought it made.

'We have to believe time has stopped,' Barbara lectured him, as convinced of the rightness of her position as a political campaigner. 'That's why I go into his room every day. Nigel can't bear it. Neither can I, really, but if I didn't go in, I wouldn't know for sure that it hadn't changed. And someone has to keep it clean.'

She climbed the remaining stairs to the first-floor landing. Simon followed her. There were four doors, all closed. One had a large sheet of paper stuck to it, on which someone had drawn a black rectangle, sides perfectly straight, and written something inside it in small black handwriting. From where he was, Simon couldn't read it.

'That's Kit's room, with the notice on the door,' said Barbara. Simon had guessed as much. As he moved closer, he saw that the sign was made of something thicker than paper – a kind of thin canvas board. And the words had been painted on, not written. Carefully; it looked almost like calligraphy. Kit Bowskill had intended the sign on his door to be more than a means of imparting information.

Barbara, standing behind Simon, recited the words aloud as he read them. The effect was unsettling, as if she was the voice of his thoughts. 'Civilization is the progress towards a society of privacy. The savage's whole existence is public, ruled by the laws of his tribe. Civilization is the process of setting man free from men.'

Beneath the quote was a name: 'Ayn Rand'. Author of *The Fountainhead*. It was one of many novels that Simon wished he'd read, but never actually fancied reading. 'This an intellectual way of saying, "Kit's Room – Keep Out"?' he asked Barbara.

She nodded. 'We did. Religiously. Until Kit told us we'd seen him and spoken to him for the last time. Then I thought, "Sod it – if I'm losing my son, at least I can get a room in my house back." I was so livid, I could have ripped the walls down.' The electric tremor in her voice suggested she was no less angry now. 'I went in there intending to strip it bare, but I couldn't, not when I saw what he'd done. How could I destroy my son's secret work of art when it was all I had left of him? Nigel says it's not art, Kit's not an artist, but I can't see any other way to describe it.'

Simon was closest to the door – two footsteps away. He could have walked in and seen it for himself, whatever it was, instead of standing outside listening to Barbara describe it obliquely, but that would have felt inappropriate; he ought to wait for her permission.

'Have you ever had your heart run over by a large truck?' She pressed both her hands to her chest. 'That's what happened to me when I opened that door for the first time in eleven years. I couldn't understand it at all – what was I looking at? *Now* it makes sense, now that I've got to know Kit a bit better, in his absence.'

Eleven years. *Number eleven again*. In spite of the heat, a cold shiver snaked down Simon's back. Barbara must have seen the question in his eyes, because she said, 'Nigel and I were banned when Kit was eighteen. He came home from his first term at university and that was the first thing he said. It wasn't just us, because we were his parents – everyone was banned. No one set foot in his room after that – he made sure of it. He didn't bring friends round often, but when he did, they stayed in the lounge. Even Connie, when the two of them used to come and visit, he never took her upstairs. They'd sit in the lounge, or the den. Kit had his own flat by the time they met – I don't think Connie knew he still had a room here, one that was more important to him than any of the ones he actually lived in. You wouldn't think of it, would you? Most people, when they move out, they move out altogether.'

Unless they had something they wanted or needed to hide, thought Simon. Most people couldn't get away with saying to their girlfriends who lived with them, 'This room's mine – you're not allowed anywhere near it.' Come to think of it, most people couldn't get away with saying that to their parents either. 'In eleven years, you weren't tempted to go in and have a look?'

'I probably would have been, but Kit had a lock fitted.' Barbara nodded at the door. 'That's a new one, with no lock, to symbolise the new admissions policy: my ex-son's room is open to the public, twenty-four seven. I'll show it to anyone who wants to see it,' she said defiantly, then giggled. 'If Kit doesn't like it, let him come back and complain.'

'You had the old door removed, the one with the lock?' Simon asked.

'Nigel kicked it down,' Barbara told him proudly. 'After the "big bust-up".' She mimed inverted commas. 'It was the only way we could get in. Nigel said, "At least it's clean", which was a bit of an understatement – it was cleaner than I could ever get a room to be, that's for sure. Kit bought his own hoover, dusters, polish, the works. He used to come round once a fortnight and spend a couple of hours in there, maintaining it – you could hear the hoover buzzing away. I don't think Connie knew what he was doing – she spent so much of her free time round at her mum and dad's, Kit could come here at weekends and she'd know nothing about it. Nigel and I used to feel sorry for her in her ignorance, shut out of something that was so important to him – as if we were the lucky ones, privy to his secrets, because we knew about his room even if we didn't know what was in it.'

Barbara shook her head as pride gave way to frustration. 'We were idiots, letting an eighteen-year-old child lock us out of a room in our own house. If I had my time again, I wouldn't let Kit *close* a door against me, let alone lock it. I'd watch him like a hawk, every second of every day.' She pointed her finger at Simon as if to fix him in place. 'I'd sit by the side of his bed all night and stare at him while he slept. I'd stand next to the shower while he washed, even stand over him while he was on the toilet. I'd allow him no privacy whatsoever. He'd be horrified if he heard me saying this, and I don't care. Privacy's the soil that nourishes all sprouting evils, if you ask me.'

'Can we have a look at the room?' Simon asked, finding her repellent. If he'd met her before what she called the 'big bust-up', he would probably have felt quite differently about her. She'd have been a different person then. Simon would never have admitted it to anyone, but he often felt disgusted by people to whom exceptionally bad things had happened; his fault, not theirs. He figured it was something to do with a desire to distance himself from the tragedy, whatever it was. If anything, it made him try harder to help them, to compensate.

'Go ahead,' said Barbara. 'I'll follow you in a minute. I don't want to get in the way of your first impression.'

Simon turned the handle. As the door swung open, the smell

of furniture polish was unmistakeable. Kit Bowskill might not have set foot in his private sanctuary since 2003, but someone had been maintaining it to his high standard since then. Barbara. It was the sort of thing only a mother would bother doing.

'Don't fall over the hoover,' she warned. 'Unlike all the other rooms in this house, Kit's actually has things in it.' She laughed. 'I got rid of the bulk of what Nigel and I owned about six months after Kit gave us our marching orders. If we didn't have a son any more, there didn't seem much point in us having anything.'

The door stood half open. Simon pushed it all the way and walked in. The room was full without being cluttered: bed, two chairs, desk, wardrobe, chest of drawers, a bookcase against one wall with a Dyson vacuum cleaner next to it. Between the bookcase and the too-small window there was a line-up of cleaning products – for glass, for wood, for carpets – next to a grey plastic bucket from which six feather-dusters protruded, a mockery of a vase of flowers.

At first Simon thought the walls were papered, because every inch of wall space was covered, and the ceiling. He quickly saw that it couldn't be paper; there was no repeated pattern. No designer, not even the most radical, would create something this convoluted and bizarre. *Photographs*. Simon realised he was looking at hundreds of photographs, melded together in such a way that you couldn't see the joins. Maybe there were none; Simon couldn't see lines where one picture started and another finished. How had Kit done it? Had he taken all these photos and had them made into wallpaper, somehow?

They were all of roads and buildings, apart from the ones on the ceiling. Those were of the sky: plain pale blue, blue streaked with white cloud, grey flecked with sunset pinks and reds; a deep blue with part of the moon in one corner, a curve of uneven glowing white.

Simon moved closer to the wall; he'd spotted a street he recognised. Yes, there was the Six Bells pub, the one near the Live and Let Live, where he'd met Ian Grint. 'Is this . . . ?' Turning in search of Barbara, he found himself looking at the books on the shelves instead. They were lined up in neat rows, their spines exactly level. From their titles, Simon saw that they had a subject in common.

'Welcome to Cambridge in Bracknell,' said Barbara.

Histories of Cambridge, books about the origins of the university, the boat race, Cambridge's rivalry with Oxford; about famous people associated with the city, Cambridge and its artists, Cambridge and the writers it inspired, the pubs of Cambridge, the gardens of Cambridge, its architecture, its bridges, the gargoyles on the college buildings, *A Cambridge Childhood*, Cambridge college chapels, Cambridge and science, spies with a Cambridge connection.

Simon saw the words 'Pink Floyd' – had he found a book that broke the pattern? No, it was *The Pink Floyd Fan's Illustrated Guide to Cambridge*.

At the far end of one shelf there was a pristine copy of the city's *A–Z* – an old one, if Kit hadn't been inside this room since 2003, but it looked brand new. On the shelf above it, Simon saw a row of Cambridge *Yellow Pages* and telephone directories.

He was aware, suddenly, of Barbara standing beside him. 'We knew he was fond of the place,' she said. 'We had no idea it was an all-consuming obsession.'

Simon was reading the road signs in the photographs: De Freville Avenue, Hills Road, Newton Road, Gough Way,

Glisson Road, Grantchester Meadows, Alpha Road, St Edward's Passage. No Pardoner Lane, or at least none that Simon had seen yet. He looked up at the pictures of the Cambridge sky. Thought about eighteen-year-old Kit Bowskill, unwilling to sleep under its Bracknell equivalent.

Connie had been wrong. She'd told Simon that Kit had been in love with someone while he was at university, someone he wouldn't tell her about, whose existence he flat-out denied. For obvious reasons, she'd suspected it was Selina Gane.

It wasn't. It was no one. The love Kit Bowskill had been intent on hiding from his wife – so strong that he either couldn't put it into words, or was unwilling to – was not for any individual inhabitant of Cambridge. It was for the city itself.

Barbara was doing her tour-guide bit, as promised. 'This is the Fen Causeway – Nigel and I used to drive along it when we went to visit. King's College Chapel you probably spotted. The Wren Library at Trinity. Drummer Street Bus Station . . .'

Simon was aware of his breathing and not much else. Like Kit Bowskill seven years ago, he could think about only one thing.

'Are you all right?' Barbara asked. 'You look a bit worried.'

18 Pardoner Lane.

Kit Bowskill, who hated to fail, had found his perfect house in his perfect city. His parents wouldn't give him the money he needed, so he hadn't been able to buy it, but someone had bought it. Someone had succeeded where Kit had failed.

Someone who, at the time, must have felt lucky.

21

Saturday 24 July 2010

'Do you have a job?' DS Alison Laskey asks me, determinedly calm in the face of my agitation. She's a slim, middle-aged woman with short, no-nonsense brown hair. She reminds me of a politician's wife from about twenty years ago – dutiful and muted.

'I have two jobs,' I tell her. 'My husband and I have our own company, and I also work for my parents.' We're in the same interview room that Kit and I were in on Tuesday, with the chicken-wire grid covering the window. 'Look, what does this have to do with Ian Grint? All I want is—'

'Imagine if you were on holiday – sunning yourself on a beach, say – and someone turned up at one of your workplaces asking for your mobile number. Would you want your mum and dad, or the people at your company, to hand over your number, so that the person could interrupt your holiday?'

'I'm not *asking* for Ian Grint's mobile number.'

'You were when you first arrived,' says DS Laskey.

'I understand why you can't give it to me. All I'm asking now is that *you* ring DC Grint and ask him to ring me. Or . . . meet me somewhere, so that I can talk to him. I need to talk to him. He can ring me at my hotel. I can be back there in—'

'Connie, stop. Whether he's interrupted by you or by me, it's still an interruption, isn't it?' DS Laskey smiles. 'And it's his day off. And there's no reason to disturb him. All police work is done on a team basis. You can talk to me about whatever's bothering you. I'm familiar with your . . . situation already, so I know the background. I've read the statement you gave us.'

'Was it you who decided there was no murder at 11 Bentley Grove? Was it your decision to just leave it, forget all about it?'

Laskey's mouth twitches. 'What was it that you wanted to tell Ian?' she asks.

'There *was* a murder,' I tell her. 'Come with me and I'll show you.'

'You'll *show* me?' Her eyebrows shoot up. 'What will you show me, Connie? A dead woman lying in a pool of blood?'

'Yes.' What choice do I have but to brazen it out? Even if the dead woman isn't there any more, the blood must be. Traces of it, at least. 'Will you come with me?' I ask.

'I'll be glad to,' says Laskey, 'but first I'd like you to tell me where we'll be going, and why.'

'What's the point? You think I'm delusional – you're not going to believe anything I say. Come with me and see for yourself, and then I'll tell you – when you'll have no choice but to take me seriously.' I push back my chair, stand up. The keys I took from the mug on Selina Gane's shelf hang heavy in my pocket.

'Sit down,' Laskey says. I hear the slump of weariness in her voice. 'It's Ian Grint's day off today, not mine. I have work to do, in this building.' She gestures around the room, as if I might be in some doubt as to what she means by 'this building'. 'I can't abandon ship unless I'm convinced there's a need. Like it or not, if you want me to accompany you somewhere, you'll have to give me a full explanation now.'

And then you'll decide I'm even crazier than you already think I am.

I fall back into my chair. I might as well get on with it, if I have no choice. I turn my head so that I can't see her, and start talking, imagining I'm addressing a more sympathetic listener: Sam, or Simon Waterhouse. I thought about contacting them instead of Grint, but what could they do? They're miles away, in Spilling.

I tell Laskey everything. She must be wondering why my delivery is so slow and jerky. I can't help it – the most important thing is to test every sentence before it leaves my mouth, check it for errors. My reasoning needs to convince her, or she won't help me. A voice in my head, one I'm trying to ignore, whispers that it won't work, however hard I try, and I'll hate myself afterwards for this demeaning attempt to impress her.

When I finish, she looks at me for a long time without saying anything.

'Will you come with me?' I say.

She seems to be trying to make up her mind about something. 'I'll tell you what I'll do. I'm going to have someone bring you a cup of tea and a sandwich, so that you can have a bit of a break, and then I'm going to come back and—'

'I don't need a break,' I snap.

'And then I'll come back, and I'd like you to tell me that story – everything you've just told me – again.'

'But that's a waste of time! Why do you want to hear it again? Weren't you listening?'

'I listened very carefully indeed. I don't think I've ever heard anything quite so . . . unusual. We police don't hear that many unusual stories – far fewer than you might think. Normally the stories surrounding the crimes we deal with are very dull.'

I see what she's driving at. 'You think I invented the whole thing, don't you? You want to hear the story again so that you can check I don't slip up and change some of the details.'

'Do you have an objection to telling me again?' Laskey asks.

Yes. It's a waste of time. I force myself to subdue my anger. 'No,' I say, then can't resist adding, 'As long as you're aware of the flaw in your logic.'

'What's that?'

'If I tell you again and my story doesn't change, you're no further forward. I might be telling the truth, or I might be a liar with a brilliant memory.'

She smiles. 'Whichever you are, you need something to eat. Your stomach's been rumbling for the last fifteen minutes. Wait here.'

At the door, she stops, turns back. 'Stealing a set of keys from someone's house is a crime, by the way. If you're planning on changing any part of your story, that's the bit I'd start with.' Still smiling, she leaves the room.

What does she mean? Is she suggesting I lie to avoid trouble? Or giving me notice that, after the food she's forcing on me, I'm going to be arrested? It didn't occur to me not to tell her that I took the keys from the mug in Selina Gane's kitchen. How can she care about that, after what I've just told her?

Because she doesn't believe you about the dead woman and never will. She probably doesn't believe you about stealing the keys either, or she'd have arrested you already.

I had to take those keys. Didn't I? What if I'm wrong, and they don't belong to Selina Gane's American friend? What if the number on the label doesn't mean what I think it means? Maybe it's a different street. The label didn't say Bentley Grove, or a name, just the house number.

No. You're not wrong.

When she talked about her American friend, Selina Gane looked straight at that mug. The keys are to the friend's house – they must be. And the number with no street name, that has to mean Bentley Grove – you'd only do that with your own street.

And the houses on Bentley Grove are more or less identical. The lounges are more or less identical . . .

Suddenly, the thought of staying here a moment longer, to be patronised and subtly threatened, makes me feel ill. I don't need this kind of help. I've got a better idea, one that doesn't involve trying to ingratiate myself with Alison Laskey.

I grab my bag and make my way out of the building as quickly as I can, then walk until I come to a phone box. Pressing the buttons, I wonder if I will always remember Kit's mobile number, even in ten or twenty years.

He answers on the second ring. 'It's me,' I tell him.

'Connie.' He sounds pleased to hear from me. His voice is thick, swollen. Has he been crying? He never used to cry. Maybe he does it all the time, now that he's got the knack. 'Where are you?'

'Where I am now is irrelevant. It's where I'm going to be in twenty minutes that matters. I'm going to be at 11 Bentley Grove.'

'What are you . . . ?'

'You know where I mean, don't you, Kit?' I talk over him. '11 Bentley Grove, not Selina Gane's house. That's where I'm going to be. *Your* 11 Bentley Grove.'

Silence from Kit.

'I've got a set of keys in my hand,' I tell him. 'I'm looking at them now.'

I put the phone down, leave the booth, panic as I try to

remember where I left my car. That's right: the multi-storey car park next to the glass-fronted swimming pool with the tube-like slides.

I move as fast as I can, knowing that Kit, wherever he was when I spoke to him, will now be making his way to the house. I couldn't explain to someone like Alison Laskey how I know this, but I do. When you've been with someone for as long as I've been with Kit, you can predict a lot of their behaviour.

I have to get there before he does. I need to let myself in and see it for myself, whatever it is. However bad it is.

What are you going to do when Kit turns up? Kill him? Say 'I told you so'?

It doesn't seem to matter what happens next. All that matters is what I'm doing now – trying to get to the house, so that I can put the key in the lock and turn it. See that it works. That's all I want out of this: the relief of proving to myself, finally that I'm not mad or paranoid. I can't think beyond that.

Every traffic light is on red. I ignore a few of them and drive straight through. Others I obey. There's no system behind my actions; my driving's worse than it's ever been, all my decisions entirely random. Lots of disconnected thoughts flash in my mind: the blue and pink hourglass dress Kit bought me, Mum's tapestry of Melrose Cottage on my bedroom wall at home, Alison Laskey's worm-lipped smile, 11 Bentley Grove's floor-plan, Nulli's certificate of incorporation in its smashed glass frame, iron railings, Pardoner Lane, the Beth Dutton Centre, the rotting cabbage Mum found in the cupboard under the stairs, the yellow key fob in my pocket, red feathers on the mug in Selina Gane's kitchen, her map of Cambridgeshire with the empty crest. *Empty Crest Syndrome*, I think, and laugh out loud.

I pull up outside the house and look at the clock on the dashboard. The journey from the multi-storey car park to here took ten minutes. It felt more like ten hours.

The key works because I don't waste time wondering if it will or won't. Of course it works. That's the part I forgot to mention to Alison Laskey: how absolutely certain I am that I'm right.

I push open the front door and walk in. The smell makes me gag: human waste. And something even worse underneath it, like an undertone. *Death*. I've never smelled it before, but I recognise it instantly.

This is *real*.

Something inside me is screaming that I should run, get out, as far away as I can. I see several things at once: the white button stuck to the top of the newel post, a telephone on a table in the hall, by the stairs, lots of blood-dotted papers scattered on the floor beneath the table, a pink denim jacket lying just inside the front door. I reach to pick it up, feel the pockets. One is empty. The other has two keys in it – one on a Lancing Damisz key-ring, the other with a paper tag attached to it, the sort you might stick on a gift. On the tag, someone has written 'Selina, no. 11'.

My mind reels as I struggle to make sense of this. Then I see that there's no mystery; it's pitifully simple: you give someone your spare key, they give you theirs. If you lock yourself out, you're covered.

Ring the police. Pick up the phone and ring 999.

Focusing on every move my body makes, I put one foot in front of the other and start to walk across the hall, keeping my eyes fixed on the end point. Twelve steps to that phone, no more. I stop when I reach an open door, aware of something in my peripheral vision, something large and red. My head is too heavy to turn and my neck too stiff. Slowly, I realign my whole body so that I'm facing the lounge.

I'm looking at my sea of blood. Mine and Jackie Napier's, I suppose I should say, since she and I were the only ones who saw it. It's darker now, dry, like crusty paint. In the centre, there's a woman lying on her front with her head to one side, facing away from me. The position of her head isn't the only thing that's different. Her hair is neater than in the photograph I saw on Roundthehouses. Almost too neat, as if someone has brushed it while she's been lying there. And she isn't wearing the green and lilac hourglass dress, she's wearing a sleeveless pink top, a skirt with a white and pink print, pink lace-up pumps. *The pink jacket in the hall must be hers too*. Lying by her side, as if it dropped from her shoulder before she fell, is a colourful flower-print canvas handbag.

No wedding ring on her left hand.

Terror jolts through me. I don't know what to do. Ring the police? Check to see if she's still alive?

Get out of the house.

But I can't. I can't just leave her here.

I don't know how long I stand there – it could be half a second, ten seconds, ten minutes. Eventually, I force myself to walk into the room. If I walk around the edge of the blood, over to the window, I'll be able to see her face. *If I walk around the edge of the blood. If I walk around the edge. Walk. Around the edge*. It's only by repeating it to myself that I'm able to do it.

When I see who it is that's lying there, I have to press both my hands over my mouth so hard that it hurts. My arms are shaking – all of me is shaking. It's Jackie, Jackie Napier. She's dead. Eyes staring, full of fear. Marks around her throat. Strangled. *Oh, my God, please let this not be happening*.

Her face is twisted, especially her mouth. The tip of her tongue is visible between her lips. I hear myself saying no, over and over.

Jackie Napier. The only other person who saw what you saw.

I drag myself towards her, as close as I can bear to go. Bending down, I touch her leg. *Warm.*

Shuddering, I back out of the room. The phone. *Ring the police.* That's it. That's what I do next: ring the police. I focus on my destination, start to make my way across the hall. As I get closer to the table with the phone on it, I see something that makes me seize up: my husband's handwriting, on one of the blood-splattered pieces of paper on the floor.

I sink to my knees, unable to stay upright. What I'm looking at makes no sense to me. It's a poem by someone called Tilly Gilpatrick, about a volcano. There's a comment beneath it, praising the poem. Underneath the praise, Kit has written that the poem is appalling, even for a five-year-old, and added a poem that he thinks is better: three rhyming verses. I try to read them, but can't concentrate.

One by one, I pick up the other scattered pieces of paper. All of them are dotted with red. There's a shopping list – someone calling themselves 'E' asking 'D' to buy, among other things, chargrilled artichokes, not a tin of artichokes. The 'not' is in capital letters. What else is here? A car insurance certificate. I notice the name Gilpatrick again; the named drivers are Elise and Donal Gilpatrick.

E and D.

A letter thanking Elise, Donal, Riordan and Tilly for a lovely weekend; an ancient-looking and angry letter from Elise to someone called Caroline, dated 1993; a poem by Riordan Gilpatrick about conkers; the same Riordan's school report;

a description of some kittens by Tilly. I push all these to one side, and find myself staring at a small blue note from Selina Gane to Elise, dated 24 July. *Today*. Did she write it just after I left? There's no blood on this one. As I read it, I'm aware of a numbness behind my eyes. I have to stop looking.

Who are these people, the Gilpatricks? What do they have to do with Kit?

Somehow, I manage to get myself upright again. I pick up the phone, then notice another piece of paper beside it, on the table. Kit's handwriting again, but just one line this time, repeated over and over. The ink is blurred where drops of water appear to have landed on it, as if it's been left out in the rain.

As if the writer was crying when he wrote it.

The words look familiar. Is it a line from the poem, the one Kit wrote beneath five-year-old Tilly's volcano poem? I bend down, look for the relevant piece of paper. Here it is. *Yes*. But why did Kit choose to write this particular line thirteen times? What does it mean? And who wrote the poem? Not Kit; he doesn't write poems, though he often quotes them – always ones that rhyme, by people I haven't heard of who have been dead for years.

I pick up the phone again, try to put it to my ear, and find I can't move my arm. There's a hand around my wrist, pulling it back. I drop the phone as metal flashes in front of my face, glinting in the sunlight flooding in through the hall window. *A knife*. 'Don't kill me,' I say automatically.

'You say it like I want to. I don't want to.' A voice I used to love; my husband's voice. The blade is flat against my throat, crushing my windpipe.

'Why?' I manage to say. 'Why are you going to kill me?'

'Because you know me,' Kit says.

POLICE EXHIBIT REF: CB13345/432/26IG

24 July 2010

Hi Elise
Just realised I haven't seen you, even in passing, for weeks. Or Donal and the kids, for that matter. And (at the risk of sounding like a nosy neighbour!) your curtains seem to have been closed for a long time, upstairs and down. Is everything okay? Are you in America for the summer? I'm assuming not, since you've not asked me to water the plants, etc (unless you've found someone else!).

I'm feeling guilty for neglecting you for too long – no excuses, but work's been frantic and I've been having a rough time recently – I'll tell you about it when I see you.

Anyway, do give us a ring (on mobile, not home) or send a text, and let's catch up really soon.

Lots of love,

Selina xxx

POLICE EXHIBIT REF: CB13345/432/27IG

Where's the Lost young man?
Where's the Lost young man?
Where's the Lost young man?
Where's the Lost young man?
Where's the Lost young man?
Where's the Lost young man?
Where's the Lost young man?
Where's the Lost young man?
Where's the Lost young man?
Where's the Lost young man?
Where's the Lost young man?
Where's the Lost young man?
Where's the Lost young man?

22

24/7/2010

'I need you to help me break into a house,' said Simon, as if it was the most reasonable request in the world.

Charlie nearly lost her grip on the three pints of lager she was carrying; somehow she managed to lower them onto the table without spilling a drop. She, Simon and Sam Kombothekra were sitting outside the Granta pub in Cambridge, by the river. Charlie had been waiting for Sam at the Brown Cow in Spilling when Simon's summons by text message had arrived. She'd had to abandon her drink and tell Sam he wasn't getting one either, not until he'd sat in a car for two hours.

'On Bentley Grove,' Simon helpfully provided more details. 'Not number 11 – the house opposite Professor Sir Basil Lambert-Wall's.'

'Why?' Sam asked. 'What's in there?'

Simon took a sip of his drink, frowned. 'Dunno,' he muttered. 'Maybe nothing.'

'Well, there's an irresistible incentive if ever I heard one,' said Charlie sarcastically.

'I'll tell you what I do know,' said Simon. 'That'll be easier. When I left Kit Bowskill's parents' house, I broke the speed limit all the way to 18 Pardoner Lane. There was no one in, so I tried number 17. The owners were as pleased to see me as they were last time I turned up unannounced, and today I accepted their offer of a coffee. I figured they'd be the people to ask about number 18 – they've lived on Pardoner Lane since 2001, and they're talkers. Especially her.'

Seeing Sam's puzzled expression, Charlie explained, 'He means they're socially adept human beings who speak and are friendly to people.' In stark contrast to Simon, who kept his head down when he entered and left the house, and could imagine nothing worse than knowing all the neighbours and having to chat to them when he saw them. Charlie had grilled him about it on numerous occasions. 'You chat to your colleagues, your mum and dad, me,' she'd pointed out, aware of the linguistic inaccuracy. What Simon did could hardly be described as chatting. 'If I talk to the neighbours once, it sets a precedent,' he'd said. 'Every time I walk out of my front door, I'll have to stop on the street and exchange pleasantries – I don't want to have to do that. When I leave the house, it's because I've got somewhere to go. When I'm on my way home, I want to get home, quickly.'

'What did Mrs Talker tell you?' Charlie asked.

'When she and her husband first moved to Pardoner Lane, number 18 was owned by the Beth Dutton Centre people – the school next door.'

Charlie wondered again about Connie Bowskill getting the address wrong. How could she have remembered every detail about it correctly apart from the house number, especially when Kit had made that joke about using the address as a name for the house?

17 Pardoner Lane, 17 Pardoner Lane, Cambridge.

But that was wrong, surely. It must have been 18 Pardoner Lane, 18 Pardoner Lane, Cambridge.

'The headmistress lived at number 18,' Simon was saying.

'Short commute to work for her – just next door. Then, in 2003, the school got into financial trouble and they sold number 18 to raise capital. The headmistress now lives in a rented flat on the next street along.'

'Mrs Talker told you that?' said Charlie.

'She and the headmistress belong to the same book group. I asked her if she knew who the house had sold to. She did: a family called the Gilpatricks. She also knew which estate agent had sold it, both in 2003 and last year, when it came up again, because she and her husband nearly put in an offer. Both times, the house was sold by Cambridge Property Shop. Estate agents' offices are open on Saturdays, so they were my next port of call.' Simon's eyes had taken on the glassy, possessed look that Charlie and Sam knew so well. 'Guess who worked for Cambridge Property Shop in 2003? And in 2009 – she only left to go to a new job in February this year.'

'Lorraine Turner?' said Charlie.

'No,' Sam said. He normally sounded tentative when he made a suggestion, but not now. 'It was Jackie Napier, wasn't it?'

'What makes you say that?' Simon asked. Charlie sighed. She was obviously wrong, if he was asking Sam to explain his thinking and not her.

'I've got a bad feeling about her,' said Sam. He turned to Charlie. 'That's why I wanted to talk to you today.' He had the grace to look contrite, at least. 'Sorry, I should have told you in the car.' All the way from Spilling to Cambridge, Charlie had tried to persuade him to tell her what had been so important that it couldn't wait; Sam had refused to be drawn, claimed he'd misinterpreted something, that it was nothing, really. 'I figured Simon knew what was going on and he'd tell us when we got here. If it was nothing to do with Jackie Napier, then my hunch was wrong – I suppose I wanted to hold off on bad-mouthing her. I've got no proof of anything.'

'Let's hear the hunch,' said Simon.

Sam looked cornered. He sighed. 'I didn't like her at all. She seemed . . . This is going to sound unforgivably snobbish.'

'I forgive you,' Charlie told him. 'Embrace your inner snob – I did, a long time ago.'

'She seemed stupid. Ignorant, but thinking she knew it all – that was how she came across for most of the interview. The sort of woman who imagines she's making a brilliant impression when actually everyone listening to her thinks she's a bigoted idiot. She came out with some classic self-righteous lines: "I live in the real world, not fantasy land", "No one pays me to worry about murders" – that sort of thing. Quoted herself a lot, too: "I always say", followed by some pearl of non-wisdom or other.'

Charlie laughed. 'God, Sam, you're such a bitch!'

Sam's face coloured. 'I'm not enjoying this,' he said.

'Go on,' said Simon.

'She had fixed ideas about herself, kept telling me what sort of person she was. "Two things about me," she said, and then she listed them. The first was loyalty – if she was on your side, then she was on your side for ever.'

'How tedious,' said Charlie. 'The people who bang on about their own loyalty are always the first to turn vicious if you send them a birthday card late.'

'She told me she wasn't "an imagination sort of person",' said Sam. 'Seemed proud of it, too. She'd just got back from staying with her sister in New Zealand. From what she said, it was clear she'd spent her time there criticising her sister's life choices and flaunting the superiority of her own – completely insensitive. But then there were times when she seemed to know exactly what I was thinking – sensitive to the point of telepathy. She was inconsistent.'

'Some people are,' Charlie felt obliged to point out.

'I know,' said Sam. 'That's what I told myself. But then she said something else, about Selina Gane's passport photo, something that struck me as . . . wrong. Gut instinct, before I'd had a chance to think about it, even. I knew I'd heard something that jarred as soon as she said it, but I couldn't work out what it was, not for ages. Then last night it came to me. She was talking about the woman who pretended to be Selina Gane and tried to put 11 Bentley Grove up for sale. "She was clever," she said. "She knew all she had to do was talk about people not looking like they do in their passports. If she made me think about all those other people, she wouldn't have to convince me – I'd do all the work myself." '

'So?' said Charlie. 'What's the problem there?'

Simon was nodding, infuriating know-all that he was. He couldn't possibly understand what Sam was getting at. Could he?

'Maybe no problem.' Sam sighed. 'That's why I kept quiet about it.'

'What might or might not be the problem?' Charlie rephrased her question, rolling her eyes at his annoying humility. 'I'm not asking you to commit to its problematicness – just tell me what it is.'

'What do you think Jackie meant when she said that the woman knew she'd do all the work herself?' Sam asked.

'She knew Jackie would immediately think of all the friends' passport photos she's seen that have looked nothing like them,' said Simon. 'All the times she's asked, "Is that really you?" '

Sam was nodding vigorously.

'The weight of your own experience always feels like solid proof.' Simon directed the comment at Charlie. Did he think she was lagging behind? 'Jackie's subconscious reminds her that in all the cases she, personally, has come across, without exception, the implausible photographs *were* of the people in question, however unlike them they looked.'

'That's exactly right.' Sam sounded relieved. 'Whoever she was, this woman didn't so much lie to Jackie as invite her to lie to herself: to think beyond the specific issue of the picture in Selina Gane's passport to what she knew to be the norm in the generic situation: that *no one* looks much like their passport photo, and yet that *never* means it's not a photo of them. It means it's a bad likeness, that's all.'

Charlie thought she'd grasped it. 'So you're saying this woman deliberately invoked one of Jackie's firmly ingrained assumptions . . .'

'One of her firmly ingrained *personal-experience-based* assumptions,' Simon amended. 'Those are always more powerful: I once met a gay man who had a high-pitched voice, therefore all men with high voices are gay. A group of Asian teenagers once stole my handbag, therefore all Asian teenagers I meet from now on must be criminals. Our minds are reassured by patterns that repeat and repeat: whenever X is the case, that means Y is also the case. That's what Jackie Napier meant: that the woman was banking on her mind, all on its own, finding that familiar groove and slotting into it – no passport photos look like their subjects, yet all passport photos are, nonetheless, *of* their subjects.'

'So Jackie was right,' Charlie concluded. 'Liar Woman was clever.'

'She might or might not have been, but that's not what matters.' Sam looked worried again. 'It's Jackie's cleverness I'm concerned with. When she told me, in passing, that this woman knew she would do all the work herself, she was making a point that was quite profound, quite subtle – a point we've just taken several minutes to unpack, and we're three pretty intelligent people. Sorry.' Sam blushed as he apologised for having awarded himself praise he perhaps didn't deserve. 'She was demonstrating that she understood and could sum up, far more succinctly than we just have, exactly why the deception had worked so well. That level of instinctive understanding of something so complex would be way beyond a hell of a lot of people. It'd be way beyond someone with the – sorry, this is going to sound terrible – with the hackneyed, below-average mindset she seemed to have the rest of the time.'

Simon downed the dregs of his pint, slammed the glass down on the table. 'There's no doubt that Jackie Napier's clever,' he said. 'She's also an expert liar. If you're bright, it's almost impossible to present yourself as the opposite – much harder than for an evil person to present himself as good. It's not only the attitudes you express that are different, it's the speech patterns, the sentence structure, vocabulary, everything. But she very nearly pulled it off. If she hadn't said that one thing, you'd have been convinced.'

Sam nodded.

'You were privileged,' Simon told him. 'She must have thought highly of you. For you, she pulled out all the stops and produced the biggest lie she's ever told or is likely to tell. She told you she wasn't an imagination sort of person. Wrong

– that's precisely what she is. She's an imagination person, but with no conscience, no empathy, very little fear, hardly any awareness of her own limitations.'

Charlie felt a shiver pass through her. The description was too familiar; other names sprang to mind. *Names of monsters*.

'Jackie Napier's the sort of person you wish had no imagination at all,' said Simon.

23

Saturday 24 July 2010

'I can't breathe,' I gasp. Kit's pressing the knife too hard against my throat. 'You're suffocating me.'

'Sorry,' he whispers. He's buried his face in my hair. I can feel his tears wetting my neck. He takes the knife away, holds it in front of my face. It shakes in his hand. His other arm is round my waist, holding me in place, pinning my arms to my sides. No way I can get away from him; I'm not strong enough.

The knife's serrated blade gleams silver.

Images flash through my mind: a teapot, chocolate cake, a plastic beaker with a lid, the blue and pink hourglass dress.

It's our knife, from Melrose Cottage. I last saw it on a wooden tray, beside my birthday cake.

Why didn't I think that Kit might be here already? How can I have been so stupid? New tears prick my eyelids. I blink, try to hold them back. Try to think. I can't die now, can't let Kit kill me. Can't let my own recklessness turn me into a news headline. People will hear the story of what happened to me and say, 'It was her own stupid fault'.

'Don't be scared,' Kit says. 'I'm coming with you. Do you really think I'd make you go alone?'

Go. He's talking about dying.

'We'll go together, when we're ready,' he says. 'We're in the right place, at least.'

When we're ready. That means not yet. He's not ready yet, not ready to kill us both – I cling to this shred of hope.

'Who was the dead woman I saw on the virtual tour?' I make a vow to myself: I might not live through this, but I won't die until I know. I won't die in ignorance.

'Jackie Napier,' says Kit.

No. That's not right. Jackie was alive on Tuesday. She walked into the room Kit and I were in. Said to Grint, *I don't know where you got her from, but you can put her back. I've never seen her before in my life*.

'It wasn't Jackie . . .' I start to say.

'It was,' says Kit. 'She wasn't dead, but it was her.'

She wasn't dead, but it was her. She wasn't dead, but it was her. Horror prickles my skin, like the thin legs of a thousand tiny spiders, all over me. I can't make myself ask if the blood was real. Don't need to. I know the answer.

I think of Mum asking what woman in her right mind would ruin a lovely dress by lying in red paint. Jackie Napier's mind must have gone badly wrong.

'She was lying in blood that didn't belong to her,' says Kit.

She still is. If you strangle someone to death, they don't bleed. 'Whose blood?' I gasp, bile rising in my throat. I can smell Kit's sweat, his desperation – a hard, rotten smell. As if his body's accepted that it will die soon and is making preparations.

'You have no idea how much I hate her,' he says. 'And I hate myself for hating her.'

But not for killing her. 'Jackie?' I say

'She'd have done anything for me . . .' The rest of his sentence loses itself as loud sobs shake his body.

When he's quiet again I ask, 'Why did you kill her?'

'Because I. Had to.' His breathing is uneven. 'There was no

happy ever after for me and her. There's no happy ever after for me and you, not now that everything's happened the way it has. It's left us no way out. We have to be brave, Con. You said all you wanted was to know, and I want to tell you. I'm sick of the loneliness of knowing and not being able to tell you.'

Terror twists my heart. I don't want him to tell me, not yet, not if killing me's what comes afterwards.

I stare at the shaking knife. Even if I could concentrate on it hard enough to make it fall out of his hand, I still wouldn't be able to struggle free. I try to make myself believe that DS Laskey will come in time. I told her the address, told her there was a dead woman here. She might have her doubts about my story, but she'll come anyway. She'll want to check.

One dead woman. Not two. Please not two.

'I'll look after you, Con,' Kit says. 'Jackie said she'd *take care* of you, but she didn't mean look after. She meant "take care of" in the other way. There's something wrong with that, don't you think? That the same words can mean both?'

Words. I hear them, but they don't seem to work. They don't translate. What's he saying?

I can smell death. Decay, decomposition. How is that possible? How long ago did Kit kill Jackie Napier? How long before a dead body starts to smell? She was still warm . . .

'What did she say about me?' I ask.

'She was going to kill you, Con.' Kit weeps into my hair. 'I couldn't have stopped her, not without . . . doing what I did.' He kisses the back of my neck. I clamp my mouth shut to keep in the scream that's ringing in my head.

'I killed her to save you,' Kit says.

24
24/7/2010

Charlie had finished her pint and needed another one, but she knew that if she went to the bar, she'd miss too much and struggle to catch up; that was her – what had Simon called it? – her firmly ingrained personal-experience-based assumption. The other two seemed to have forgotten that there were thirsty bodies attached to their brains; Charlie tried to do the same.

'Remember your point about simple solutions, in Spain?' Simon said. 'When there's an unknown, a puzzle, the simplest answer's usually the right one?'

'You disagreed with me,' said Charlie. 'We managed to pack some interesting arguments into our half-hour honeymoon,' she told Sam.

'Jackie Napier was banking on Ian Grint subscribing to your way of thinking, not mine,' said Simon. 'Like a lot of highly imaginative people, she assumes most people she comes into contact with have more straightforward, prosaic minds than she does, and she's right. Grint finds that someone's hacked into Lancing Damisz's computer network – who's the obvious non-suspect? Jackie Napier. Why would she need to hack in when she works there and can access the system legitimately whenever she wants? If a woman might or might not have been murdered at 11 Bentley Grove, who's the obvious non-suspect? Jackie Napier again – she drew herself to the police's attention, saying she'd seen the body, supporting Connie Bowskill's story, a story no one would have wasted five minutes on if Jackie hadn't come forward – Connie would have been dismissed as a delusional neurotic. It was thanks to Jackie that Grint moved on the possible murder, did the whole forensic bit, found out about the computer hacking. Simplistic assumption? That Jackie can't have been responsible for any of it. The possibility that she might be wouldn't occur to Grint or to anyone – no one draws their own crimes to the police's attention, crimes they would otherwise get away with.'

'But . . . you're saying Jackie did?' Sam asked.

'I think so, yeah,' said Simon. 'I'm not sure why, though.' He looked angry. 'I might be an imagination person, but I'm nowhere near her level.'

'You're talking as if you know for a fact that Jackie's a liar,' said Charlie.

'I do. If you'd come with me to Lancing Damisz and the Cambridge Property Shop today, you'd know it too.'

Charlie didn't point out that he had neither told her where he was going nor invited her to join him.

'For starters, Jackie hasn't been to New Zealand any time recently, and she hasn't got a sister,' said Simon. 'The holiday part was true. She took her disabled mother to a B&B in Weston-super-Mare. She does it every summer, apparently.'

Weston-super-Mare. New Zealand. The distance between the lie and the truth was enough to make anyone feel jet-lagged.

'Jackie sold 18 Pardoner Lane to the Gilpatrick family in 2003,' said Simon. 'In 2009, they decided they wanted to move again. Jackie, still working for Cambridge Property Shop, sold them another house: the one opposite Professor Sir Basil Lambert-Wall's. She bought their old house herself.'

'What?' Charlie wasn't sure she'd heard right.

'Jackie Napier bought 18 Pardoner Lane, in March last year,' said Simon. 'She was the agent handling the sale, she put the house on the market – and then bought it herself.'

'So . . . why bother putting it on the market?' asked Sam.

'Did she have to pay herself commission?' said Charlie.

'No idea.' Simon looked away; he hated not knowing. 'But that's where Jackie now lives – in the house Kit Bowskill was gagging to buy in 2003, the house he wanted so much that he allowed his proud mask to slip and begged his folks for fifty grand.'

Charlie looked to Sam for help, saw her confusion mirrored in his face.

'In February this year, Jackie switched jobs – she moved to Lancing Damisz,' said Simon. 'I spoke to Hugh Jepps, one of Cambridge Property Shop's senior partners. He's felt guilty ever since about the glowing reference he wrote her, and was only too willing to let me hear his confession. The reference was only glowing because he was keen to get rid of Jackie – he'd have sacked her, except that then the story of what she'd been up to might have come out. Jepps wasn't sure the firm could weather the bad publicity. He also couldn't have proved anything against her, though he knew exactly what was going on.'

'More than can be said for me and Sam,' Charlie muttered.

'Every house Jackie was selling, soon as an offer came in, there would be a counter offer – a little bit higher,' said Simon. 'Usually this would lead to a bidding war, with each side offering two grand more each time, sometimes five or ten grand more each time, depending on how desirable the property was. Eventually someone'd drop out. So far, so normal, Jepps said – happens all the time with house sales – except that, with the houses Jackie Napier was selling, there was one constant: Kit Bowskill. Bowskill was the one who made the second offer, every time, and started the bidding war. Funnily enough, he was never interested in any of the houses anyone else was selling. It was only the houses on Jackie's list that inspired him to bid the price up and up, high as he could. Invariably, the inspiration was short-lived; Bowskill was always the one who dropped out, leaving the other bidder several tens of thousands of pounds worse off, sometimes, but feeling chuffed as anything, thinking he or she had won.'

'So . . . you're saying Kit Bowskill never had any intention of buying any of these houses?' said Sam. 'He wanted to inflate their prices artificially. Why?'

'So that Jackie Napier would get more commission,' Charlie said with certainty. Someone ought to invent a word, she thought, to describe this very particular kind of eureka moment: when the penny drops and you realise two people you haven't previously connected are having an affair. *Jackie Napier and Kit Bowskill. Olivia Zailer and Chris Gibbs.*

'Same thing's been happening at Lancing Damisz, since Jackie changed jobs,' said Simon. 'She's not been there long enough for anyone to notice, but when I told Lorraine Turner what Hugh Jepps had said, she was concerned enough to have a rummage around Jackie's desk. She found two letters from Jackie to Bowskill, confirming his offers on two different houses she was selling, explaining that there was another potential buyer interested in each case who'd offered more than he had, and did he want to offer more at this stage?'

'That's illegal,' said Sam. 'It's fraud.'

'Yeah, it is,' Simon agreed. 'A fraud that's close to impossible to prove, as long as Kit Bowskill sticks to his story: since 2003, he's been looking for a place in Cambridge. He's put in offers on a stack of houses, got into bidding wars – starting with 18 Pardoner Lane, the only one that was genuine – but, so far, he's always pulled out. Why? He's a perfectionist – that's actually true, so it bolsters the lie pretty effectively. No one can hack into his mind and prove his motivation: that he never had any intention of buying any of those houses, and it's all a scam. And if Jackie's colleagues ask any questions – as Hugh Jepps did, several times – she turns on the charm and says, "Poor Mr Bowskill – he just can't commit." '

'Hugh Jepps didn't believe her, though,' said Charlie.

'Course he didn't. The coincidence of Bowskill only ever going for houses Jackie was selling wasn't plausible. Jackie didn't care, though – she brazened it out. It's not her fault, it's nothing to do with her, she says. Mr Bowskill's a stranger to her, and coincidences do happen. Jepps considered getting a private investigator onto her, see if he could prove a connection between her and Bowskill. In the end he decided he just wanted shot of her, and packed her off to be another firm's problem instead. He said her unjustly accused naïve waif act was scarily convincing.'

'That wasn't the act I saw,' said Sam. 'She wasn't naïve with me, she was more . . . the weary, put-upon woman of the world who thinks she knows a thing or two.'

'I doubt she's short of personas,' said Simon. 'The woman at number 17 described her as "a warm, lovely girl".'

'So if Jackie lives at 18 Pardoner Lane, Mrs Talker at number 17's her neighbour,' said Charlie.

'Neighbour and good friend,' Simon said. 'Oh, she's known Jackie for years, she told me – since long before Jackie moved to Pardoner Lane. She's also friendly with Elise Gilpatrick, though she's not seen Elise for a while.' He emphasised this as if he thought it was significant. Charlie was about to ask him what he was implying when he said, 'Jackie's a close friend of Elise too – used to go for dinner at the Gilpatricks' house all the time. That's where Number 17 Woman met her. Which is why she wasn't suspicious when she saw Jackie and her boyfriend letting themselves into number 18 on weekday afternoons.'

Jackie Napier and Elise Gilpatrick, close friends. Charlie frowned. Jackie had sold 18 Pardoner Lane to Elise Gilpatrick in 2003. Were they already friends at that point? They must have been. No one befriends the estate agent who sells them their house.

'Number 17 Woman made the same mistake Basil Lambert-Wall made,' said Simon. 'You see someone let themselves in with a key and you assume they're legitimate. Intruders don't have keys: they have stockings over their faces and sacks labelled "Loot" in their gloved hands. Number 17 Woman didn't even twig when Elise Gilpatrick confided in her that she couldn't shake off an irrational feeling that 18 Pardoner Lane wasn't hers, somehow. She said she felt like an intruder or a squatter, even though she and her husband had bought the place fair and square. She had nightmares about another family turning up and telling her she had to leave. One day she ended up in tears and admitted that she was worried the house was haunted, even though she knew it couldn't be and didn't believe in ghosts. Still, Number 17 Woman didn't make the link.' A mixture of disbelief and disdain hardened Simon's voice. 'Even when she was telling me, she presented the two as unconnected: Elise Gilpatrick's sense that number 18 wasn't really hers, and Jackie Napier and her boyfriend turning up at the house in the daytime, when none of the Gilpatricks were in. I showed her the photo of Kit Bowskill that Connie gave me – she confirmed that was who she meant by Jackie's boyfriend.'

Sam looked as if his eyes were about to fall out of his head.

'18 Pardoner Lane wasn't haunted,' said Simon. 'It was invaded. They're unlucky, the Gilpatricks. The house they moved to in March last year, opposite Basil Lambert-Wall – that's been invaded too.'

'Day Man and Day Woman,' Charlie said, remembering the scant information Simon had given Sam over the phone, while she'd been driving. 'That's them too – Kit Bowskill and Jackie Napier.'

Simon nodded. 'Though Jackie told the professor her name was Connie, short for Catriona. At first I wondered if Day Woman might be Connie, but it's not possible. On Tuesday 29 June, when Day Woman was apologising to Basil Lambert-Wall for Day Man's rudeness, Connie Bowskill was at her mum and dad's shop in Silsford all day – I checked.'

'Jackie was playing at being his wife,' Sam said. 'I get that part, but not the Gilpatricks.' He looked up, at Simon. 'Why do Bowskill and Jackie want to have sex in their house – in two of their houses – while they're out? Is it some sort of sexual obsession thing?'

'Simon.' Charlie's voice caught in her throat, which was horribly dry. 'Fuck. I think I've just . . .'

'What? What?' Simon always demanded to know everything before she'd had a chance to get her thoughts in order.

'The house opposite the professor's – what number is it?'

Simon screwed up his face, trying to remember.

'It's number 12, isn't it?'

'That's strange. Just before you said that, I was thinking

"12". I suppose it must be. I half remember seeing it on the door.'

'I think Alice misunderstood what Connie Bowskill told her,' said Charlie, tripping over her words in an effort to get them out quickly. 'About Kit's joke name for 18 Pardoner Lane. I think the joke was calling the house 17 Pardoner Lane when the address was *18* Pardoner Lane. It wasn't the duplication that made it funny – 17 Pardoner Lane, 17 Pardoner Lane, Cambridge – it was the idea of confusing the postman by giving the house, as a name, a different address on the same street. Not only annoying the postman, but annoying the people who lived at number 17 too – Mr and Mrs Talker.' The memory of Alice's words came suddenly into sharp focus. 'Annoying people was on Kit Bowskill's mind when he was making his stupid suggestions,' Charlie said, certain now that she was on to something. 'He asked Connie if she thought it'd annoy the Beth Dutton people, them calling their house the Death Button Centre.'

'17 Pardoner Lane, 18 Pardoner Lane, Cambridge,' said Sam slowly.

'You're right,' Simon said. 'It works as a joke. Might even be a better joke.' Humour wasn't his area of expertise, and he knew it. 'It'd also explain why Connie misremembered the address, all these years later – if the joke stuck, if 17 Pardoner Lane became her and Bowskill's nickname for the house . . .' Simon pulled his mobile phone out of his pocket, pressed some keys, then thrust it into the space between Charlie and Sam so that they could both see it. 'Proust's not Proust in my phone – he's "Snowman". Nicknames, pet names – they stick. Don't they, Stepford?'

Sam cringed visibly at the nickname Colin Sellers and Chris

Gibbs had devised for him when they hardly knew him and found his unwavering politeness frustrating.

'Forget about teasing Sam,' Charlie said impatiently. 'Don't you see what I'm saying? Kit Bowskill did it again – he repeated his nickname trick, so proud was he of his little in-joke. He's never had any connection with Selina Gane, or with her house – hers wasn't the house he had in mind when he put 11 Bentley Grove into his SatNav as home.'

Simon's eyes were wide, unfocused. Charlie could see that he was getting it. '11 Bentley Grove is his name for *12* Bentley Grove,' he said eventually. 'His private name for his and Jackie's . . .'

'"Love-nest" is the word you're looking for,' said Charlie pointedly.

Simon was biting the inside of his lip. 'If he cares enough about that house to give it a special name . . . No, it doesn't work. If he's obsessed with 12 Bentley Grove now, it's only because the Gilpatricks bought it. It's a massively less attractive house than 18 Pardoner Lane, and Kit Bowskill wouldn't be prepared to compromise on the aesthetics. Which means it's not about the house any more . . .' Simon's eyes narrowed. He drummed his fingers on the table.

'We've lost him,' Charlie said to Sam, who looked worried.

'You can't dismiss 11 Bentley Grove as irrelevant,' he told her. 'That's where Connie Bowskill saw the woman's body.'

'Why did they buy new curtains?' Simon demanded, startling Charlie and Sam with the volume of his question. 'No one buys curtains for a house they don't own. Basil Lambert-Wall said the new curtains hadn't gone up yet, but today, when I went to the house and rang the bell, all the curtains were drawn – closed. Sunny day like this, why wouldn't you let the light in?'

'You went to 12 Bentley Grove today?' said Charlie.

'I was hoping to talk to some or all of the Gilpatricks,' Simon told her. 'Seven years ago, they got what Kit Bowskill wanted. I wanted to check they'd survived their victory. No one answered the door.'

'So you thought you'd enlist our help to smash it down,' said Sam with a shudder he tried, unsuccessfully, to hide.

'The woman at 17 Pardoner Lane told me where Elise Gilpatrick works,' Simon said. 'The Judge Business School. I couldn't get through to them on the phone – they're probably closed Saturdays. If I'd got through, I'd have asked when Elise last turned up for work.'

'Aren't you leaping to rather extreme conclusions?' said Charlie.

'Who was the dead woman Connie Bowskill saw on Roundthehouses?' Sam asked her. She inferred from the question that he shared Simon's concern for Elise Gilpatrick's welfare.

'You could wrap a body in a pair of curtains,' Simon said in a monotone. He seemed to be talking to a point beyond Charlie's shoulder. 'The prof said Jackie Napier's car was full of them, curtains wrapped in plastic – so many she'd had to put the back seats down. Wrap a dead body in curtains, cover the whole lot in plastic, make it airtight with parcel tape so that the neighbours don't smell anything . . .' Simon was pressing buttons on his phone. The same button, three times: number 9. 'We've got enough,' he said. 'No breaking and entering required.' A few seconds later, Charlie and Sam heard him ask to be put through to the police.

25

Saturday 24 July 2010

'You can still save me,' I say to Kit, as calmly as I can. 'Saving me doesn't mean killing me. You must be able to see that.'

He's behind me, his face pressing against the back of my skull. When he shakes his head, I feel it. 'You don't understand anything,' he says, his words indistinct, muffled by my hair. 'Nothing.'

The knife moves beneath my chin. I lift my head, try to pull my neck back.

'Listen to me, Kit. You've always told me I'm clever. Remember?' This is what I have to do: I have to talk. There can't be silence, or space for him to think. *Space for him to act.*

'You're not as clever as Jackie,' he says flatly.

I want to scream at him that I'm cleverer than Jackie, that she's lying lifeless in someone else's congealed blood and I'm still alive.

I'm clever enough to find a key labelled 'No. 12' in a mug with a red feather design, and remember about 17 Pardoner Lane, 18 Pardoner Lane. *11 Bentley Grove, 12 Bentley Grove.*

If only I'd been clever enough to stay away – to be satisfied with knowing, instead of having to prove it to myself.

How can Jackie Napier have wanted me dead? She didn't know me.

'Please listen,' I say evenly. 'There's no way out of this, you're right, but there is a way *through*. If we face up to what's happened, take responsibility . . .'

Kit laughs. 'Did you know there are no prisons in Cambridge? I Googled it yesterday. There's one in March, one in a place called Stradishall, near Newmarket. Postcode's CB8 – sounds like Cambridge, but it's not.'

I open my mouth, but no words come. It's not what I was expecting him to say. He searched for prisons in Cambridge. On the internet. *Why?*

'We were idiots – we shouldn't have wasted our time on the villages,' he mumbles. 'Should have stuck to the city. Those tiny hick places – Horningsea, Harston – they're not Cambridge, they're not civilisation. Might as well stagnate in Little Holling. Reach, Burwell, Chippenham – you might as well be in Newmarket, once you've gone that far.'

My teeth are chattering. Is it still hot outside? It can't be; I'm freezing. Kit's body feels cold too. *Freezing each other to death.*

'We wasted so much time,' he says sadly. He's talking about 2003, our house search.

Seven years ago. Gone, finished. There's no past and no future, no point talking about either. There's nothing but now, and scared of dying, and silence piling up around me, suffocating, spreading like blood.

Blood that disappeared when Kit sat down to look.

I breathe in sharply. Knowledge rushes at me, before I have time to doubt it. *The blood wasn't the only thing that disappeared.*

I try to push my fear aside and think in an ordered way, but I can't think – all I can do is see what's no longer in front of me, like a film playing in my head: Kit sitting at my desk, staring at the laptop. Me standing behind him, scared I'll see the horrific picture again, even though he's saying it isn't there; Nulli's certificate of incorporation lying on the floor in its smashed frame . . .

'I know how you did it,' I say. 'Everyone kept asking me why you didn't see the woman's body, when you looked at the same virtual tour that I looked at, the one I started. I kept having to explain what I thought must have happened.'

Kit makes a noise, a small exhalation. Somehow, I can tell that he's smiling.

I can feel the expression on his face without seeing him: does that mean I know him?

'It was a good theory,' he says. 'A virtual tour with a variable that comes up only once in every hundred or thousand loops.'

'I was wrong, though, wasn't I? You were looking at a different tour. When you first went into the room, I stayed outside.'

Shaking on the landing. Kit on the other side of the closed door, complaining. *Great. I've always wanted to look at a stranger's dishwasher in the middle of the night.*

'You closed down the lot,' I say. 'The tour, the internet, everything. One click and it was gone. On the desktop, you had the other tour ready to go – the original one.' *You got it from her, from Jackie.* 'Another click and it started playing. There was the lounge, with no woman's body in it.'

Kit says nothing. I don't think he's smiling any more.

'When I came back into the room, there was no Roundthehouses screen behind the virtual tour box, only the desktop screen. Before I woke you up, when I was watching the tour on my own, the screen behind it was the Roundthehouses screen. The address was there – 11 Bentley Grove – and the Roundthehouses logo.'

Why has it taken my memory so long to produce this detail?

Because you can't see everything at once. You can't see your husband's face when you're staring at the knife in front of your own.

'When you got angry with me and went back to bed, I sat there and stared for a few minutes, just stared. Watched one room after another turn in slow motion. Every time the lounge came back, it was the same – no woman's body. Then I closed the tour down – your tour. I decided to start from scratch, in case that made a difference. All I could think about was how the dead woman could possibly have disappeared. I didn't ask myself why I was having to reconnect to the internet – I was barely aware of doing it.'

'You didn't wake me up,' says Kit quietly.

Of course I didn't. 'No. You were awake. Doing a convincing impression of somebody asleep.' *Those long, slow breaths, the stillness . . . Both of you, you and Jackie, lying still, pretending. Lying.*

'You knew I went to Cambridge on Fridays, looking for you, looking for evidence of your other life at 11 Bentley Grove. You must have known long before I told you.' I feel disorientated as I pull the story, piece by piece, out of the darkness. I still can't grasp what it means, still can't see the full picture. It's as if I'm shining light on one fragment at a time, trying to connect each new part to the others I've managed to gather together.

'You didn't go every Friday,' Kit says. 'I could always tell. Some Thursday nights you'd be massively on edge – you'd ask me what time I was setting off to London in the morning, what time I'd be back at the end of the day. You wanted to know how long you had.'

I close my eyes, remembering how exhausting it was – pretending to have one motive, concealing another. I needn't have bothered.

Needn't bother with anything, ever again.

No. Keep talking. Keep telling the story, before the chance slips away. Kit has spent so long and worked so hard trying to keep my reality separate from his. I need to tear down the barrier. We are going to die here, together; I want us first to live, just for a short while, in the same world.

'Jackie knew exactly when 11 Bentley Grove went on the market. She works for Lancing Damisz. Worked,' I correct myself. 'She'd have known all the details. You both knew that when I went to Cambridge that Friday, I'd see the "For Sale" board outside the house for the first time and be desperate to look inside. I rang them, you know.'

'Who?' Kit brings the knife closer to my throat.

'Lasting Damage.' I hear a noise, a manic laugh, and realise it's coming from me. 'I wanted someone to show me round there and then. The woman I spoke to told me no one was available, it was too short notice. Was it Jackie who told me that?'

Kit says nothing, and I know I'm right. I shiver: cold feathers on my neck.

'You knew I'd come home and go straight on the internet to look at the pictures. That's why . . .' I stop, sensing the presence of an obstacle without knowing what it is. Then it comes to me. 'How did you know I wouldn't go to an internet café? I thought about it. If I'd known where one was . . .'

'We figured you were bound to,' Kit says. *We*. Him and Jackie. 'Didn't matter. We knew you'd look again at home, soon as you could. You were so suspicious and paranoid by then, once wouldn't have been enough for you – you'd have had to check, in case you'd missed something.'

'You stuck to me like glue when I got home, all evening, right until we went to bed. I remember thinking it was odd that you didn't do any of the things you normally do: watch the Channel 4 news headlines, go for a quick pint before dinner. All you seemed to want to do was talk to me. I wasn't suspicious – I was flattered.' *After six months of not trusting you, I still loved you.* 'When we went to bed, you read your book for ages – much longer than usual. Did you agree a time with Jackie, beforehand?'

Through my hair, against the back of my head, I feel Kit nod. I wait for him to say something. All I hear is ragged breathing.

'You needed it to be late at night,' I say, thinking out loud. 'You needed the body and the blood to appear and disappear quickly – I was supposed to be the only one who saw them.' My mind snags on something, but I force it out of the way. 'Jackie hacked into the website and put the new tour up just before one. You gave her step-by-step instructions how to do it. She wouldn't have needed to hack in, except it had to look as if an outsider had done it. At one o'clock, you pretended to fall asleep, knowing exactly what I'd do and exactly what I'd see.' Rage flares up inside me, breaks through the fear. 'How did it feel, to know so much when I knew nothing?'

The knife swerves towards me, nicks the skin on my neck. I feel a trickle – thin, like a tear.

Is that the best you can do?

If he wants to silence me, he'll have to kill me. 'Did you lie in bed waiting for my scream?' I can't remember, now, whether I screamed or not. I hope I didn't, if that was what Kit was waiting for. I hope I disappointed him. 'You knew I'd wake you up as soon as I'd seen it. I wouldn't want to be alone with . . . *that*, in the middle of the night – of course I'd wake you. Must have been a fairly safe bet for you that I wouldn't want to go anywhere near my computer afterwards, that I'd send you in there on your own to look, so that I didn't have to see it again.'

'I knew only you . . . that you'd only come in once I'd told you there was nothing there,' Kit whispers. He stumbles over the words, struggling with what must feel like a second language to him and not his mother tongue: the language of rationality.

'You went in, closed down my tour, clicked on yours on the desktop screen and started it playing,' I say, numb inside. 'You called out to me that you were looking at the picture of the lounge and there was no dead woman in it.'

'Stop,' says Kit. There's a hollow tiredness in his voice. 'None of this is my fault,' he says. 'Or yours, or Jackie's.'

If I tried to struggle free, would I stand a chance? No. Not yet. Kit's arm is still pinning me against him. Maybe later, when he's held the position for even longer and his muscles are aching. If I try and fail now, I might not get another chance – Kit might decide to hurry things along.

How long was he here with Jackie before he killed her?

'Why have the original tour waiting on the desktop? Why not just text Jackie and tell her to change it back?' I'm asking myself, not Kit. I'm asking the person I trust. When the answer presents itself, I feel as if I've cheated and it must be the wrong one. How can I know, if I didn't know before?

I hear Alice's voice in my head: *Usually what we're seeking comes to us. It's just a matter of how long it takes to reach us.*

'You *did* text Jackie,' I say. 'You heard me scream, or you heard the sound of glass smashing when I knocked Nulli's certificate off the wall – either way, you knew I'd seen what I was supposed to see and you texted her then. But you couldn't bank on her being able to change the tour back to the original quickly enough, could you? And you couldn't risk me seeing the woman's body more than once.'

'Stop, Con.'

I recognise begging when I hear it. But there's no need for Kit to beg. He's the one with the power, the one with the knife. I ignore him. 'Any more than once and it wouldn't have been so easy to make everyone believe that I imagined it: a split-second visual delusion, gone in the blink of an eye. That's what you wanted them all to think – the police, my family, Alice. You wanted me to feel that the whole world was against me, that no one believed me . . . but . . .' I stop, aware of the flaw in what I'm saying. 'Jackie. She came forward. She said she'd seen it too. Ian Grint only took my story seriously because of her.' It makes no sense. If Kit and Jackie wanted me not to be believed . . .

'Stop!' Kit shouts, finding his energy. He's moving, dragging me with him. I try to make a big enough noise to immobilise him as he pulls me towards the stairs, but terror steals the sound, and all that's left is a long, low moan. Did I think I could keep him at bay for ever? That if I carried on talking, I could make time stand still? I reach out, close my fingers around the top of the newel post, the white death button, but Kit pulls me away, yanking me roughly up the steps, one at a time. My arms and legs feel floppy and uncoordinated, like a rag doll's.

Does he have a plan for what happens next, or did his plan

run out a long time ago? Is he going to do it in one of the bedrooms? A bitter liquid fills my throat. I haven't got the strength to swallow; I can hardly breathe.

On the landing, the bad smell gets stronger. Kit starts to panic. I can feel it, like electrical charges all over his body, pulsing through to mine. *He doesn't want to be up here*. He can't keep still. The blade of the knife keeps touching my face; each time, I jerk my head away. Kit mumbles apologies, one after another. *Sorry, sorry, sorry*. I'm too frightened to speak, unable to tell him that no amount of sorrys will ever be enough. 'It's not your fault, any of this,' he says. 'I'll show you whose fault it is.'

He moves us towards the only closed door on the landing; all the others are slightly ajar.

'No,' I manage to say. 'Please, I don't . . . no, don't . . .' *This is the room. He's going to kill me in this room.*

Using the tip of the knife, Kit pushes hard near the handle and the door swings open with a click. He tightens his arm around my waist. I try to focus on the idea of breathing easily, without restriction. Kit yelps like an animal in a trap as he forces me over the threshold. *He doesn't want to do this. He hates everything he's doing*. The stench of putrefaction in the room makes me gag. I notice nothing but the black humming, the double bed in front of me, and on top of the bed . . .

No. No. Nopleasenopleasepleaseno.

Four large plastic parcels, each one several feet long, with brown parcel tape wound around them and sealing the ends. Four stinking cocoons, with a cloud of black flies buzzing around them – three lying side by side, and the fourth, the smallest, nestling in a groove made by the curved sides of the two biggest. Through the transparent plastic, I see material – a pattern of flowers and leaves, a paisley pattern . . .

'We had to wrap them like mummies,' says Kit. 'Stop them smelling, stop the flies getting in – that's what Jackie said. See how well it worked? This is her idea of the flies not getting in.'

Now. Now's when I should run, but my body is boneless and limp. Kit bends down, taking me with him. There's a roll of brown parcel tape on the floor, by the leg of the bed. 'Pick it up,' he says, freeing one of my arms. 'Tape your mouth shut, then wind the tape twice round your head, so that your mouth's properly covered.' The knife blade slices into the air in front of my eyes. One inch more and it would cut my eyeball in half.

I feel something pouring down my legs. I try to deny to myself what this must mean, but the knowledge is there and I can't get away from it. *I've wet myself*. I try to turn my head so that I don't have to watch my shame soak into the carpet. Whoever finds my body will know that I died terrified and humiliated.

'Pick up the tape,' Kit says again, as if he can't understand why the thing he wants to happen isn't already happening. 'Tape your mouth shut, then wind the tape twice around your head.'

But I can't do anything, nothing at all. I can't comply and I can't resist. 'Just kill me,' I say, sobbing. 'Get it over with.'

26

24/7/2010

'Plenty of Cambridge students stay on after they finish their degrees,' said Charlie. 'Why didn't Kit Bowskill, if he was so in love with the place?' She was sitting in the back of Simon's car, having abandoned her own outside the Granta pub. The traffic was heavy; Sam had already suggested once that they get out and walk. Charlie was starting to think he might have a point. The car had been in the full glare of the sun all the time that they'd been in the pub, and so far the air-conditioning hadn't had much effect. The back of Charlie's top was wet with sweat.

'You're looking at it the wrong way,' said Simon. 'Don't think of Bowskill as an ordinary bloke who sets out to achieve something, succeeds, then pats himself on the back for a job well done. Think of him as a wanting machine, programmed to do nothing but enhance its wanting skills. He's spent his whole life practising. He can want longer and harder and deeper now than he could five years ago. He's so good at wanting that no amount of getting can ever be enough for him.'

'So he avoids the things he wants so that he can do more wanting?' Sam said.

'Basically, yeah,' said Simon. 'Though if I was being picky, I'd say that there's no such thing as "the thing he wants". Charlie's right – if living in Cambridge was what he wanted, he could have stayed after he finished his degree. That might have involved taking any old job, though, and living in a shithole for a while, which for Bowskill wouldn't have been an option. It'd have been too much of a comedown for him, after three years as one of the city's elite – accommodation in historic college buildings, studying at one of the world's best universities. Not that he'd have been happy during his student years either. He wouldn't have been able to relax enough to enjoy any of it, knowing it was temporary.'

Charlie shook her head. 'I still don't see how taking a job in Rawndesley would move him any closer to his—'

'I do,' Simon cut her off. 'I can guess what his strategy was: get a job with a reputable firm, one with good promotion prospects and branches all over the country – specifically, one with a branch in Cambridge – and wait for the opportunity to transfer. Meanwhile, you might be living in Rawndesley, but you've got a plan to get back to where you want to be. And you can start working your way up the corporate ladder, so that when you *do* transfer to Cambridge you can afford a decent house there. For as long as you're living in Rawndesley, it's easy to accept that your current life is a compromise – Rawndesley's a compromise kind of place. What Bowskill was unwilling to do was compromise in Cambridge – to him, Cambridge represents perfection, and he's only willing to be there when the conditions are perfect. In the unlikely event of that ever happening, he'd find he felt worse than ever – big shock to his system. The day Kit Bowskill's forced to admit that no detail of his life could be improved – that's a dangerous day for him. He'd have to recognise that the problem's internal – that's *he's* the detail he needs to change. Probably at that point he'd have a breakdown.'

'So . . . before applying for a job at Deloitte Rawndesley, he'd have applied to Deloitte Cambridge?' said Charlie.

'Yeah – and all the other firms he'd decided were worthy of him,' said Simon. 'He could probably have coped with an entry-level salary and a tiny flat if he'd had a job he was proud of, and could see a clear way to the top. Maybe there were no openings, or maybe he had interviews and lost out to other people – either way, Deloitte Rawndesley was the best he could do. He might have set himself a deadline: transfer to the Cambridge branch within two years, five years, whatever.'

'Clearly he failed,' said Charlie.

'No. You still don't get the way his mind works. Someone like Bowskill never fails. He's always en route to realising his master plan. Success and victory are always just round the corner.'

Charlie made a face at the back of Simon's headrest. If she wasn't entirely familiar with every nuance of Kit Bowskill's dysfunctional psyche, that could be because she'd never met the man. Simon had only met him once, yet he seemed to be an expert on Bowskill's particular brand of unquenchable dissatisfaction. Charlie wondered if this was something she ought to worry about.

'Whatever Bowskill's transfer-to-Cambridge plan was, he changed it when he met Connie,' said Simon. 'From the second he met her, moving to Cambridge without her would have felt like a terrible failure.'

'You're saying he fell in love with her?' Charlie enjoyed trying to make Simon say the word 'love'.

He neatly avoided it. 'I doubt he's capable of normal emotions,' he said. 'Everything he feels is couched in terms of a want. He'll have decided he wanted Connie as much as he wanted Cambridge, but she had strong roots in Silsford – she was a Monk before she married Bowskill, as in Monk & Sons. Her family's lived in Little Holling for generations. It won't have taken Bowskill long to realise that prising Connie out of the Culver Valley was going to be hard. Connie told me herself: the whole ethos of no one ever leaving is woven into the fabric of her family. There was a glimmer of hope for Bowskill, though – he quickly saw that Connie's parents drove her insane. She was desperate to get away from them. Cleverly, he didn't put any pressure on her or try to persuade her. He encouraged her to spend time with her parents, telling her what a great thing a close family was – he said that all the time, Connie told me. He was relying on her getting so sick of the Monks that *she'd* suggest moving away. He probably had to wait longer than he'd initially hoped, but it happened eventually – one night they went out for dinner and Connie told him how bored of the Culver Valley she was. Bowskill wasted no time in telling her he'd been offered a job by Deloitte Cambridge, a promotion—'

'Too much of a coincidence,' Charlie cut in.

'Not a coincidence – a lie,' said Simon. 'If I ring Deloitte Cambridge on Monday and ask, I know what they'll tell me: they didn't offer Bowskill anything. He went to them, soon as he could after finding out Connie wanted to move, and told them they had to let him transfer. Not a promotion, necessarily – any job, though I suppose it could have been a promotion. I'm sure Bowskill had spent years, by then, making sure he impressed all the relevant people. Deloitte must have agreed to the move, because Bowskill and Connie started looking at houses in Cambridge. They found the perfect house.'

'18 Pardoner Lane,' said Sam.

'All the "perfects" seemed to be lining up,' Simon went on. 'Perfect city, perfect woman, perfect house, perfect job. Someone like Bowskill's happiest when he's tantalisingly close to realising his dream – before it comes true, and he wakes up the next day to find that he's still the same sad fuck he was before. Fuck, is this traffic ever going to move?' Simon banged the window angrily with his fist. 'I can't even take the pavement route, not without killing fifty tourists. You know Cambridge better than I do, Char – shall we get out and run? How far are we from Bentley Grove, on foot?'

'This is the worst bit,' Charlie told him. 'Let's sit it out. Once we get to that roundabout ahead, we'll be okay.'

'It must have been a big blow, when he didn't get 18 Pardoner Lane,' said Sam.

'He could have got it, if he'd been less arrogant,' Simon told him. 'There was someone else interested, but when Hugh Jepps broke the news to Bowskill, Bowskill accused him of lying, said he didn't believe this other buyer existed, that it was a ruse to bump up the price. He walked away – told Jepps to get back to him once the other bloke had lost interest. You can see where the idea for his and Jackie's fake bidding-war scam came from.' The car swerved sharply to the left; the wheel scraped the kerb.

'Simon, don't,' Charlie groaned. 'The pavement's not an option – let it go.'

'By the time Bowskill worked out that the other buyer story was true, a deal had been done,' Simon said. 'The Beth Dutton people were selling to the Gilpatricks. Bowskill would have had a hard time accepting that. That's where Jackie Napier came in. Hugh Jepps had told Bowskill the house was sold, there was nothing that could be done, but Bowskill sensed that Jackie was more sympathetic to his cause.'

'Which, if she wanted to shag him senseless, she would have been,' Charlie chipped in cheerfully.

'She was.' Simon's solemn tone cut through her frivolity. 'She rang the vendors and asked them to reconsider – probably told them how keen Bowskill was, that he'd be willing to pay more than the price they'd agreed with the Gilpatricks. The Beth Dutton people were torn – they were against gazumping on principle, but they saw a chance to get their hands on more money. They told Jackie that if Bowskill could go fifty grand above what the Gilpatricks were going to pay, he could have the house.'

'They were *so* principled that their sell-out mark-up was that much higher,' Charlie muttered scornfully.

'We know what happens next,' said Simon. 'Bowskill's folks won't stump up the cash and he cuts them off. Meanwhile, Connie's been quietly going to pieces. Much as she wants to move, she's also panicking. Bowskill can't tell her the truth about 18 Pardoner Lane and admit he failed, so he rewrites the story. In his fictional version of events, he reclaims his power – instead of being at the mercy of circumstance, he's in control. He pretends he's changed his mind for the sake of Connie's health, and tries to enthuse her about his new plan: their own business, a beautiful house in the Culver Valley – a new dream, a fake one.'

'It came true, though,' Sam pointed out. 'I've seen their place in Little Holling. It's pretty amazing – the archetypal idyllic country cottage. And they *did* start their own business – something to do with data and databases. It's called Nulli Secundus. I get the impression it's a success.'

'Oh, yeah, Bowskill made it all happen,' said Simon. 'But it was never his dream – only a stage on the way to the real goal.'

'You don't know that,' Charlie said irritably. The heat was getting to her. She wanted to open a window, but if she did,

Simon would demand she close it for the sake of the too-feeble-to-make-a-difference air-conditioning. 'Maybe the new dream was real.'

'You wouldn't say that if you'd seen that bedroom at his mum and dad's place,' Simon told her. 'For as long as there's breath in his body, there's no way Kit Bowskill's settling for living anywhere but Cambridge.'

'But he *has* settled,' Charlie argued. 'Or else he's changed his mind: he was fixed on Cambridge once, but then he had a rethink and—'

'You didn't see what I saw,' Simon interrupted her. 'It wasn't the bedroom of someone planning a rethink – take my word for it. The cottage in Little Holling was a stepping stone. Starting his own business was a good move: if you work for yourself, you can relocate head office when it suits you – you're not dependent on Deloitte or any other firm having an opening at the right time.'

'But . . . Connie told me he's obsessed with the Little Holling house,' said Sam. 'She said he's commissioned an artist to paint its portrait.'

'Yuck,' said Charlie. No need to say any more when one word summed it up.

'Obsessives remain obsessive, but they sometimes change the focus of their obsession, don't they?' Sam asked.

'Not Bowskill,' said Simon irritably. He hated it when other people's inconvenient questions got in the way of his certain knowledge. 'Changing his mind about the best place to live would feel like failure to someone with his mindset – it'd involve admitting he'd been wrong for years. He feels humiliation acutely and easily. Imagine him pulling all those pictures off the walls of his Bracknell bedroom, thinking about the fool who put them up in the first place.'

Sam and Charlie exchanged a look. Neither wanted to point out that none of this could be known for sure.

'While he and Connie were looking for their Little Holling house and starting up their business, Bowskill was dwelling on where he'd gone wrong,' said Simon. 'First mistake: walking away from 18 Pardoner Lane and expecting it to come back to him. Not believing in the Gilpatricks. Second mistake: letting Connie see his enthusiasm for moving, once she'd suggested it. His certainty and determination scared her off – she fell into the role of the one who panicked and applied the brakes. He became the reassuring adult and she was the frightened child. Her hair started falling out, she was sick with nerves all the time – it was all wrong – Bowskill didn't want to be in Cambridge with a bald invalid wife who felt she'd been steamrollered into moving and resented it. Finding out that there was no way of him getting his hands on 18 Pardoner Lane was what convinced him: one by one his "perfects" were falling away, and it was better to pull out and wait.'

Sam and Charlie waited. The traffic had started to inch forward.

Simon didn't move, not until the car behind beeped its horn. He was too focused on his thoughts; the outside world, with its baking heat and its traffic jams, had receded.

'Second time round, Bowskill planned to do it differently,' he said. 'He told Connie he'd changed his mind, he had no desire to move to Cambridge – told her to forget all about it, they could be just as happy in Silsford. It was classic reverse psychology, and it worked. Connie started to resent him for giving up on the Cambridge dream. Thinking he'd abandoned it, she claimed it as her own. Bowskill, meantime, was waiting for 18 Pardoner Lane to come up for sale again – he was prepared to wait as long as it took. The longer the better – he knew Connie would get progressively unhappier, caught in the Monk family trap. When the house finally came on the market again, Bowskill would be ready with his pre-emptive offer – enough money to make sure the Gilpatricks accepted, whatever that took. He's the director of a successful company now – no question of him having to go begging for handouts. Once his offer's been accepted, he tells Connie, "Oh, by the way, a mate of mine in Cambridge says our house is for sale again – pity we're so happy here." Then he sits back and lets her enthusiasm for their original dream do the rest. Aided and abetted by her desperation to get out of the Culver Valley and never go back.' Simon said this last part with feeling, as if he knew how she felt. Charlie was puzzled. He'd always given the impression of being wedded to Spilling until death did them part – his death, presumably, since Spilling was as dead as it was ever going to be, at least until the sun made the world explode, or whatever it was that was eventually going to happen to put a stop to everything; science had never been Charlie's strong point.

'So, second time round, Connie's in the role of enthusiastic driving force?' said Sam.

'Yeah,' Simon said. 'And Bowskill's the doubter, the one who has to be persuaded – because he loves his Little Holling cottage so much, or so he's made Connie believe – he's even commissioned a portrait of it.'

'Yuck,' Charlie said again.

'From the minute he missed out on getting 18 Pardoner Lane in 2003, Bowskill threw his heart and soul into his pretence of loving all things Silsford,' said Simon. 'He had to – to create the necessary resistance in Connie. Meantime, he's working on the other strand of his plan, the one based in Cambridge.'

'Jackie Napier,' said Sam.

'Jackie Napier,' Simon repeated. 'Clever, unscrupulous, and keen to claim Bowskill as her own. Here's a question for you: if Bowskill hated to be seen to fail, how come he ended up involved with a woman who must have known exactly how gutted he was not to get the house he wanted? He'd have had to tell Jackie he couldn't raise the fifty grand. For someone as proud as Bowskill to end up in an . . . affair with a woman who'd witnessed his defeat in that way – how was it possible for him?'

'You're the one who knows him so well,' said Charlie drily. 'Tell us.'

'All right.' No problem for Simon, who of course knew everything. 'Jackie's smart enough to pick up very early on that Bowskill needs to see himself as a winner. She says to him, "You haven't lost the house – you just haven't got it *yet*. You'll get it in the end, but we need to play a longer game." She comes up with a plan. First step? She makes a copy of the keys to 18 Pardoner Lane before handing them over to the Gilpatricks on completion of the sale. She uses her fake charm – which would have been hard to resist – to befriend Elise Gilpatrick, so that she can find out as much information as possible, including much that's of interest to Bowskill: the Gilpatricks have a young baby and they're not planning to stop at one. 18 Pardoner Lane doesn't have a garden. Sam, would you and Kate ever buy a house without a garden?'

'We wouldn't,' Sam said. 'With kids, you need a garden.'

'And Jackie Napier would have told Bowskill that the Gilpatricks would realise this, probably sooner rather than later,' said Simon. 'She also found out that no one was at home on weekdays – Elise and Mr, whatever his name is, worked full-time, and the baby was at nursery. Wouldn't it be a laugh, Jackie says to Bowskill, if we used their house as if it was already ours? Almost like staking a claim as the true owners – the ones who know what's going on, in contrast to the deluded Gilpatricks who only *think* they're in control and don't realise that the house isn't really theirs. Now do you see why Jackie made sure to befriend Elise Gilpatrick? She needed to be seen at the house, often, with Elise, so that no one suspected anything when they saw her there in the daytime. Friends have each other's keys, don't they?'

'She'd also have wanted to guarantee that, if and when the Gilpatricks decided to move to a house with a garden, they'd ask her to handle the sale of 18 Pardoner Lane instead of going to another estate agent,' Sam pointed out.

'Right,' said Simon. 'Which they duly did, last year. That's when Jackie's plan started to cave in around her ears. When she tells Bowskill the Gilpatricks are finally moving, he doesn't react as she expects him to. She's all proud of herself, bragging about how clever she was, finding her friend Elise the perfect house. Instead of saying, "Great, nice job" and buying 18 Pardoner Lane, Bowskill starts asking about the house the Gilpatricks are moving to. By now his envy of the Gilpatricks has become ingrained – he's lived with it for six years. All that time he's been reading the letters they've left lying around, rifling through their personal stuff – he knows what's in their bathroom cabinet, what's in their *minds*, probably. If they're happy, he senses their happiness. It disturbs him. Enrages him. But he can't stop, can't help immersing himself in their life and envying it. They have a real life and he doesn't – he's attracted to what he knows he's incapable of being and . . . having. The Gilpatricks are the usurpers, the winners who bagged the big prize. If they've suddenly found somewhere they think is better, what does that say about 18 Pardoner Lane? Maybe it's not the perfect house after all, if the winners no longer want to live there. Sam, you mentioned a transfer of obsession – this is the moment when it happened, the transfer moment: Bowskill decides it's not about the house any more, it's about triumphing over the Gilpatricks by getting the thing they want.'

'So he's a nutter, then, Kit Bowskill?' said Charlie. 'A fully fledged nutter.'

'That's one way to look at it,' Simon said. 'Another is to see him as practical. Adaptable. Think about it: if he doesn't divert his obsession at this point and start to obsess about 12 Bentley Grove, what does he do? Buy 18 Pardoner Lane? Connie's the one he wants to be with, not Jackie. Jackie boosts his ego and works well as a means to an end, but Bowskill knows the difference between a quality product and a piece of shoddy crap – he knows Connie's the first and Jackie's the second. If he and Connie buy 18 Pardoner Lane and move in, what does he tell Jackie? "Sorry, thanks for all your help, but my wife will take over now"? Jackie's not going to sit back and take that, is she? She's going to tell Connie about the affair, do her best to destroy the marriage.'

Charlie tried not to mind that Simon had described Connie Bowskill as a quality product.

'So Bowskill transfers his obsession to 12 Bentley Grove . . .' Sam began tentatively.

'He persuades Jackie to buy 18 Pardoner Lane,' said Simon. 'Tells her it's a way of them having both houses, tells her to copy the keys for 12 Bentley Grove before she hands them over, and they can start the whole adventure again – invade the Gilpatricks' new house like they invaded the old one. Jackie does as she's told, and they get into a new routine – weekday meetings at 12 Bentley Grove, maybe the odd one at 18 Pardoner Lane too, to help Bowskill believe in his Cambridge empire. And a new impossible perfection-centred goal, because he has to maintain the fantasy, always, that he's working towards the ultimate victory. He asks Jackie if, theoretically, she thinks she could persuade the Gilpatricks to move again. By this point, if she's got common sense as well as brains, she'll be starting to doubt him. All the years he's spent telling her he wants to live with her at 18 Pardoner Lane – he must have said that, to keep her onside – and now he has the chance to do just that and he isn't taking it. Nor is he leaving Connie, as he no doubt promised he would. Jackie sticks with him, but she's not happy. Unlike Bowskill, she's not addicted to the idea of unreachable perfection – she wants the result she wants, as soon as she can get it: her and Bowskill living together in Cambridge. She starts thinking of ways to make that happen.'

'Didn't he see that there was no way of resolving his dilemma?' Charlie asked. 'Even if the Gilpatricks did move again, what's to stop Bowskill deciding 12 Bentley Grove's no longer good enough, and fixating on whatever house they're moving to?'

'That's exactly what he would have done,' said Simon. 'He won't have allowed himself to dwell on that, though – or on the choice he'll have to make as soon as he moves to any house in Cambridge: Connie or Jackie. If he chooses Connie, Jackie brings his whole world crashing down. If he chooses Jackie, he's with the wrong woman – one of his "perfects" is missing. Deep down, he knows he can never square the circle, either of the circles, but he also can't adopt a more realistic mindset. His whole life's been a flight from reality. If he allows himself to see things as they truly are, he faces instant annihilation, or at least that's his fear.'

'So what does he do?' asked Sam. The stilted chug of traffic had become a flow; they were nearly at the roundabout. Finally, the air-conditioning was doing its stuff.

'He takes it out on Jackie,' said Simon. 'Loses his temper with her whenever she tries to point out to him that the Gilpatricks are unlikely to move again any time soon, having found the perfect family home with garden. Bowskill insists that they might decide to sell – that's what he's waiting for and it's what he's going to be waiting for until it happens. Jackie doesn't like the sound of this, but what can she do? If she ends the relationship, she doesn't get what she wants: Bowskill.'

'So she puts up with his lunacy because she loves him?' said Charlie. Here, at last, was psychology she could understand.

'While she's putting up with it, the unexpected happens,' said Simon. 'Connie Bowskill finds an address she doesn't recognise, claiming to be "home". In a pitiful attempt to make his fantasy feel more real, Bowskill's given 12 Bentley Grove a nickname – one that reminds him of a happier time, when he came within touching distance of his dream. 17 Pardoner Lane, 18 Pardoner Lane – a joke he made years ago, when he still believed perfection was attainable. He's not convinced any more, but maybe if he repeats the same joke, he'll get the old feeling back. He programmes 11 Bentley Grove into his SatNav – just to see how it feels, because that's what he'd do if the house was his.'

'And Connie finds it,' said Charlie.

'Right. Connie finds it, and doesn't believe him when he says it's nothing to do with him. Suddenly Bowskill's got a new problem to contend with – not only is he struggling to manage

Jackie's expectations and nurture his own fantasy, he's now also trying to cope with a wife who doesn't trust him – who doesn't believe a word he says, no matter how much effort he puts into lying to her.'

They were on Trumpington Road, minutes away from Bentley Grove.

'Don't ask me what happened next, because I don't know.' Simon sounded dissatisfied. 'I can speculate, if you want me to.' Without waiting for encouragement, he went on: 'With Connie so suspicious, Bowskill and Jackie probably steered clear of 12 Bentley Grove. Or maybe they only met there when they knew Connie was busy, but how could Bowskill have known for sure that she wouldn't turn up when he least expected her to, to try and catch him out? He can't have. Jackie will have been piling on the pressure, saying, "Forget Connie, forget 12 Bentley Grove – it's all getting too difficult. Come and live at 18 Pardoner Lane with me, happily ever after." ' Simon sighed. 'At some point, with everything closing in on him, Bowskill reached his limit.'

'And did what?' Sam asked.

'Went to number 12 and killed the Gilpatricks,' said Simon. 'Who else could he blame for the mess he was in? I think we're about to find their bodies, wrapped in curtain material and plastic.'

Sam made a strange noise as they turned left onto Bentley Grove.

'What's up?' Charlie asked him.

'That's Connie Bowskill's Audi,' he said, pointing. 'Shit. She's in there too.'

Simon was out of the car within seconds, running.

POLICE EXHIBIT REF: CB13345/432/28IG

11BG worth 1.2/1.3 million
Minimum deposit £400,000? (Nulli? C sick leave – stress)
Borrow 800,000/900,000
Life insurance for full amount borrowed
Acc/su – policy pays out full amount
(Check su clause – may have to be acc)
1.2 mil house for 400 K

OR
1 mil/900K if price reduced?
As above, but min depos 250 K
1.2 mil house for 250 K – not bad!

Same house, but much bigger garden, southfacing – more desirable – OBVIOUS AND UNDENIABLE – MEANT TO BE!!

(Officially acc – poss su, unprovable. Guilt at 4 murders – obsessed with Gils since Pardoner 2003. Wanted 11 for view of 12, to watch them? PARANOID AND DELUSIONAL SINCE JAN, WHEN PUT ADDRESS IN SATNAV!! 11BG, 12BG – say her joke all along.)

Viewing (Frenches? Talbots?) Find SG in – stalker has gone step further, put house up for sale
Woman who met and gave keys – describe C

Letters, stuff through letterbox?
Nitromose car?

LANCING DAMISZ, UNIT 3 WELLINGTON COURT
CAMBRIDGE CB5 6EX, 01223-313300

Virtual tour – Gil bodies? Something else?
Advise 1 mil/900 v quick sale
Need C passport for buy/sell

C DNA AT 12

Police – C access 12 using key found at 11 – easy

HOW GOT KEY TO 11? Important?

Suicide understandable – avoid punishment?

Rent out 11, live at Pardoner – 11 rent 2500 pcm

27

Saturday 24 July 2010

I can't move or speak. There's parcel tape wrapped round my head, sealing my mouth shut. Once he'd done that, Kit taped my wrists together behind my back and forced me down on the floor. There might have been a chance for me to get away, but I didn't take it, if there was, and now I'm going to die. When Kit's ready. And if not being dead gets any worse than it is now, I know how to speed up the process – all I have to do is let myself cry. I'd be unable to breathe within minutes, and I'd suffocate.

'I didn't want to kill them, Con.' He has to raise his voice to make himself heard over the noise of the flies. 'Four lives, two of them kids. It wasn't an easy decision, not until I thought about us. Our future children. This is the home our children deserve.'

I don't want to listen, but I force myself. I wanted to share Kit's reality. This is Kit's reality. This man, this monster, is my husband. I loved him. I married him.

'I didn't want to kill Jackie either,' he says. 'She wasn't judgemental when I told her what I'd done. She didn't panic like I did. The wrapping was her idea, to keep the smell to a minimum. Airtight, she said.' He stops, looks over at the bed. 'I don't know why the flies came,' he says vaguely. 'Do you think maybe they're not airtight?'

Looking at me, he remembers the tape that's preventing me from answering him. Remembers that he was in the middle of telling me a story, about Jackie not panicking. 'She went into their emails,' he says. 'Contacted their works saying there was a family emergency, that they wouldn't be in for a while. And the school. She kept their mobiles charged, monitored them – when texts arrived from friends and family, she'd text back, pretending to be . . .' His body judders, as if a current's running through it. 'Pretending to be Elise Gilpatrick,' he says eventually. *The name of the woman he killed for no reason.*

'I was falling apart, Con. It was Jackie who kept me in one piece, Jackie who had a plan. I went along with it because I was a coward, and because . . . how could I not help her, after everything she'd done for me?'

I flinch as he lunges at me, starts scratching at the tape on my mouth. 'Why don't you say something?' he hisses in my face. His fingernails dig into my skin. Apart from hurting me, it has no effect. Kit picks up the knife, looks at it, then puts it down again and leaves the room. I count. Seven seconds later, he's back with a pair of nail scissors. I keep as still as I can as he hacks at the tape, but he's shaking too hard and ends up cutting my mouth. 'Sorry,' he breathes, sweat running down his face and neck.

A few more seconds and he's cut all the way through the tape – I can speak again, if I want to. Blood trickles down my chin. My new cuts start to throb, gathering more pain with each beat.

Kit stands back and stares at me. 'Say something,' he orders.

I shouldn't allow myself to hope, but the hope is there, allowed or not. He taped my mouth shut, then cut the tape away. It's a clear reversal, one that allows me to believe that he might put his intention to kill me into reverse as well. 'What did Jackie want to do to me?' I ask. 'Did she want you to kill me too?'

'No. She'd have done it herself. She knew I'd never be able to do it.'

I'd never be able to do it. I'd never be able to do it. I cling to those words.

'A lot had to happen before she could kill you,' Kit says. 'She had to set it all up first, so that you'd be blamed for the . . .' He glances over at the bed. 'The others, you know,' he says. 'I don't know how she could think clearly, but she did. Do you want to see?'

'See?' I repeat blankly.

Kit smiles, and for a moment I'm dropped back into our old life together, our normal life. I've seen this smile many times before: when Kit makes a joke that he's pleased with, when I say something that impresses him. 'I'm offering you proof,' he says. His smile has vanished. His voice is harsh.

'Show me,' I say.

Kit nods, turns his back on me. I hear him run downstairs. When he comes back, he's holding a battered sheet of white A4 paper. There's spidery handwriting on it. *Jackie's handwriting.* Kit holds it in front of my face. I read it three or four times. I shouldn't be able to understand. I try pretending I don't, but it doesn't work. I know immediately what Jackie meant when she wrote these words.

I feel defiled, claustrophobic, as if I'm trapped inside her warped mind, unable to escape the tainted swirl of her thoughts. I have no choice but to admit that this is real, since it's here in front of me. All the same, I can't believe it. Until four days ago, I had no idea Jackie Napier existed.

I'm glad she's dead.

'None of it was my idea,' says Kit.

'You killed the Gilpatricks.'

He cranes his head away from me, as if I've tried to hit him. 'That wasn't an *idea*. It wasn't planned, it . . . Jackie was the planner, not me.' He lets go of the paper. It falls to the floor. 'She seemed to be able to anticipate everything, and I couldn't even see the next step.'

Did she anticipate you strangling her?

'She predicted that you wouldn't be able to stay away from Cambridge, after you found the address in the SatNav,' Kit goes on. 'I didn't believe her – I thought there was no way you'd travel all that way in the hope of catching me out. Jackie laughed when I said that. Called me a naïve idiot. She said she'd prove it to me: she took two weeks off work and staked out Bentley Grove. Soon as the Gilpatricks left in the morning, in she'd go to number 12, to wait for you. She knew what you looked like – she must have spent hours on Nulli's website, staring at your photograph. She envied you like crazy.'

Envied me. Who wouldn't want to be married to a deranged killer?

'Two Fridays running, she saw you. Then we knew – even I worked it out. Friday was the day you'd go, if you went at all. Mondays and Wednesdays there was a chance I'd be at home, Tuesdays and Thursdays you were at Monk & Sons. Friday was your only free day when I was in London for sure.'

I nod, trying to ignore the sick feeling spreading through me. How does Kit expect me to respond?

'Sometimes Jackie followed you,' he says. 'To Addenbrooke's, or into town. I told her she shouldn't take the risk – I couldn't stand the thought of you noticing her and confronting her in case she gave something away, but she just laughed at me. "I only get noticed when I want to," she said.'

'She was wrong,' I say, shocked by the hoarse sound of my own voice. 'I knew someone was following me.'

I mentioned it to Alice when I first went to see her – that once or twice, in Cambridge, I'd heard footsteps behind me. She prescribed me a remedy for that precise delusion: Crotalus Cascavella.

Wrong.

I didn't need a brown bottle full of something dissolved in water. I needed Jackie Napier to die.

Obsessed with Gils since Pardoner 2003. There's only one thing that can mean.

'The Gilpatricks bought 18 Pardoner Lane, didn't they?' I say. 'When you . . . when *we* wanted it.'

I don't need an answer – I can see it in Kit's face.

'You pretended you didn't want it any more, blamed it on my . . . problems. You must have loathed the Gilpatricks. And then . . . what, they moved? They bought 12 Bentley Grove, and . . .'

Rent out 11, live at Pardoner.

'Jackie. Jackie bought 18 Pardoner Lane.' I'm still working it out as I say it. 'You probably gave her some of the money.'

'How could I do that?' Kit says angrily. 'I don't have any money that you don't know about.'

'I was too much of a mess to move away from my family, but that wasn't a problem for you,' I say, thinking aloud. 'You could live in Cambridge with Jackie. The two of you had been waiting for 18 Pardoner Lane to come up for sale again, but when it did, you didn't want it any more – Jackie did, enough to buy it, but you . . .' *Yes. It has to be.* 'You wanted whatever house the Gilpatricks wanted, and that wasn't 18 Pardoner Lane any more – it was 12 Bentley Grove.'

Disjointed ideas clash in my mind. What did Kit say about Jackie waiting in number 12, watching for me, knowing I would come looking? *Soon as the Gilpatricks left in the morning* . . . So they weren't dead at that point. And if Kit hadn't killed them yet . . . 'How did Jackie get the keys to this house?' I ask. 'Was she . . . ?' *Her pink denim jacket, a Lancing Damisz key-ring in the pocket. Her black spider handwriting, on Lancing Damisz paper.* 'She was an estate agent, wasn't she? Did you meet her in 2003? Did she sell this house to the Gilpatricks?'

Kit doesn't answer. He looks away.

'She did, didn't she? And she kept a copy of the front door key.'

'We used to meet here, when they were out,' Kit mutters, eyes down. 'It was a stupid game we played, but it was better than the real life she wanted us to have together. I couldn't bring myself to set foot in the Pardoner Lane house, not once she'd bought it. She wanted me to move in there with her, but how could I? I lived in Little Holling, with you – at Melrose Cottage.' He says it as if I don't know already – as if I'm a stranger he's introducing himself to. *Telling me about his life.* 'I never loved Jackie. The one thing I knew for sure was that I wanted to live with you, wherever I lived but . . . the game had gone too far by then. And . . . it was more than a game. I wanted . . .' He clears his throat. 'I didn't see why the Gilpatricks should have what I wanted. That was when it all started to go wrong, when they bought our house.'

I wait.

'Jackie and I had terrible rows,' Kit goes on eventually, so quietly I can barely hear him. 'I didn't really want this place . . .'

he gestures around him '. . . but it was easier to pretend I did than admit the truth. Jackie knew it was bullshit – she went on and on at me, telling me the Gilpatricks wouldn't be selling anytime soon, that this was their forever home, trying to get me to admit that I'd stop wanting it anyway as soon as I could have it, even if they did decide to move again. She was furious with me – how could I have let her buy 18 Pardoner Lane if I wasn't planning to live there with her? The rows got worse and worse, and then . . .' He shakes his head.

This time I can't guess. I have to ask. 'Then what?'

'The SatNav thing happened. And Jackie decided it was destiny – the solution to all our problems.'

'How? *How*, Kit?'

'Number 11,' he whispers, folding his hands into a tight ball. 'Everything pointed to it. Eleven was what we called this house – you remember the old joke?'

I bite my lip to stop myself from screaming.

'There were keys in a bowl in the kitchen with a label on that said "Selina, no. 11", and after the SatNav disaster, you thought I was shacked up with someone at number 11 – nothing I said could persuade you it wasn't true. One day Jackie asked me if I knew how much bigger number 11's garden was than the garden here.' Kit jerks his head in the direction of the window. 'I didn't know what she was talking about. She had this strange expression on her face. It scared me. I realised then: she was halfway to being mad.'

'She'd used the keys from the kitchen and let herself into number 11,' I say.

He nods. 'She wanted to check out the house where I was supposedly leading my double life. She thought it was hilarious.'

I glance down at the sheet of paper on the floor,

remembering Jackie's words: *Same house, but much bigger garden, southfacing – more desirable – OBVIOUS AND UNDENIABLE – MEANT TO BE!!*

'She thought she'd found the perfect solution.' Kit shrugs. 'We could buy a house almost identical to the Gilpatricks' but better, on the same street. "You'll be able to lord it over them," she said. "All we need to do is persuade this Selina woman to sell." She started talking about putting shit through the letter-box, Nitromosing her car . . . I didn't even know what Nitromose was. I told her not to be ridiculous – even if we could drive the owner out of her home, we'd never be able to afford a house on Bentley Grove, this one or number 11. I was seconds away from telling Jackie I couldn't go on the way we were when . . .' He breaks off.

A heavy sense of calm spreads through me, like a drug. I fight the urge to close my eyes. 'When she explained to you exactly how it could work,' I finish Kit's sentence. 'If I died at the right time, with the right price on my head, then you could afford it. What was her plan? First, get me out of the way at Nulli. All the stress I was under after finding that address in your SatNav – you were supposed to suggest to me that I stop working for a while, hand everything over to you. And then, what, sell Nulli, with Jackie passing herself off as me to sign the relevant papers? She looked like me, superficially – shoulder length dark hair, slim. With my passport, and a solicitor who'd never met me—'

'I didn't, though, did I?' Kit snaps. 'I never suggested you give up work – everything I did from that moment on was to protect you from this . . . this madwoman I'd got us involved with. You don't have to believe that, but it's the truth.' He lets out a bitter laugh. 'Jackie accused *me* of being the crazy one.

To her it was so obvious, so simple – we sell Nulli, buy 11 Bentley Grove with a huge mortgage and a whacking great life insurance policy, with her posing as you, then . . .' Kit covers his face with his hands. Groans.

'Then kill me, cash in, and get a house worth 1.2 million for two hundred and fifty to four hundred grand, depending on how low Selina Gane was willing to go to get rid of her house quickly,' I say, aware of the uselessness of my words, wishing they were knives. 'The house where she'd been persecuted by someone she didn't know, for no reason that was anything to do with her. So, what did you say? Did you say, "No, I don't want Connie dead"? Did you say, "I'm going to the police"?'

'I couldn't go to the police. I . . . I did my best to stall her by . . .'

I wait.

Kit changes tack. 'Anyway, her plan wouldn't have worked,' he says defensively. 'Who'd have given us a mortgage for that amount once we'd sold Nulli and had nothing?' Is he daring me to call him a liar, or has he forgotten about Melrose Cottage because it suits him to do so? He and Jackie would have got their mortgage – someone would have given it to them, especially if whoever bought Nulli kept Kit on as CEO on some exorbitant salary.

'I had to pretend to go along with it, pretend we'd do it eventually, once we'd got the details right. Jackie enjoyed the planning. We stopped fighting. Completely. Sometimes I thought – I hoped – that working on the details might keep her happy for ever, that she'd never need to . . . take it any further.'

'So your aim was to guarantee Jackie's everlasting happiness?'

'No! You don't understand,' Kit sobs.

'I do,' I tell him. 'I wish I didn't, but I do.'

I watch as he struggles to compose himself.

'Jackie could and would have ruined my life if I'd said no. I had to give her something to hold on to. I never loved her, Con. She was more like . . . I don't know, a colleague I felt I had to be loyal to. She loved me, though – I was in no doubt about that. You know she . . . she cried for nearly two hours after we . . . did the filming.'

Is he talking about the virtual tour?

'She insisted on wearing my wedding ring to do it – she wouldn't explain why. Just kept saying it would be funny, but that wasn't the real reason. If it was funny, why did she go to pieces when I asked for it back afterwards? I felt worse taking that ring off her than I did . . .' His mouth sets in a line, as if to stop the words escaping: *than I did strangling her to death.*

'How bad did you feel about butchering an innocent family? Where does that fit in, on your scale of guilt?'

'If it'll make you feel any better, I'll tell you something I never told Jackie, not even at the end,' Kit says, ignoring my question. 'I thought about telling her, but I didn't. It would have been vindictive.'

I wish he'd told her, whatever it is, if it's something that would have hurt her. I wish he wouldn't tell me, but I say nothing to stop him.

'The address in my SatNav?' he raises his voice, as if afraid I might not hear. 'I programmed it in.'

'I know that,' I say, starting to cry at the stupidity of it all – him telling me something that I've been telling him and that he's been denying for six months. 'I've known all along.'

'I did it deliberately,' he says. 'I knew you'd take my car that day, because of the snow. I *wanted* you to find out, Con. I wanted you to stop me. Why didn't you stop me?'

~

I didn't kill the Gilpatricks. I didn't kill them. It's not my fault that the Gilpatricks are dead.

I don't know how much time has passed since Kit and I last spoke to one another. There's a hole in my mind and I can't find where it ends. The flies are still buzzing. The smell is worse.

Did I imagine it, or did Kit tell me the rest of the story? He wanted it to stop, all of it. I couldn't stop it for him, so he killed the Gilpatricks – it was their fault he was in the predicament he was in, so they deserved to die. Did Kit say that, or am I imagining what he might have said?

It was easy for Jackie after that – she had him exactly where she wanted him. She could help him escape the four murders he'd committed, but only if he agreed to a fifth. Only if he accepted that I had to die.

Jackie copied the key to number 11, let herself into Selina Gane's house with some prospective buyers, and told a pack of lies about a woman who looked very much like Selina's strange stalker woman putting the house on the market, pretending to be Selina. Maybe she did other things to drive Selina out too – maybe she Nitromosed her car, whatever that means. Whatever she did, she got the result she wanted: number 11 went on the market.

Why the next part, though? I don't have the energy to ask Kit. They must have moved everything out of the lounge at number 12, where the blood was, and replaced it with the contents of number 11's lounge. Risky; someone could have seen them. They'd have had to move furniture and pictures across the street. But no one did see them, or else they'd have gone to the police. Of course no one saw them; Bentley Grove is the sort of street where people make a point of not noticing – the kind of street that makes a stalker feel entirely comfortable. No one around during the day apart from one very old man who sleeps most of the time.

Jackie had access to the right kind of camera, and to the Lancing Damisz website. Jackie lay down in the Gilpatricks' blood, and she and Kit made an alternative version of the virtual tour for me to see, so that I'd go to the police and talk about blood and murder. I would be hysterical – exactly the sort of person who might, later, suffer an accident that may or may not be suicide. Kit must have done the filming. Was Selina Gane supposed to find out that someone was claiming there had been a murder in her house, the house she was already desperate to get shot of, and lower the price?

When was I supposed to have my accident? Not before Kit and Jackie, posing as me, had bought 11 Bentley Grove. The police wouldn't have had too much trouble working out the chain of events: I'd been obsessed with the Gilpatricks since 2003, when they had bought the house I'd set my heart on. I was so obsessed that I'd persuaded Kit to buy 11 Bentley Grove, directly opposite the Gilpatricks' new house, so that I could spy on them, but it turned out that spying wasn't enough for me – one day I cracked and killed them, all of them. I was so deranged that I killed two young children.

She kept hassling the police with some made-up story about a dead body on a website – everyone knew it was a lie. There was no evidence of any blood on the carpet – the police checked.

The guilt had driven her mad.

They found her DNA all over number 12, you know. All over the bodies.

'What?' says Kit, making me jump.

Did I say something?

'I made it easy for her,' I tell him. 'Jackie. She didn't have to pretend to be me so that the two of you could buy 11 Bentley Grove – I came up with a plan of my own to buy it.' A chill seeps into my bones as I realise what this means. 'That's why you killed her, isn't it? Once I'd . . . Once *we'd* bought the house, she'd have wanted to move on to the next stage.'

I think of what Kit said before: *I killed her to save you*. By insisting on buying 11 Bentley Grove, I was bringing forward my execution date. And signing Jackie's death warrant.

'When you said you wanted to buy it, you know what went through my mind?' Kit says. '"This can't be happening," I thought. "Jackie never said this would happen." How pathetic is that?'

'No one can predict everything, not even Jackie.'

'No,' he agrees. Listening to us having this conversation, I can't believe we are about to die. Maybe we're not. Kit hasn't touched the knife for a long time. Or at least, I think it's a long time. Perhaps it isn't; perhaps it's just a few minutes.

'No way she could have known about Mr and Mrs Beater and their Christmas tree,' he says. 'She got a massive kick out of going to the police and treating them like idiots, saying she'd seen what you'd seen, but it wasn't part of the original plan.'

I don't know what he means.

Kit must be able to see that I'm confused, because he says, 'The police didn't check out your story like they were supposed to – they didn't see any reason to mention to Selina Gane that someone was claiming to have seen a picture of a slaughtered woman in her house.'

And so there was no reason for her to lower her asking price from 1.2 million to the nine hundred thousand that Jackie had in mind.

'Jackie's colleague Lorraine explained to them that the carpet in number 11's lounge was the same one that had been in when she'd last sold the house – and there was the stain to prove it. That was it, end of story – Grint wasn't going to take it further on your word alone. Once Jackie threw her hat into the ring, he thought again – Christmas tree stain notwithstanding. If two people, entirely unconnected to one another, see the same dead woman on the same website at the same time—'

A shrill ringing sound cuts across Kit's voice. We both jump. I start to shake uncontrollably. *The doorbell. The police.* 'Hello? Kit? Connie? Are you in there? Open up.'

Not DS Laskey. Simon Waterhouse.

Kit picks up the knife and points it at my throat. The tip presses against my skin. 'Don't say anything,' he whispers.

'Mr Bowskill, can you open the door, please?' That's Sam Kombothekra.

'We're coming in anyway,' Simon Waterhouse yells. 'You might as well let us in yourself.'

Hearing their voices sharpens my mind. There are still things I don't understand, things I want to understand while Kit and I are alone together. I don't know what's going to happen to either of us, but I know for certain that we won't be in a room together, just the two of us, ever again.

'Grint asked Jackie if I was the one who pretended to be Selina Gane and put 11 Bentley Grove up for sale.' My words tumble out too fast. 'She said no.'

'If she'd said yes, you'd have known she was lying. Grint had no reason to doubt Jackie when she came forward to say she'd seen the body, but if you'd told him she was a liar, he might have taken a closer look at her.'

'And found the connection to you.' Yes. That makes sense.

'Bowskill! Open up! Don't do anything stupid. Connie, are you all right in there?'

The knife cuts the bottom of my neck. It makes me realise my lips are still bleeding. I wonder how much blood I've lost. Thinking about it makes me feel weak.

'What about the dress?' I ask Kit.

'Dress?' He enunciates the word oddly, as if it doesn't belong in our conversation. He's beyond lying now; I don't think he knows what I'm talking about.

'My birthday present.'

'That was nothing. I told you it was nothing,' he says impatiently. 'I had to buy you a birthday present, and I bought Jackie a present at the same time – I liked that dress, that's all. I bought one for you and one for her.' He sniffs, wipes his nose with the back of his hand. 'All I wanted was for all this . . . *shit* to end well – for all three of us. All the shit that wasn't my fault, or yours, or Jackie's. None of us deserved any of this – they're the ones who deserve it.' He jerks his head towards the bed. 'Do you want to see them? Do you want to see their smug faces?' He takes hold of me, pulls me to my feet.

'No!' I scream, thinking he's going to show me the bodies. Instead, he drags me down the stairs and into the lounge. There's a lock on the door. Kit slides it across. He puts down the knife, walks over to a cupboard and opens it. He pulls out a photograph, throws it at me. It lands on Jackie, face up. *It lands on Jackie, dead. Dead Jackie.* A man, a woman, a boy and a girl. On a bridge, eating ice creams. Laughing.

I know the woman's face. Elise Gilpatrick's face. How can I know it? It makes no sense.

What makes sense? Jackie's body lying here like rubbish – does that make sense?

Kit walks slowly towards me, holding the knife in front of him. Where's Simon Waterhouse? Where's Sam? Why can't I hear them any more? I try to send a message to them, knowing it's useless: *Please come. Please.* There's nowhere for me to go, no way of getting away from Kit. He's fire, a tidal wave, a cloud of toxic air – he's everything bad there's ever been, coming for me. He's not looking at me any more; his eyes are on the photograph, on his victims' faces. Nothing is their fault – I know that perfectly well – but they are the reason.

I'm going to be killed because of a family called the Gilpatricks.

There are four of them: mother, father, son and daughter. 'Elise, Donal, Riordan and Tilly.' Kit tells me their first names, as if I'm keen to dispense with the formalities and get to know them better, when all I want is to run screaming from the room. 'Riordan's seven,' he says. 'Tilly's five.'

Shut up, I want to yell in his face, but I'm too scared to open my mouth. It's as if someone's clamped and locked it; no more words will come out, not ever.

This is it. This is where and how and when and why I'm going to die. At least I understand the why, finally.

Kit's as frightened as I am. More. That's why he keeps talking, because he knows, as all those who wait in terror know, that when silence and fear combine, they form a compound a thousand times more horrifying than the sum of its parts.

'The Gilpatricks,' he says, tears streaking his face.

I watch the door in the mirror above the fireplace. It looks smaller and further away than it would if I turned and looked at it directly. The mirror is shaped like a fat gravestone: three straight sides and an arch at the top.

'I didn't believe in them. The name sounded made up.' Kit laughs, chokes on a sob. All of him is shaking, even his voice. 'Gilpatrick's the sort of name you'd make up if you were inventing a person. Mr Gilpatrick. If only I'd believed in him, none of this would have happened. We'd have been safe. If I'd only . . .'

He stops, backs away from the locked door. He hears the same footsteps I hear – rushing, a stampede. They're here. The police are finally here. Holding the handle of the knife with both hands, Kit drives it into his chest. The last thing he says is, 'Sorry'.

POLICE EXHIBIT REF: CB13345/432/29IG

Caroline Capps
43 Stover Street
Birmingham

24/12/93

Dear Caroline

Sorry if this letter is blunt, but some of us prefer to be straightforward than two-faced – not you, obviously. You told me you believed me, but now Vicki and Laura are telling me you don't – apparently you only said you did to be polite, and because you feel sorry for me.

Luckily, I don't need your sympathy. In my eyes, you're the one who needs pity, if not full-blown psychotherapy. I have been dumped several times in my life, and have never had a problem admitting to it. And I have NEVER sent dozens of photos of myself to an ex-boyfriend either – why would I? Do I seem that insane to you?

Your boyfriend is the insane one around here – he's a loony as well as a liar. He took the photos you found – he's obsessed with me, though I've spoken to him for a total of about ten minutes. Why don't you prove it to yourself?

Follow him one day – it won't take you long to catch him pursuing me round Cambridge with a camera. By the way, if you could ask him to stop, I'd be very grateful.

And just to clarify one more thing: yes, I'm saying he didn't dump me, but I'm not claiming I dumped him, as you seem to think I am. No one dumped anyone – THERE WAS NO RELATIONSHIP IN THE FIRST PLACE!!! I shouldn't have to tell you this – if your radar hasn't detected that I'm your friend and he's a creep, there's no hope for you.

Elise

Friday 17 September 2010

I ought to sit down, relax, but I can't. I stand by the lounge window, next to the Christmas tree stain. Waiting. Still twenty minutes before she's due to arrive. When I see a car pull up outside, I assume it can't be her. When a tall redhead with a long, elegant neck gets out of the car, I tell myself she can't be Lorraine Turner, she must be someone else.

I'm wrong. 'Sorry I'm so early,' she says, shaking my hand.

'I'm glad you are,' I tell her. 'Come in.'

She crosses the threshold tentatively, as if afraid she might regret it. 'I can't pretend to understand,' she says. Giving me the chance to explain if I want to.

I don't. I smile, say nothing.

'You're absolutely sure you want to sell the house?' she asks.

'Yes.' She can't question me for too long without seeming rude. Knowing a little of what I've been through, she won't want to upset me.

She makes one last effort to get me to talk. 'When did you complete on the purchase?' she says. Estate agent language.

'Yesterday. I rang you straight away.'

She gives up then, goes upstairs to start taking her photographs. The second she's left the room, I regret my reticence. She seems nice, and I need to stop assuming everyone's untrustworthy. Most people aren't Kit Bowskill and Jackie Napier.

Nobody is Kit Bowskill, and nobody is Jackie Napier – not any more.

When Lorraine comes downstairs, perhaps I'll tell her. I'm not ashamed of any of it. I bought 11 Bentley Grove because I promised Selina Gane that I would. How could I let her down, after giving her my word? When I made the promise, I thought I'd be able to live in number 11, because nothing bad had happened there – because it wasn't number 12. Maybe I would have been able to, if things had turned out differently – if I hadn't ended up in that room with the flies and the wrapped bodies, helpless with terror . . . But after what I went through, I can't live on Bentley Grove. It would be impossible.

So I'm putting my new house up for sale, having bought it only yesterday. And when I sell it, I'll buy a house on a different Cambridge street. I've seen a few things on Roundthehouses that look promising, but I'll wait to see which college I end up at, and maybe try to buy somewhere nearby. Fran rang yesterday and said she'd heard about a Cambridge college that's specifically for mature women students. Her encouragement goes some way towards making up for Mum and Dad's silence on the subject of my belated university education.

11 Bentley Grove isn't all I'm selling. London Allied Capital are in the process of buying Nulli from me, for about half of what it's worth, but the amount of money isn't important – my freedom is all I care about. A new start.

I hear Lorraine moving around upstairs. She'll be down soon. I open the bag I've brought with me. *One more piece of unfinished business to attend to*. I take out the print Kit gave me all those Christmases ago – the laughing girl sitting on the steps of King's College Chapel – and slot it in between the wall and the sofa that Selina Gane didn't take with her. It's a nice picture, and I can't bring myself to throw it away even though I don't want to keep it. Maybe the house's new owner will find it and be pleased. He or she will see the '4/100' on the mount and believe, as I did, that it's a print.

It isn't. Kit took the photo himself. The girl in it is eighteen-year-old Elise Gilpatrick. Or Elise O'Farrell, as she was then, when she and Kit were undergraduates together and she made the fatal mistake of rejecting his advances.

I can't leave her behind the sofa; it feels wrong. I pull the frame out and put it on the mantelpiece, lean it against the wall where Selina Gane's antique map of Cambridgeshire used to hang. That's better.

'Goodbye, Elise,' I say. 'I'm so sorry.'

Footsteps on the stairs. Lorraine's on her way down. I get ready to smile and offer her tea or coffee.

Acknowledgements

As always, I am profoundly grateful to Peter Straus and Jenny Hewson at Rogers Coleridge & White, and to Carolyn Mays, Francesca Best, Karen Geary, Lucy Zilberkweit, Lucy Hale and everyone at the continuously brilliant Hodder & Stoughton. I thank my lucky stars several times a day that I ended up with all of you – and then I decide it was fate, not luck.

Thank you to Liz and Andrew Travis for donating their business to the good cause of fiction, to Beth Hocking for passing on a useful contact, and to Guy Martland for supplying the necessary gruesome facts about malodorous bodies and mummification. Thank you to Anne Grey for teaching me everything I know about homeopathy, to Lewis Jones for referring to someone as 'Gummy' in my presence, to Heidi Westman for mentioning a minor incident involving a SatNav that, as far as I know, was never satisfactorily resolved and therefore remains rather suspicious (though far be it from me to cast aspersions . . .) Thank you to Mark Worden for the Pink Floyd book, to Paul Bridges for the surname anthology (which immediately fell open at the name 'Gilpatrick'), to Tom Palmer, James Nash and Rachel Connor for editorial advice in the early stages, and to Stuart Kelly, who introduced me to the concept of the mobilising grievance – mine is that I didn't think of it myself.

Thanks to Dan for the Christmas tree stain (ahem) and the unconventional house name ideas. Thank you to Phoebe and Guy for the lovely cards and presents when I finished the book, and for their crucial insights regarding *Ben 10* aliens.

Major thank-yous to John Jepps and Peter Bean, for all the usual reasons, and this time for an extra reason too, which will only make itself apparent if they read the book.

Thanks to Geoff Jones, and to the mysterious (and, I have no doubt, non-fictional) 'Mr Pixley', who kept offering just a bit more money than I did. Hmm . . . Thank you to the Jill Sturdy Centre for giving rise to an intriguing plot possibility.

I can only imagine how sick of me the estate agents of Cambridge are. They might be pleased to know that I found the right house in the end, or they might simply shudder and growl at the thought of me. Whichever is the case, thank you anyway to Nick Redmayne, Chris Arnold, Oliver Hughes, George Moore, Stewart Chipchase, James Barnett, Richard Freshwater, Robert Couch, Michael Higginson, Zoe and Belinda from Carter Jonas and the rest. I promise I won't move again soon.

Thank you to my virtual spiritual home, the Rightmove website (on which I can safely say there are no images of dead bodies, having examined every single house and each floorplan in great detail). I'm not an addict; I could stop anytime I wanted to. And besides, it's not bad for you if you do it in moderation, and I'm down to an hour a day. Thank you to both Trinity College and Lucy Cavendish College in Cambridge – my non-virtual spiritual homes.

Thank you to Will Peterson for being amazing and lovely, to Morgan White for the bench plaque witticism, to Jenny and Ben Almeida for the new married surname idea.

Finally, I would like to thank Alexis Washam, Carolyn Mays, Francesca Best and Jason Bartholomew for rallying round during the fraught (nay nightmarish) Chapter 27 emergency. Without your help, Chapter 27 would never have pulled through.

The poem 'When First My Way to Fair I Took' is by A E Housman.